Prologue

August 1807, Yorkshire

F itzwilliam Darcy did not know how far he walked, watching the sky shift from a soft pink to brilliant amber and finally to a bright, clear blue. The Yorkshire moors stretched endlessly before him, bathed in the golden light of early morning, and a delicate mist hovered over the heather-clad hills. Approaching the river that separated the local village from the untamed countryside, he breathed in the earthy scent of damp grass and distant wildflowers—a faint promise of the warmth the day would bring. The gentle rush of water moving over the rocky riverbed offered a soothing cadence, and for a fleeting moment, the tension he carried seemed to ease slightly from his shoulders.

His uncle meant well; that much was certain. Since his father's death some six months prior, Lord Matlock had proved himself to be a steadfast pillar of strength, guiding Darcy through the labyrinthine responsibilities of his estate's management. But more importantly, he had become a true confidant—an unexpected ally in the most personal of matters.

Darcy's cousin, Richard Fitzwilliam, had been no less constant. Fitzwilliam, with his irreverent humour and his calm, steady presence was as close as any brother could be, and there was no one Darcy would rather have by his side on this journey north.

Yet, however grateful he was for their unwavering support, his uncle's constant vigilance and his cousin's overbearing solicitude bore down on him, tightening like an invisible restraint.

Staring out at the horizon, he exhaled deeply, the breath leaving his body in a long, weary sigh. Within a fortnight they would reach their destination, and he would learn his fate—whether he would be granted a chance at an ordinary existence or condemned to an uncertain future. The thought sent a shiver down his spine, one that had little to do with the lingering morning chill.

A sudden sound—the sharp snap of a twig perhaps—wrenched Darcy from his thoughts; his head lifted, his gaze alert as he surveyed the silent terrain.

It was only then that he realized how far he had wandered, well beyond the village's borders.

And more unsettling still, he was no longer alone.

MORE THAN YOU KNOW

More Than YOU KNOW

A PRIDE & PREJUDICE VARIATION

JENNIFER ALTMAN

More Than You Know. Copyright © 2025 by Jennifer Altman.

All rights reserved.

No part of this publication may be reproduced, distributed, or transmitted in any form or by any means—including photocopying, recording, or other electronic or mechanical methods—without the prior written permission of the author, except in the case of brief quotations embodied in critical reviews and certain other noncommercial uses permitted by copyright law.

Without in any way limiting the author's exclusive rights under copyright, any use of this publication to "train" generative artificial intelligence (AI) technologies to generate text is expressly prohibited. The author reserves all rights to license uses of this work for generative AI training and development of machine learning language models.

This is a work of fiction. Names, characters, places, and incidents are products of the author's imagination or are used fictitiously. Any resemblance to actual persons, living or dead, is entirely coincidental and not intended by the author.

Front cover image: *Still Life with Flowers* by Ambrosius Bosschaert the elder. Public domain.

Cover Design by Susan Adriani at CloudCat Design.

ISBN 979-8-9929814-0-7 (paperback)

For my father, in loving memory

The girl was on the opposite bank, following the curve of the river. Darcy paused, his eyes narrowing as he took in the solitary figure moving briskly in his direction. The distance between them was such that he was unable to make out her features, but he could discern that she was young, perhaps no more than sixteen or seventeen years of age. Her gown, a simple sprigged muslin, rippled softly as she walked, and her bonnet dangled from one hand, swaying in rhythm with her steady gait. She moved with quiet confidence, seemingly absorbed in her own thoughts, her face tilted slightly towards the sky, as if savouring the morning sun. He tore his gaze away, scanning the area for any sign of a companion, but the countryside lay silent and deserted. No distant figure appeared along the winding path, nor did any sound suggest the approach of any other company.

The girl was alone.

Darcy continued to move in her direction, and when their paths aligned, he stopped, calling out across the rush of the river.

"Pray, excuse me, madam. Might I be of some assistance?"

At the sound of his voice, the girl halted, her posture stiffening at the unexpected address. A flash of wariness sparked in her eyes, and for a moment, he thought she would not answer. But then she smiled, calling back to him, "No, sir, I thank you. I am quite well."

With that said, she dipped into a shallow curtsey before resuming her steps—though her pace had quickened. Watching her retreat, Darcy frowned, unsettled. From her speech and mode of dress, it was evident that the young lady was gently bred, yet she roamed the countryside at daybreak, unaccompanied. Such behaviour was far from customary.

A moment of hesitation gripped him, but it swiftly gave way to a decision. Adjusting his stride, Darcy veered from his original path, matching her pace on the opposing bank.

It did not take long for the girl to notice his altered course. She regarded him with a quizzical expression, yet she neither spoke nor lengthened her stride, as though weighing his intentions.

They proceeded in this silent parallel for several moments until, at last, she stopped, turning to face him with a lifted brow.

"Forgive me, sir, but were you not walking the opposite way?"

"I was," Darcy answered, his tone clipped.

"I see." Her head tilted ever so slightly. "And, may I be so bold as to ask why you have decided to change direction?"

Darcy straightened, instinctively drawing himself to his full height. "I should think that would be obvious," he replied, his voice cool. "I am offering you my protection. You should not be out walking alone in such a desolate area. Any number of hidden dangers might befall a young lady in such a circumstance."

To Darcy's astonishment, the girl gave a light, incredulous laugh. "And how am I to know that *you* are not one of those hidden dangers?"

Darcy sucked in a breath, offended at such a slight. "I assure you, madam, I pose no threat to you. I simply could not, in good conscience, leave you to walk on unaccompanied. I am bound, as a gentleman, to attend you."

The girl regarded him for a moment, as though weighing his words. At last, she gave a slight, almost imperceptible nod. "Very well. As you wish."

And so, they walked—divided by the river, the faint burbling of the water filling the silence between them.

The girl's steps were light, her gown brushing the tops of the grasses along the bank, while Darcy maintained his measured pace, glancing now and again across the flowing water to observe her progress.

In time, the river narrowed, its steady current settling into the quiet meander of a gentle stream. Pausing her strides, the young lady called out, asking whether there was a place ahead where she might cross the water.

Darcy tilted his head but answered evenly, "I believe there is a bridge about half a mile upstream."

She nodded in acknowledgement and continued onwards, her steps sure and unhurried.

They walked until the bridge gradually came into view, rising over the stream below.

As they reached it, Darcy slowed his steps, watching as the girl began to cross. The soft tap of her half-boots echoed faintly on the smooth surface. When she reached the centre of the structure—mere yards from where he stood—she suddenly startled, her gaze locking on something in the near distance.

"Oh!" she cried, and without another word, she lifted her skirts and broke into a run.

Darcy blinked, momentarily taken aback. His eyes followed the line of her vision, settling on a patch of vivid colour among the grasses—a wide expanse of purple wild-flowers swaying in the breeze.

Recovering himself, Darcy exhaled slowly, and after a brief hesitation, he began to follow in the direction of the blooms.

When he reached her, she had already sunk to her knees amidst the sea of wildflowers, her bonnet carelessly discarded in the grass. She leaned forwards with an air of reverence, her fingers grazing the tops of the delicate blossoms.

"Are they not glorious?" she murmured. "They look like perfect little pincushions! I have never seen them in such abundance in Hertfordshire."

Hertfordshire, Darcy mused, silently observing her. So, the young lady came from the south.

"Indeed?" he replied, stepping forwards to better examine the amethyst blooms. "They are devil's-bit—a flowering plant of the scabious family. They thrive in damp soil, so I am not surprised to see them flourishing along the riverbank."

She tilted her head to regard him, and under the weight of her steady gaze, Darcy could feel a surge of heat rising along his jaw.

"Devil's-bit?" she repeated, a faint smile playing upon her lips. "What an unfortunate name for something so lovely."

"If you would prefer the Latin," he replied seriously, "its scientific name is *Succisa pratensis.* The common appellation derives from the shape of its roots. They appear truncated, as though bitten off—a misfortune legend ascribes to the devil himself."

For a moment, she merely blinked up at him, and Darcy inwardly winced, feeling foolish for going on in such a pompous manner. But then her lips curved into a bright, unrestrained smile, and he was startled by the strange stirring within his chest.

"Goodness, you certainly know a great deal about flowers," she teased lightly.

Darcy, unsure how to respond, watched as she reached into the hidden folds of her gown and withdrew a small penknife.

"Wait!" he blurted, surprising himself with the vehemence in his tone. "I neglected to mention a most important detail—the blooms are poisonous to the touch."

She recoiled instantly, eyes widening in alarm, and a rich chuckle escaped his throat.

"Forgive me," he said at once, though a smile still pulled at the corners of his mouth. "That was badly done. I was only teasing. The flowers are perfectly harmless, I assure you."

Her frown deepened, but Darcy crouched down and, with deliberate ease, snapped one of the stems, running his thumb along the cluster of tiny petals.

"See? You have nothing to fear. In truth," he continued, "plants in the scabious family have been used for centuries to treat ailments of the skin. So these blossoms are far more likely to heal than to harm."

He rose and extended the flower in her direction. She hesitated only briefly before accepting it with a crooked smile.

"Well then, I shall have to hold on to this one," she said archly, twirling the stem between her fingers.

For a lingering moment, they simply stood there, the quiet hum of the countryside surrounding them. But soon, a flicker of awareness crossed her features, and she glanced towards the horizon, where the sun had climbed higher in the sky.

"Oh! It is later than I thought," she exclaimed, hastily gathering her discarded bonnet. "I must go. If my relations wake to find me missing, they will worry."

She lifted her skirts and set off towards the footbridge at a brisk pace. Instinctively, Darcy followed, lengthening his stride. Noticing his intent, she flushed delicately.

"You need not trouble yourself. I am bound only for the inn across the square."

She inclined her chin in the direction of the nearby village, now visible beyond the trees. Darcy followed her gaze before nodding his agreement. The girl resumed her measured pace, and Darcy hesitated before calling out impulsively, "Wait! Will you walk this way again tomorrow?"

As soon as the words left his mouth, he could feel his cheeks heating at the boldness of his question, but the girl merely looked back at him with a guileless expression.

"I may," she answered simply, "if the weather holds."

And with that, she offered him a fleeting, luminous smile before her steps carried her across the bridge and out of sight.

That night, Darcy scarcely slept. But, for once, it was not his own troubles that caused his restiveness. His mind was consumed by the enigmatic young lady he had encountered along the riverbank. Her image lingered in his thoughts—the way the morning light had caught the loose tendrils of her hair, the bright curiosity in her eyes, the lilting tone of her laughter. There was an unstudied ease about her, a liveliness so genuine that it unsettled him.

In truth, he could not recall the last time anyone—be it lady or gentleman—had so thoroughly captivated his attention. He, who prided himself on his restraint and discernment, had behaved with uncharacteristic familiarity. What had possessed him to speak in such an open, sportive manner? And worse, what reckless impulse had driven him to arrange another assignation? The very idea was beyond reason!

Was he not the same man who had cautioned her against walking alone in such a remote place? Then, in the next breath, he had encouraged her to do precisely that. It was madness!

He turned restlessly on the thin mattress, the bedsheets twisting around his body as if to ensnare him in his own folly.

And yet—he could not bring himself to regret his boldness. Not when the promise of seeing her again stirred something within him, something he could not even name. The lady—a virtual stranger—had sparked an almost visceral need to know her better, to unravel the mystery of her bright, knowing eyes and easy smile.

But what if she did not come? The thought gnawed at him, causing him a moment of utter panic. He did not even know her name. If she failed to appear, would he be able to find her again in this unfamiliar corner of Yorkshire? How could he explain his need to seek her out when he did not understand it himself?

Darcy exhaled sharply, running a hand through his already dishevelled hair. It was senseless to dwell on such things, and yet sleep would not come. His thoughts circled endlessly, an uneasy blend of anticipation and dread. He had risked too much already, and still, the thought of returning to that quiet stretch of moorland and finding it empty distressed him in a way he could not describe.

Eventually, exhaustion overtook him, and he drifted into a restless slumber, his mind haunted by the fleeting image of a young woman's smile and the uncertain promise of tomorrow.

Darcy was out of his bed before the clock struck six. They had not arranged a specific time to meet, and he could not bear the thought of missing her.

As he strode through the pale morning light, his mind raced with troubling thoughts. Not only had he encouraged the young lady to walk out alone, he had practically insisted upon it. The very idea unsettled him. How would he ever forgive himself if harm should befall her as a result of his recklessness?

The cool morning air was sharp against his skin when Darcy took up his post near the footbridge. He paced restlessly along the river's edge, scanning the near distance for any sign of her. Minutes stretched interminably, until at last, a movement captured his attention. Finally, the girl approached.

"Good morning," he called when she had drawn close enough to hear him.

Her lips immediately curved into a bright smile, and Darcy felt an unexpected warmth bloom inside his chest, as though some long-dormant part of him had quietly awakened.

"Good morning," she replied, dipping into a graceful curtsey.

Darcy inwardly recoiled, realizing he had neglected to offer the same courtesy. He hastily bowed, mortified by the lapse.

Recovering himself, he inclined his head, gesturing towards the path ahead. "If you are not opposed," he began, "I thought we might walk in this direction today. I passed a thicket full of blackberries that looked ripe for the picking."

A flicker of surprise crossed her features, but after a moment she nodded her agreement, and they set off together.

"I had not expected to come upon you so soon," she remarked lightly as they walked. "When we met yesterday, it was at least a mile downriver."

Darcy inclined his head, acknowledging the truth of her observation; but he could hardly admit that he had arrived in the village nearly an hour ago and had spent the intervening time pacing the path between the river and the inn.

"I thought it prudent to wait near the bridge," he answered. "I did not wish for you to venture too far on your own."

A low laugh escaped her lips. "Ah yes, I had forgotten that you frown on young ladies scampering about the countryside unchaperoned."

Darcy's mouth tightened at her teasing tone, but he did not reply.

They walked on in amicable silence, the rhythmic crunch of dirt beneath their boots blending with the gentle rustle of the breeze through the wild grasses. Darcy's thoughts churned, but his watchful gaze remained attentive to the terrain.

He was just about to point out the blackberries in the distance when he noticed the young lady's steps had begun to veer towards the edge of the water.

"Miss—!" Darcy stopped abruptly, realizing he knew not what to call her.

She turned to him, waiting, and he coughed lightly into his fist. "There is moss along the riverbank. It is slick, so pray, be cautious."

She nodded, glancing down and stepping carefully around it. "Thank you, sir. That might have been unfortunate."

They walked on in the direction of the bushes for some moments before Darcy stopped, looking back at her.

"Forgive me for shouting earlier, but I realized that I had no proper way to address you. I still do not know your name."

A slow, serene smile spread across her face, her eyes glinting with quiet mischief.

"No," she agreed, "that is true. As I do not know yours."

She turned to resume their walk, but Darcy called after her, "I beg your pardon, but if we are to continue in one another's company, I believe I must know what name I may use."

She stopped, one brow arching in silent defiance, and Darcy exhaled in quiet frustration.

"Very well," he said at last. "If you will not tell me your name, then I shall be forced to invent one for you."

The girl gazed back at him as Darcy glanced about for inspiration. At length, his eyes settled on the slow trickle of water by their side, and he turned back to her triumphantly.

"I shall call you Miss Rivers."

Her laughter, light and musical, rang out, and he found himself oddly arrested by the sound.

"*That* is hardly a river, sir," she said, playfulness evident in her tone. "Why, it is scarcely more than a stream."

"Yes," he conceded, "but Miss Stream lacks a certain elegance, do you not think?"

She laughed again, the sound so genuine that it made his chest tighten.

"Very well. You may call me Miss Rivers if it pleases you. And what shall I call you?"

Darcy hesitated. He had been the one to request an introduction, but now he realized the risk of revealing his true identity. The name Darcy was well-known in polite society, and his Christian name, Fitzwilliam, no less so.

His gaze drifted towards the horizon as he considered inventing a name—perhaps something as simple as Stone or Meadows. Yet when his eyes met hers once more, he found himself giving her a very different answer from the one he had intended.

"You may call me William," he said quietly.

Her eyes widened in response, a light flush creeping into her cheeks. Clearly, she was well aware of the impropriety of being asked to address him in such a way, but after a pause, her usual composure returned, and she smiled.

"Well then, *William*, perhaps you might lend me your handkerchief. It would be a shame not to collect at least some of those berries before the birds have their feast."

Darcy chuckled, withdrawing his handkerchief and offering it to her with a formal bow, and they approached the briars at a lively pace.

For Darcy, the next hour passed in a contented haze. They moved among the brambles, plucking ripe berries and speaking of everything and nothing. Darcy could scarcely recall a time when he had felt so unencumbered, so free from the cares that had long rested upon his mind.

At last, the sun had risen a fair way into the sky, and they found themselves back at the footbridge. The girl turned to him, offering a polite curtsey before setting off for the village beyond.

"Miss Rivers," Darcy called after her, "will you walk again tomorrow?"

She paused, turning to look back at him, a gentle frown furrowing her brow.

"I am not certain," she answered slowly. "We leave tomorrow."

The words struck him with unexpected force, a knot immediately forming in the pit of his stomach. He had nearly forgotten that he and his relations were also meant to resume their journey.

"Before you go, then," he called, more urgently than he intended. "I can meet you at the usual time."

She hesitated, then offered a small smile.

"I cannot promise anything," she called back to him, "but I shall try."

And with that, she turned and retraced her steps, vanishing from view.

§

That night, exhaustion weighed heavily upon Darcy, dragging him into the deepest slumber he had known in weeks. No restless turning, no dark thoughts to plague his mind—only the comforting stillness of oblivion.

He awoke to the sweet trill of birdsong, the golden light of morning stretched leisurely across the floorboards of his chambers. He rolled onto his side before his eyes snapped open, and for one disorienting moment, he could not comprehend the hour. Then the dreadful realization struck —the sun stood high in the sky.

"God above!" he called out in a choked whisper, flinging aside the bedclothes.

Panic clawed at him as he stumbled towards the washstand. He had overslept—on the one morning he could not afford to do so.

Without thought for his appearance, he tugged on his clothes, scarcely bothering to fasten his cravat properly. Snatching up his coat, Darcy tore from the room, his footfalls echoing sharply along the narrow corridor. His lungs burned as he raced across the grass, his strides eating up the distance to the river.

His heart thundered in his chest, each beat louder than the last. How long had she waited? Or worse—had she gone already? The footbridge loomed ahead, still frustratingly distant. His breath came in ragged gasps as he scoured the opposite bank.

Then he saw her.

A solitary figure, moving along the water's edge. Relief crashed over him, nearly buckling his knees.

"Miss Rivers!" he bellowed, but the wind and the river's steady rush swallowed his shouts.

Heedless of his new Hessians, he strode into the swirling shallows. Ice-cold water surged over his boots, soaking through to his stockings. The swift current dragged against his legs as he pressed on, struggling to maintain his footing. Cupping his hands around his mouth, he called out to her again, his voice desperate and raw.

The figure stilled. Slowly, she turned, her head tilting in surprise as her eyes searched for the source of the sound.

He knew the moment she saw him, as her posture instantly straightened. "William!" she called, lifting her skirts as she approached him at a run. "Forgive me—I waited as long as I could."

"No, the fault is mine," Darcy managed. "I meant to be here over an hour ago."

Scrambling up the rocky embankment, he came to an abrupt halt before her. His heart raced, the words he wished to say tangled on his tongue.

For a moment, they just stood there, rooted in place.

"I am so sorry," she said at length. "I must go. I am already late."

Darcy gave a rigid nod, a knot tightening at the back of his throat.

Then, without warning, she reached out, pressing her

palm gently to his chest, just over his heart. Her touch sent a thunderbolt racing through his body.

"Goodbye, William."

She turned away, moving towards the village at an accelerated pace. Several moments passed before panic seized him. "Wait!" The word tore from him, raw and urgent. "Will you not tell me your name?"

She hesitated before turning to face him. Then she smiled, calling out in a strong clear voice.

"Jane. My name is Jane."

And then she was gone.

Chapter One

Late August 1811, London

The carriage jostled over London's uneven cobblestones as Fitzwilliam Darcy leaned back against the leather squabs. His eyes, heavy-lidded from lack of sleep, took in the familiar sprawl that rose up around him as the distant cries of vendors selling their wares drifted through the open window—yet none of it registered.

Darcy was bone-weary, in both body and mind. The past few weeks had been nothing short of a crucible—a relentless series of trials that had left him dangerously close to the end of his tether. And to think, it had all begun with a single, unforgivably audacious letter.

His aunt, Lady Catherine de Bourgh, had never been one for subtlety, but even by her standards, the express she had sent was nothing short of extortion. She had threatened

—threatened!—to publish an announcement of his supposed engagement to her daughter, Anne, in the London papers if he did not immediately present himself at Rosings to sanction the match.

Darcy's jaw tightened at the memory. The scheme had been as absurd as it was insulting. Did she truly believe he could be so easily coerced? Yet, to his begrudging acknowledgement, the letter had achieved its purpose; it had stirred him from the quiet sanctuary of Pemberley, compelled to put an end to the entire farce, something he should have done long ago.

But fate, in its capricious manner, had intervened. For had he not been forced to travel into Kent to confront her ladyship, he never would have had the fleeting instinct to stop in Ramsgate where his sister, Georgiana, was spending the summer under the care of her newly appointed companion, thereby averting disaster. Even now, his fingers clenched at the thought of how close Georgiana had come to utter ruin. His sweet, trusting fifteen-year-old sister, persuaded into an elopement by that scoundrel, George Wickham. Had he arrived a day later—well, he dared not even consider the consequences.

But amid the fury and the shame, Darcy could not help but feel an unbidden, bitter gratitude. Lady Catherine's imperious summons, meant to further her own ambitions, had inadvertently saved his sister, and for that, he owed his aunt more than he cared to admit.

The carriage slowed, turning into Grosvenor Square and drawing him back to the present. Moments later, the conveyance came to a halt, and a footman hurried forwards to open the door. Descending onto the pavement, Darcy could feel the weight of the city pressing in around him as he slowly climbed the steps, where his long-serving butler greeted him with a bow.

"Welcome home, Mr Darcy. I trust your journey was without incident?"

Darcy acknowledged him with a curt nod, already tugging off his gloves as he stepped into the hall. "Yes. Thank you, Carleton. Please see to my trunks. And send Pierce to my chambers."

"Yes, sir."

Darcy resumed walking, but Carleton remained at his elbow.

"Sir, if I may—"

Halting mid-step, Darcy turned to his butler with thinly veiled annoyance. "Yes, Carleton, what is it?"

Carleton, ever composed, gave a discreet cough before saying evenly, "I thought it prudent to inform you that Colonel Fitzwilliam is currently in residence. He arrived yesterday afternoon."

Darcy startled, turning towards his butler with a narrowed gaze. "Richard is here?"

"Indeed, sir," Carleton confirmed. "I believe he might presently be found in the saloon."

For a moment, Darcy's thoughts raced. His cousin was meant to be escorting Georgiana and his mother, Lady Matlock, to their family's country estate in Derbyshire. What the deuce was he doing sitting in Darcy's saloon?

Without another word, Darcy pivoted sharply, abandoning his original course. His boots echoed against the marble floor as he crossed the hall.

Pushing the door open with force, his eyes scanned the

room until they settled upon the familiar figure slouched comfortably in a high-backed chair, a tumbler of brandy already in hand.

Richard Fitzwilliam looked up, a flicker of surprise crossing his features as Darcy strode towards him, already beginning to speak in an agitated manner.

"Fitzwilliam, what do you do here? Are you not meant to be on your way to Matlock by now?"

"Relax, Cousin, you will do yourself an injury," Richard replied in measured tones, rising to his feet and holding out a hand in placation. "I assure you, all is well."

Darcy dragged his fingers through his hair and forced himself to draw a steadying breath. Moving farther into the room, he came to stand before his cousin as Richard continued, "The ladies are on their way to Briarwood, as planned. His lordship accompanied them."

"His lordship? I thought my uncle had resolved to remain in town?"

Richard's mouth twisted into a wry smirk. "He had—until I mentioned that you were bound for Rosings to put an end to Lady Catherine's schemes concerning your supposed engagement to Anne. Then, quite miraculously, he recalled an urgent matter in Derbyshire that required his immediate attention."

A low laugh escaped his cousin as he returned to his seat, taking a leisurely sip of brandy before placing his glass on a nearby table. "As such, I saw no reason to make the trip myself. So, I elected to wait here for your return."

Relief loosened the tightness in Darcy's chest as his heart slowly returned to a steady rhythm. "Good," he murmured, pivoting towards the sideboard to pour himself a drink. The crystal decanter clinked against the glass as he filled it halfway with the amber liquid.

"And the other business?" Darcy asked quietly. "Regarding Wickham?"

Even the act of forming the blackguard's name left a bitter taste on Darcy's tongue, and he quickly took a long swallow of brandy to wash it away.

Across from him, Richard darted a glance at the tumbler before saying, "Everything has been arranged, exactly as we discussed."

Darcy nodded grimly, crossing the room to sink into the winged chair opposite his cousin. The brandy burned a slow path down his throat, and Darcy closed his eyes, savouring the feeling. He rarely drank any sort of spirits, but at times like this, he was willing to take his chances.

He opened his eyes to find Richard studying him with a pensive expression. "Not that I am surprised, but you look like the very devil. I hesitate to enquire but...how did matters unfold at Rosings?"

Darcy grimaced, twisting his glass and watching the liquid swirl. "Much as I had anticipated. Anne stared at her shoes for the duration of the interview, while Lady Catherine nearly brought down the walls with her tirade on duty, honour, and family loyalty. Still, I have no regrets. The conversation ought to have occurred long ago."

Richard smothered a sigh. "What, exactly, did you say to her?"

"What could I say? I told her the truth." At Richard's narrowed gaze, he continued, "At least as much of the truth as I was at liberty to share. I simply informed Lady Catherine that as soon as Georgiana was settled, I would be leaving England and that I had no intention of taking a wife before I went."

Richard gave him a long, measured look, and Darcy sighed, running a finger along the rim of his glass.

"I am only sorry it has taken me this long to speak my piece. Anne is seven-and-twenty! She deserves the chance to marry and raise a family, if that is her desire. I have done her a great disservice by not making my position clear years ago."

Richard released a breath, rubbing a hand over his face. "I know you and our cousin would never have made a love match. But…given the circumstances, could you not have seen your way to marrying Anne? You know she would not talk, and once you were wed, surely Lady Catherine would do everything in her power to keep your confidence."

"Certainly not!" Darcy replied, appalled at the very thought. "I have told you—I shall never marry. I could not condemn any woman to such a fate. Besides, Anne deserves some happiness in this life, and she will not find that with me."

"You and your blasted principles," Richard muttered, and Darcy scowled back at him.

"Pray, do not laud me for my principles. There is little honour in what I have done. For years, I allowed our aunt to perpetuate this fiction because it suited my purposes. But it was cowardice, not virtue. Had Lady Catherine not threatened to announce the engagement, I might never have bothered to end the masquerade."

Richard regarded him steadily. "Well, I can hardly fault you for going to Rosings. If you had not stopped in Ramsgate, Georgiana would be bound to that degenerate

Wickham as we speak." He took another slow drink, his expression hardening. "But Anne... I still say you should have left that well alone. You know how much influence Lady Catherine wields in society. Now you have turned an ally into an enemy. And there is no telling what she would do for her daughter's sake."

Darcy's grip tightened around his glass. His cousin spoke the truth, and yet—what choice had he truly had?

"We must hope," he said quietly, "that your father can keep her in check. At least until Georgiana's future is fixed."

Richard's eyes narrowed thoughtfully, but he said nothing more.

They sat in silence for some moments before Darcy, seeking a change of subject, made a faint sound at the back of his throat.

"I do not believe I have properly thanked you for persuading your mother to have Georgiana to stay at Briarwood. After being so deceived by Mrs Younge, I am in no hurry to entrust her care to another paid companion. And I must confess, after this debacle with Wickham, I fear I find myself completely out of my depth where my sister is concerned."

"Oh, that was nothing," his cousin replied, waving Darcy's gratitude away with a flick of his wrist. "You know how Mother is. She cares deeply for Georgiana, and she does love to be of use."

Darcy hesitated, then asked cautiously, "And you did not...tell her anything?"

"About Ramsgate?" Richard's expression sobered. "Certainly not. The fewer people who know about that, the better. And from what I have gathered, Georgiana wants nothing more than to put the entire ordeal behind her. So, I do not think we have anything to fear from that quarter."

Darcy nodded slowly. As Georgiana had scarcely said two words to him since he had dragged her back to town, he would have to take his cousin's word for her state of mind.

"And what of Wickham?" Darcy continued. "Are you certain he will not talk?"

"Not if he wishes to retain all his limbs. I threatened him within an inch of his life.

I still wish you had let me run him through."

Darcy exhaled sharply. "You know full well why I could not—much as I might have wished it. We cannot risk drawing attention to the matter. Georgiana's reputation is in a precarious enough state as it is."

Richard muttered something unintelligible under his breath before slumping back in his chair. "I still say you let him off far too easily. But at least the commission I purchased for him—or I should rightly say the commission *you* purchased for him—places him under the command of Colonel Bartholomew, one of the most exacting officers in His Majesty's Army. Wickham will find no leniency there."

"Good. As much as it galls me to have had to spend yet another sum of money on that reprobate, at least this time I know he will not gamble or drink it away. Perhaps the army will teach him a lesson or two."

Richard smirked darkly. "Doubtful. But at least we have got him out of the way, for now. In any case, one good thing has come of this entire disaster—it has flushed you out of hiding. How long do you intend to remain in town?"

Darcy's shoulders stiffened. "No longer than necessary. I shall depart for Pemberley as soon as Walsh returns."

"Ah, yes. I meant to ask how you were faring without your faithful shadow. Where has he gone off to, again?"

Darcy forbore to comment on his cousin's sarcastic tone, saying only, "He is in Bedfordshire, visiting relations. He will return to London on Tuesday week."

Regarding him with a thoughtful expression, Richard began slowly, "Hmm…that does not give us much time, but we shall make the best of it. Granted, the Season is well and truly over, but there must still be a few soirées we can attend. I believe Lady Copley's ball takes place on—"

"No," Darcy cut in sharply.

Richard blinked back at him. "Oh, very well. A ball might be a bit much, but surely—"

"Richard, desist!" Darcy's tone was clipped. "Once and for all, the answer is no—to all of it. I have no intention of going out into society."

Richard stared at him for a long moment before leaning back with a sigh. "Then, might I be so bold as to ask, what *do* you intend to do while you are in town? Lock yourself away in your study?"

Darcy said nothing, setting his glass down with a quiet thud. Moving to the window, he pulled back the heavy curtains, staring out at the street below. His thoughts, however, were far from London.

"I thought I might travel to Hertfordshire for a few days…"

His voice faltered, and behind him, Richard mumbled an oath under his breath.

"Not this again! Darcy, you must abandon this folly. I

27

should imagine you have searched every inch of that county by now, and to what purpose? There must be a thousand women named Jane in Hertfordshire alone. And even if—by some miracle—you did stumble upon the one you seek, what then?"

Allowing the curtain to fall back into place, Darcy turned once again to face his cousin. "I do not know. I simply wish to see her. I cannot explain it."

Richard sighed heavily, shaking his head in exasperation. "And she gave you nothing else to go on? No surname, no mention of her family?"

"No. I only know that she came from Hertfordshire and was travelling with her aunt and uncle. She did not even reveal her Christian name until the moment before she left."

Richard quirked a brow. "She must have been quite a beauty to leave you in such a state after all these years. Of course, you know what they say about country girls," he added with a wink and an exaggerated smirk.

Darcy narrowed his gaze. "Do not be crass."

He turned away, staring into the cold, empty hearth. He could hardly expect Richard to understand when he did not. But it had not been Jane's physical beauty that had so captivated him—though she had been undeniably handsome. No, it was something else...something far more elusive, something in her very bearing that was impossible to name.

"She was different," he said quietly, choosing his words with care. "I do not know how to explain, exactly, but she was so lively and clever. She did not dissemble, nor put on airs. And she noticed things—things that would have seemed insignificant to the ordinary person. She had the most expressive countenance..."

Richard snorted, breaking the moment. "You sound like a lovesick schoolboy."

Darcy stiffened, but his cousin pressed on. "Honestly, Darcy, I think you have built her up into some paragon inside your mind. If you ever did find her, I doubt she would live up to the fantasy you have created. For all you know, she could be the daughter of a shopkeeper or a tradesman," he continued with a theatrical shudder. "You said yourself her manner of dress was not that of someone in the first circles."

Darcy's frown deepened. "She was out for a morning walk. One could hardly expect her to be dressed in satin and lace."

"Yes, a morning walk," his cousin repeated, "without even a maid to accompany her. That alone says something about her upbringing."

A flicker of annoyance rose in Darcy's chest. While he had thought the same himself upon their first meeting, it sat ill with him to hear his cousin speak so disparagingly of the lady he admired.

His jaw tightened. "Say what you will, but as you have made abundantly clear, the point is moot, as I shall likely never see her again."

Richard opened his mouth to speak, but before he could reply, a sharp knock echoed through the room, granting Darcy a welcome reprieve.

"Enter," Darcy called out curtly.

The door opened to reveal Carleton, ever the model of

composed efficiency. The butler inclined his head in a respectful bow.

"Forgive the interruption, sir," Carleton intoned smoothly, "but a Mr Bingley is calling. Shall I inform him that you are not at home?"

Inwardly, Darcy stifled a groan. How the devil had Bingley discovered his presence in town so quickly? He had only just arrived! Darcy sighed. Despite his weariness and general distaste for company, he could not bring himself to turn his friend away. Bingley's good-natured persistence was difficult to rebuff.

"No," Darcy replied, schooling his expression. "Show him into the library. I shall be with him directly."

Carleton bowed once more and withdrew, the faint click of the latch marking his departure.

Out of the corner of his eye, Darcy saw his cousin lean slightly forwards in his chair, a curious glint in his eyes.

"Well, this is unexpected," Richard mused. "An outsider permitted entry into your sacred hermitage? Who is this Bingley? Your solicitor or some such?"

"No," Darcy responded tersely. "He is an old friend. We were at university together."

Richard cast him a sidelong glance. "At Cambridge? I cannot recall you ever mentioning him. In fact, I was under the distinct impression that you had no friends beyond Walsh and myself."

Disregarding his cousin's gibe, Darcy stood, adjusting his cuffs with measured precision.

When it became clear he had no intention of elaborating, Richard continued, "How did he know you were in town? The knocker is not on the door."

"I haven't the vaguest idea. But I know Bingley—if I do not see him now, he will only come back again."

Richard frowned. "I cannot see that as a problem. If you wish to avoid the connection, why not simply instruct Carleton to say you are not at home?"

Darcy exhaled slowly, pinching the bridge of his nose. "I am not trying to avoid the connection, precisely. Bingley is a good man, and we were quite close at one time...before circumstances interfered. In any case, we have maintained a correspondence. Last summer, he and his sisters visited Pemberley for a few days when they were travelling to some relations in Scarborough."

Across from him, Richard straightened in his chair, surprise flickering across his face. "You had guests at Pemberley?"

"Only for a brief stay. Bingley requested permission to break their journey there, and I could see no polite way to refuse."

Richard gave a low whistle. "Well, I'll be... I should have paid good money to see that. You, entertaining guests."

Darcy shot him a withering look. "As much as I would love to stay and listen to more of your witty rejoinders, I believe I have kept Bingley waiting long enough. If you will excuse me?"

He turned towards the door, but before his hand closed around the latch, Richard was already rising to his feet.

"I believe I shall accompany you," his cousin declared, straightening his coat with a practised tug. "After all, we would not wish to take any chances. And besides, I think I should rather like to meet this Mr Bingley."

Darcy sighed, inwardly resigned. There was little use arguing when his cousin's curiosity was piqued.

"Very well. But do try to behave yourself."

Richard chuckled, falling into step beside him. "When have I done otherwise?"

Darcy merely pressed his lips together and led the way from the room.

The cousins had scarcely crossed the library's threshold before an enthusiastic Bingley sprang to his feet, bounding in Darcy's direction and pumping his hand with a boyish grin.

"Darcy! Well met, old friend!"

Turning to his cousin, Darcy proceeded to perform the necessary introductions, and the three gentlemen then made their way to a cluster of comfortable sofas in the centre of the room.

"Well, I must say, this *is* a surprise!" Bingley began as soon as they were seated. "When Caroline told me she had seen your carriage, I thought she must have mistaken the matter, but then my sister has always possessed a sharp eye, and an even sharper memory—particularly where gentlemen of good fortune are concerned."

He laughed lightly at his own jest, though Darcy could not quite suppress the flicker of irritation at Miss Bingley's meddlesome attentions. Yet, despite this, the familiar ease in Bingley's demeanour tugged at Darcy's composure, tempering his usual reserve. Although they had drifted apart over the years, Bingley's open and affable nature remained unchanged—a trait that had always made him well-liked in every company.

"I trust you do not mind my calling unannounced,"

Bingley continued with his usual exuberance. "Caroline was most emphatic that I pay my respects as soon as may be."

Darcy felt the corners of his mouth twitch upwards despite himself. "No, I am glad you came," he admitted, surprised to find the words sincere. "My stay in London will be brief, but it is always agreeable to see old friends."

Bingley's expression instantly brightened. "Well I do hope you will be here long enough to dine with us in Berkeley Square."

Obviously noting the shift in Darcy's expression, Bingley added eagerly, "Ah, yes! I do not believe I mentioned—my sister Louisa is recently married to Mr Arthur Hurst. We are making use of his townhouse for the time being. You must come—we are practically around the corner."

After extending his good wishes to the newly wed Mrs Hurst, Darcy replied, "As for dining, I thank you for the invitation, though I am not certain it will be possible. My time in town is limited, and I have several matters that require my attention."

Bingley's expression faltered only slightly before his natural optimism recovered. "That is a pity," he said, though his tone remained light. "Although this is not the fashionable time to be in London, there are still some delightful diversions to be found. Why, not a fortnight ago, I attended an assembly and met the most enchanting young lady! Truly, Darcy, she is an angel! And I have every reason to believe—"

Darcy sank deeper into the cushions, allowing Bingley's rhapsodizing to wash over him. His friend had not changed in the least when it came to women. Even through their infrequent correspondence, Darcy had counted no fewer than half a dozen 'angels' who had captured Bingley's fleeting affections since their university days. It was, in truth, a wonder the man had not been leg-shackled long ago.

The sudden sound of his cousin clearing his throat jolted Darcy from his inattentive reverie. He straightened abruptly, realizing with some embarrassment that Bingley had ceased speaking and was now regarding him expectantly.

Drawing a steadying breath, Darcy attempted to slow his rapidly beating heart.

"Pray, forgive me, Bingley," he began with as much equanimity as he could muster, "my mind was elsewhere. What was it that you were saying?"

"Bingley was speaking of Lady Copley's ball," his cousin supplied, lounging back with practised ease. "He and the enchanting young lady he has just been telling us about will be in attendance, and he wonders whether he might have the pleasure of seeing you there."

"Ah. I am afraid not. Walsh is travelling with me, and I am only in town until he returns from a brief sojourn to Bedfordshire. We depart for Pemberley within the week."

To Darcy's mounting irritation, Richard's lips curled into a slow, knowing smirk. "How fortunate then that the ball is in two days' time."

Darcy cast his cousin a withering glance, but Bingley remained blissfully unaware, his enthusiasm undimmed.

"I hear it will be a grand occasion!" his friend declared eagerly. "Of course, my sisters and Mr Hurst will be joining me. Caroline, especially, would be most pleased to see you again."

Inwardly, Darcy suppressed a groan, but Richard fairly beamed his approbation.

"Splendid! We shall both be delighted to attend."

"Richard." Darcy's tone was low, clipped, and laced with warning. "I believe you are well aware of my feelings on the matter."

At last, Bingley seemed to sense a shift in the air, glancing cautiously between the two cousins. However, Richard, undeterred, leaned forwards with a conspiratorial gleam in his eye.

"Darcy has been studiously avoiding all social engagements of late—too many ambitious mamas thrusting their marriageable daughters into his path." He chuckled, casting a wink in Bingley's direction. "But never fear, Cousin. I shall be on hand to keep you out of trouble."

Darcy's jaw tightened, the muscle in his cheek twitching, but Bingley's broad smile only widened.

"Well, it is settled, then! We shall see each other at the ball!"

Darcy exhaled slowly, resigned to his fate.

"Indeed," he muttered, though his tone suggested anything but enthusiasm.

Richard said nothing more, merely settling back with a look that suggested he had won far more than the argument.

ॐ

"I do not know why I let you talk me into this," Darcy

muttered two days later as their carriage jolted through the crowded London streets.

"Yes, you do," his cousin replied with a satisfied grin. "It is important for you to be seen, for Georgiana's sake, if not your own. People are beginning to talk."

"Well they will certainly have something to talk about if this goes wrong!" Darcy spat back at him. "You will have to take Georgiana abroad to find a husband, for I shall be in Bedlam."

"Nonsense," Richard replied with his usual good humour, "all will be well. As I have already told you, you need not dance. But it will be good for you to be seen while you are in town. We agreed on the importance of laying the groundwork for Georgiana's Season, and you will have to begin sometime. The longer you stay away, the more difficult it will be."

To this, Darcy gave no answer, merely staring out of the window at the passing carriages. He knew Richard was right, but that did not make the prospect of spending the evening being gaped at like a public curiosity any more palatable.

Turning away from the darkened glass, he looked back at his cousin. "What is it they say about me?" he asked with some trepidation.

"I beg your pardon?"

Darcy sighed, barely refraining from rolling his eyes. "You said people were beginning to talk. What do they say?"

"Oh, you know, just the usual," Richard replied with a wave of his hand. "That you are a recluse, that you think yourself superior to the rest of polite society, that you are consumed by grief."

Darcy frowned. Although he had been close to both his parents, his father had been gone above five years now, and his mother had died three years before that. It hardly seemed likely that he would still be mourning their deaths. However, he supposed when it came to his avoidance of society, grief was a preferable explanation to some of the other alternatives.

"Nothing else? Nothing about Walsh, or…?"

Richard's eyebrows lifted. "No. But you will not be able to bring him with you when you return for Georgiana's Season. It would be noticed. I shall request leave so that I can accompany you whenever you go out. No one will think anything of that. I am Georgiana's second guardian, after all."

Once again, Darcy sighed, sinking farther into the plush squabs. "Perhaps I ought not to come at all. As you said, we share guardianship of Georgiana. You could be the one to escort her to all the necessary events…" He lapsed into silence as his cousin stared at him incredulously.

"You cannot be serious. It is one thing for me to accompany you, but *you* are her nearest relation! How would we explain your absence?"

When Darcy did not answer, his cousin leaned in, resting his elbows upon his knees. "Darcy, you promised you would see this to completion. You must make more of an effort. If you ask me, you have already left it too long. It was one thing the year or two following your father's death. Back then, it was easy to make excuses—you were grieving, and you had Georgiana to look after and Pemberley to manage. But you have scarcely been seen in public these last five years. Georgiana will never make a suitable match if you have the reputation of being some sort of recluse."

"It is preferable to anyone learning the truth," Darcy muttered. "Besides, Georgiana has a dowry of thirty thousand pounds—she will have no trouble finding a husband."

"Is that what you want for her? A fortune hunter? Another George Wickham who will marry her for her money and make her life a misery?"

"Of course not!" Darcy snapped, his countenance hot with anger. "Why do you think I am sitting in this carriage, even now!"

He turned away, drawing a ragged breath before fixing his cousin with a steely gaze.

"Very well, I shall keep my promise. I shall do everything in my power to see Georgiana settled. But mark my words—if we are successful in this, I shall leave England the moment she is married. And I will *not* be coming back."

The heat of the ballroom pressed in from all sides, thick and suffocating. As they made their way through the shifting crowd, Darcy tugged at his cravat, though the gesture did little to ease the constriction in his throat. The air was heavy with the mingled scents of beeswax, perfume, and too many bodies packed into too small a space. Candles blazed from the chandeliers overhead, their flames flickering against the gilt-framed mirrors and casting sharp, unrelenting light that caused beads of perspiration to instantly dampen Darcy's brow. He could not recall the last time he had been in a ballroom. Certainly not since his father's death, and everything that had followed.

Beside him, Richard navigated the crowd with confident familiarity, offering clipped greetings and charming smiles. But at length, he glanced back at Darcy, and his expression faltered.

"Are you well?" Fitzwilliam murmured, and Darcy responded with a curt nod.

His cousin regarded him with a wary expression before saying, "Well, let us get out of this crush, in any case. We shall find Lady Copley and pay our respects, then adjourn to the card room. It will be quieter in there."

Again, Darcy nodded, his mind on steadying his breathing as his cousin led the way through the throng of merrymakers. The swell of conversation and the strains of the orchestra tangled into a cacophony that grated on his already frayed nerves. All around him, ladies in richly-coloured silks and men in stiff evening coats moved in an endless, glittering tide. Laughter rang out in shrill bursts, ribbons of gossip curling through the crowd like smoke. Over the din, he could hear the sharp gasps and hushed whispers that followed their slow progress, and it was all he could do to keep his gaze fixed upon his cousin's back.

They were halfway to the edge of the room when the sound of his name being called caused Darcy to startle, his head snapping up instinctively.

"Fitzwilliam! I thought that was you!"

A gentleman in military dress emerged from the crowd, striding towards Richard with unmistakable good cheer.

"Captain Hargrove," Richard greeted him heartily, clasping the man's hand. "What the devil are you doing in town?"

Darcy exhaled, feeling foolish. Of course, it was Richard who was being addressed, not him; no one here would be calling out his Christian name.

Fitzwilliam, ever the gentleman, turned to perform the necessary introductions. But after offering a polite bow and the briefest greeting civility would allow, Darcy promptly angled his body away. He had never been comfortable making conversation with strangers, and tonight, more than ever, he wished to remain unnoticed.

Hoping his cousin's conversation would be mercifully brief, Darcy let his eyes drift across the crowded ballroom. Although many faces were unfamiliar, several stood out. Across the room, he spotted Bingley's two sisters standing beside a portly gentleman with a ruddy complexion—Mr Hurst, Darcy presumed. As he watched, Miss Bingley lifted her fan, leaning in to whisper something to her elder sister. Mrs Hurst frowned, glancing towards the dancers as her younger sister's feathers bobbed emphatically with a determined tilt of her chin.

Darcy followed her gaze.

There was Bingley, beaming as he led his partner through the steps with easy confidence. His friend's face was flushed with good cheer, his smile broad and unguarded.

Darcy's attention shifted to the lady at Bingley's side. He could not make out her features at this distance, but there was something about her—the effortless poise in her movements, the graceful tilt of her head—that caught him off guard. She was slender, light on her feet, moving through the dance with practised ease.

Something about the lady seemed familiar… Unsettlingly so.

The music swelled and then slowed, signalling the dance's end. Bingley leaned in, saying something that made the lady laugh. Then, as though sensing eyes upon him, Bingley glanced up. Darcy felt his cheeks burn to be caught staring, but his friend's face brightened instantly, and he murmured a few more words to his companion before offering his arm and leading her in Darcy's direction.

Darcy straightened at once, casting a glance at Richard, who was still engrossed in conversation and heedless of the rest of the room.

The crowd seemed to part as Bingley approached, the unknown lady's head tilted towards his as the pair engaged in quiet conversation.

Darcy's pulse quickened, a disquieting tension settling in his chest.

And then she looked up, and their gazes locked.

Darcy froze.

A jolt—sharp and startling—shot through him as recognition struck with blinding clarity.

His breath caught, and before reason could intervene, the name tore from his lips in a ragged whisper.

"Jane!"

Chapter Two

F or one agonizing moment, silence stretched between them. Darcy remained rooted in place as the echo of his voice seemed to hang in the air.

Jane.

He had spoken the name aloud—blurted it, in fact—without a shred of decorum or thought. The word had burst from him with all the restraint of a startled schoolboy, and now it lingered in the space between them.

The young lady blinked, her expression flickering—first with surprise then something unreadable—before her gaze dropped demurely to the floor.

Beside him, Bingley's bright countenance creased in visible confusion, his eyes darting between his companion and Darcy. The silence grew heavier, threatening to become oppressive, before Bingley gave a low chuckle, breaking the tension.

"Forgive me, I have quite forgotten my manners!"

He turned eagerly to the young woman at his side, offering her a broad smile.

"Miss Elizabeth Bennet, may I present my good friend Mr Fitzwilliam Darcy of Pemberley in Derbyshire to your acquaintance?"

Attempting to regulate his emotions, Darcy offered the lady a shallow bow, but he did not miss the light flush that infused her countenance, nor had he failed to note the flash of recognition in her eyes when their gazes met.

So, he had not been mistaken. It *was* her.

"Miss Bennet," he murmured, his voice hoarse despite his effort to steady it.

The lady—Elizabeth—curtsied, though her movements were a shade more hesitant than they ought to have been.

"The pleasure is mine, Mr Darcy," she replied politely, but her eyes looked everywhere but at his.

He gave a low murmur of acknowledgement before adding, "Miss Bennet, pray forgive my informal—and erroneous—manner of address just now. You remind me a good deal of someone I met in Yorkshire some years ago."

At his words, her colour deepened, yet there was a slight quirk to her lips as she replied lightly, "Someone you thought well of, I hope?"

"Indeed."

Their gazes held for a long moment before Richard joined them, and Darcy was forced to look away as Bingley once again performed the necessary introductions.

"Well," Bingley continued, "I had best be returning Miss Bennet to her relations."

Once again, the young lady dropped a curtsey, but before they could step away, Darcy heard his own voice call out, "Miss Bennet, if you are not engaged for the next, might I request the honour of your hand?"

Out of the corner of his eye, he could see his cousin's eyebrows jump, but his attention remained fixed on the object of his interest.

To Darcy's relief, she flushed prettily before answering in the affirmative, taking the arm he offered and allowing him to lead her to where the next set was forming.

Quickly taking their places at the end of the line just as the music began, they moved through the figures of the dance. Around him, Darcy could hear startled murmurs as the other guests took note of his presence, but his focus never strayed from his partner.

"So, *Miss Bennet*, is it? Miss *Elizabeth* Bennet," he finally intoned as the steps brought them face-to-face.

Once again, the lady flushed slightly, but her gaze was steady as she answered, "Yes," in a calm, clear voice.

"Not Jane, then," Darcy persisted.

"No."

The pattern forced them to turn away from each other, leaving Darcy several moments to seethe in silence at the unaffected manner of her reply.

"And might I be so bold as to ask *why* you gave your name as Jane, when in fact it is Elizabeth?" he enquired when they were again in close proximity.

The lady arched one delicate brow. "I should imagine you know why," she answered, and once again Darcy was left to stew as the steps drew them apart.

"I am afraid I do not," he responded stiffly, as soon as he was able, and Elizabeth seemed to take pity on him, saying mildly, "We were scarcely more than strangers to one another, sir. It would have been imprudent of me to have shared my Christian name."

They changed partners then, and Darcy was forced to focus his attention on the pattern of the dance.

"Then why give me any name at all?" he hissed back at her as soon as opportunity allowed. "I should have preferred to go on thinking of you as Miss Rivers than to have been taken for a fool."

Elizabeth's eyes widened slightly at the vehemence in his tone, and she briefly looked away.

"I assure you it was not maliciously done." She paused for a moment before adding, "Jane is my sister's name. It was she who was travelling with me that summer."

"Ah. Of course," Darcy replied, making no effort to disguise the bitterness in his voice. "You gave me her name instead of your own so that if any negative repercussions were to have arisen from our meetings, your sister would have been the one who bore the blame."

To Darcy's chagrin, the young lady looked genuinely offended.

"Certainly not! Besides, my aunt and uncle would never have believed that Jane was out walking before breakfast, let alone conversing with an unknown gentleman."

Darcy opened his mouth to answer, yet was forced to hold his tongue as she spun away from him. But when the dance again brought them together, it was Elizabeth who spoke.

"I apologize for deceiving you, sir. However, I do not see what difference it can make now."

"It does make a difference! I wish to know why you felt the need to lie to me," he pressed. Attempting to steady his breathing, he continued in a gentler tone, "I know we were not well acquainted, but I always believed you to have been truthful."

"Oh?" she replied with an arch expression. "The way you were truthful with me, *William?*"

"That is entirely different!" Darcy sputtered, but he could not help but note the heat of a flush he felt climbing up his neck. "William is an abbreviation of my given name. It is not a bald-faced fabrication."

Elizabeth frowned up at him, but he could see the heightened colour in her cheeks. Once more, the couple was forced to endure another separation. However, when the pattern reunited them, he could see that her expression had softened.

"Mr Darcy, pray let us not quarrel. It was long ago. I am certain neither of us had any expectation of seeing the other after we parted ways. But now that we have met again, I hope we can put the past behind us and continue as...friends?"

Darcy stared into her upturned face, her dark eyes flashing with a mixture of humility and hope, and a vice clamped tightly around his heart. *Friends? Dear God, he did not want to be her friend. He wanted to gather her in his arms and crush her to his chest and never let her go!*

He realized too late that the music had stopped, and Elizabeth was now looking at him, a light furrow creasing her forehead.

Immediately, Darcy stepped back, releasing her gloved hands and bowing stiffly. He needed to gather his wits; he was already wading into dangerous waters in more ways than one.

"Forgive me, Miss Bennet, my mind was elsewhere. Yes, of course. You are right. It was long ago."

At his words, Elizabeth seemed to relax, and a delicate smile curved her lips.

"Come," she urged gently, tilting her chin towards the edge of the ballroom. "I shall introduce you to my aunt and uncle—they are just over there."

Following the subtle motion, Darcy's eyes settled on a fashionably dressed couple of middle years. The lady was deep in conversation with a woman Darcy did not recognize, but the gentleman's gaze was another matter—firm, unwavering, and fixed directly upon him.

Darcy's pulse quickened.

Turning back to Elizabeth, he replied crisply, "I thank you, Miss Bennet, but I am afraid I must decline."

Her smile faltered, the faintest shadow crossing her features. Before she could enquire further, Richard reappeared, accompanied by Bingley, who eagerly offered Elizabeth his arm, which she accepted with grace.

Darcy watched her go, an inexplicable hollowness opening within him as though something precious was slipping beyond his grasp.

It was only when Richard's hand came to rest lightly on his shoulder that Darcy stirred.

"Darcy?" Richard's voice was low but edged with concern. "Are you certain you are well? You look as if—"

"No, it is only a headache," he replied, dismissing his cousin's dubious expression, "but I have had enough. Stay if you wish, but I am going home."

Without waiting for a reply, Darcy turned sharply on his heel, striding towards the door, leaving behind the stifling heat, the press of bodies, and the haunting memory of Elizabeth Bennet's eyes.

§&

Mercifully, aside from one brief enquiry regarding Darcy's health, Richard remained silent during the carriage ride back to Grosvenor Square. The steady percussion of the horses' hoofs and the muted hum of London's streets did little to soothe the turmoil in Darcy's mind. He sat stiffly, his eyes trained on the shadowed lanes beyond the window, though their shapes wavered and passed unnoticed.

Once inside the marbled entrance hall, Darcy bade his cousin a good night with the curt assurance that his headache required only rest. Without further word, he stalked towards the sanctuary of his chambers, eager to escape Richard's silent scrutiny. But even as he settled into the vast solitude of his bed, he knew sleep would elude him.

For every time he closed his eyes, he saw her.

Elizabeth.

Her eyes—dark, bright, and impossibly expressive— seemed to be seared upon his consciousness, and her voice, light and teasing, echoed faintly in his mind.

For four long years, the woman he had known only as *Jane* had haunted his thoughts. Not a day had passed when she had not, in some form, occupied his mind. Yet seeing her again, standing poised and radiant in the ballroom, had shaken him to his very core.

Striking his pillow, Darcy rolled onto his back, staring at the embroidered canopy above. Richard had been right, of course. He had been a fool to search for her; he knew that now. What had he hoped to gain? Had he truly believed that finding her after all this time would bring him peace? That he might simply satisfy some lingering curiosity and walk away unscathed?

Darcy sighed. Perhaps, he thought bitterly, some part of him had hoped to find her happily settled. That she would appear on another gentleman's arm, a ring upon her finger, smiling with the ease of a woman content in her life. Perhaps that sight would have extinguished the stubborn flame he still carried for her, leaving him free to walk away without regret.

Or perhaps he had foolishly believed that time had dulled her brilliance. That her beauty and spirit were embellishments of his memory, mere imaginings of a heart too long starved of affection.

But he had been wrong.

Painfully wrong.

If anything, Elizabeth Bennet was even more captivating than he remembered. The girlish delicacy of her features had given way to refined elegance; her cheekbones more defined, her complexion radiant. Her figure, once slight, now bore the graceful curves of a woman grown. Yet the essence of her remained unchanged. Her eyes still danced with intelligence and mischief, her smile still stole the breath from his lungs, and the brief touch of her gloved hand had only made him long for more.

Darcy groaned quietly, dragging a hand down his face. And now, of all things, she was being courted by Bingley!

He wondered briefly whether his friend would offer for her. He had to think not. Bingley's affections were notoriously fleeting, his heart easily swayed by a pretty face.

Yet Elizabeth was no ordinary young lady. Her wit, her poise, her undeniable spirit—of course Bingley was drawn in, as any man would be. And the mere thought of it made Darcy's stomach twist.

He sighed, knowing that, in the end, it did not matter. Whether it was Bingley or another, Elizabeth would marry. Somewhere out there was a gentleman who would one day have the right to claim her as his own. To know the softness of her skin beneath his hands. To lose himself in the warmth of her breath. To wake beside her each morning, and to fall asleep each night tangled in her arms.

A sharp, unrelenting pain tightened in his chest.

For Darcy knew one thing with absolute certainty: that man would never be him.

"Well, Darcy, we have done it! Our scheme was a success!"

Darcy glanced up from his coffee as Richard strode into the breakfast room, his smile triumphant. A folded newspaper was held aloft, brandished like a battle standard.

Darcy merely lifted his cup to his lips, silently willing the strong brew to dull the pounding in his temples.

Undeterred by his cousin's silence, Richard helped himself to a generous serving of kippers, settling into the opposite chair. With a flourish, he tapped the paper he had laid upon the table.

"According to this, your appearance at Lady Copley's ball is the talk of the town. Every drawing room in London is rife with chatter, speculating on the identity of the mystery woman you deigned to honour with a dance. I have to give you credit, Cousin, you certainly know how to play your cards."

Darcy forbore to answer, but Richard just grinned broadly, shovelling a heaping helping of kippers onto his fork. "I must confess, I doubted the wisdom of our early departure, but it seems to have worked in your favour. Your abrupt withdrawal only stoked curiosity. And your decision to dance—when all of society knows how you detest the activity! Of course, I cannot think it would be prudent to—"

"It was her."

Richard paused, his fork halfway to his mouth. "I beg your pardon?"

Pressing his lips into a tight line, Darcy set his cup down with a muted clatter. "The woman I danced with. It was her. Jane."

Richard blinked back at him, confusion briefly clouding his features. "Bingley's young lady? Surely not! Did Bingley not introduce her as—"

"Miss Elizabeth Bennet," Darcy finished grimly. "Yes. It seems the name she gave me was false. I have spent the better part of four years searching for a woman who did not even exist."

Richard leaned back in his chair, stunned into momentary silence. Then, recovering, he let out a low whistle. "Well, I'll be..." He paused, but in a matter of moments, his customary smirk returned. "Though the woman I saw was certainly no figment of the imagination," he added with a suggestive expression.

Darcy scowled as his cousin leaned back in his chair.

"So, *that* was Jane."

When Darcy did not answer, he continued, "What will you do, now that you have finally found her?"

Darcy looked down, assiduously adjusting his cuffs.

"Do? Nothing. I have seen her, and that is the end of it."

"The end of it?" Richard echoed, regarding him incredulously. "You cannot be serious! You have spent four years searching for this girl, and now that you have found her, you will do...nothing?"

Darcy's gaze shifted away. "I should think you would be pleased. After all, you were the one who told me it was pointless to look for her. Besides, she lied to me," he muttered, his voice heavy with resentment.

"Lied?" Richard blinked. "Oh, you cannot possibly mean the matter of her name?"

"Of course I do," Darcy snapped, irritation creeping into his tone. "Our entire acquaintance was built upon a lie."

Richard chuckled dryly. "Ha! That is rich, coming from you."

Darcy's scowl deepened as he abruptly pushed back his chair, stalking to the sideboard.

"Oh, come now, Darcy," Richard pressed. "Did it never occur to you that she might have been protecting herself? A young lady, alone on the moors—she would have been a fool to reveal her identity to a virtual stranger. And as I recall, she only gave you her name when you parted. That hardly seems the work of a deceitful woman."

Darcy returned to his seat, a fresh cup of coffee in hand, a muscle twitching in his cheek. "I suppose," he grudgingly agreed. "But nevertheless, you were right. It was foolish of me to search for her. I can offer her nothing."

Richard opened his mouth but soon closed it again, staring back at his cousin with a weary sigh.

"Very well. I know better than to argue when your mind is fixed like iron. But you cannot brood in this house all day. You will go mad. Come—what say we do something to distract you from your troubles? A ride in the park? Or mayhap a match at Gentleman Jackson's?"

Darcy's jaw tightened. If by "troubles" his cousin referred to Miss Elizabeth Bennet, Heaven only knew *that* was a hopeless task.

"You are well aware that I do not ride in public," he curtly replied. "And Gentleman Jackson's is out of the question."

Richard winced. "Ah. Yes, of course. Forgive me, I was not thinking... Well then, one of your clubs? That should be safe enough. You cannot remain hidden until Walsh returns. You have made a start. Now you must continue to be seen."

Darcy grimaced. Every fibre of his being recoiled at the thought, yet he could not deny the truth in Richard's words. He had endured the ball, despite his misgivings, and if not for the encounter with Jane—damn it all, *Elizabeth*—he might have managed without incident.

"Very well," he relented abruptly. "We shall go to White's. But do not expect this to become a regular occurrence."

Richard's grin was all satisfaction. "Splendid. I shall order the carriage."

Darcy merely sighed, already regretting his concession.

&

"Darcy! I say, this is becoming a regular occurrence!"

Darcy turned at the sound of his name to see Bingley striding across the Axminster carpet, looking for all the world like the cat that got the cream.

Darcy rose from the corner table where he and Richard had ensconced themselves, offering a brief nod in greeting. Richard, ever amiable, clasped Bingley's hand with a hearty grin.

A liveried waiter appeared as if by instinct, swiftly producing another chair for their guest.

Once they were comfortably seated and pleasantries exchanged, Bingley leaned in with a conspiratorial air, lowering his voice only slightly.

"Tell me, Darcy, how are you feeling today? Miss Bennet was quite concerned. She remarked that you did not look well at all by the end of your dance."

Darcy stiffened, his grip on his glass tightening before he forced himself to relax.

"It was nothing of consequence," he replied evenly, his tone clipped. "Only a trifling headache. As you see, I am in perfect health."

A flicker of concern crossed Bingley's features, but it was gone almost as soon as it appeared.

"Well, I am glad to hear it, though I was sorry you could not stay longer last evening. I had hoped you would have had the opportunity to become better acquainted with Miss Bennet. You know how much I have always relied upon your guidance in such matters."

Darcy blanched before saying slowly, "So, your intentions towards her are serious, then?"

Bingley blinked at him, seemingly surprised by the bluntness of the question.

"Well... I—I cannot say for certain," he admitted, his tone turning thoughtful. "But I find her quite charming. And she is certainly one of the most agreeable young ladies of my acquaintance." His brows knitted together briefly. "Of course, Caroline is against the match. She feels I should align myself with someone who might elevate my standing in society, but I have little patience for her schemes. Miss Bennet's father is a gentleman with an estate that has been in his family for generations—which is certainly more than my own family can profess."

Bingley leaned in eagerly, his entire countenance aglow. "Oh! That reminds me—I have not even told you the best part! Last night, when I mentioned my desire to find a suitable property to let, Miss Bennet told me there is a manor not three miles from her family's home in Hertfordshire! Is that not the most marvellous stroke of luck? It is almost as if fate itself has conspired to bring us together."

Bingley stared back at him, his eyes bright, and Darcy was forced to look away.

It had not occurred to him—*not truly*—that Bingley might entertain serious intentions towards Elizabeth.

It would be difficult enough to let her go after encountering her again; but to witness her being romanced by his friend, to see her marry him and to know that it would be Bingley who would grow old with her, Bingley who would take her to his bed and father her children... An involuntary shudder raced up Darcy's spine as he attempted to gather his wits.

Across from him, Richard coughed into his hand, and Darcy lifted his gaze to take in Bingley's crestfallen expression.

"Do not tell me you disapprove of her also?" Bingley murmured dejectedly.

"No, not at all," Darcy replied with as much enthusiasm as he could muster. "She seems a very pleasant young woman."

From the corner of his eye, Darcy could see Richard suppressing his laughter, but Bingley brightened at once, clearly relieved.

"That means a great deal to me, coming from you," his friend replied earnestly. "And I must say, I am especially glad of it, for I have a favour to ask." At Darcy's quizzical expression, he continued, "Would you come to look at Netherfield with me? That is the name of the estate in Hertfordshire. I cannot think of anyone I trust more to advise me on its suitability, and it is no more than a half day's journey from town."

Darcy's breath stilled as Bingley gazed at him expectantly.

Certainly, he could not go to Hertfordshire, to the very spot Elizabeth called home.

Although, had that not been his intention all along? To see the place and the people that had shaped her into the remarkable young woman she was?

Perhaps once he had satisfied his curiosity, it would be easier to let her go—as he knew he must.

His eyes darted briefly in his cousin's direction, and when he spoke, the words sounded distant to his own ears.

"Very well, I shall accompany you—but only to advise you on the property. Walsh will return to London shortly, then we must leave for Pemberley without delay."

Bingley's face lit up with gratitude, his good humour restored. "Excellent! I am most obliged, Darcy. You will not regret it, I am sure!"

But it was not Bingley's effusive appreciation that unsettled him; it was the knowing smile on his cousin's face that caused Darcy to flush with quiet shame.

Chapter Three

"Lizzy, can it be true? William? *Your* William, after all these years? I can hardly credit it!"

Elizabeth glanced over at her sister Jane, who sat gracefully upon the window seat in their shared bedchamber at Longbourn, her hands folded neatly in her lap.

Elizabeth, in contrast, gave a dramatic sigh and collapsed back against the pillows of her bed, staring up at the ceiling.

Although she had only returned to Hertfordshire that very afternoon, she had wasted no time in whisking her dearest sister upstairs to the privacy of their room, eager to describe every astonishing detail of her unexpected encounter at Lady Copley's ball.

Of course, Jane had long known of Elizabeth's first meeting with Mr Darcy. The sisters shared nearly everything, and Elizabeth had not hesitated to recount the tale in hurried, whispered fragments during their return journey from Yorkshire, and later in full detail once they were safely ensconced at Longbourn.

To her credit, Jane had never scolded her for such reckless behaviour—though she had, in the gentle manner of a caring elder sister, cautioned Elizabeth about the dangers of walking out alone and conversing freely with strangers. Fortunately, Elizabeth's earnest descriptions of *William's* quiet integrity and gentlemanly conduct had seemed to soothe most of Jane's concerns.

In the years that followed, the sisters would occasionally revisit the subject, wondering aloud who the mysterious stranger might have been and whether Elizabeth might ever chance to meet him again. But if Elizabeth continued to weigh every eligible gentleman she encountered against the impossible standard set by that fleeting acquaintance, she wisely kept *that* particular reflection to herself.

"He is hardly *my* William," Elizabeth said now, her tone dry. "In fact, he is not *William* at all. He is Mr Fitzwilliam Darcy of Pemberley, and he is as far above me as the moon. According to my aunt Gardiner, his family owns half of Derbyshire, and he is as wealthy as Croesus." Her lips twisted wryly. "Besides, he made it quite clear that he has no interest in reviving the acquaintance. He could scarcely endure an entire set before fleeing the ballroom."

Across from her, Jane's brows drew together in confusion. "But why should he cut you in such a way? From all you have told me, he was always courteous and well-mannered. You said he never behaved with anything short of kindness and respect."

Elizabeth exhaled, her gaze drifting to the ceiling once more.

"Yes," she murmured, more to herself than to Jane. "That is true. The William I knew four years ago in Yorkshire was kind. Or at least, I believed him to be. Perhaps I have merely fashioned him into the man I wished him to be in my imagination. In any case, the gentleman I encountered at Lady Copley's ball bore little resemblance to the one I remember."

Jane regarded her sister with quiet thoughtfulness. "I find that difficult to believe. People do not change so materially in a few short years—at least, not in essentials."

"Perhaps," Elizabeth admitted quietly. "But...there is something else. Something I have never told you."

Her throat tightened, but at Jane's gentle expression, she continued with quiet resolve.

"I...I lied to William—that is, to Mr Darcy. About my name. And at the ball, he found out. It seemed to anger him. Clearly, he is not a man who tolerates disguise of any sort."

Jane blinked, clearly puzzled. "Your name? But I thought you said you never exchanged names. You told me he called you Miss Rivers."

Elizabeth nodded, biting her lip. "He did. At first. But that last morning, when I knew we were leaving..." Her voice faltered, and she looked down at her hands clasped tightly in her lap. "As I was leaving, I turned back to him. And...there was something in his expression. Suddenly, I wanted him to know me—truly know me. But when I opened my mouth, it was not my name that came out. It was...yours."

"Mine?" Jane repeated, her eyes wide with astonishment.

"Yes." Elizabeth's voice was barely above a whisper. "I
gave him your name. I told him I was Jane."

Jane stared at her in disbelief. "But why? Why would
you give him my name instead of your own?"

Elizabeth buried her face in her hands before finally
replying, her voice strained. "I do not know! It was not
deliberate. I had no intention of telling him anything at all.
But the way he looked at me—with such admiration—no
gentleman had ever looked at me in that way. It…it was the
way gentlemen have always looked at you. And I suppose,
for that one fleeting moment, I wanted to *be* you. To be the
kind of lady that men admired in such a way."

"Oh, Lizzy," Jane breathed, her voice tinged with quiet
sorrow.

Elizabeth winced. "I know. It was foolish and wrong. I
regretted it the instant the words left my mouth, but I could
not take them back."

To her surprise, Jane rose and gracefully crossed the
room, settling beside her on the bed. She wrapped her arms
around Elizabeth's shoulders in a steady embrace.

"No, Lizzy, you misunderstand me. I am not angry. I
am only saddened that you should feel the need to be
anyone other than yourself."

Elizabeth choked out a laugh, wiping her tears with the
back of her hand. "Can you truly not understand? You are
the one who never puts a foot wrong. You are always so
calm and composed. You never speak thoughtlessly as I do.
And you are the one gentlemen admire. Not that I
begrudge them—you are by far the loveliest and kindest

young lady in Hertfordshire—but is it truly so surprising that, for a single moment, I wished to step into your shoes?"

Jane's gentle expression softened further as she studied her sister. Slowly, she turned her head to gaze out of the nearby window, watching the late afternoon sun casting shadows across the garden below.

"I do not see things that way," Jane replied after a thoughtful pause. "Gentlemen may notice me, yes, but you are the one who truly captivates. Your intelligence, your wit, and your lively spirit draw people in. Consider this Mr Bingley you mentioned in your letters. He seemed utterly charmed by you."

Elizabeth knitted her brow in mild protest. "If he was, it is only because *you* were not with me in town. Besides, I am not certain his attentions indicated any particular regard. Mr Bingley is amiable and obliging—I dare say he would be equally content with any agreeable young lady."

Jane shook her head, a rare firmness in her expression. "Lizzy, you told me he called upon you three times in Gracechurch Street—and even brought his sister. That is hardly the conduct of a man who is indifferent."

Elizabeth's gaze faltered, and she sighed. "Mr Bingley is everything a young lady could desire in a gentleman. He is good-humoured, sensible, and unaffected. And he is quite handsome, which a young man ought to be, if he possibly can," she added with a faint smile. "Yes, I liked him very well indeed. But whether his interest will endure now that I am no longer in London…that remains to be seen."

Jane studied her carefully before speaking with quiet

hesitation. "And…have your feelings for him changed upon seeing Mr Darcy again?"

Elizabeth paused, her fingers absently twisting the corner of her handkerchief. "No," she answered slowly. "At least, I do not wish them to. There is no future where Mr Darcy is concerned. Even if he could forgive me for misleading him, knowing who he truly is has extinguished any foolish notions I may have entertained. Mr Bingley is a much more suitable prospect for me. I would do well to remember that." She paused before saying lightly, "Besides, it is unlikely that I shall cross paths with Mr Darcy again. Mr Bingley mentioned he is to return to Derbyshire soon, and it seems he rarely leaves his estate."

"And Mr Bingley?" Jane asked. "Do you believe he will lease Netherfield Park?"

Elizabeth offered a gentle shrug. "I cannot say. He appeared eager when I mentioned it, but whether he will stir himself from town to view the property is another matter."

The sisters spoke quietly for some time longer, their voices gradually fading into an easy silence. By the time they left their room to join the rest of the family for the evening meal, Elizabeth felt her spirits lifted, her usual good humour restored. She had resolved—quite firmly—not to waste another thought on Mr Fitzwilliam Darcy.

Fitzwilliam Darcy turned sharply on his heel, his dark eyes narrowing into a withering glare.

"Absolutely not. It is entirely out of the question! What could possess you to suggest such a thing?"

Colonel Fitzwilliam leaned back in his chair, impervious to his cousin's sharp tone.

"Give me one good reason why we should not go. What else have you to occupy your time? And spare me the tired refrain about Pemberley. You have an exceedingly capable steward to oversee the estate, and Georgiana is safely settled at Briarwood until Christmastide. You are free, Darcy—free to go to Hertfordshire."

Darcy's jaw tightened. "Was it not enough that I accompanied Bingley to inspect the property? I have given him my counsel, my approval. That is the extent of my obligation. I will not suffer through weeks of observing his courtship of Miss Elizabeth Bennet."

Richard's lips quirked upwards on one side. "Perhaps if you were there, you might put an end to his courtship altogether."

Darcy's scowl deepened. "I have no desire to put an end to it. As painful as it is to imagine her marrying Bingley, he is a good man—worthy of her. They are alike in temperament—amiable, cheerful, and sociable. He can provide for her, and more importantly, he will treat her with the respect she deserves. In truth, I ought to be pleased."

"But you are not."

The words hung in the air, heavy and knowing. Darcy averted his gaze, unwilling to let his cousin glimpse the turmoil roiling within him.

"My feelings are irrelevant," he said at last, his voice low and clipped. "I have done what I intended. I have seen her. I know she is well. That must be enough. Now, it is time she moved forward with her life —and I must do the same."

Richard's expression sobered. "Ah, yes. Your scheme to see Georgiana married and then flee the country to live as a hermit in some remote corner of the globe."

Darcy shot him a black look, but Richard merely smirked, undeterred.

"Very well," his cousin continued, folding his arms. "Let us assume that you will carry out your plan—what is to stop you from spending a few weeks in Hertfordshire before everything is put in motion? Georgiana is taken care of for the time being, and she will not make her come out until the spring. So, if you are in earnest about remaining on English soil until she is married, you have some time at your disposal. Why not give yourself a few happy memories before you go?"

"You know why," Darcy replied darkly. "I would be taking too great a risk, staying at Netherfield for an extended period."

Richard shrugged. "All of life is a game of chance when you come down to it. I take greater risks every time I step onto the battlefield, and yet I go, willingly. Besides, did you not say that Walsh was delayed in Bedfordshire due to that business with his aunt's jointure? And I still have a fortnight before I must return to my regiment. I dare say I might enjoy a sojourn to Hertfordshire."

"Miss Bingley will be there," Darcy muttered, and Richard barked out a laugh.

"If that is all the ammunition you have in your arsenal, then I consider the battle won."

"You do not know what she is like! She will attach

herself to me like a barnacle. I shall not have a moment's peace!"

"Oh, come now. She cannot be as bad as all that. Bingley introduced us at the Copleys' ball, when you were dancing with Miss Bennet, and I found her rather charming."

"Of course she was charming," Darcy snapped. "You are the son of an earl! I am warning you—you would do well to keep your guard up while we are at Netherfield, or she will have you in the parson's mousetrap before the year is out."

Richard's brows lifted, his lips pulling up into a familiar smile. "So, we are going, then?"

Darcy looked away, releasing a heavy sigh.

"I am certain I shall live to regret this, but yes. We shall go."

"Mr Bennet! Jane, Mary, Lizzy—pray, come at once! For I have such news to share!"

The sound of Mrs Bennet's shrieks of joy preceded the matron and her two youngest daughters into Longbourn's front parlour, where Jane and Elizabeth sat with their needlework.

Exchanging glances, the two sisters stood as Mrs Hill, their housekeeper, bustled in, relieving the three ladies of their wraps.

"Oh, where is Mr Bennet?" their mother continued. "And Mary? Lizzy, go and fetch them this instant, for you will never guess what I have just learned from Mrs Long."

"What is your news, Mama," Jane dutifully enquired once Mr Bennet and their sister Mary had been found and brought to the parlour.

Mrs Bennet paused, looking around to make sure all eyes were fixed in her direction before saying in a hurried breath, "Netherfield Park is let at last! Mrs Long says that it is taken by a young gentleman of large fortune from the North. Can you imagine, Mr Bennet? What a fine thing for our girls!"

Mr Bennet, who had seated himself and retrieved a newspaper from a nearby table, barely glanced up. "Oh?" he drawled lazily. "And how, precisely, is this event to benefit them?"

Mrs Bennet huffed, her cheeks flushing with impatience. "Good gracious, how can you be so tiresome! But I forget myself—I have not even told you the best part!"

"He is single!" Lydia cried, her youthful voice ringing throughout the room. "And Mrs Long says he has five thousand a year!"

"Not only that," Kitty interjected eagerly, "but he is bringing a large party to Netherfield with him—a sister and three other gentlemen!"

Mr Bennet's mouth twitched, his expression laced with quiet amusement. "How marvellous. And pray, are these other gentlemen married or single?"

"Oh, single, to be sure!" Mrs Bennet cried, flapping her handkerchief in obvious delight. "And rumour has it that one of them is the grandson of an earl!"

Across the room, Elizabeth and Jane exchanged a subtle glance, Jane's usually serene expression tinged with curiosity.

"Mama," she began with quiet composure, "do you know the gentleman's name—the one who has taken the lease?"

"What? Oh yes, did I not say?" Mrs Bennet paused only long enough to catch her breath. "His name is Bingley. And Mr Bennet, you must call on him as soon as he arrives! For Sir William will surely visit, and I will not have Charlotte Lucas taking precedence over our girls."

"Mama—" Jane tried again, but Mrs Bennet swiftly silenced her with a wave of her hand.

"Now, now, I know what you will say. Charlotte is a sweet girl, I grant you. But Jane, one does not often see a young lady with your beauty. I am quite certain Mr Bingley will favour you above all others in the neighbourhood—if only your father will call on him and secure us an introduction!"

"But Mama, that is what I have been trying to tell you," Jane continued patiently. "Papa need not call, for we are already acquainted with the gentleman. Or at least Lizzy is. Lizzy met Mr Bingley in town. It was she who recommended Netherfield to him."

At Jane's words, Mrs Bennet's eyes grew round, and her lips parted slightly as she surveyed her second-eldest daughter.

"Lizzy, is this true?" Without giving Elizabeth a chance to answer, she rushed on, "Oh, but this could not possibly be any better! Now we have a perfectly acceptable reason to invite him to tea, and we must do so forthwith," she added, in an aside to Mr Bennet, "*before* Sir William Lucas goes to visit. Once Mr Bingley sees Jane, I am certain he will not even look at any other young lady!"

"Mama!" Jane cried, her cheeks aflame, "I believe it is for *Lizzy's* sake that Mr Bingley has come to Hertfordshire. He called on her several times when she was in town."

Mrs Bennet's mouth dropped fully open then as she stared at Elizabeth in unconcealed astonishment.

"But...how can this be? My sister Gardiner mentioned nothing about it in her letters. Well, no matter. You have done well for yourself, Lizzy. Now, you must work to secure him while he is in the neighbourhood. And Jane," she continued, "do not fret, for I am certain that Mr Bingley is *nothing* to the grandson of an earl! If this Bingley has five thousand a year, his friend very likely has more. Oh, Mr Bennet! Just think—our dear Jane, the granddaughter of an earl!"

Chapter Four

N etherfield Park was precisely as Darcy remembered it—a large, sprawling estate, well situated amidst the Hertfordshire countryside yet bearing subtle signs of neglect. Its elegance remained, but the house was undeniably past its prime, its charm dulled by the passage of time.

Leaving his valet to unpack, Darcy crossed into the small sitting room that connected his bedchamber to his cousin's. Pulling a book at random from a nearby shelf, he settled into an armchair near the window, but his mind was far too occupied to read. Being here—so close to the place Elizabeth called home—filled him with a disquieting mixture of anticipation and unease. He knew he had no business feeling either, but the knowledge that she was near unsettled him more than he cared to admit.

The faint creak of the door opening broke through his thoughts, and Darcy looked up to see his cousin striding into the room.

"There you are!" Richard declared, brushing off the

sleeves of his coat. "I have been looking everywhere for you."

Darcy lifted a brow, his tone dry. "You cannot have searched very thoroughly, considering I am seated not ten feet from your door."

Richard smirked, undeterred. "Well, I sincerely hope you do not intend to remain cloistered in here for the duration of our stay. That would rather defeat the purpose of our coming, would it not?"

"I had no purpose in coming," Darcy replied curtly. "This was your doing, if you recall."

The colonel straightened his shoulders. "Be that as it may, we are here now. Let us at least make ourselves known to our hosts."

With a sigh heavier than necessary, Darcy placed the unopened book aside and rose to follow his cousin. They moved through a short corridor and descended the broad staircase into the hall below.

But Darcy's steps faltered at the sharp, unmistakable tones of Caroline Bingley's voice echoing off the polished marble floors.

"Really, Charles! When you said you intended to lease an estate, I had hoped you would exhibit the good sense to use Pemberley as your example. I am astonished that you would settle for a house in such deplorable condition!"

Darcy's mouth tightened, and he nearly beat a hasty retreat back to his chambers, but Fitzwilliam prodded him forwards. When they entered the drawing room several moments later, Miss Bingley's critical expression instantly smoothed into one of practised sweetness as she glided in their direction.

"Oh! Mr Darcy, Colonel Fitzwilliam!" she cooed. "How delightful of you both to join us. I trust your chambers are satisfactory?"

Darcy frowned as Colonel Fitzwilliam, ever the model of gallantry, bent over her hand with effortless charm. "More than satisfactory, madam. I can scarcely recall when last I was a guest in so charming a home."

Miss Bingley blinked, apparently caught off guard by the unexpected compliment. However, she quickly recovered, offering a gracious murmur of thanks before turning to Darcy with a calculated flutter of her lashes.

"And you, Mr Darcy? If there is anything I can do to make your stay more comfortable, I hope you will not hesitate to inform me."

Darcy inclined his head politely, offering little more than a perfunctory, "Thank you, Miss Bingley."

But Richard, with a glint of mischief in his eye, interjected smoothly, "Oh, Darcy is perfectly content with his accommodations. We shall be fortunate if we can coax him from his rooms."

Darcy shot his cousin a pointed glare, but before he could respond, Bingley garnered everyone's attention, rubbing his hands together and saying with animation, "Well! Now that we are all settled, I thought I might ride into Meryton. Perhaps I shall call upon Miss Elizabeth Bennet while I am out. What say you, Darcy? Will you accompany me?"

Darcy's breath caught, his mind scrambling for a response.

"Do you not think it a little soon? You have only just arrived," he finally replied, levelling Bingley with a steady gaze. "In any case, it is customary for Mr Bennet to pay the first call to welcome you to the neighbourhood."

Bingley waved off the objection with a flick of his wrist. "I do not see why that should matter. It is not as though Miss Bennet and I are not already acquainted. Besides, it feels only right to call upon her as she was the one who recommended Netherfield to me."

Darcy sighed. "Very well, go if you must, but it is too late in the day for a call. You will have to wait until tomorrow."

Bingley's shoulders drooped slightly, though he gave a nod of resignation. "Yes, I suppose you are right. But you will accompany me, will you not? You are acquainted with Miss Bennet as well, and I am sure she would be most pleased to see you again."

"No." Darcy's tone was clipped. "You and Miss Bingley may go. My cousin and I shall remain here to await Walsh's arrival."

"Oh, yes," Caroline Bingley drawled. "I had quite forgotten that your man would be joining us. Your steward, is he not?"

Darcy's jaw tightened, though he answered with practised civility. "Walsh is a trusted advisor, not a steward, and a valued friend besides. We were at university together, along with your brother."

"Upon my word, Caroline," Bingley scolded, "you have heard me speak of Walsh many times, and you were even introduced to him at Pemberley last summer." Turning to Darcy he added, "I am glad he has been able to conclude his business in time to join us here at Netherfield."

Darcy nodded his appreciation before Bingley once

again turned to address his sister. "Now, what say you? Will you accompany me to Longbourn tomorrow?"

"Oh, I could not possibly leave Netherfield so soon," Miss Bingley replied airily, smoothing the folds of her gown. "I have a thousand things to see to, and as mistress of the house, I must be here to welcome Mr Darcy's friend."

Bingley's lips pressed together in a thin line, then parted, but it was Colonel Fitzwilliam who spoke next.

"Well, I for one should very much like to go," he announced, glancing slyly at Darcy. "I am eager to make the acquaintance of the rest of the Bennet family. I believe Miss Elizabeth has a sister or two?"

Darcy shot his cousin a withering look, but Bingley brightened. "Indeed, she has four sisters in all, though I have only had the pleasure of meeting her aunt and uncle in town."

Turning eagerly to Darcy, Bingley added, "Come, Darcy, will you not join us? It need not be an extended call. And Caroline will be here to greet Walsh should he arrive before our return."

Darcy's glare towards Richard deepened, but he knew he was cornered. He certainly would not stay behind at Netherfield with only Miss Bingley for company.

"Very well," he replied curtly, "but a quarter of an hour will suffice. If you intend to stay longer, you may return without me."

Richard smirked, clearly satisfied, while Bingley grinned broadly. Darcy, however, could only wonder what he had just agreed to—and why he felt a flicker of hopeful anticipation despite his best intentions.

·❧·

On Monday morning, Elizabeth woke early, as was her custom, donning a simple day dress and hurrying through her morning ablutions. Although she always enjoyed her time in town, she had been glad to return to her morning rambles—the chance to wander through the Hertfordshire countryside during the crisp, cool hours of the day when the world was quiet and still.

She had not been home more than a quarter of an hour when the distant rumble of carriage wheels could be heard echoing up the drive. Pausing in the hall, Elizabeth moved to the window, drawing back a corner of the curtain in time to see a fine lacquered coach coming to a halt before the house. A footman leapt nimbly down, and the moment the door was opened, a familiar figure descended.

Mr Bingley!

Elizabeth watched as he stepped onto the gravel, his expression bright with cheerful interest as he took in the house's façade. Just then, another figure emerged from the carriage—Colonel Fitzwilliam, whom she recalled meeting briefly at Lady Copley's ball. But it was the tall, imposing gentleman who followed that caused her pulse to falter.

A quiet gasp escaped her lips as she hastily dropped the curtain and stepped back, her mind racing. What was Mr Darcy doing here? Had Mr Bingley not told her that he was to return to Derbyshire?

Unthinking, Elizabeth turned on her heel and hurried towards the music room, where Mary sat dutifully at the pianoforte, labouring over some sombre melody.

"Mary, come quickly! We have callers!" Elizabeth's voice was low but urgent.

Mary's fingers stilled mid-chord, and she looked up in startled confusion. But before she could utter a word, Elizabeth grasped her arm, gently but firmly pulling her up from the bench and guiding her swiftly into the front parlour.

They had barely arranged themselves on the settee when the sharp clattering of the door knocker rang through the house. Moments later, footsteps crossed the hall, and the drawing-room door was opened and their guests announced.

Mr Bingley led the way, followed by Colonel Fitzwilliam. Mr Darcy brought up the rear, looking serious and subdued, a stark contrast to the ease and affability of his companions.

Rising to greet the gentlemen and introduce them to her sister, Elizabeth was careful to direct most of her attention to Mr Bingley, who promptly claimed the armchair nearest to her. His open expression spoke of his joy at their reunion, in contrast to Mr Darcy, who appeared serious and subdued, his gaze carefully averted, as though he were determined to keep himself removed from the conversation.

Elizabeth clasped her hands tightly in her lap, willing herself to remain composed, even as she felt Mr Darcy's silent presence weighing upon her senses.

"I am afraid you find us on our own this morning," Elizabeth began, infusing her voice with as much equanimity as she could muster. "My father had business with his steward, and my mother and sisters have gone into Meryton."

"Ah, then I must thank you for receiving us," Mr

Bingley replied with his usual good humour before saying in a rush, "although I certainly look forward to calling again when the rest of your family is at home."

Elizabeth acknowledged his words with a small smile. "I should like to say my mother and sisters will return soon, but I fear they may be some time yet. They have been known to spend an entire morning at the haberdashery alone!" She continued amiably, "There is to be an assembly on Thursday, so it only follows that new ribbons and shoe roses must be procured for the occasion."

Mr Bingley chuckled. "And what of you and Miss Mary? Have you no need of ribbons and shoe roses?" he asked with evident curiosity.

"Mary is not particularly fond of shopping," Elizabeth replied. "As for myself, I was out walking when the party set off, so I shall have to be content with what I have already."

Colonel Fitzwilliam then entered the conversation with the readiness and ease of a well-bred man, enquiring as to Meryton's distance from Longbourn, the size of the town, and the types of shops that might be found there.

Elizabeth and Mary spoke at length about the neighbourhood, with Mr Bingley eagerly adding his share to the conversation.

Mr Darcy said nothing, merely watching the proceedings with a slight frown, until at length his civility appeared to be awakened, and he turned to address Elizabeth.

"You are fond of walking, I believe."

Elizabeth blinked, momentarily startled by his sudden interjection. She noted the faint flush that crept into his cheeks as he added, "You mentioned earlier that you were out walking when the rest of the party left for the town. Do you walk often?"

"I do," Elizabeth replied evenly, though she could not entirely suppress her curiosity at the turn in the conversation. "I walk most mornings, provided the weather is not too disagreeable."

Mr Darcy nodded, his expression unreadable. "Is there a particular path you favour?"

Elizabeth felt a brief ripple of surprise but quickly schooled her features into neutrality. "My destination varies with the season and my mood. However, if you are asking for your own amusement, I can recommend Oakham Mount. The view is particularly lovely this time of year."

Mr Darcy inclined his head in acknowledgement but offered no further comment, leaving Elizabeth to redirect her attention to Mr Bingley.

"And how are you finding Netherfield, sir?" she asked. "I hope you are not regretting your decision to enter the neighbourhood?"

This prompted an animated recitation from Mr Bingley. He enthused about the comfortable appointments of the house, the agreeable situation of the grounds, and the excellence of the stables. Everyone he had met thus far had been unfailingly kind and attentive, and he declared his joy at fully immersing himself in country life.

Elizabeth listened attentively, keeping her expression open and encouraging. When he paused for breath, she said lightly, "I am glad to hear it. I hope we shall have the pleasure of your company at the assembly on Thursday?"

"Indeed you will!" Mr Bingley replied with enthusiasm. "And I hope I might take this opportunity to solicit your hand for the first two dances, if you are not already engaged?"

Elizabeth hesitated for the briefest of moments, her eyes flickering to Mr Darcy. His countenance remained stony, his frown deepening ever so slightly, but she could not fathom what might cause such an expression. Pushing the thought aside, she returned her attention to Mr Bingley and offered him a gracious smile.

"I would be delighted, sir."

"And Miss Mary," Mr Bingley continued, turning to her sister with the same geniality, "I hope you will honour me with a dance as well?"

Mary's eyes widened, her complexion turning a brilliant shade of crimson. She looked as though she might refuse outright, but after an awkward pause, she managed a faint nod.

Mr Bingley beamed, clearly pleased with the arrangements, while Colonel Fitzwilliam opened his mouth as though to extend a similar invitation. However, before he could speak, Mr Darcy abruptly rose, his movements sharp and deliberate.

"I believe we have taken up enough of the ladies' time," he declared in a clipped tone.

The suddenness of his action prompted Mr Bingley and the colonel to rise as well, though the latter cast a puzzled glance in his cousin's direction. Still, Mr Bingley's spirits were not dampened, and he extended his usual effusive promises.

"It has been a great pleasure to call upon you, Miss Bennet, Miss Mary. I look forward to seeing you both at the assembly."

Elizabeth and Mary offered their courtesies, though Elizabeth could not suppress her lingering curiosity about Mr Darcy's strange demeanour. His bow was perfunctory, his expression guarded as he turned to lead his companions from the room.

As the door closed behind them, Elizabeth allowed herself a small sigh of relief. "Well," she said at last, turning to Mary with a faint smile, "it seems we shall be well acquainted with our new neighbours before long."

Mary merely nodded, her cheeks still flushed, while the echo of the gentlemen's departure lingered in the quiet of the parlour.

Darcy spent the remainder of the day in brooding silence.

He never should have agreed to call at Longbourn.

Watching Elizabeth Bennet turn her radiant smile on Bingley had been every bit as torturous as he had imagined, and the mention of a local assembly had been the final blow. The idea of standing on the periphery, watching Bingley dance with Elizabeth—not to mention enduring the ceaseless chatter of Meryton's fortune hunters—was unthinkable. Thankfully, he had managed to cut their call short before his tenuous self-control had fractured and he had done something irredeemably foolish, like soliciting Elizabeth's hand for a dance.

Upon their return to Netherfield, Darcy had feigned a headache and retreated to the sanctuary of his chambers. There, he paced restlessly, alternately berating himself for his earlier lapse in judgment and dreading the prospect of dinner. Yet even solitude brought little relief, for his mind relentlessly conjured images of Elizabeth: the graceful curve of her figure as she rose to greet them, the gentle cadence of her voice as she conversed with Bingley, and the sharp intelligence that glimmered in her eyes when she answered his own clumsy questions about walking paths.

He was shaken from his reverie only by the sound of Walsh's arrival late in the afternoon. Darcy immediately went to greet him, though the encounter was brief; there was no time for more than a quick exchange of pleasantries before they were both obliged to dress for dinner.

By the time Darcy descended to the drawing room at the appointed hour, he felt as though every nerve in his body had been drawn taut. Walsh was already there, standing near the hearth with an expression of affable composure as he acknowledged their hosts. When Darcy entered, however, Walsh's eyes flicked towards him, and within moments, the man had gravitated to his side, offering a respectful bow of his head.

"Has all been well?" Walsh asked in a low voice.

Darcy gave a curt nod. "Yes, quite. There have been no incidents since your departure."

"Good," Walsh replied simply, his sharp gaze lingering on Darcy's face for a moment, as if weighing the truth of the statement.

Before either man could say more, Miss Bingley's voice rang out from across the room. "Mr Darcy, Mr Walsh, do let us adjourn to the dining parlour! The soup will not wait."

Darcy suppressed the desire to roll his eyes as he

moved towards the dining room, Walsh falling into step beside him.

❧

"Mr Walsh," Miss Bingley began, as soon as everyone had been seated, "it is so good of you to join us. I trust you had a pleasant journey?"

"Yes, I thank you, madam. Both for your kind words and your hospitality. It is good of you to have me on such short notice."

"Nonsense!" she exclaimed with a tinkling laugh. "Mr Darcy is practically family, so any acquaintance of his is always welcome. Is that not so, Charles?"

"Certainly," Bingley replied jovially. "Darcy is doing me a great service coming all this way to advise me. I fear, without his help, I should not know up from down when it comes to the running of an estate."

"What are your plans for Netherfield?" Colonel Fitzwilliam asked, taking a swallow of claret before digging into his ragout.

Across from him, Bingley chuckled. "I suppose I must rely upon Darcy to tell me that. Although I have already spoken to the proprietor about making some improvements to the stables. They are quite large, but I believe the roof could do with repairing."

"The stables? Honestly, Charles!" Miss Bingley interjected, her tone laced with exasperation. "The upstairs sitting room is simply ghastly, and the principal bedchambers look as though they have not been redecorated since the turn of the century. Yet here you sit, fretting over the accommodations for your precious horses. Sometimes I think you care more for ponies than for people."

"Perhaps I do," Bingley replied amiably. "I do not recall any of my horses overspending their allowance." He laughed heartily at that before adding, "Besides, I did not hear you complaining when I purchased that chestnut gelding for you last spring."

Caroline Bingley turned a deep shade of scarlet, her lips tightening as she muttered something unintelligible under her breath before offering to refill Colonel Fitzwilliam's glass.

"Mr Darcy," she continued with forced brightness, "may I pour you some more claret? Oh! But you have not even touched yours. I hope the vintage is to your liking?"

"I am certain it is excellent," Darcy replied evenly, "but I find I am prone to headaches, which alcohol only exacerbates, so I rarely indulge."

"Charles!" Miss Bingley cried, turning towards her brother with an indignant scowl. "Why did you not tell me that Mr Darcy does not care for wine?"

"Ah, yes, pray forgive me, Darcy. I am afraid I had quite forgotten. Shall I see whether there is any ale...or... tea?"

"I thank you," Darcy replied stiffly, "but there is no need to bother anyone. I shall take tea after dinner."

"Nonsense! You cannot mean to sit through the meal without drinking anything at all!" Miss Bingley pressed, leaning in his direction with an air of theatrical concern.

The back of Darcy's neck prickled as all eyes turned towards him. He opened his mouth to speak, but Richard intervened with a disarming grin. "You must excuse my cousin his quirks, Miss Bingley. I am afraid it is a family trait. Both my aunt Lady Catherine, and his lordship—that is to say my father, the earl—eschew beverages with meals. However, your excellent wine will not go to waste, as I am more than willing to drink Darcy's share."

With that said, Richard drained his glass, holding it out to Miss Bingley, who refilled it with a confused smile before turning her attention to Walsh.

"And you, sir? More wine?"

"I thank you, madam, but I am afraid I must keep a clear head. Darcy and I have some business dealings to discuss later this evening."

"Business! But you have only just arrived! Surely whatever you have to discuss can wait until tomorrow?"

Darcy shot Walsh a grateful look before replying with practised seriousness, "I am afraid it cannot. We must go over some estate matters so that I might write to my steward first thing tomorrow."

Across the table, Miss Bingley drew her lips into an exaggerated pout, clearly displeased. "But I was so looking forward to entertaining you all at the pianoforte this evening! Though I would not be at all surprised to learn that the instrument in the drawing room is hopelessly out of tune."

"Now, Caroline," Bingley began, exasperation creeping into his tone, "I shall have you know—"

As Bingley launched into a defence of Netherfield's furnishings, Darcy leaned closer to Richard, his tone low and reproachful. "What were you on about just now?" he murmured. "You know full well that Lady Catherine never takes a meal without her beloved sherry, and I have personally witnessed his lordship polish off an entire bottle of burgundy before the second remove!"

Richard responded with a mischievous expression. "Yes, but *they* do not know that. If Miss Bingley believes abstinence to be fashionable, she is far less likely to pester you. I shall be surprised if we see another bottle of wine on the table for the remainder of our stay."

With a barely concealed sigh, Darcy cast his cousin a look of exasperation as Richard took another leisurely sip of claret.

Turning his attention back to the conversation at large, he was just in time to hear Miss Bingley say in plaintive tones, "Well, I do hope you will both make some time for amusements while you are here. I know how fond Mr Darcy is of music."

Darcy forbore to answer, leaving Bingley to jump into the breach with his usual enthusiasm.

"I, for one, intend to take advantage of all the diversions the neighbourhood has to offer! In fact, we learned earlier today that there is to be a local assembly on Thursday, which should provide an excellent opportunity to become better acquainted with our new neighbours."

"Oh, Charles, really," Miss Bingley replied with a faint sneer. "I shudder to think what might pass for an assembly in a place like this."

Bingley bristled, his amiable demeanour hardening ever so slightly. "I am sure I do not know what you mean. I have found everyone I have met so far to be exceedingly pleasant. In any case, you may do as you wish, but I shall certainly attend. In fact, I have already secured Miss Elizabeth Bennet's hand for the first set."

Colonel Fitzwilliam, who had been following the conversation with a trace of amusement, raised his glass with a rakish grin. "Hear, hear! To local assemblies!"

Miss Bingley's gaze widened, and a small crease formed between her brows. Although she was clearly unwilling to contradict the son of an earl, even one serving as a commissioned officer in His Majesty's Army, she remained resolutely unmoved. Turning instead to Darcy, she said, "I can no doubt guess your feelings on the matter, sir. I do not imagine you would wish to pass an evening in such company."

In truth, Darcy had every intention of declining. With very few exceptions, he avoided large gatherings at all costs, and a crowded, overheated assembly room in a provincial town was the last place on earth he wished to find himself. While he had narrowly escaped disaster at Lady Copley's ball, he had no desire to tempt fate.

But to his consternation, he found himself fixing the lady with a level gaze and replying coolly, "You are quite mistaken, madam. It will be my honour to attend."

Miss Bingley let out a startled gasp, her carefully arranged composure faltering for a moment. Across the table, Darcy caught the subtle shift in Walsh's expression and the unmistakable twinkle of amusement in Richard's eyes.

"Then we shall all go," the colonel supplied cheerfully. "I dare say it will be an exhilarating evening."

Darcy felt the weight of his cousin's unspoken jest, but he kept his expression impassive. Whatever the consequences, he could not deny that the prospect of seeing Elizabeth Bennet again—even in so unlikely a setting—was proving impossible to resist.

Chapter Five

As expected, the Meryton assembly rooms were
modest, cramped, and overheated, and Darcy felt the
familiar stirrings of unease the moment he crossed the
threshold. The low hum of chatter mixed with the strains of
a lively tune from the quartet in the corner, and the press of
bodies moving through the narrow corridors made his heart
pound faster inside his chest. To make matters worse, Miss
Bingley, who had declared herself too superior for such an
event, was making her displeasure known at every possible
opportunity.

"What a dreadful little room," she scoffed beneath her
breath as she walked beside Darcy. "I cannot fathom why
Charles insisted upon coming here. I doubt there is a single
accomplished young lady to be found in such a place. And
the decoration—good heavens! The colour on these walls is
positively atrocious."

Darcy clenched his jaw. While he could not entirely
disagree with her judgment, at least he had the decency to

keep such opinions to himself. Attempting to disregard her ceaseless chatter, he let his eyes drift over the throngs of townspeople, most of whom had their gazes fixed upon his party as they slowly progressed through the series of rooms. The novelty of the newcomers—the wealthy Mr Bingley and his sophisticated companions—seemed to have created a buzz of anticipation, and Darcy felt the weight of dozens of curious stares.

The group had just entered the ballroom when a beaming gentleman detached himself from a nearby group, bounding in their direction.

"Ah, Mr Bingley! Welcome, welcome!" The rotund man of middling height dressed in slightly outdated evening wear grasped Bingley's hand and began pumping it vigorously as he continued, "Such a pleasure to see new faces at one of our local gatherings."

"Sir William," Bingley responded cheerfully, "it is delightful to see you again."

The older gentleman turned, gesturing expansively as he began to introduce Bingley to everyone in the general vicinity. Miss Bingley stood by his side, a false smile fixed to her countenance, as Fitzwilliam and Walsh affably greeted the locals.

As the pleasantries dragged on, Darcy allowed his attention to wander, scanning the crowded ballroom in search of a distraction—and then he saw her.

Elizabeth Bennet stood on the far side of the room, surrounded by a small group of women, her figure framed by the flickering candlelight from the chandeliers above. She wore a simple blue gown, its unadorned elegance setting her apart from the more elaborately dressed ladies in attendance. Her dark curls were neatly arranged, and a smile played upon her lips as she engaged in conversation with the woman beside her.

Instantly, his breath hitched, and his chest tightened with emotion. How was it that she managed to hold his attention so completely, even in such a place as this?

"Ah, I see Miss Bennet!" Bingley's voice suddenly called out, breaking through Darcy's reverie. "Let us go over and greet her relations."

Before Darcy could muster a reply, Bingley was already threading his way through the crowd, leaving the rest of their party little choice but to follow in his wake.

§♠

As the principal matron in the area, Mrs Bennet had always felt it her duty to be among the first to arrive at local gatherings. Thus, by the time the Netherfield party entered the Meryton assembly rooms, she had already determined that Mr Bingley—along with his eligible friends—must be considered the rightful property of one or another of her daughters.

Armed with this intelligence, she wasted no time in seeking out her two eldest, who had gravitated to a quiet location at the edge of the room. With Mary trailing behind her, Mrs Bennet bustled in their direction, her face alight.

"Lizzy! Jane!" she called out, making her way towards them at a rapid pace. "Have you seen that the party from Netherfield has arrived at last? Oh, but why ever are you hiding away in this corner when— Well, never mind, for now I can tell you all that I have learned," she added in a rush, pausing only long enough to draw breath before continuing eagerly, "I have just been speaking to Mrs Long, who heard Sir William telling Lady Lucas that *Mr Darcy,* the tall, distinguished looking gentleman, has a clear *ten thousand a year*, and one of the largest estates in Derbyshire! He is also the grandson of the *Earl of Matlock.* But that is not all! His cousin, the one in uniform, is the earl's second son! Can you imagine two more eligible gentlemen? Now Jane, you must waste no time in securing a dance with one of them."

Jane flushed a delicate pink but was saved the trouble of forming a reply by the approach of their friend and neighbour Charlotte Lucas, who was greeted warmly by the entire party.

"Ah, Charlotte," Mrs Bennet began, "you are looking very well this evening, very well indeed."

Charlotte murmured her thanks before turning to Elizabeth with a knowing smile. "So, Lizzy, I understand that you are no stranger to the Netherfield party. Papa visited Mr Bingley shortly after his arrival, only to learn that he and the other gentlemen had paid a call at Longbourn the previous morning."

This time it was Elizabeth's turn to blush, but it was Jane who answered easily, "Lizzy and Mr Bingley met when she was lately in town, visiting my aunt and uncle. It was on her recommendation that Mr Bingley came to view Netherfield."

"Well, then I suppose we have you to thank for everyone's good spirits, Lizzy," Charlotte replied. "I do not recall such a stir at an assembly since Mr Goulding's pigs escaped and drank all the punch."

The Bennet sisters chuckled at this, but Mrs Bennet, who had gone back to scrutinizing the newcomers, said, "I dare say that must be Mr Bingley's sister. Oh! Just look at her gown! Have you ever in your life seen anything more elegant? Why, the lace alone—"

"Charlotte," Elizabeth interrupted, "do you know who the other gentleman is? The one in the blue coat? He is not known to me, and he was not of the party when the gentlemen called at Longbourn."

Charlotte tilted her head to get a better look through the shifting crowd before answering, "I believe he is an acquaintance of Mr Darcy's, but I do not know his name. Though they appear to be speaking with Papa, so I am certain we shall all be made aware of his identity soon enough."

Elizabeth returned Charlotte's wry smile as Mrs Bennet leaned in towards Elizabeth and Jane and cried impatiently, "Oh, I do wish your father had agreed to come this evening! He takes such delight in vexing me. If I could but see one of my daughters happily settled at Netherfield, and all the others equally well married, I should have nothing to wish for!"

"*Mama*," Elizabeth hissed in abject mortification upon seeing that Mr Bingley and his party were now advancing at a rapid pace.

But Mrs Bennet had already turned her attention to her eldest daughter, adjusting the bodice of her gown and prodding her forwards before saying in a shrill whisper, "Remember Jane, *ten thousand a year!*" just as the newcomers drew to a halt before them.

❧

"Miss Elizabeth, how good it is to see you again," Bingley declared with his usual good cheer upon reaching the ladies. "I hope you will do me the honour of introducing me to your acquaintances?"

Stepping up to stand beside his friend, Darcy briefly captured Elizabeth's gaze, noting the deep flush that had crept up the column of her neck before she seemed to gather her composure enough to make the requested introductions to her mother, eldest sister, and neighbour.

"A pleasure," Bingley replied, greeting the entire party with a ready smile, though Darcy could not help but notice that his gaze remained fixed on the eldest Miss Bennet for far longer than was appropriate. It was only when Colonel Fitzwilliam pointedly cleared his throat that Bingley remembered his duty and performed his own set of introductions.

Once greetings were exchanged, Mrs Bennet quickly seized hold of the conversation, turning to Bingley and saying stridently, "It is very good of you to join us so soon after arriving in the neighbourhood, sir! I do hope you and your friends have come prepared to dance?"

"Why yes, of course!" Bingley answered in an instant. "I have already secured Miss Elizabeth and Miss Mary's hands for the first and second sets, but it would be my pleasure to partner Miss Jane Bennet for the third, if she is not otherwise engaged?" He then turned back to the eldest Miss Bennet with a besotted stare that caused that lady to flush with obvious embarrassment while her mother preened.

"No, sir, I am not engaged," Miss Bennet murmured, and Bingley's grin widened in response.

Several moments went by before he once again remembered himself, tearing his gaze away from Miss Jane Bennet to address the ladies' mother.

"And did Mr Bennet accompany you?" he eagerly remarked, turning to survey the throng as if the gentleman might suddenly appear before him. "I should very much like to make his acquaintance."

"Ah! Well...you see..." the matron began to stammer, "that is..."

"My father does not enjoy assemblies, sir," Miss Jane Bennet finished for her, prompting a short burst of laughter from Elizabeth.

"But that is not so, Jane," she answered sweetly before turning to face Mr Bingley. "In truth, I would say that my father looks forward to our local assemblies more than anyone in the neighbourhood, for they are the one occasion where he may be assured of an empty house."

Beside her, Mrs Bennet frowned but was saved from having to reply by Colonel Fitzwilliam, who asked whether the other Miss Bennets were in attendance.

"Oh, goodness, yes!" the lady hastened to reply. "My two youngest are just there, conversing with some of our neighbours," she remarked, waving her handkerchief in the general vicinity of the dais, where the musicians had begun to gather.

Darcy shifted his gaze in the direction she indicated just in time to see a stout, well-grown girl release a raucous cry before snatching a hair ribbon from one of her companions and racing off into the crowd. Next to him, Miss Bingley sucked in a breath, her lips twisting into something very like a sneer before she addressed Mrs Bennet in a biting tone.

"Goodness, five daughters out at once! Why, the youngest hardly appears old enough to have left the schoolroom!"

Mrs Bennet beamed, clearly insensible to Miss Bingley's rebuff, saying heartily, "How clever of you to notice! Indeed, my Lydia is not yet sixteen. But really, I think it would be very hard upon my two youngest not to have their share of society just because their elder sisters have yet to marry. Lydia especially, for she is the liveliest of all my girls, and a great favourite of the gentlemen in the neighbourhood. Although her beauty may not be equal to Jane's, I would not be at all surprised if Lydia were the first to marry. One does not often see a figure such as hers," she concluded with a suggestive lift of her brows.

Beside him, Caroline Bingley audibly gasped, and Darcy could only grimace at such flagrant vulgarity. A furtive glance at the eldest Miss Bennets showed that they were, as he had surmised, deeply mortified, but he could not know whether it was by their sister's behaviour or their mother's indecorous comments.

An awkward silence momentarily ensued, but fortuitously, the musicians had finally finished tuning their instruments, and the room was soon filled with the first strains of a country reel.

"Well," Colonel Fitzwilliam heartily exclaimed, breaking the tension, "I for one look forward to enjoying tonight's amusements! Miss Bingley, would you do me the honour of joining me for this set?"

The lady acceded with alacrity, and Darcy sent a grateful look in his cousin's direction—both for his precipitous interjection as well as for his generosity in asking Miss Bingley to stand up with him so that Darcy would not be forced to do so himself.

To his surprise, Walsh then turned to Miss Lucas to request her hand for the opening dances—an invitation that was accepted with obvious pleasure.

"And what about you, Mr Darcy?" Mrs Bennet called out, her voice easily carrying across the room. "I hope you enjoy dancing as much as your friends. I am certain you cannot refuse the amusement when so much beauty is before you?" This last was followed by a not-so-subtle nod towards her eldest daughter, who turned an even deeper shade of pink before casting her eyes to the threadbare carpet.

Turning to regard the matron, Darcy's jaw tightened, and he answered in clipped tones, "Forgive me, madam, but I have not the least intention of dancing."

And then, with a cursory bow to the eldest Miss Bennet, and a crisp, "If you will excuse me," he stalked off in the direction of the refreshments.

Two hours and one tepid cup of lemonade later, Darcy found himself standing alone in a dimly lit corner of the assembly room, observing the swirl of dancers.

As it turned out, Miss Jane Bennet had secured a partner for the first set—an ungainly youth in an ill-fitting coat—and for every set thereafter. Her graceful manner and classic beauty clearly made her the object of much admiration among her neighbours; though, for Darcy's part, her serene countenance could not compare to Elizabeth's livelier expression.

Walsh had danced the first with Miss Lucas, then resumed his usual place at Darcy's side, following him about the room until Darcy assured his friend of his wellbeing, sending him off to enjoy the evening's entertainment.

Richard, likewise, had sought Darcy out between sets, and Bingley had come over once to admonish him for standing about in what he called a "stupid manner" when so many agreeable young ladies were in want of partners. But Darcy had deflected his friend's entreaties easily enough.

Miss Bingley, however, was another matter. Her relentless attempts to secure his attention forced Darcy to shift about the room at regular intervals, his sole aim being to avoid her transparent advances.

Yet through it all, Darcy's eyes rarely strayed from Elizabeth Bennet.

As arranged, she had danced the first set with Bingley, and Darcy could not help but notice how easy they appeared in one another's company. Bingley leaned down often to speak into her ear, and more than once, whatever he said caused her to laugh—a sound that Darcy found both enchanting and irritating in equal measure. An unfamiliar pang of something he refused to name rippled through him each time her smile turned in Bingley's direction.

It was also painfully clear that Elizabeth had been avoiding him for most of the evening. He could hardly blame her. He knew he had appeared churlish by declaring himself unwilling to dance, but it could not be helped. As much as he ached for the feel of Elizabeth's hands in his, he had no interest in gratifying Mrs Bennet's schemes when it came to Miss Jane Bennet. Not to mention that once he had danced with one of her daughters, he would be expected to partner all of them, as well as Miss Bingley. As it was, it would be difficult to avoid standing up with his friend's sister. No, it was far better to endure the discomfort of remaining on the periphery, as he was accustomed to doing.

Pulling himself from these musings, Darcy scanned the room, only to realize with some alarm that he had lost sight of Elizabeth. The last he had seen, she had been near the refreshment table, engaged in conversation with Walsh and Miss Lucas. Now, however…

His gaze swept the crowded room, searching. At last, he caught sight of a flutter of pale blue muslin disappearing through a doorway at the rear of the room.

Setting his cup on a nearby table, Darcy moved quickly to follow. Slipping outside, he stepped onto a spacious terrace overlooking the quiet garden beyond. The air was crisp and refreshing after the stifling heat of the assembly room.

The sound of the door closing behind him caused Elizabeth to startle. She turned abruptly, her features briefly registering surprise before settling into composed indifference.

"Oh, it is you," she said primly.

Coming to stand beside her, Darcy frowned. "Were you expecting someone else?"

"Of course not! I came out here for a moment of quiet and a breath of fresh air. And before you lecture me on the evils of venturing out of doors alone, I can assure you that I am perfectly capable of taking care of myself."

"I beg your pardon. It has never been my intention to lecture you. If I have spoken out of turn in the past, it has only ever been out of concern for your well-being."

Elizabeth regarded him in silence for a moment, her expression unreadable, before turning and resting her forearms on the stone balustrade. She stared out into the gardens, her profile softened by the silvery glow of the moon.

"I was surprised to see you here—in Hertfordshire," she finally offered. "In London, Mr Bingley led me to believe that you were to return to your estate within the week. In fact, he said you rarely left Derbyshire."

Darcy's gaze followed hers. "That is true, I do not. And indeed, I intended to return to Pemberley as soon as my business in town was concluded. I am in Hertfordshire at Bingley's request."

"I see," she answered, her tone cool.

When she said no more, the silence stretched between them, broken only by the faint strains of music filtering through the open windows.

"Is something troubling you?" he finally asked, turning to look at her.

"No. Yes!" Elizabeth burst out, her eyes flashing. "Why did you refuse to stand up with Jane?"

Feeling the heat rise up his neck, Darcy stiffened. "I meant no offence. As I said to your mother, I have no intention of dancing this evening."

Elizabeth narrowed her gaze. "You came to an assembly with no intention of dancing?"

Darcy looked away, but Elizabeth pressed on. "And it is not only that. Your manners have been dreadful all evening —stalking around the perimeter of the room or standing by yourself in such a ridiculous manner. You looked for all the world like someone who thinks himself above his company."

Darcy's posture straightened, his shoulders rigid. "Forgive me if you have found my behaviour wanting. I do not generally attend assemblies such as this. And I never dance."

"Oh? While I cannot speak to the first, I know the second statement to be untrue. You danced with me at Lady Copley's ball."

Darcy hesitated, momentarily caught by the fullness of her lips, the spark in her eyes under the moonlight. The memory of their dance swept through him, sharp and vivid.

That was because I was utterly desperate to be near you —to look into your eyes, to hear the laughter in your voice. I would have sold my very soul for the chance to touch your hand.

"That was because it was the only way I could speak to you with any degree of privacy," he said aloud, his voice quieter but no less firm. "It was an isolated occurrence. I assure you it will not happen again."

Elizabeth sharpened her gaze. "If those are your feelings, may I be so bold as to enquire why you chose to come here tonight?"

Why do you think I came? I am here because of you. The words surged unbidden in his mind, teetering on the edge of his tongue. For a moment, he feared he had spoken them aloud, but Elizabeth was still watching him, waiting for his response.

Schooling his features, Darcy replied crisply, "I have spent the evening asking myself that very question. You and your older sister were the only handsome women in that ballroom. And I certainly did not come here to give consequence to young ladies who are slighted by other men."

Elizabeth gasped softly, her lips parting in shock. The weight of his words settled between them like an insurmountable wall.

Darcy opened his mouth, desperate to explain, but Elizabeth was already retreating. Her back was straight, her steps swift as she crossed the terrace without a word.

"Jane! That is, Elizabeth—Miss Bennet!" Darcy called after her, his voice tight with regret. But it was too late. The door to the assembly rooms slammed behind her emphatically, leaving him alone beneath the starlit sky.

The Bennet ladies returned from the assembly to find Mr Bennet still awake and sitting in Longbourn's front parlour, a glass of port in his hand and an open book upon his lap.

"Oh! My dear Mr Bennet," cried his wife upon entering the room, "we have had a most delightful evening! I wish you had been there. All our girls were so admired, and Mr Bingley is the most charming gentleman! He danced the first two with Lizzy, and then the two next with Mary. Then the two third with Jane and the two fourth with Charlotte Lucas. And after that—"

"Mrs Bennet, pray desist!" her husband cried, setting aside his book. "For God's sake, say no more of Mr Bingley's partners, I beg you!"

Mrs Bennet huffed but gratified her husband by replying, "Well, in any case, I am quite delighted with him. Oh! And Mr Darcy! He is so exceedingly handsome! And his cousin, Colonel Fitzwilliam! I never saw such happy manners. So much ease with such perfect good breeding. He danced every dance, as did Mr Bingley."

"And Mr Darcy danced none," Lydia added with a throaty giggle. "Not even Jane was handsome enough to tempt him."

Beside her, Mary nodded primly. "I thought his behaviour was most uncivil. He acted as if it would be a punishment to stand up with any of us."

"Hush, child! What would you know of such things?" said Mrs Bennet with a wave of her hand. "Great men like Mr Darcy are always a little whimsical in their civilities. It is of no significance if he was not disposed to dance."

"I thought him very proud," said Kitty causing her mother to glower in her direction.

"And what if he is? Is it any wonder that such a fine young man with family, fortune, everything in his favour should think well of himself? He has the right to be proud! Goodness, a gentleman such as Mr Darcy must be invited to the most exclusive balls in town!"

"Then he ought to know how to behave at one," said Lydia with a snort.

Mrs Bennet frowned but forbore to chastise her youngest daughter, who had always been her favourite.

"Never you mind about that. In any case, I could tell he

admired Jane, for who could not? She was easily the most beautiful woman in the room."

"I thought he spent far more time gazing at Lizzy than at Jane," Kitty remarked.

"And Mr Walsh seemed quite taken with Charlotte Lucas," Lydia added. "He danced with her twice."

"Charlotte was in especially good looks tonight," Mrs Bennet conceded. "I suppose I give Mr Walsh leave to like her, for he is only Mr Darcy's man of business and no match for any of the other gentlemen in the party."

"I thought Mr Walsh was very kind," Jane offered, briefly catching Elizabeth's eye. "And he spoke highly of Mr Darcy. He said they were at university together."

"There, you see!" Mrs Bennet trilled. "With friends such as that, and a cousin as charming as Colonel Fitzwilliam, I am sure Mr Darcy cannot be so very bad."

Mr Bennet, who had been listening to all of this in silence, at last turned to his second eldest, who had the distinction of being his particular favourite.

"You are very quiet, Lizzy. What have you to say about the gentleman?"

Elizabeth briefly looked away, carefully avoiding her older sister's gaze, before turning to address her father with cool indifference.

"I assure you, I have nothing whatsoever to say about Mr Darcy. As *Mr Bingley* is the object of my affection, his friend's likes and dislikes are of no concern to me. Now, if you will excuse me, I am going to bed."

Chapter Six

❧❧❧

That the Miss Lucases and the Miss Bennets should meet to talk over a ball was a custom of long duration. However, on the morning following the Meryton assembly, Elizabeth awoke with no inclination to revisit the previous evening's events.

Rising at her usual early hour, she donned a simple day dress and a woollen pelisse, intent on a solitary ramble through the Hertfordshire countryside. Slipping quietly out of the rear door that led to the garden, she inhaled the crisp, cool air, her feet instinctively carrying her towards Oakham Mount.

Although she had quit Longbourn's parlour the night before without voicing her opinion on Mr Darcy's conduct, the truth was she had been deeply disappointed—and embarrassed—by his behaviour. To see the gentleman who had occupied her thoughts for so many years act in such an uncivil manner had wounded her pride and unsettled her far more than she cared to admit. And to hear her younger sisters speak of him with such disparagement had only heightened her discomfort. If she had been silent, it was only because she was forced to concede that her sisters' criticisms were not entirely without merit; Mr Darcy had behaved poorly.

But once she had sought the privacy of her chambers and allowed her thoughts to settle, her indignation had begun to recede. She had found herself wondering whether his actions had not been without some provocation. True, it had been unconscionably rude of him to refuse to stand up with Jane, but her mother's mortifying behaviour could hardly be overlooked. Mrs Bennet had loudly extolled Mr Darcy's wealth and rank, all but demanding that he partner Jane for a set with no regard for the gentleman's feelings or preferences. Could it be any wonder, then, that he had declined to indulge her expectations?

As Elizabeth wound her way along the familiar path, her thoughts turned to a new and unsettling possibility: Could Mr Darcy's refusal to dance with Jane have been motivated by...loyalty? Despite her better judgment, her pulse quickened at the thought. Could it be that, beneath his reserved demeanour, Mr Darcy still harboured some tenderness towards her? The notion was absurd, of course. And yet, the mere suggestion stirred something within her that she had long tried to suppress.

A sudden snapping of a twig nearby pulled Elizabeth from her musings. Startled, she spun in the direction of the sound, her breath catching as a tall figure emerged around a bend in the path, framed against the morning sun.

"Mr Darcy!" she exclaimed, her tone a mix of surprise and annoyance. It seemed almost as though her thoughts had conjured him, the very object of her ruminations appearing before her as if by design.

At her cry, the gentleman halted, removing his hat with deliberate precision before offering her a formal bow.

"Miss Elizabeth," he said, his voice as steady as ever. "Pray, forgive me. I had no intention of startling you."

Regaining her equilibrium, Elizabeth released a low chuckle. "I am afraid I was lost in my own thoughts and did not hear you approach. I am also unaccustomed to seeing anyone on my morning walks, especially the day after an assembly. I am certain most of the neighbourhood is still abed."

Across from her, Mr Darcy studied her with a serious expression. "I have always been an early riser, and I also enjoy a morning walk, as you may remember."

Elizabeth's skin prickled at the tacit allusion to their first meeting, but it was his previous remark that garnered her immediate attention. "You cannot mean that you walked here? From Netherfield?"

When the gentleman nodded his confirmation, her eyes widened. "But that is above four miles! You must have left before daybreak!"

Mr Darcy shrugged lightly, as if travelling such a distance in the chill of an October morning—not to mention near darkness—were a matter of no consequence. "I remembered you saying this was one of the places you liked to walk, and I wished to speak with you. I did not like the way we parted last evening."

Elizabeth regarded him with a measured gaze. Choosing to overlook his last remark, she answered instead, "I only meant that I am surprised you did not ride. Surely

Mr Bingley could spare a horse from his stables if you did not bring your own?"

Much to her astonishment, Mr Darcy responded with a faint, slow smile. "Indeed. I dare say Netherfield's stables are bursting at the seams. However, I do not ride unless circumstances require it."

"Oh, I see," she replied, though in truth she did not see at all. "Well, you have come a long way on foot, so I suppose it would be churlish to refuse to listen to whatever it is you have to say."

Mr Darcy inclined his head, his gratitude evident. Extending his hand to indicate they should proceed along the path, the pair ambled in silence for several moments before he began haltingly, "I must first beg your forgiveness for my manner of address as you were leaving the terrace. Using your sister's name when I called after you was unpardonable. I do not know what took hold of me."

Studying him from the corner of her vision, Elizabeth shrugged. "You have no need to apologize for that. It is how you were accustomed to thinking of me, after all. Besides," she added lightly, "you are certainly not the first gentleman to have done something similar. Growing up with a sister as beautiful as Jane has its disadvantages at times."

Mr Darcy blinked at her, his brow furrowing. "Your sister seems a pleasant young lady, but I hope you are not insinuating that my addressing you by her name indicates any partiality towards her. It is simply, as you said, that I have not yet accustomed myself to thinking of you as Elizabeth—that is, Miss Elizabeth," he hastily amended.

"Very well," she replied with a faint smile. "And as I

have also said, you need not have come all this way to apologize for a slip of the tongue."

"I thank you, but that is only one of the things I wished to speak to you about," Mr Darcy said earnestly. "I owe you an apology for my behaviour as well. I do not have the talent of conversing easily with those I have never seen before, and I have not been much in company these last five years. It was never my intention to slight your sister. It is just that…" He paused briefly, his gaze fixed on the horizon, before continuing, "I do not do well in ballrooms. All the candles and the noise… I cannot fully explain. Suffice it to say that I was not prepared to dance last evening. But you were right to chastise me. If I was unwilling to participate, it would have been better not to attend."

Looking up into Mr Darcy's dark, expressive eyes, Elizabeth felt a sudden surge of emotion. Jane was forever telling her that allowances must be made for differences in situation and temperament. Not everyone was at ease in company, particularly when surrounded by strangers eager to pass judgment. Even she, who had glimpsed facets of Mr Darcy's character during their first meeting all those years ago, had been swift to assume the worst. What distressed her further was her silence when her friends and family had spoken harshly of him; she had offered nothing in his defence.

Suddenly, all the anger and resentment she had harboured against Mr Darcy since his arrival in Hertfordshire seemed to melt away, leaving her with only a deep sense of humiliation for her own bad behaviour.

"I shall accept your apology, Mr Darcy, if you will accept mine. I should not have been so severe upon you last night. It could not have been easy to walk into a room full of unfamiliar people to find oneself the object of such scrutiny. As for standing up with Jane…" She paused, then offered a wry smile. "Let us just say that I cannot place the blame entirely upon your shoulders. My mother's behaviour would have put almost anyone out of countenance."

Mr Darcy's brows lifted slightly at her remarks, though he soon concealed his amazement, offering her a sombre nod. "Thank you. I am glad we have had this opportunity to clear the air. I have been hoping to find a moment to speak with you privately since Lady Copley's ball."

"Have you?" Elizabeth asked, her curiosity piqued.

He nodded. "It is why I followed you out to the terrace."

They walked on in silence for a few moments before Mr Darcy continued. "I hope you know that I was pleased to encounter you again in town. We parted with such haste that day in Yorkshire, and I have always regretted not offering you a proper farewell. I have thought of you often these past four years."

At his words, a frisson of exhilaration coursed through Elizabeth's veins. He had thought about her? Taking a calming breath, she forced herself to reply evenly, "Well, I am glad to hear it. Though I should not have imagined a gentleman of your consequence would have had any cause to reflect on an inconsequential meeting with a stranger," she added with a quiet chuckle.

Mr Darcy halted, turning to face her with a puzzled expression. "That was never how I viewed our acquaintance. I have always considered you a friend."

"Ah, but that was before," Elizabeth quipped. "Before you knew I was not the daughter of a peer but rather an insignificant country miss of no particular importance."

"No, of course not! That is…" He paused, visibly flustered. "Although I now know your station in life is decidedly beneath my own, it changes nothing. I think as highly of you now as I did before."

A startled laugh slipped from Elizabeth's throat. *How was it possible for this man to be so endearing one moment and so exasperating the next?* "How magnanimous of you," she replied sardonically. "I am gratified to know that my humble origins will not affect our friendship."

Mr Darcy exhaled heavily, briefly removing his hat to rake his fingers through his hair. "You are twisting my words."

"Am I?" she countered, her voice tinged with amusement. "Well then, pray tell me, what are you trying to say, sir? If it is for my sake that you have followed Mr Bingley into Hertfordshire, you would do well to make your intentions clear."

The moment the words left her lips, Elizabeth regretted them. Not only was it highly improper to seek validation from a gentleman in such an overt manner, but she already suspected she would not like his reply.

Across from her, Mr Darcy blanched, his countenance a study in pained mortification. He briefly looked away before saying gravely, "I hope you know that I would never think of pursuing any young lady who already had an understanding with another gentleman, let alone one whom I consider a close personal acquaintance. But even if Bingley were not a factor in the matter, I would not wish to give you false hope. You should know that I am not free to marry."

At his words, Elizabeth's heart sank, and it was all she could do to lower her gaze lest he see the shock and humiliation in her eyes. *Good God! He is already married! Of course he is!* How could she have been so foolishly naïve as to think a gentleman of Mr Darcy's consequence would be unattached? *Stupid, stupid girl!*

Fighting to school her features, Elizabeth managed a thin smile, though she could not meet his eyes. "I beg your pardon, sir. I should have realized..."

She turned away to further hide her embarrassment, but a moment later, she felt the warmth of Mr Darcy's gloved hand on her arm. "What should you have realized?" he asked quietly.

"That-that there must be a Mrs Darcy," Elizabeth stammered. "Naturally, someone of your social standing—"

"There is no Mrs Darcy," he interrupted. His voice was firm but tinged with frustration. "It is...a complicated situation. Forgive me. I wish I could explain, but I am not at liberty to say more."

Elizabeth blinked, searching his face for answers, but he turned his head, staring off into the distance. "I should not have come here," he murmured, more to himself than to her, and Elizabeth sensed that he did not merely refer to Oakham Mount.

She was still composing a reply when he offered her a rigid bow. "Miss Elizabeth, forgive me for taking up so much of your time. I hope you will accept my best wishes for your health and happiness."

And with that, he lifted his hat and strode off in the

direction of Netherfield, leaving Elizabeth alone, her emotions in turmoil.

Darcy marched along the rutted path, his racing thoughts keeping time with the pounding of his heart. Although his eyes took in the rolling hills and bright blue sky, all he truly saw was Elizabeth's lovely countenance and the sanguine expression in her clear brown eyes when she had asked him if it was on her account that he had followed Bingley to Netherfield.

Devil take it! He never should have let his cousin talk him into coming into Hertfordshire. No good could come of it—for anyone.

Veering from the lane, he forged through standing puddles, crossing field after field at a brisk pace. His booted heels sank into the damp earth as he turned their conversation over and over in his mind.

After the way they had parted the previous evening, he had been prepared for Elizabeth's ire. What he had not anticipated was the fleeting vulnerability in her gaze when she questioned his intentions—the swift betrayal of emotion before she turned away. It haunted him, that look; not merely wounded pride, but something deeper, more intimate.

Could it be that she had once cared for him—as he had, and still did, for her? The thought unsettled him more than he liked to admit.

And more disquieting still was the way she had spoken of her sister's beauty. While her tone had been light, her eyes told a different story.

Darcy frowned. He knew all too well what it was to be measured against another only to be found wanting. He had lived in the shadow of George Wickham for most of his youth.

But the thought that Elizabeth—whose beauty, to his mind, eclipsed all others—might view herself as lesser than her sister pained him deeply. And yet, despite his own inclinations, there was no denying that Jane Bennet was an extraordinarily handsome young lady. Darcy had not missed the look on Bingley's face upon their introduction at the assembly, nor the way his friend's gaze had strayed to her again and again as the evening wore on.

What would it do to Elizabeth's spirit and self-worth if Bingley were to withdraw his attentions in favour of her sister?

The mere thought made Darcy's stomach clench with fury. Not only would Elizabeth be deeply wounded, but she would be made to look a fool before the entire neighbourhood.

Climbing over a stile that marked the boundary between Netherfield's property and the neighbouring estate, Darcy walked on, his agitation mounting with every step. He had long since accepted the things he could not change. For him, there would be no marriage, no children. He could not give Elizabeth—or any woman—the future she deserved.

But Bingley could. Bingley could provide Elizabeth with a good life. He could offer her financial security and a happy home—a future filled with comfort and ease.

And Darcy would be damned if he allowed Jane Bennet, or any other woman, to take that away from her.

He had scarcely reached Netherfield's curving drive when he was greeted by the sight of Richard advancing at a rapid pace. The colonel's face was set with equal parts irritation and relief, and he called out in strident tones, "Darcy, thank heavens! Where have you been? Walsh and I have been searching everywhere—we were worried sick!"

Drawing to a halt, Darcy's mind wrenched back from its single, blinding focus on Bingley—on all that must be said, and soon—only now realizing that he had been gone far longer than he intended.

"Forgive me," he replied, attempting to regulate his fractured emotions. "I woke early and went for a walk. I had not realized how late it had become."

"A walk?" Richard echoed, incredulity written across his features. "With no one to accompany you? And without leaving so much as a note? Do you have any idea how frantic we have been? Walsh has ridden into Meryton to search for you!"

Feeling the familiar stirrings of impatience, Darcy resumed his strides towards the house, his boots crunching against the gravel. "Once again, you have my apologies. Pray, send a footman after Walsh to apprise him of my safe return. As you can see, I am perfectly well."

From the corner of his eye, he caught his cousin's sceptical expression as he fell into step beside him.

"You do not look perfectly well," the colonel muttered, his voice low. "Did something—?"

"No," Darcy cut him off, his voice sharp as he turned to fix his cousin with a dark, forbidding glare. "Leave it, Richard. As I said, there is nothing amiss. Now, if you will excuse me, I must speak to Bingley as soon as may be."

Without waiting for a reply, Darcy stalked off in the direction of the house, leaving his cousin no choice but to follow in his wake.

❧

"Darcy! There you are!" Bingley exclaimed with his usual exuberance as Darcy entered the breakfast room some moments later, Fitzwilliam close at his heels. "Your cousin has been in quite a state. Another quarter of an hour, and I think he would have sent half the household to search for you," he concluded with a hearty chuckle.

Darcy frowned, momentarily diverted by Miss Bingley, who sprang to her feet at his entrance, her movements too eager by half.

Darting a glance in his cousin's direction, Darcy returned his gaze to his friend before saying in a clipped tone, "I have already made my apologies to Fitzwilliam, but pray forgive me for causing you any undue concern. I felt the need for some fresh air and neglected to leave word with one of the servants before setting out. For that, I am sorry."

He might have said more, but Miss Bingley interrupted with an exaggerated gasp. Turning once again in her direction, Darcy saw that her wide eyes were now fixed dramatically on the hems of his trousers as she cried out in a shrill voice, "Good heavens, Mr Darcy, what an ordeal you must have been through! To have walked out so early and in such dreadful weather! How thankful we all are for your safe return."

Darcy followed her gaze and noted, with no small

measure of embarrassment, that his trousers were at least six inches deep in mud—a glaring testament to his expedition across the sodden countryside. But there was nothing to be done about it now. Acknowledging Miss Bingley's outburst with a curt nod, he returned his attention to her brother.

"Bingley, there is a matter of some urgency that I must discuss with you. Now, if you please."

Bingley's eyebrows shot up at the firmness in Darcy's tone, but when he replied, it was with his characteristic amiability. "Of course, Darcy! But first, you must have some breakfast. Caroline is quite right—you do not look well. Here, let me pour you some tea."

"I thank you, no," Darcy replied through tight lips.

"Coffee, then? Or if you require something stronger, I—"

"Bingley, pray, desist!" Darcy snapped, his patience wearing thin. "I am in want of nothing save an explanation for your behaviour at last night's assembly. What were you about, showing such marked attention to Miss Jane Bennet?"

Bingley blinked, visibly startled. "I-I beg your pardon?" he stammered. "I do not believe I paid any undue attention to Miss Bennet."

"Oh no?" Darcy retorted, his voice a low thunder. "Your eyes practically fell out of your head when you were introduced, and you could scarcely look away from her for the remainder of the evening."

Bingley coloured slightly before saying, "I was merely being cordial. Though I cannot deny that Miss Jane Bennet is uncommonly pretty. Even you must have noticed that."

Darcy's scowl deepened, though he forbore to enquire into the meaning behind his friend's insinuation. "I suppose she is handsome enough if one is attracted to that sort. For my part, she lacks Miss Elizabeth's vivacity. And she smiles too much."

"Smiles too much?" Bingley echoed, his tone incredulous. "I hardly think—"

"No," Darcy interrupted, his voice rising. "It is abundantly clear that you do not! *That* is the problem."

A tense silence fell over the room as Darcy's words hung in the air. Beside him, Richard exhaled sharply, and Miss Bingley let out a nervous titter, but Darcy paid them no heed. His gaze remained fixed on Bingley, his eyes narrowed.

"How many young ladies have you paid court to since our days at university?" he pressed on. "How many 'angels' have there been before Miss Elizabeth Bennet? And now you would throw her over because her elder sister has captured your attention? It is beyond the pale, and I will not stand for it!"

"Darcy," Fitzwilliam murmured, his tone heavy with caution, but neither his cousin's warning nor Bingley's stunned expression could stem the flow of words now that they had begun.

"Can you not see that you have given rise to certain expectations where Miss Elizabeth Bennet is concerned? Not only did you pay court to her in London for all the *ton* to see, but then you followed her here to Hertfordshire, leased an estate not three miles from her home, and called upon her the very moment you arrived! It is a wonder Mrs Bennet has not had the banns read by now!"

"Darcy," Richard said loudly, his voice cutting through the tirade, "might I speak to you a moment?"

Darcy opened his mouth to protest, but his cousin had already taken hold of his arm, steering him out of the door and into the adjoining entrance hall.

"Good God, man, what are you about?" the colonel hissed as soon as they were out of earshot. "For someone who professes to have no interest in Miss Elizabeth Bennet, you certainly are making a display of your feelings. Did you not see the notice Miss Bingley was taking of the conversation?"

Heat prickled at the back of Darcy's neck. In truth, he had been so caught up in his righteous indignation that he had scarcely given a thought to anyone beyond Bingley.

Straightening his cuffs, he replied churlishly, "I care nothing for Miss Bingley's opinion. I will not have Elizabeth humiliated!"

Richard darted a glance in the direction of the breakfast parlour before dragging Darcy farther across the hall. "Can you not see that you are blowing this entire situation out of proportion? I did not notice anything improper in Bingley's behaviour towards Miss Bennet last evening, and I dare say neither did anyone else until you just called attention to it!"

"That is because you do not know Bingley as I do! He would throw Elizabeth over in favour of her sister in a trice if the mood struck. And I will not have her made a laughingstock."

Richard released an irritated huff. "Be that as it may, you cannot wear your heart so plainly on your sleeve. Not if you wish to persuade the good people of Meryton—or our hosts, for that matter—that you do not have feelings for the lady yourself."

Darcy's anger began to dissipate as his cousin's words took root, and his shoulders slumped. He regarded Richard, regret tightening his throat.

"Very well. I shall concede that I should have insisted on a private audience with Bingley rather than airing my grievances in the breakfast room. But I stand by what I said. Bingley has already raised expectations where Miss Elizabeth is concerned. If he does not mean to continue to court her, he would do better to leave the neighbourhood entirely."

"And is that what you truly want?" Richard asked, with a narrowed gaze. "For Bingley to continue to court Miss Elizabeth Bennet?"

Darcy briefly looked away before answering, "They seem well suited. He would make her a good husband."

"Mayhap. But that does not answer my question," Richard replied gently.

Darcy kept his eyes averted but straightened his shoulders, his jaw tightening.

"Elizabeth deserves to be happy, and Bingley can give her what I cannot. So yes, if she is his choice, then I wish them well. Now, if you will excuse me, this conversation is at an end."

After taking a few moments to collect himself, Darcy re-entered the breakfast room with the colonel. Once past the threshold, he wasted no time in approaching his friend.

"Pray, forgive me, Bingley. I had no right to speak to you in such a way," he began, his tone contrite, before turning to offer similar words to Bingley's sister. "Miss Bingley, I also owe you an apology for my lack of decorum."

Bingley began to stammer his own expression of regret, clearly embarrassed by the earlier confrontation, but before he could say much, his sister's voice rose above his.

"Mr Darcy, I was just telling my brother that you were quite right to chastise him for his conduct towards dear Eliza Bennet." Turning to face her brother, she continued with exaggerated disapproval, "Really, Charles, you have treated the poor girl quite infamously."

Visibly abashed, Bingley shifted awkwardly in his seat. "I assure you, it was not my intention to show any prefer-ence for Miss Jane Bennet, and I feel dreadful to think I may have caused Miss Elizabeth any distress. I have just been speaking to Caroline about how I might make amends." Turning back to his sister, he added eagerly, "Per-haps you might invite Miss Elizabeth to tea? You did mention wanting to get to know her better."

Whether or not Miss Bingley was in favour of this scheme remained unclear, for Darcy interjected before she could reply.

"Singling out Miss Elizabeth in such a way will only add fuel to the fire. Unless you are prepared to make her an offer of marriage, you would do well to cease showing her such marked attention."

"Yes, you are right," Bingley agreed, his shoulders slumping. "The last thing I would want is to cause her any undue discomfort."

He paused, staring into space for a moment before suddenly straightening his spine. "I know! Why not invite the entire Bennet family to dine with us? That way, we might all come to know one another better without giving rise to any particular expectations where Miss Elizabeth is concerned."

"All of them?" Miss Bingley cried out, her voice rising in alarm. "Really, Charles, I have no objection to becoming better acquainted with Miss Eliza Bennet, and Miss Jane Bennet does seem like a sweet girl, but the younger sisters are intolerable! And the mother!"

Disregarding his sister's objections, Bingley continued, undeterred. "Perhaps I shall invite the Lucases as well. Sir William has been exceedingly hospitable, and it would be a friendly gesture."

This suggestion was met with approval from the two remaining gentlemen. Colonel Fitzwilliam, in particular, looked amused as he responded, "A fine idea, Bingley. The more the merrier."

Miss Bingley, however, drew a sharp breath, clearly struggling to mask her displeasure, though her expression remained pinched. In the end, she could do nothing but consent, albeit grudgingly.

With the matter settled, Bingley wasted no time in seeing that the invitations were written and dispatched without delay.

Chapter Seven

T he morning of the proposed dinner party brought
with it a driving rain that kept everyone confined
indoors for the duration of the day. Colonel Fitzwilliam was
not particularly bothered by the weather—he had endured
far worse in his time as a soldier—but the enforced idleness
of the household set him on edge.

After a late breakfast, he followed the rest of the party
into the morning room, considering how best to pass the
time. Darcy, predictably, declared his intention to write
letters and ensconced himself at a small secretaire in the
corner. Bingley, all easy contentment, claimed one of the
armchairs by the fire. As for himself, Fitzwilliam
welcomed the opportunity to resume the chess match he
and Walsh had abandoned the night before. With a nod to
his opponent, he moved towards the board, already contemplating his next move.

Meanwhile, Miss Bingley drifted restlessly about the
room, alternately peering over Darcy's shoulder and glaring

at the streams of water cascading down the front windows. Her sighs grew progressively louder as the morning wore on, marked by the measured ticking of the clock. At last, she turned to her brother with a sour expression.

"I really think we must cancel, Charles. This is hardly the sort of day to be hosting our first soirée!"

"Nonsense," Bingley replied from behind his newspaper. "It is only a spot of rain. Besides, it may very well stop before this evening."

"But think of how muddy the lanes will be! What if the Bennets' carriage should get stuck on the way here? Assuming they even have a carriage," she added under her breath, her disdain evident. With an exaggerated gasp, she pressed on. "Goodness! You do not think they intend to walk? They will arrive here drenched to the skin and dripping dirty water all over the carpets!"

At this, Bingley slowly lowered his paper, frowning thoughtfully. "I am quite certain they keep a carriage," he replied evenly, "but you do raise a valid point. With the entire family attending, they will either need to make two trips, or they will be quite crowded indeed."

He brightened suddenly, climbing to his feet. "I shall send one of my own carriages to ease the burden! This way, they may all travel to Netherfield in comfort and at the same time. Thank you for thinking of it, Sister!"

Miss Bingley's glare was sharp enough to curdle milk, but before she could summon a protest, her brother had already made his way to the door, calling for a servant to deliver a note to Longbourn at once.

At this, the lady snapped her fan shut with a loud crack, muttering something unintelligible before taking up a chair as close to Darcy as propriety would allow. With her gaze fixed intently on his writing hand, she began to supervise the progress of his letter, at intervals calling off his attention with messages for his sister.

Fitzwilliam did his utmost to stifle his amusement at the lady's perpetual effusions—lavishing praise on his cousin's handwriting, the evenness of his lines, and the superior quality of his ink. To each, Darcy offered only the briefest of acknowledgements, his replies growing terser with every passing moment.

After more than a quarter of an hour of this one-sided dialogue, Darcy finally appeared to have reached the end of his patience. Pushing his chair back with a screech, he rose abruptly to his feet.

"If you will excuse me, madam," his cousin intoned, "I am afraid my quill has broken. With your permission, I shall retrieve another from my writing box and finish this letter in my chambers."

"Oh!" Miss Bingley exclaimed, springing from her chair with alarming rapidity. "But there is no need to leave! You must allow me to mend your pen. I mend pens remarkably well."

It was all Fitzwilliam could do to school his expression as his cousin replied stiffly, "Of that, I have no doubt. However, I am afraid this one is beyond repair."

With a curt bow, Darcy turned to Walsh. "Would you care to accompany me? I believe there were still some matters of business requiring our attention."

Walsh, obviously sensing his cue, nodded and rose to his feet. "Of course," he answered with measured civility, before both gentlemen excused themselves from their company.

Miss Bingley gaped after them as they strode briskly from the parlour, their departure swift enough to discourage any further attempts at detainment.

From his seat by the fire, Fitzwilliam chuckled to himself, watching his cousin's retreating form as Darcy and Walsh made their way towards the stairs.

Coward, he thought with an amused smirk, turning his attention back to his hostess. Miss Bingley, now bereft of her primary target, had taken herself to the pianoforte in the corner of the room, where she sat on the rosewood bench, plucking out a melancholy tune with one hand.

Settling deeper into his chair, Fitzwilliam stretched his legs and watched the lady's restless performance. After a moment, he let out a deliberate cough, breaking the awkward silence.

"You are wasting your time, you know."

At the sound of his voice, Miss Bingley startled, her fingers stilling on the keys. She turned to face him, her forehead creased in evident confusion. "I beg your pardon?"

"With Darcy," he replied, his lips curling into a sardonic smile.

Her eyes widened, and a mottled flush suffused her countenance before she eventually looked away, feigning indifference. "Indeed, sir, I do not have the pleasure of understanding you."

"Oh, come now, Miss Bingley. Disguise does not suit a woman of your obvious intelligence."

She turned back to him then, one brow arched in challenge. "Perhaps you give me more credit than I deserve. I am afraid I must plead ignorance in this matter."

"Very well," Fitzwilliam said with a shrug. "Then I shall speak plainly. I refer to your obvious attempts at flirtation with my cousin. If you are hoping Darcy will make you an offer of marriage, I am afraid you are bound to be disappointed."

Miss Bingley's cheeks flushed crimson, and she began to sputter a denial, but Fitzwilliam waved her protestations aside with an easy gesture.

"Now, now, there is no need for all that. If I may be honest, I am not entirely insensible to your plight. It has long been my opinion that ladies face an unfair disadvantage when it comes to courtship and marriage. You are not granted the authority to choose your life's partner—only the right of refusal. So how are you to have any influence over your destiny but to use your God-given feminine wiles to ensnare the object of your affection?"

Miss Bingley gasped lightly, her hand flying to her throat, and Fitzwilliam chuckled in response.

"I beg your pardon if I have offended your feminine sensibilities, madam. That was not my intention. I only meant to warn you that, in the particular case of my cousin, your efforts will come to nought. Darcy, you see, is a confirmed bachelor. He has told me on many occasions that he is not inclined to marry, now or in the future. And even if you were to contrive some way to force his hand, I guarantee the two of you would make each other miserable."

Miss Bingley drew herself up with a diffident tilt of her chin. "But you must be mistaken, sir! How can a man of Mr Darcy's consequence refuse to take a wife? Surely a gentleman with an estate like Pemberley must be in want of an heir."

Fitzwilliam shrugged lightly. "Pemberley is not entailed. If Darcy does not produce an heir, the estate will pass to his sister, then to her children if she is so fortunate as to have any."

"Even so!" Miss Bingley exclaimed, her indignation plain. "I cannot comprehend why Mr Darcy should have such an aversion to marriage. It is most unusual."

After a moment of silence, she rose from the pianoforte and crossed the carpet to perch on a nearby settee, her demeanour more composed. "Certainly you do not hold the same views as your cousin?" she asked coyly. "A wife with a generous dowry would be a valuable asset to a gentleman in your position."

Fitzwilliam barked out a laugh, clearly startling the lady. "Oh no! Do not set your sights on me. While it is true that I cannot afford to marry without some attention to money, I would like to think I am not so mercenary as all that. Moreover, I should never risk making any woman a soldier's widow—and I am very happy in my work. I have no intention of resigning my commission for many years to come."

Miss Bingley frowned, her gaze shifting to the window and the rain pelting the glass. "Why are you telling me all this?" she finally asked, her voice quiet.

Fitzwilliam relaxed into his chair, turning the conversation over in his mind. "I do not rightly know. I suppose I simply cannot countenance anyone expending so much effort with no hope of the desired result."

The lady turned her face away, her jaw tight, but

Fitzwilliam pressed on. "Miss Bingley, I know you have not asked, but might I give you some advice?"

When she did not answer, he continued, gentling his tone, "You are a handsome, capable lady of some means, but no gentleman wishes to feel that he is being hunted like prey. You would do much better to apply your natural intelligence than to resort to these manufactured arts and allurements. After all, one is far more likely to accomplish by kindness what cannot be achieved by force."

Miss Bingley remained silent for several moments before rising stiffly to her feet. Her expression was unreadable, but her voice was steady as she said, "I thank you for your candour, sir, but if you will excuse me, I seem to have lost track of the time. I have the dinner to prepare for."

And with a brief curtsey, she turned on her heel and walked quickly from the room, leaving the colonel to watch her retreat with quiet contemplation.

The Bennet and Lucas carriages, followed directly by Mr Bingley's barouche, arrived promptly at the appointed hour.

Although the rain had ceased late that afternoon, at Darcy's suggestion, Bingley had instructed his footmen to lay down a carpet retrieved from the attic, ensuring the ladies could alight without dirtying the hems of their gowns. The gesture, though merely practical, was met with glowing approval from Mrs Bennet, who loudly proclaimed her gratitude as she stepped out of the carriage with a flutter of lace and ribbons.

The Netherfield party had gathered in the front hall to

greet their guests. Darcy, however, made a deliberate point of standing near the entrance to the drawing room, where he could observe the proceedings without drawing undue attention to himself. It had been nearly a week since his conversation with Elizabeth at Oakham Mount, and although he had spent the intervening time preparing himself for this evening's encounter, he found himself torn between anticipation and unease. He was eager to see her again, but after his precipitous departure from their last meeting, he was also apprehensive about what her reception might be.

As expected, Bingley was the picture of geniality, welcoming each guest with unrestrained warmth and good humour. His enthusiasm extended to every member of the Bennet family, from the radiant Jane to the spirited Lydia, who preened under the attention. Walsh, as ever, was reserved but courteous, though Darcy noticed a flicker of animation in his expression as he greeted Miss Lucas—a subtle but telling departure from his usual stoicism.

Richard, ever the charmer, greeted everyone with practised ease, bowing over the ladies' hands and enquiring after their health with such sincerity that even Mrs Bennet was momentarily rendered speechless. Darcy could not suppress a wry smile at his cousin's effortless ability to win favour wherever he went.

Miss Bingley, meanwhile, wore a mask of forced civility. She simpered over Miss Bennet and Elizabeth with excessive sweetness, bestowed a half-hearted welcome to the family patriarch, and all but overlooked the remainder of their guests. When Miss Lydia's voice rose in a particularly exuberant exclamation, Miss Bingley's lips pressed into a thin line, though she managed to maintain her composure long enough to usher the entire party into the drawing room to await the dinner bell.

Upon entering the parlour, it was Mrs Bennet who spoke first, declaring the room charming and effusing over everything from the furnishings to the prospect from the windows. Lady Lucas bobbed her head in rapid agreement, her murmured affirmations blending with Mrs Bennet's enthusiastic commentary.

Sir William Lucas, eager to insert himself into the conversation, began comparing the room to one of the parlours at St James's, though the younger girls seemed more entertained by their own whispered remarks, interspersed by bursts of giggles. Meanwhile, Mr Bennet, leaning casually against the back of an armchair, surveyed the scene with a sardonic twist to his lips, offering no comment of his own.

"Indeed, I do not know a place in the country that is equal to Netherfield," Mrs Bennet proclaimed loudly over the din. "You will not think of quitting it in a hurry, I hope," she added, fixing her attention on Bingley with a pointed look.

"Whatever I do is done in a hurry," Bingley replied with an easy smile. "If I should resolve to quit Netherfield, I should probably be off in five minutes. At present, however, I consider myself quite settled here." He turned his gaze towards Elizabeth, the sincerity in his expression unmistakable.

Mrs Bennet positively glowed at the marked attention to her second-eldest daughter, clearly already planning the wedding. She then turned to Mr Darcy with a more calculating expression. "And you, sir? I hope you are enjoying your sojourn in the neighbourhood. Do you and your cousin intend to stay long?"

Although Darcy kept his eyes on the matron, he was acutely aware of Elizabeth's gaze, the scrutiny of her expression sharper than any question Mrs Bennet might pose. Taking a measured breath, he replied, "I am afraid, madam, that my cousin's time is not his own. He is due back at his regiment within the fortnight. As for myself"— here he risked a fleeting glance in Elizabeth's direction— "at present, my plans are not firmly fixed."

Mrs Bennet's eyes sparkled with interest, and she opened her mouth to press the matter further, but just then, the dinner gong sounded, and a flurry of movement followed as the party made their way to the dining room, saving Darcy—at least temporarily—from further discourse on the matter.

Elizabeth placed her hand lightly upon Mr Bingley's sleeve, allowing him to escort her to Netherfield's large dining room.

In the days since the assembly, Mr Bingley had called upon her more than once, and Elizabeth always received his attentions with great delight. The gentleman's manners were universally admired by the ladies at Longbourn, for it was plain that he took genuine pleasure in their company, a quality that only served to recommend him further to their good opinion.

As for Mr Darcy, Elizabeth had not laid eyes on him

since the morning he had walked away from her at Oakham Mount. Although she could not deny a peculiar mixture of frustration and curiosity whenever she thought of him, she was resolved to set those feelings aside and enjoy her evening at Netherfield to the fullest.

Conversation flowed in an easy manner as everyone took their seats. Elizabeth noted with mixed emotions that she and Mr Darcy had been placed as far apart as possible —she at one end of the long table beside Mr Bingley, and he at the opposite end with Miss Bingley seated to his left. *At least I shall not have to endure his sombre looks or reproachful airs tonight,* she thought uncharitably as Mr Bingley assisted her into her chair.

The meal began well enough. The food was plentiful and expertly prepared and the company pleasant. Mr Bingley and Colonel Fitzwilliam kept up a lively discourse that drew out even the more reserved members of their party, and Elizabeth was relieved to see that her mother and youngest sisters appeared to be on their best behaviour.

To her surprise, Miss Bingley said little, though her watchful gaze continually shifted between Mr Darcy and Mr Walsh, who was seated at her other side. It was not until the second remove that their hostess finally found her voice. Turning to Mr Darcy's friend, she spoke at a volume calculated to draw the attention of the entire table.

"I hope you are enjoying your stay at Netherfield, sir," she began, with a brittle smile. "Though from all appearances, you might still be in Derbyshire. You and Mr Darcy have been so very industrious since your arrival—always shut away in some corner of the house. I do hope it is not all dreadful accounts and estate papers?"

Beside her, Walsh inclined his head, his expression politely neutral. "A necessary evil, I am afraid. Mr Darcy and I have taken advantage of the quieter moments to attend to a few matters long delayed. It is not the most cheerful use of one's time, perhaps—but it keeps me out of mischief."

Miss Bingley tittered lightly, but her eyes sharpened. "Indeed, you and Mr Darcy appear to be quite inseparable. As I recall, you were in residence at Pemberley when my family and I visited last summer."

Across the table, Elizabeth sat straighter in her chair, her curiosity piqued as much by Miss Bingley's tone as by her words. She cast a sidelong glance at Mr Darcy, who was clearly unamused, his features taut with displeasure. Mr Walsh, by contrast, looked entirely at ease as he replied, "Indeed, madam, I spend most of my time at Pemberley and often travel with Mr Darcy. As I am employed to oversee his affairs, it generally makes matters more efficient."

"I see," Miss Bingley said, her tone suffused with feigned curiosity. "Pray forgive my ignorance, but is it common for a business advisor to work exclusively for a single gentleman? My brother retains a man in London, but I dare say he could not support himself on Charles's custom alone."

"Caroline," Mr Bingley interjected from the opposite end of the table, his voice coloured with exasperation, "I hardly think you can compare my fortune to Darcy's."

"No, you are quite right, Miss Bingley," Walsh replied smoothly. "It is, indeed, an unusual arrangement. But as I am sure you can imagine, Mr Darcy's holdings are vast, so there is more than enough to keep me occupied."

Elizabeth observed the conversation with a growing sense of discomfort, not for the first time marvelling at Miss Bingley's persistence in attempting to elevate herself in Mr Darcy's esteem while subtly denigrating others in the process.

A brief silence settled over the room, broken only when Sir William Lucas jovially called out, "I say, that reminds me of the last time I was in London—"

But he got no further before Miss Bingley, her gaze still fixed on Mr Walsh, continued loudly, "I believe, sir, that you were visiting relations in Bedfordshire before travelling to Netherfield, were you not?"

Mr Bingley was frowning openly at his sister now, but Mr Walsh merely replied in the affirmative, to which Miss Bingley tilted her head in an exaggerated manner.

"You must correct me if I am mistaken, sir, but is not Bedfordshire to the north? Would it not have been more advantageous for you to travel straight to Pemberley rather than journey in the opposite direction to join Mr Darcy here in Hertfordshire?"

"Caroline!" Mr Bingley hissed loudly, but Charlotte gave a delicate cough, turning towards Mr Walsh with a bright smile.

"Bedfordshire has some lovely countryside," she offered, plainly attempting to redirect the conversation. "My mother has a sister in Dunstable."

Mr Walsh grinned back at her with obvious pleasure. "Truly? I come from Bedford, but the majority of my relations reside near Luton, no more than five miles away. Do you visit often?"

"Indeed we do, sir," Lady Lucas interjected as Sir William added, "We shall stop there at Christmastide if the weather allows it."

"Well then, I shall wish for temperate conditions on your behalf," Mr Walsh replied graciously. He then turned back to their hostess, adding, "And Miss Bingley, to answer your question—yes, Bedfordshire is to the north. So, indeed, it would have been more convenient for me to return directly to Pemberley. However, Mr Darcy and I had several matters of business to discuss, so in truth, it was far more expedient for us to meet here, rather than relying on the vagaries of the post—or worse yet, postponing our work until Mr Darcy was at liberty to return to his estate."

Lifting his glass, he took a measured sip of claret before concluding, "Although I do thank you for your concern, as well as your generous hospitality."

"Well, we are very glad to have you," Mr Bingley interjected, casting his sister a dark look before turning to Sir William and asking him to resume his story.

Sir William eagerly took up the thread, and the conversation flowed once more. It was not until the dessert course that the weather was mentioned again. This time, Jane turned to Mr Bingley, her voice soft and sincere.

"It was very kind of you to send your carriage for us earlier. I was particularly struck by your fine pair of horses. It was a true joy to behold them in motion."

Mr Bingley's expression brightened immediately, and he replied with great animation. "They are a marvel, are they not? I defy anyone to find a better-matched team in the entire kingdom. And they are as even-tempered and sure-footed as they are handsome! I acquired them only last spring from a gentleman who refused to drive them together as they are both mares. Thought it unmanly—can you imagine that?"

Elizabeth smiled. "You seem quite the authority when it comes to horseflesh, sir. Has this long been an interest of yours?"

Mr Bingley had just opened his mouth to reply when Mrs Bennet called out from halfway down the table, "If you are fond of horses, you have certainly come to the right place. There is no finer countryside for riding, and the stables at Netherfield are among the largest in the county!"

"Indeed!" Mr Bingley replied, his enthusiasm undimmed. "It was one of the reasons I leapt at the chance to lease the estate. That and the proximity to such charming neighbours," he added, flashing an easy smile in Elizabeth's direction.

Glaring at Mrs Bennet, Miss Bingley replied shrilly, "Pray, do not encourage him, ma'am. Once Charles begins speaking of horses, there will be no other topic of conversation for the remainder of the evening!"

"I am certain Jane would not mind that," Elizabeth quipped, exchanging a teasing glance with her sister.

Mr Bingley looked eagerly between her and Jane before turning to the latter. "Are you also partial to horses, Miss Bennet?"

"Oh yes, very much so," Jane answered, a light flush rising to her cheeks. "I have a mare, Buttercup, that I quite dote on. I ride out as often as I can, though not as often as I would wish."

"Why, then we must organize a riding party! With your father's approval, of course," Mr Bingley added hastily, nodding to Mr Bennet. "I should love to see more of the countryside, and I have a full stable if anyone requires a mount. What say you, Miss Elizabeth?"

Beside him, Elizabeth laughed lightly. "I am afraid Jane is the horsewoman in the family. I do not ride, unless circumstances require it," she replied, darting a glance at Mr Darcy.

But if the gentleman noticed her subtle reference to their conversation at Oakham Mount, his expression did not betray it. Elizabeth's attention was soon claimed by Mrs Bennet, who cried out, "Nonsense, Lizzy! Of course you must go. You will enjoy the opportunity to show Mr Bingley around the neighbourhood."

Turning to Mr Darcy, Mrs Bennet continued, "And what of you, sir? I am certain you will wish to be of the party. Jane would greatly enjoy your company. And although I do not like to boast of my own child, one would be hard-pressed to find any young lady who is a more skilled equestrian than my Jane."

Across the table, Elizabeth noted the tightening of Mr Darcy's jaw, but he was spared the obligation of a reply as Mrs Bennet turned her attention to Colonel Fitzwilliam.

"And you, Colonel? Surely you are quite at home in the saddle. Lydia, my love," she called loudly, "would you not wish to ride out with Colonel Fitzwilliam?"

Lydia wrinkled her nose in obvious displeasure. "Oh no, not I! I have no desire to return home smelling of a stable yard!" she exclaimed, laughing loudly at her own jest. "Let Mary go. She cares nothing for such things."

Mrs Bennet opened her mouth to respond but seemed at a loss for words. The silence was filled by Mr Bingley's hearty chuckle.

"Perhaps you are only in want of a gentleman who enjoys the scent of a stable, Miss Lydia," he replied lightly. "I, for one, find the aroma of horses and hay exceedingly agreeable."

For a brief moment, his gaze met Jane's, and Elizabeth saw her sister flush prettily before lowering her lashes.

It was at this moment that Miss Bingley shoved back her chair, announcing that it was time for the ladies to withdraw, and so, the conversation was at an end.

Chapter Eight

I t was not long before the gentlemen joined the ladies in the drawing room. At Sir William Lucas' suggestion, card tables were set up, and the younger girls, along with Mrs Bennet, Colonel Fitzwilliam, and Sir William and Lady Lucas, all sat down to a game of whist, while Mr Bennet contented himself with a book he procured from a nearby shelf and took up residence by the fire.

After exchanging a brief word with Mr Darcy, Mr Walsh crossed to the small settee where Charlotte was seated. Elizabeth could not help but notice the sweet smile and becoming colour that suffused her friend's countenance at his approach. However, she had little time to dwell on the matter as Mr Bingley soon joined her and Jane on the larger sofa.

Across the room, Elizabeth observed Miss Bingley's eyes instantly drawn to Mr Darcy as he entered. After a brief hesitation, she advanced upon him, enquiring about his preference for tea or brandy. Mr Darcy declined both offers with his usual reserve before approaching their party and seating himself in a winged chair, which he angled away from the nearby fire.

For her part, Elizabeth felt all the awkwardness of being placed between Mr Bingley's cheerful attentions and Mr Darcy's stern, unrelenting gaze. While the former engaged her and Jane in pleasant conversation, the latter's rigid expression unnerved her. What could Mr Darcy be about, staring at her so intently? If he had no interest in her himself, he had no right to silently rebuke her for her attentions towards his friend.

Finally, when the talk turned to the estate, Elizabeth faced the dour gentleman with a pert expression. "Mr Darcy, what think you of Netherfield? Mr Bingley has mentioned that he is counting on you to advise him on its management."

Mr Darcy started, clearly surprised to be addressed directly, but he soon replied, "I have seen nothing to cause me concern. The estate is well situated, and the soil appears fertile. Although the gardens and fields on the north side of the property show some signs of neglect, I have no doubt these difficulties could be easily remedied with the appointment of a new steward."

"I see. And is it your recommendation that Mr Bingley remain at Netherfield to oversee these improvements?" Elizabeth asked.

"That, I am afraid I cannot answer."

"Cannot, or will not?" Elizabeth challenged with an arched brow.

Mr Darcy stared back at her with an inscrutable expression before saying deliberately, "May I ask, Miss Elizabeth, to what these questions tend?"

"Merely to the illustration of your character," Elizabeth replied sweetly, endeavouring to maintain her composure. "I am trying to make it out."

"And what is your success?"

"I am afraid I do not get on at all. Since the beginning of our acquaintance, I have perceived such contradictory conduct that it puzzles me exceedingly."

"That I can readily believe," Mr Darcy answered gravely. "I am well aware that I am apt to display many inconstant traits. Therefore, I would wish, Miss Elizabeth, that rather than attempting to sketch my character, you might simply take me at my word."

Elizabeth blinked at him, chastened by the severity of his tone, but before she could muster a reply, Miss Bingley interjected.

"Oh, my dear Eliza, your tea has gone cold. Let me pour you a fresh cup."

Her thoughts still with Mr Darcy, Elizabeth turned to her hostess, but before she had the opportunity to accept or decline Miss Bingley's offer, the lady snatched up Elizabeth's teacup so rapidly that the delicate piece teetered precariously upon its saucer, splashing its contents on the hem of Elizabeth's gown before toppling to the floor.

"Caroline, have a care!" Mr Bingley cried as Jane let out a gasp of surprise.

"Oh! How clumsy of me," Miss Bingley tittered, her smile strained.

Mr Darcy shot her a stern look before turning to Elizabeth with evident concern. "Miss Elizabeth, are you hurt? You have not been burnt, I hope?"

"No, no. As Miss Bingley said, the tea was cold, so there was no harm done. In any case, I am afraid it is the carpet that has borne the brunt of the damage," Elizabeth said lightly, brushing at her skirt.

Mr Bingley immediately assured everyone that the carpet was of no concern as Jane bent to retrieve the cup and saucer.

"But we must do something about your gown," Miss Bingley interjected in an agitated tone. "Pray, let us go and tend to it before the stain has a chance to set."

"Here, take my handkerchief," Jane offered, opening her reticule, but Elizabeth waved her sister's concern away with a small smile.

"Yours is far too pretty to ruin. Besides, it was only a few drops. 'Tis already dry."

Jane looked back at her with mild concern, but she acquiesced, setting the delicate linen square on a nearby table.

"Why, that is remarkable!" Mr Bingley exclaimed as he picked up the handkerchief to admire the intricate embroidery. He held it aloft, revealing the delicate likeness of a horse's head encircled by a wreath of yellow buttercups. "Did you stitch this yourself?"

"Indeed, she did, sir," Elizabeth replied on her sister's behalf. "Jane is by far the cleverest of all of us with a needle."

"It is always amazing to me," Mr Bingley said earnestly, "how young ladies have the patience to be so accomplished. You paint tables, cover screens, net purses, and I know not what!"

At Mr Bingley's praise, Jane flushed, her expression alight with modest pride. "In this case, I am afraid I cannot take all the credit. Lizzy sketched the image—I am merely responsible for the needlework."

Mr Bingley began to reply, but it was Mr Darcy's deep baritone that cut through the conversation. "It is a remarkable portrayal. Only someone with a true understanding of the natural world could have captured such detail so faithfully."

Although it was unclear which lady he addressed, Elizabeth's gaze lifted instinctively, only to find his eyes fixed on hers.

A brief, awkward silence fell over the room until Miss Bingley rose abruptly, addressing Elizabeth. "Miss Eliza Bennet, might I persuade you to take a turn about the room? I assure you it is most refreshing after sitting so long in one attitude."

Elizabeth lifted a brow at the sudden invitation but could see no reason to decline. Rising from her seat, she excused herself from the rest of the party and hesitantly took the arm Miss Bingley offered. Together, they began a slow promenade around the perimeter of the room. It was not until they reached a quieter corner that Miss Bingley began speaking in a low tone.

"Let me recommend you, Miss Eliza, as a friend, that you ought not to set your cap at Mr Darcy. I have it on excellent authority that he has no interest in taking a wife, so I must assure you that any hopes you may have in that quarter will come to nought."

A ripple of mortification coursed through Elizabeth, but she kept her expression neutral, replying serenely, "I thank you for your concern, Miss Bingley, but may I ask what makes you think I have any designs on Mr Darcy?"

"Oh, my dear Eliza! You must know it is evident to anyone who observes the two of you together. However, if you spent less time trying to capture the gentleman's attention and more time studying his activities, you would see where his true interest lies."

With that, Miss Bingley tilted her head meaningfully towards the opposite side of the room, where Mr Darcy now stood by the darkened windows in quiet conversation with Mr Walsh.

"Of course," Miss Bingley continued, "there have been rumblings about it in town for some time. Personally, I try to avoid such mean-spirited gossip, and as he is my brother's particular friend, I have always given him the benefit of the doubt. But you know what they say—where there is smoke, you are almost certain to find fire."

Elizabeth stopped walking abruptly, forcing Miss Bingley to halt as well. Fixing her companion with a steady gaze, she said evenly, "Forgive me, Miss Bingley, but I, too, make it a point to avoid mean-spirited gossip. I do not know where these accusations tend, but so far, I have heard you reproach Mr Darcy for nothing worse than remaining unmarried and maintaining a close personal friendship with a trusted advisor—neither of which are…"

She paused, searching for the right word, but Miss Bingley interrupted with a patronizing laugh.

"Oh, my dearest Eliza, do not be so naïve! Why else

would a gentleman of Mr Darcy's age, wealth, and connections never so much as look at marriageable young ladies? It is well-known that he eschews social gatherings, and not once has his name been linked with any lady, save his cousin Miss Anne de Bourgh—and even that has come to nothing. Why, he rarely leaves his estate! He is all but a recluse. Do you not find that rather…odd?"

"A recluse?" Elizabeth replied with a startled laugh. "I certainly have seen no evidence of that. I met Mr Darcy recently at a ball in town, and now he is here at Netherfield, visiting your brother. Perhaps he only appears misanthropic to those individuals he wishes to avoid."

Elizabeth was gratified to see Caroline Bingley's countenance turn a vivid shade of scarlet at this remark, though the lady quickly masked her embarrassment with an affected smile.

"Be that as it may," Miss Bingley countered, her voice clipped, "I have it from his own cousin Colonel Fitzwilliam that Mr Darcy will not marry. And you need do no more than look across the room to see why that is."

Elizabeth felt heat rise in her cheeks at the insinuation, but she maintained an air of calm indifference. When she spoke, her tone was measured and devoid of emotion. "I am certain I do not know what you are implying, Miss Bingley, but I can assure you that Mr Darcy's personal affairs are of no concern to me."

Miss Bingley's eyes narrowed as she regarded Elizabeth. "In that case," she said at last, her voice honeyed but sharp at the edges, "pray excuse my interference. It was kindly meant."

And with that, she dropped Elizabeth's arm and flounced off to take a seat beside Colonel Fitzwilliam on the far side of the room.

§&

That night, Elizabeth lay awake in her bed, staring at the ceiling, reliving the events of the evening over and over in her head. Every glance, every word exchanged, and every unspoken tension lingered in her mind like the faint, enduring scent of flowers pressed between the pages of a forgotten book. How had the evening unravelled into this tangled mess of feelings she could scarcely name?

She pressed her palms against her eyes, willing herself to banish the image of Mr Darcy's sharp, dark gaze, which seemed to find hers at every opportunity. Why did it matter? Why should she care what Mr Darcy thought—or whom he might care for? She, who had always prided herself on her discernment and good sense, found it maddening to be so consumed by thoughts of a man whose regard she had neither sought nor encouraged.

Elizabeth struck the pillow in frustration, rolling over in the wide bed. She had never possessed the romantic sensibilities of her two youngest sisters, who spent hours imagining the dashing gentlemen who would one day sweep them off their feet. However, had she ever truly paused to consider such matters, she might have admitted that the sort of gentleman she envisioned as a future husband bore a striking resemblance to Charles Bingley.

Mr Bingley was all that was amiable and kind. He was

cheerful, easy-going, and genuinely good-natured. His manners were engaging, his countenance pleasant, and he possessed a natural charm that made him agreeable to everyone he encountered. Elizabeth knew that should she be lucky enough to secure such a gentleman as her husband, she would have no reason to repine. As her father had aptly noted after one of Mr Bingley's visits, their tempers were by no means unalike, and she could have no doubt of them doing very well together.

By contrast, Mr Darcy was a puzzle that resisted solution. Despite his wealth and status, he seemed perpetually uncomfortable in company, as though he stood on a distant hill, content to watch the world unfold beneath him without ever fully engaging with it. His manners, while perfectly proper, were far from inviting. He was aloof, fastidious, and at times maddeningly inscrutable. While Mr Bingley was universally liked, Mr Darcy had an almost unerring talent for offending wherever he went.

Yet why was it that when Elizabeth allowed her mind to wander into the hazy unknown of her future, it was not Mr Bingley but *Mr Darcy* she saw at her side…?

The question stayed with her like an unwelcome guest, and Elizabeth sighed heavily, shifting on the mattress and pulling the quilt higher around her shoulders. Much as she hated to admit it, Miss Bingley's insinuations had struck a nerve. Could it be true, what the lady had suggested? That Mr Darcy's unwillingness to marry arose from some deep, unspoken attachment that he was not permitted to name?

Elizabeth had heard the gentleman's own words at Oakham Mount: "I am not free to marry." His reasons, he

had said, were "complicated". If it were something simple
—an entanglement, a prior engagement—surely he would
have shared it? And yet, he had remained enigmatic,
leaving her to wonder, to fill the gaps with her own restless
imagination.

She did not like idle gossip, she reminded herself
fiercely. She never had. She knew too well the sting of
baseless assumptions and unkind speculations. She would
not indulge in such meanness herself—not even when the
subject was Mr Darcy. Still, she could not deny that Miss
Bingley's words had unsettled her.

"Why?" she whispered aloud to the shadowed room.
"Why does it bother me so?"

The answer came almost immediately, unbidden and
unwelcome.

Because your vanity was wounded.

Elizabeth closed her eyes, a rush of heat rising to her
cheeks even in the privacy of her own thoughts. She had
spent weeks convincing herself that she felt nothing for Mr
Darcy—that his reserved demeanour, his brooding silences,
and even his occasional sharpness had left her untouched.
Yet, somehow, she could not bear the thought of him
harbouring tender feelings for anyone but her.

A groan of frustration escaped her lips as she turned her
face into her pillow, as though the fabric might absorb the
clamour of her emotions. Perhaps she was no better than
Miss Bingley in her jealousy and pride. But even if Miss
Bingley's insinuations were baseless, the truth remained:
regardless of his reasons, Mr Darcy did not wish to marry
her. He had made that point abundantly clear. Only a fool

would set their sights on something they could never have, and Elizabeth Bennet was no fool.

By the time slumber finally found her, she knew one thing for certain: Mr Darcy was her past, whereas Mr Bingley—steady, cheerful, and ever kind—might very well be her future. If only she could bring herself to let him into her heart.

Chapter Nine

The fortnight that followed was marked by fair weather and lively activity in Hertfordshire.

Bingley grew ever more frequent in his visits to Longbourn, often accompanied by Colonel Fitzwilliam, and on occasion, Walsh or Miss Bingley. However, despite repeated invitations, Darcy declined to join in any of these calls, choosing instead to remain at Netherfield to focus on estate matters with the new steward Bingley had recently hired.

The proposed riding expedition took place, with Bingley and Richard escorting the two eldest Bennet sisters to a park near Hertford, where they admired the picturesque scenery and paused to view the ruins of a medieval priory. The party returned in high spirits, with Bingley declaring it the most delightful excursion of the season.

As the days wore on, Bingley's fondness for Elizabeth became ever more apparent. His sentiments, voiced with unrestrained enthusiasm, left no one in doubt—but Darcy, for his part, was quietly thankful he need not bear constant witness to their every encounter. Finally, after twice delaying his departure, Colonel Fitzwilliam was at last compelled to return to his regiment. Bingley, eager to keep the remainder of the party at Netherfield, was quick to offer the colonel the use of a mount from his stables to carry him to his destination of Northampton—an offer that was gratefully accepted.

So it was that on a bright morning, three days before Fitzwilliam's intended removal, Darcy sat in Netherfield's sparsely stocked library, attempting to immerse himself in a study on agricultural innovation. The quiet hum of the house provided a reprieve from the increasingly chaotic atmosphere of Bingley's plans and the lingering tension of his own conflicted thoughts. But Darcy's concentration was broken when his host bounded into the room some moments later, with his characteristic enthusiasm on full display and his countenance alight.

"Ah, Darcy! Just the man I have been looking for," Bingley began without preamble. "I have just returned from Longbourn, and I thought you should be among the first to know—I have heeded your counsel regarding Miss Elizabeth, and I could not be happier! You have my deepest gratitude."

Darcy slowly lowered the thin volume, gazing back at his friend with mild perplexity. "Forgive me, Bingley," he began cautiously, "but to what do you refer? I cannot recall offering any particular counsel to do with Miss Elizabeth Bennet."

Indeed, Darcy could not remember speaking of Elizabeth for some time. If anything, he had made a determined effort to avoid participating in any conversations that centred around the object of Bingley's affections—chiefly because those discussions had grown increasingly difficult to endure.

"Oh, come now, Darcy," Bingley replied with an easy laugh. "Surely you cannot have forgotten how you chastised me for raising expectations with Miss Elizabeth before being sure of my own mind? Well, I have taken your words to heart and acted accordingly. And now"—his expression grew almost bashful—"I have just spoken to Mr Bennet, and all is settled. I hope you will congratulate me on my good fortune."

The words struck Darcy like a physical blow, though he fought to keep the sense of dread that immediately washed over him from showing in his expression. Lowering his gaze, he busied himself with adjusting his cuffs before saying carefully, "Ah, I see. So you have made Miss Elizabeth an offer of marriage, then?"

For a moment, Bingley was silent, and Darcy looked up, noticing that his friend's animation had faltered slightly.

"Well, no," Bingley replied, "not as such. I thought that might be a bit precipitous, given the recent nature of our acquaintance. But I did feel it important to state my intentions plainly, so I have made it clear to Miss Elizabeth—and her father as well—that I wish for this courtship to end in marriage, and they both seemed to share my desire."

A rush of conflicting emotions swept over Darcy, and it was all he could do to keep the tremor from his voice as he answered, "Well then, you have my best wishes." He hesitated briefly before adding, "I assume this means you have conquered your feelings for Miss Jane Bennet?"

At Darcy's question, a faint flush crept up Bingley's cheeks, though his tone remained even as he answered. "Miss Bennet is lovely, of course. And perhaps if circumstances had been different..." He fell silent, his gaze growing distant. Then, with a brisk shake of his head, he seemed to collect himself, saying, "In any case, it does not signify. I have thought on all you said, and you were right —my loyalty must be to Miss Elizabeth. Besides," he added with a sheepish grin, "we are well suited, I think. And Caroline seems to have grown rather fond of her. I hope she will be pleased with my choice."

Darcy grunted in reply, suppressing a grimace. He doubted Miss Bingley's professed fondness for Elizabeth extended beyond ensuring that the lady was not a threat to her own romantic ambitions.

Rising to his feet, Darcy extended his hand and Bingley clasped it eagerly. "I am happy for you, Bingley. Truly. I do not think you could have chosen a worthier woman."

His friend's face lit up at the words, his obvious delight causing Darcy to avert his gaze. Clearing his throat, Darcy added, "Also, I am glad we have found a moment to speak, as I wished to inform you that you need not trouble yourself over my cousin's departure. I have received a letter from my steward, and my immediate presence is required at Pemberley. So, I shall be able to carry Fitzwilliam as far as Northampton. We shall depart in two days' time."

Bingley's expression immediately fell. "Must you go so

soon? Of course, I understand you have many demands upon your time, but... Well, I have come to rely upon your guidance in the running of the estate. There is still so much I do not know."

"I am afraid it cannot be helped. Besides, the new steward is fully apprised, and I shall, of course, be happy to continue to advise you. All you need do is write." He drew a breath before concluding, "Now, if you will excuse me, I must make the necessary arrangements for our journey."

With that, Darcy strode from the room, his measured pace belying the tumult of his feelings. He did not dare look back, knowing full well the dejected expression he had left on Bingley's face. It was better this way, he told himself. Better to leave now before his resolve weakened further.

But as he climbed the stairs to his chambers, Darcy could not shake the image of Elizabeth Bennet from his mind, nor the nagging thought that he would be surrendering something infinitely precious when he went.

"Leaving?" Richard repeated, incredulity plain in his voice as Darcy stepped into the small sitting room that adjoined their chambers. "What has prompted this sudden change of plans? You have mentioned nothing of it until now. And before you attempt to lay the blame at my door, I shall remind you that Bingley was only too delighted to offer me transport to my destination, so I shall not be your scapegoat."

Darcy frowned, folding his arms across his chest. "I do not have to justify my decision. I simply see no point in lingering. Bingley's steward is more than capable of managing the estate, and I have pressing business at Pemberley."

"Ah, yes. Pemberley," Fitzwilliam drawled, his tone laden with disbelief. "So, this abrupt departure has nothing at all to do with Bingley finally reaching a decision regarding Miss Elizabeth Bennet?"

Darcy stiffened despite himself, an instinctive response that elicited a knowing grin from his cousin.

"I ran into Bingley at the stables as I returned from my morning ride," Fitzwilliam supplied. "He seemed positively euphoric."

"As well he should be," said Darcy, his voice clipped. "He appears to have secured the affections of one of the most estimable women in the kingdom. I am happy for them both."

And he was—for the most part. But that did not mean he could bear to stand by and watch his friend lay claim to the woman he loved. Leaving Hertfordshire was not only prudent—it was necessary. If it could have been managed, he would have departed that very afternoon.

Fitzwilliam studied him for a moment, his expression uncharacteristically sober. "Very well," he said at last, his tone quieter. "I can see your mind is made up. I only hope you are not making a decision you will one day come to regret."

The morning after Mr Bingley shared his wishes for the future, Elizabeth and Jane were sitting alone in Longbourn's front parlour when the sound of an approaching carriage drew their attention.

Glancing up from her book, Elizabeth peered out of the nearest window, immediately recognizing the landau as one of Mr Bingley's, and felt a smile instantly coming to her lips.

Noticing Elizabeth's diversion and the rhythmic clatter of wheels upon the drive, Jane rose and stepped into the entrance hall to summon Mrs Hill, requesting that a tea tray be brought up. She had scarcely returned to the parlour when the knocker sounded, and moments later, three of the gentlemen from Netherfield were announced.

The ladies stood to greet their visitors. Elizabeth welcomed Mr Bingley and Colonel Fitzwilliam with gracious affection, but her expression faltered for the briefest moment when her gaze fell on Mr Darcy standing at the back of the group. Their eyes met fleetingly before Elizabeth, quickly recovering herself, turned to usher everyone into the sunlit parlour.

"I am afraid you find us on our own this morning," she began lightly once everyone was seated. Mr Bingley and Colonel Fitzwilliam responded with cheerful politeness, lamenting the absence of the other ladies, while Mr Darcy remained silent, his manner subdued.

Mr Bingley soon steered the conversation towards plans for renovating Netherfield's library, and the topic was thoroughly canvassed as the tea tray arrived. Jane stepped up to pour, her movements graceful and assured. Mr Darcy, however, remained taciturn, idly fiddling with his teacup and casting disinterested glances about the room. After several moments, he abruptly cleared his throat.

"Colonel Fitzwilliam and I have come to take our leave of you," he announced, his tone clipped. "We shall depart Netherfield on the morrow."

Elizabeth blinked at the unexpectedness of his declaration, momentarily at a loss for words. Even Mr Bingley looked mildly surprised by his friend's brusque statement. At length, it was Jane who recovered first.

"So soon?" she asked, her tone tinged with genuine remorse. "But it feels as though you have only just arrived."

Colonel Fitzwilliam offered a low laugh. "I am afraid I must shoulder the blame for our abrupt departure. I am due back at my regiment within the week, and my cousin has kindly offered to convey me to my destination." He paused for a moment before adding, "Walsh, I am certain, will be here later to pay his respects. He was with the steward this morning, else he would have accompanied us."

The ladies murmured their understanding before Jane turned once again towards Mr Darcy and the colonel.

"Well, you will all be greatly missed, though we wish you a safe journey."

Mr Darcy nodded curtly, saying, "Walsh and I have already been away from Pemberley longer than anticipated. It is prudent for us to go now, before the weather worsens."

Elizabeth's eyes narrowed slightly at his tone, but she replied with calm composure, "Of your duty to Pemberley, sir, I would not presume to speak. But if the state of the roads is your chief concern, I should think you have ample time before conditions become severe."

Mr Darcy frowned. "While it is true that the climate remains temperate here, the same cannot necessarily be said of Derbyshire. Autumn rains can make the roads impassable, and by midwinter, the hills about Pemberley are often thick with snow."

"Well, I envy you that," Elizabeth replied easily. "I adore the snow. I hope to experience a great deal of it when Jane and I travel northwards for Christmastide."

"Ah," cried Mr Bingley, clearly eager to lighten the mood, "I had not realized you were planning to remove from Longbourn for the festive season, Miss Elizabeth. Will your entire family be travelling?"

"No," Elizabeth answered, her smile softening. "Only Jane and I. My aunt Gardiner has a brother in Yorkshire, and they have arranged a reunion of sorts. She and my uncle have graciously invited us to join their party."

"You are travelling to Yorkshire in the dead of winter?" Mr Darcy interjected, fixing Elizabeth with a disapproving gaze. "What can your relations be thinking? The roads will be abominable. You will be lucky to make the journey in less than a fortnight."

Despite her best efforts, Elizabeth bristled. For someone who had made it clear he had no intentions towards her, Mr Darcy certainly seemed determined to offer unsolicited opinions. But then again, he was precisely the sort of man who likely never hesitated to impose his will on those around him.

Attempting to moderate her tone, she replied coolly, "I am afraid, Mr Darcy, that we are not all at liberty to come and go as we might wish. My uncle Gardiner finds it increasingly difficult to leave his business, and my uncle

Harper is a physician rarely able to abandon his patients. In any event, we are to go no farther north than Derbyshire. My aunt and her brother have arranged to meet in a village called Lambton, where they passed much of their youth."

At the mention of their intended destination, Mr Darcy's eyes widened ever so slightly, and Colonel Fitzwilliam exclaimed, "Lambton! Why, that is not five miles from Pemberley! I had no idea your relations were from Derbyshire, Miss Elizabeth. Does your aunt still have family in the area?"

A warmth crept up Elizabeth's neck as she turned towards the colonel. "No, sir. I believe she and my uncle have some acquaintances there, though they have not seen them in some time. We are to stay at an inn in the village."

"An inn? At Christmas?" the colonel echoed in mock horror. "Surely not?"

He then shot a pointed look at Mr Darcy, which immediately caused Elizabeth distress. Oh, why had she mentioned the village by name? Now it would appear as though she had deliberately spoken of their plans in the hopes of securing an invitation to Pemberley! And while she could not deny her curiosity about the estate, she would sooner rip out her fingernails than have Mr Darcy think her so ill-mannered as to solicit his hospitality—especially after he had made it abundantly clear that he harboured no interest in furthering their acquaintance.

Lost in her musings, Elizabeth did not realize the conversation had continued without her until Jane's gentle touch brought her back to the present. Her sister's measured tones filled the room, saying, "That is very considerate of you, Mr Darcy, but we would not wish to intrude upon your family, especially at Christmas. I am certain we shall be quite content at the inn."

"Nonsense," Colonel Fitzwilliam interjected. "If the inn in question is the Queen Anne, I hear the place is fairly crawling with bedbugs. You will be lucky to escape unscathed. No, you will be far more comfortable at Pemberley."

Elizabeth darted a glance at Mr Darcy, but his expression, as always, remained unreadable. Turning back to the colonel, she replied, "It is an exceedingly generous offer, but I believe my sister and I must apply to our relations, as we are at their disposal."

Colonel Fitzwilliam opened his mouth, no doubt to press the matter further, but to Elizabeth's surprise, it was Mr Darcy who spoke with quiet civility. "I hope you will tell them that they would be most welcome. I assure you, it will be no inconvenience. The house is large, and we expect no other guests. We shall be a small family party for Christmas, consisting only of myself, Walsh, and my younger sister, Georgiana, who is not yet out."

At the mention of Mr Walsh, Elizabeth felt an unwelcome pang of recollection as Miss Bingley's insinuations about Darcy's private affairs flitted briefly through her mind. Quickly, she looked away, determined to banish such thoughts.

"We shall certainly pass on your kind request," Elizabeth replied, meeting Mr Darcy's steady gaze. "Might my uncle write to you, should he have any questions?"

"Of course. Bingley can provide my direction."

"Gladly!" Mr Bingley immediately interjected, clearly

pleased to assist. Elizabeth turned to him with a pleasant smile, eager to shift the conversation.

"And what of you, sir? Will you remain at Netherfield, or have you made other arrangements for yourself and your sister?"

The gentleman's lips curled in mild amusement. "Truth be told, I had not given the matter much thought, though Caroline will likely insist upon returning to town. She is not particularly fond of the country, and I imagine she will wish to spend Christmas with our eldest sister, who is recently married."

He paused, regarding her with a thoughtful expression. "I suppose I shall join her, though now that I think of it, I do have an aunt near Leeds whom I have been meaning to visit…"

His words faded into silence, and Mr Darcy stared back at him with a lifted brow. "An aunt near Leeds? I do not recall you ever mentioning any relations in that area."

Mr Bingley flushed under his friend's steady gaze. "Ah, well, she is my great-aunt, really, on my mother's side. We have never been particularly close, but she has written recently. She is getting on in years and is not in the best of health. Perhaps I ought to visit her for Christmastide."

"If she is so unwell, perhaps you should not wait," Mr Darcy replied drily.

Mr Bingley began to stammer an explanation, but Mr Darcy appeared to relent, tempering his tone. "Of course, if you do decide to make the journey, you are more than welcome to break your trip at Pemberley, along with the Miss Bennets and their relations."

Mr Bingley's face brightened, and he cast an enthusiastic glance in Elizabeth's direction. "Perhaps we might all travel together? I should very much enjoy becoming better acquainted with your aunt and uncle."

Elizabeth smiled gently. "I am certain they would enjoy that as well," she replied. While their stay at Pemberley was by no means assured, the prospect seemed far less daunting if Mr Bingley were to accompany them.

As if buoyed by her response, Mr Bingley sprang to his feet, his enthusiasm palpable. "Then it is settled! I shall write to my aunt without delay!"

"Jane! Lizzy! Was that Mr Bingley's carriage I just saw turning onto the lane?"

Mrs Bennet swept into the parlour, Mary trailing behind her, barely pausing to draw breath as she continued, "I told Mary it must be his, lacquered to a shine as it was and with such a fine team of horses." She paused for a moment before saying thoughtfully, "It was not the barouche we rode in when we dined at Netherfield, of course, but a gentleman of Mr Bingley's means must have several carriages at his disposal, I am sure!"

Elizabeth cast Jane a glance of silent exasperation, but her sister, ever composed, answered gently, "Yes, Mama. He came with Mr Darcy and Colonel Fitzwilliam, who wished to take their leave of us. They depart Netherfield tomorrow."

"Leave?" Mrs Bennet exclaimed, her voice rising an octave. "But they have only just arrived! Oh, why did I choose today to visit my sister Philips? If I had been here, I am certain I would have thought of some way to detain them!"

"That seems unlikely, Mama," Elizabeth interjected with measured calm. "Colonel Fitzwilliam must return to his regiment, so you could hardly——"

But Mrs Bennet's attention had already shifted to the tea service laid out on the low table. "Oh, Jane! I hope you had the sense to serve the good tea and did not stint on the sugar. Ah! And I see you offered them biscuits, at least. How fortunate they are fresh as today is Dobson's baking day."

"Yes, Mama," Jane replied with quiet patience.

Mrs Bennet's mind darted to the next pressing matter. "And what of Mr Bingley? He is not leaving the neighbourhood as well, I hope?"

"No, Mama," Jane assured her. "He intends to stay at Netherfield at least until mid-December."

"Well, thank heavens for that. Lizzy, that gives you ample time to secure an offer! Why the gentleman has not come to the point yet I shall never know… Oh, but I did have my heart set on Mr Darcy for Jane! And Colonel Fitzwilliam! How often does one have the son of an earl sitting in their parlour—and an unmarried gentleman at that!"

She paused briefly, as if to catch her breath, before continuing, "Of course, I do not suppose Mary is handsome enough to tempt him, but Kitty or Lydia might have done well. Lydia would so enjoy being escorted to balls by a man in uniform…"

Elizabeth seized the opportunity presented by her mother's brief silence, saying hurriedly, "Mama, where are my younger sisters?"

With a distracted wave of her handkerchief, Mrs Bennet replied, "They remained in Meryton to visit the shops with Maria Lucas. But Lizzy, you must listen to me." Her tone grew urgent. "You must use all your feminine wiles to elicit a proposal from Mr Bingley as soon as may be. Once you are married, you will be able to introduce Jane to all manner of wealthy gentlemen. Perhaps you might even secure an invitation to Pemberwood! I am quite certain Mr Darcy would fall hopelessly in love with Jane, if only he spent more time in her company."

"*Pemberley*, Mama," Elizabeth corrected with a sigh. "Mr Darcy's estate is called Pemberley, and it appears I need not marry Mr Bingley to secure an invitation. Mr Darcy has already extended his hospitality when we travel to Lambton with Aunt and Uncle Gardiner this winter."

Mrs Bennet let out a delighted shriek, causing Elizabeth's heart to sink. As was often the case, she had spoken in haste and realized too late that she had only made everything worse.

"Oh, Lizzy! Jane! Why did you not tell me this at once?" cried Mrs Bennet. "This could not be better if I had planned it myself! To think, my own daughters, guests of Mr Fitzwilliam Darcy—and during the festive season, no less! You must stay until Twelfth Night at least. Perhaps Mr Darcy will host a ball…"

"Mama, please!" Elizabeth replied, her voice laced with frustration. "I should not have mentioned it. Nothing is decided. I told Mr Darcy that we must apply to Uncle Gardiner for his approbation."

"Nonsense!" Mrs Bennet declared with a gleam in her eye. "Of course you will stay at Pemberley. I shall see to it."

With that, the matron swept out of the room, her mind clearly spinning with schemes. Elizabeth watched her mother's retreating form with resignation. It was clear there would be no avoiding it now. To Pemberley, they would most assuredly go.

Chapter Ten

꧁꙰꧂

Mid-December 1811, Derbyshire

D arcy stood before the tall windows of Pemberley's front parlour, his sharp gaze fixed on the carriage making its slow approach along the tree-lined avenue. As it rolled to a stop in the circular drive, he turned from the glass, moving through the grand entry hall and out of the front doors with determined strides.

The coach and four halted just as he reached the bottom of the steps. A liveried footman moved to open the door, but Darcy motioned him aside, stepping forwards to assist the occupants himself.

A gloved hand emerged, and he grasped it with a tenderness that belied his usual reserve. The young lady smiled up at him, and Darcy's heart swelled with a rare warmth.

"Georgiana," he murmured, leaning down to press a gentle kiss to his sister's cheek. "It is so good to see you again, my dearest. I trust the journey was not too taxing?"

"No, not at all," Georgiana replied softly. "The distance from Matlock is not great, and Cousin Richard ensured that I was well looked after."

As if summoned by the sound of his name, Colonel Fitzwilliam poked his head out of the open door, his broad grin a stark contrast to Georgiana's restrained demeanour.

"Darcy!" he called cheerfully before jumping down. The two men exchanged a firm handshake, Darcy expressing his gratitude for his sister's escort.

After offering his arm to Georgiana, Darcy led the way into the house, where the servants hurried to relieve them of their coats. Once inside, his sister professed fatigue and asked to be excused, and while Darcy promptly acquiesced, he could not help feeling a pang of disappointment. Apparently, her time at Matlock had done little to lift her spirits; if anything, she seemed more withdrawn than ever.

"You will find your rooms ready," he told her gently. "Dinner will be at the usual time, and there is no need to dress formally. It will only be the three of us."

Georgiana nodded before ascending the staircase, and Darcy's frown deepened as he watched her go.

"She will regain her spirits in time," Richard remarked as if reading his thoughts. "Now, let us retire to the library. I, for one, could use a drink."

Darcy swiftly agreed, following his cousin to the familiar sanctuary, where a low fire crackled in the hearth. Sinking into a leather chair, Darcy watched as Richard made his way to the sideboard.

"So," his cousin began, lifting one of the crystal decanters and pouring himself a generous portion of brandy, "only the three of us for dinner? Where, pray tell, is Walsh?"

"Bedford," Darcy replied with a faint sigh. "Or somewhere thereabouts. He left the day before yesterday."

Richard regarded him sceptically as he settled into the chair opposite. "Again? And with guests expected at Pemberley? I thought he was to remain here for Christmas."

"As did I," Darcy answered. "He announced his intention to travel a fortnight ago."

Richard studied his cousin's expression before saying slowly, "And you did not try to stop him? Surely you could have persuaded him to stay."

"What would you have me do?" Darcy remarked irritably. "He is not one of my servants. If he wishes to go, that is always his prerogative."

"True," Richard acknowledged, swirling his glass thoughtfully. "I just find it somewhat surprising, given the circumstances." After a slight hesitation, he continued, "Have you thought about how you will manage? Shall I write to Father and tell him I intend to stay?"

Darcy immediately shook his head. "You have already done me a great service in bringing Georgiana here. I cannot ask you to miss Christmas with your family."

Richard opened his mouth, clearly prepared to argue, but then seemed to change tack. "There is another solution, you know. If you were to take Georgiana into your confidence—"

"No," Darcy interrupted sharply. "And I am not having

this discussion. I have already told you—it is out of the question. I will not have her worrying over me, or worse yet witnessing—" He broke off, unable to finish the thought. The very idea twisted his stomach. Shaking his head to dispel the unwelcome image, he forced himself to smooth his tone. "In any case, I would prefer to speak of Georgiana's state of mind. How is she, really? I have not been able to glean much from her letters." Darcy exhaled heavily, raking a hand through his hair. "I suppose I had hoped she would have put this business behind her by now."

Richard shrugged, taking a measured sip of his brandy. "She seems well enough to me. Mama said she has been a bit dispirited, but I suppose that is to be expected after... everything. In any case, she was perfectly convivial on the journey here."

"Was she?" Darcy asked, surprise evident in his tone. "Did she speak at all about... Ramsgate?"

"A bit," Richard admitted. "In a roundabout sort of way. But if you must know, we spoke mainly of you."

"Me?" Darcy replied, taken aback.

"Yes, you, Cousin," Richard said, his exasperation plain. "You and your scheme to marry her off at the earliest opportunity."

"*My* scheme?" Darcy repeated, his voice rising. "You were in agreement when last I took note!"

"Yes, well, I am no longer convinced it is a good idea," Richard shot back. "Can you not see that this whole affair with Wickham would not have happened if you had been more forthcoming? She never expected that you would be *angry* with her. She believed herself to be doing as you would wish—securing a husband."

Darcy huffed, his temper flaring. "As if I would ever condone acquiring a husband in such a way! And Wickham, of all people! No one in the entire country would be a less suitable match."

"And how was Georgiana to know that? Since you have never thought it prudent to confide in her about *anything*, all she knows is that George Wickham was a favourite of her father's and a friend to you. Can you blame her for thinking that you would be pleased with the arrangement?"

Darcy's jaw tightened as he turned away, pacing to the hearth. "This entire misadventure is your fault," he muttered darkly. "You were the one who convinced me to remove her from school."

"Now hold on a moment! I suggested you take her from school so the two of you could spend more time together. I did *not* tell you to bundle her off to Ramsgate with only a companion of dubious repute for company!"

"Mrs Younge came with an impeccable character!" Darcy sputtered, his face heating. "How was I to know she was a reprobate—and in George Wickham's pocket to boot?"

Richard set down his glass with a weary sigh, rubbing his hands over his face. "Well, there is no sense arguing about it now. What's done is done. I just wish you would reconsider bringing Georgiana out next spring. It is too soon. What happened in Ramsgate should have convinced you of that."

A muscle ticked in Darcy's neck, tension simmering just

below the surface, but when he replied, it was in measured tones. "We have been through this a hundred times already, and you know my reasoning. The sooner she is settled, the better." After a pause, he added with a note of defiance, "Besides, Georgiana is sixteen now. Plenty of girls marry at such an age."

"Yes, girls whose circumstances force it upon them, or empty-headed romantics like the youngest Miss Bennets," Richard bit back. "I am telling you, Darcy, Georgiana is in no way ready to be a wife. You have kept her cloistered all these years—first in the care of nursemaids and governesses, then at school. She knows nothing of her own family, let alone the rest of the world! Marrying her off now, simply to suit your own interests, would be like sending a lamb to the slaughter."

Darcy stiffened. "You exaggerate. All Georgiana needs is an opportunity to gain a bit more confidence. I have already taken steps to engage another companion. There is a respectable lady—the widow of a clergyman—who has recently come to my attention. Someone like that could provide just the sort of steadying presence she requires."

Richard huffed out a sigh of frustration. "That is all well and good, but she needs more than a companion—she needs a brother! A brother who is open and honest with her. One who confides in her and shows her some affection!"

"Enough," Darcy snapped, his voice sharp. He felt perilously close to the end of his patience.

Across from him, Richard exhaled heavily, his shoulders slumping in defeat. "Very well," he said, his tone resigned. "I did not come here to argue. Since we clearly cannot agree, let us set the topic aside and speak of pleasanter things—like the impending arrival of your guests.

Georgiana was positively agog at the prospect of visitors at Pemberley. When she was not filling my ears with talk of you, she was pestering me with all manner of questions about the eldest Miss Bennets."

Darcy frowned. "I hope it will not be too much for her. When I extended the invitation, I had not considered the fact that she would be required to act as hostess..." He hesitated before continuing thoughtfully, "Although, perhaps it will prove educational. I think she will enjoy the company of the Miss Bennets, and Bingley is already known to her. At least she will be spared *Miss Bingley's* effusions."

Colonel Fitzwilliam smirked back at him. "I must confess, I am rather shocked that Miss Bingley will not be of the party. I cannot imagine what would possess the lady to forgo an invitation to Pemberley."

Darcy shrugged, though he had to admit he had been equally perplexed.

"According to Bingley, she chose to travel to Scarborough with the Hursts for Christmas. They left town a fortnight ago."

Richard quirked a brow. "Travelling to Scarborough in the dead of winter? I hope you saw fit to pen a strongly worded letter of protest."

Darcy shot his cousin a withering glance, but Richard merely took a generous swallow of his brandy, the twitch at the corner of his mouth betraying his amusement. "And what of your own guests?" he remarked casually, reclining further into his chair. "I do hope they arrive before I am forced to return to Briarwood. I am especially looking forward to seeing Miss Elizabeth Bennet here at Pemberley," he added, casting a sidelong look in Darcy's direction.

"I am certain you are, considering *you* were the one who invited her."

"True," Richard replied, "but as I recall, you did not waste any time in echoing the suggestion."

Darcy turned away, unable to meet his cousin's teasing gaze. Of course, Richard was correct. When faced with the prospect of having Elizabeth at Pemberley, he had indeed leapt at the opportunity. And in the weeks since his return to Derbyshire, he had imagined her here—her laughter filling the halls, her keen eyes observing every detail of the estate—more times than he could count. If he were honest with himself, it was the only thing that had brought him any joy in longer than he cared to admit. But it was all an illusion; Elizabeth's place would never be by his side. There was no future for them at Pemberley or anywhere else. And he would do well to remember that.

Shifting his attention back to his cousin, Darcy began slowly, "Richard, I know you have the best of intentions, and I appreciate your concern for my welfare—truly, I do. But I must ask you to cease playing Cupid. It serves no purpose. You well know my plans, and I have already spoken to Miss Elizabeth. She is aware that I cannot marry."

"*Will not* marry," Richard corrected, leaning forwards in his chair. "And does she know why?"

"Certainly not! Nor will she, if I have anything to say about it. And if I find that you have breathed one word to her—"

Richard held up his hands in mock surrender, his

expression one of feigned innocence. "She will hear nothing of that from me. While I do not agree with your... choice, I have long accepted that it is yours to make. Still, I could not see the harm in inviting her to Pemberley, not when she was to be in Lambton already. Surely, you would not wish to deprive yourself of her company when she is but five miles down the road."

Darcy groaned, running a hand over his face in frustration. "But can you not see? The longer we are in company, the more difficult this becomes! Now, not only am I to play host to Miss Elizabeth, her sister, and her aunt and uncle but to Bingley as well. So I shall have the dubious honour of watching their courtship play out before my very eyes." He turned away, his voice lowering to a mutter. "I would not be surprised to learn that he and Elizabeth are already betrothed."

"Doubtful," Richard said easily, setting his glass aside. "Would Bingley not have written of such a momentous development? Besides," he added more gently, "that was what you wanted, was it not?"

Darcy looked away, a surge of emotion tightening his throat and making it momentarily difficult to speak. No, it was most certainly *not* what he wanted—not by a long shot. But it was the wisest course, for everyone involved.

Straightening his shoulders, he met Richard's gaze with feigned composure. "Of course. Now, if you will excuse me, I shall see whether Georgiana is settled."

The remainder of the day passed uneventfully. During dinner, Georgiana scarcely spoke, though Colonel Fitzwilliam carried the conversation with his usual charm, regaling his cousins with lively tales from his latest posting in Northampton. When the meal concluded, their small party retired to the saloon, where Georgiana played the pianoforte for nearly an hour. Her music filled the room with a gentle warmth, but even as she performed, her quiet demeanour remained unchanged. At last, she pleaded exhaustion and excused herself. Darcy and Fitzwilliam likewise retired early, though Darcy spent a restless night, his dreams troubled.

The following morning, Darcy entered the breakfast parlour to find his cousin already seated, a newspaper spread before him and a steaming cup of coffee in hand. He looked up at Darcy's approach, rising briefly to extend the usual courtesies.

They had just settled when Georgiana entered, her movements subdued. Darcy turned to her with eager anticipation, determined to lift her spirits.

"Ah, Georgiana. Good morning. I trust you slept well?" he began with forced cheer, while Fitzwilliam rose to assist her into her seat.

"Yes. Thank you, Brother," she murmured, her gaze fixed on the table before her. The two gentlemen exchanged worried glances behind her back.

Determined not to let the mood dampen further, Darcy moved to the sideboard, filling a plate with the simple fare he knew she preferred, as well as a second one for himself. He returned to his seat across from her, searching his mind for a way to engage her.

Drawing a steadying breath, he began tentatively, "I enjoyed your playing last evening. It is such a balm to have music filling Pemberley again. I have missed that—and you —more than I can say these last few months."

Georgiana lifted her eyes briefly, nodding shyly. "It is good to be here," she replied. Then, after a slight hesitation, she added, "Thank you for having me."

Darcy exchanged another glance with Fitzwilliam, who gave a barely perceptible shrug. Turning back to his sister, he said gently, "You need not thank me, Georgiana. Pemberley is your home, and it always will be. I would welcome you here at any time."

She nodded again, her focus returning to her plate.

Darcy shifted uneasily in his chair, his hand tugging at the inside of his collar, which seemed to have grown suddenly tight. He tried again, his voice low but steady. "It is only that, as you are preparing to come out, it seemed sensible for you to remain with your aunt and your female cousins for the time being. Your aunt, especially, has written of her eagerness to have you in town with them this spring, and I have secured several masters to attend you in the new year. You will enjoy that, I hope?"

"Yes, Brother," she murmured, though her response was faint and unconvincing.

Darcy sighed, his gaze searching hers for any sign of the vivacity she had once possessed. Leaning forwards slightly, he gentled his tone even further. "Georgiana, I know I have written this before, but now that you are here, I must say it again. I bear you no ill will for what happened in Ramsgate. You must believe that none of it was your fault. If I had only been more direct about my feelings for

Mr Wickham, or if I had not been so utterly deceived by Mrs Younge's character—"

"Yes, Brother," Georgiana interrupted, her voice a whisper.

A muted noise from Fitzwilliam drew Darcy's notice. His cousin gave a slight shake of his head, his expression cautionary. Darcy nodded in acknowledgement, swallowing back the words he had been so desperate to express. Instead, he reached for his coffee, taking a large swallow— only to grimace at the realization that it had long since gone cold.

"Well, in any case," he continued, setting his cup down with forced cheer, "let us speak of other things. What should you like to do today? The weather is temperate. Perhaps a ride, if you are not still fatigued from your journey?"

At this, Georgiana's countenance brightened, and Darcy was rewarded with the first genuine smile he had seen from her since her return.

"Oh, yes! I would like that very much," she replied.

Exhaling in relief, Darcy grinned at her. "Splendid! I shall send a note to the stablemaster. I am certain he will be happy to escort you."

Across from him, Georgiana's expression faltered. Her gaze dropped to the edge of her teacup as she traced its rim with a finger. "Oh, I see. I suppose I hoped...that is, I thought perhaps *you* might accompany me?"

Darcy instantly stiffened. "No. I cannot," he said, wincing at the gruffness in his voice. He turned away, masking his discomfort as his mind raced for a plausible explanation. But it was Richard who stepped in smoothly.

"What your brother means is that he will be busy preparing for your guests, who, as I understand it, are expected any day. However," he added with a pointed glance at Darcy, "I would be only too happy to ride out with you, if you will allow it. I can think of nothing I should like better."

Georgiana offered her cousin a weak smile, her voice timid yet earnest. "Thank you. I would enjoy that."

"Good! Then it is settled," Fitzwilliam declared with enthusiasm. "And we may go as early as you like, ensuring that we return in time to rescue your poor brother from the dreaded task of performing for strangers."

This last remark was accompanied by an exaggerated waggling of his brows, which elicited a small giggle from Georgiana.

"But they are not strangers at all, are they?" she asked, turning her gaze on her brother. "You are acquainted with them, are you not?"

Pleased to see the topic of their guests had sparked some interest in his sister, Darcy relaxed in his seat.

"Most of them, to some degree," he began thoughtfully. "You have, of course, met Bingley, though this time he will be without his sisters, thank providence." Georgiana smiled at this, and Darcy continued readily, "The Miss Bennets, I have had the pleasure of meeting previously, and I believe you will enjoy their company. Miss Elizabeth is spirited yet amiable and warm. Her kindness is unaffected—a natural inclination rather than a performance for society's benefit. Miss Jane Bennet reminds me of you in some ways. She is gentle and sweet tempered, though somewhat quieter and more reserved than her younger sister."

Darcy paused briefly, considering his words before speaking further. "As for their aunt and uncle Mr and Mrs Gardiner, they live in London. I have encountered them once, at a ball, and Mr Gardiner and I have exchanged letters, but they are otherwise not known to me. Lastly, there is a gentleman called Harper—Mrs Gardiner's brother. He is a physician in the North, though he will not be arriving until a later date."

As Darcy spoke, he noted a light flush spreading across Georgiana's cheeks, her eyes shining with a liveliness he had not seen in far too long. He allowed himself a small smile at the sight. Glancing briefly at his cousin, Darcy observed that Fitzwilliam, too, appeared pleased, reclining comfortably in his chair with an expression of quiet satisfaction.

Despite his usual wariness of his cousin's meddling, Darcy found that, in this instance, he could not bring himself to object. If the prospect of their guests' arrival could inspire such a response in his otherwise reticent sister, he would certainly not repine.

Chapter Eleven

✿

As it transpired, Pemberley's houseguests did not arrive until the following day. The decision had been made for the entire party to travel together to Derbyshire. Mr and Mrs Gardiner were obligated to stop at Longbourn, both to collect their two nieces and to deposit their four young children, who would remain in the Bennets' care. Mr Bingley had chosen to send his coach and team of horses ahead so that he might travel with the rest of the party, and thus it was arranged that they would change conveyances each time they stopped. To everyone's satisfaction, the weather remained fair and the roads in good condition—despite Mr Darcy's dire warnings—and their journey progressed with much good cheer and agreeable conversation.

On the day they were to reach Pemberley, Elizabeth sat near the window on the forward-facing seat, watching for the first appearance of the manor house with some perturbation. The park, as it turned out, was very large and contained a great variety of ground. They entered it at one of its lowest points and drove for some time through a beautiful wood, stretching over a wide extent.

Mr Bingley pointed out various landmarks as they went, and even though Elizabeth's mind was too full for conversation, she saw and admired every remarkable spot and point of view.

At last, they found themselves at the top of a considerable eminence, where the wood ceased, and all eyes were instantly drawn to Pemberley House, situated on the opposite side of the valley. Elizabeth noted that it was a large, handsome stone building, backed by a ridge of high woody hills; and in front, a stream of some natural importance ran —reminding her of the little Yorkshire river where she had first encountered Mr Darcy.

Inside the carriage, the Bennets and Gardiners were all enthusiastic in their admiration, and Mr Bingley, who had stayed at the house several times, assured them that they would find the manor warm and welcoming despite its proportions.

They descended the hill, crossed the bridge, and drove to the door, all while Mrs Gardiner indulged in reminiscences about visiting the park as a child, and Mr Bingley continued to regale them with descriptions of some of the principal rooms. However, Elizabeth could scarcely attend to the lively discussion, as all the apprehension she had attempted to stifle immediately leapt to the forefront of her mind. She was quietly thankful that Jane, with her usual poise, had the presence of mind to keep Mr Bingley's attention engaged, as she had done so effortlessly throughout their journey.

In due course, the carriage drew to a halt, and before their groom could so much as step down to open the door, several liveried footmen appeared, followed by a senior member of the household whom Elizabeth assumed to be the butler—and there, close at that gentleman's heels, came Mr Darcy himself!

Elizabeth cast an anxious glance at her sister as their uncle descended the carriage steps, met by a deep bow from their host.

"Mr Gardiner, I presume?" Mr Darcy offered in his deep baritone, and their uncle dipped his chin in reply.

"Mr Darcy—a pleasure, sir! I know we have exchanged letters, but I must thank you once again for your hospitality. Not every gentleman would open his home to near strangers in this way, and at such a time of year, no less! You have my gratitude."

"It is my honour, sir. Bingley is a friend of long duration, and I know the Bennets have made him feel very welcome in Hertfordshire. It was the least I could do, on his behalf."

By this point, Mr Bingley had also left the coach, and the two friends clasped hands before Mr Gardiner turned back to assist the ladies.

Mr Darcy received each one of them in turn, offering quiet civilities as a stream of servants came forwards to discreetly unload the luggage.

Amidst their party's cheerful chatter, their host led the way into a vast entrance hall where the butler and two footmen were on hand to divest the visitors of their great-coats and pelisses. Once this was accomplished, they were ushered into a nearby drawing room, where Elizabeth was pleasantly surprised to find Colonel Fitzwilliam sitting beside a young girl who could only be Mr Darcy's sister. Introductions commenced, and soon they were all seated around the comfortable parlour, which Elizabeth noted was neither gaudy nor uselessly fine.

Miss Darcy was tall, and on a larger scale than Elizabeth, but her appearance was womanly and graceful. She was less handsome than her brother, but there was sense and good humour in her face, and her manners were perfectly unassuming and gentle. Although she spoke little, Elizabeth could easily discern that it was due to embarrassment and an innate reserve rather than any sort of vanity or pride.

Colonel Fitzwilliam was as cordial and agreeable as Elizabeth had ever known him to be. He enquired after the rest of her family and looked and spoke with the same good-humoured ease as he had always done.

For his part, Mr Darcy was more civil and free from self-consequence than Elizabeth had previously observed in Hertfordshire, and she began to catch glimpses of the gentleman she remembered from their first meeting.

When tea arrived, Miss Darcy stepped up to pour, and though clearly eager to please, she approached the task with obvious trepidation. To Elizabeth's surprise, Mr Darcy was instantly at her side, speaking to her in gentle tones and passing around the teacups as his sister performed her duties.

After half an hour of pleasant conversation, Mr Darcy rang the bell, and the housekeeper, Mrs Reynolds, arrived to show them to their chambers. Mr Bingley, who had visited the house recently and knew the location of his rooms, chose to stay behind to converse with his hosts, but the Bennet ladies along with their aunt and uncle proceeded out the way they had come.

As they moved through the hall and then ascended the great staircase, Elizabeth saw with delight that while the rooms they glimpsed all appeared to be well proportioned and handsomely furnished, like the drawing room, they spoke less of splendour and more of real elegance, rendering the ambience hospitable and inviting.

Elizabeth, while usually of a cheerful and communicative disposition, found herself too overcome to speak. However, Mr Gardiner, whose manners were easy and pleasant, had no trouble engaging the housekeeper in conversation as they walked.

"Is your master much at Pemberley in the course of the year?" he enquired, and Mrs Reynolds smiled back at him with genuine civility.

"Oh yes, sir. He is quite attached to the place and rarely leaves. Miss Darcy is always down for a fortnight during the summer months, though her primary residence is in London. She is to make her curtsey in the spring, so, of late, she has been spending much of her time with her aunt, who will present her at court."

"She seems very young," Elizabeth ventured, at last finding her voice.

Mrs Reynolds nodded her agreement. "She is just sixteen, ma'am, though many might take her for older with her tall stature and pleasing figure. And she is so accomplished! She plays and sings all day long. She will do the master proud and make a fine match, I am sure of it."

Mrs Gardiner smiled. "I imagine it will be difficult for her brother to see her go. He seems deeply devoted to her."

"Oh, indeed, ma'am," Mrs Reynolds readily affirmed. "Whatever can give Miss Darcy any pleasure is sure to be done in a moment. He is as fine a brother as one could wish."

Elizabeth briefly caught her sister's eye, silently acknowledging the housekeeper's words. Whatever else could be said of Mr Darcy, his devotion to his sister appeared to be beyond reproach.

Mrs Reynolds, either out of pride or genuine attachment, seemed to take immense pleasure in speaking of her master and his sister. She continued with enthusiasm, "Though I do not know that it will be Miss Darcy who goes away. My master has always maintained that he hopes she will make Pemberley her home, even after she weds."

"Has Mr Darcy plans to travel, then?" Mr Gardiner asked as they reached the spacious lobby at the top of the stairs.

Mrs Reynolds' smile faltered briefly, though her tone remained composed. "He has often said as much, sir. At least, that is what I have been made to understand. Once the young miss marries, it is his intention to leave Pemberley. Where he is to go, I cannot say—but a dark day it will be for us all when that time comes."

She paused then, as if realizing she had said too much. Her expression turned cautious, and when she resumed speaking, her manner was deferential once more.

"Ah, here we are," she announced, gesturing towards an open door. "This way, ladies, if you please."

❧

Elizabeth and Jane were shown into a very pretty sitting room with doors leading to private bed chambers on either side, while their aunt and uncle were taken to a similar apartment farther along the corridor.

Thanks to the efficiency of Mr Darcy's footmen, their trunks had already been delivered, and moments after entering, a young housemaid appeared to assist with the unpacking. Mrs Reynolds informed them that dinner would be served at five o'clock, allowing the sisters ample time to rest, bathe, and dress for the evening.

At the appointed hour, they met the Gardiners at the top of the grand staircase. A footman waited there to escort them to the drawing room, where the rest of the party had already assembled.

It was not until they proceeded into the dining parlour and took their places around the long, polished mahogany table that Elizabeth noticed that someone she had expected to see was conspicuously absent. Turning to their host, she enquired, "Is Mr Walsh not joining us this evening, sir? I recall you mentioning he would be with you at Pemberley for the festive season."

"Ah, no. That is, yes, I had expected it to be so, but he informed me some days ago that he would travel to his relations in Bedfordshire this year," Mr Darcy replied gravely.

"Oh, I see. Well, we shall miss his society, though I am happy he can be with his family at such a time."

Mr Darcy's response was little more than a thoughtful frown, but Colonel Fitzwilliam interjected cheerfully,

"Hopefully the pleasure of *my* company makes up for the lack of his."

Elizabeth laughed lightly. "It was indeed a pleasant surprise to find you here, sir. Do you stay at Pemberley for long?"

"Alas, no," the colonel replied with a good-humoured smile, nodding to a footman, who stepped forwards to fill his glass. "I am to return to Matlock for Christmas, but I could not resist the temptation of enjoying such delightful company once more before I go."

Their conversation was interrupted by the arrival of the first course, which boasted nearly a dozen fine dishes: two soups, platters of pike and trout, and an impressive array of meats, all roasted to perfection.

Bowls were passed, roasts were expertly carved, and wine flowed freely as the conversation meandered comfortably among the diners. Mr Darcy—who seemed far more relaxed in his own home—spoke easily with Mrs Gardiner of her time in Lambton, while Mr Gardiner chatted amiably with Mr Bingley and Colonel Fitzwilliam.

Miss Darcy, at first, said little, content to focus on her dinner while listening with wide-eyed interest to the conversations unfolding around her. However, it was not long before Elizabeth and Jane began to draw her out, gently enquiring after her favourite books and music. Although Elizabeth seldom allowed her gaze to drift towards Mr Darcy, seated farther down the table, whenever she did, she noted his watchful expression. Though whether his gaze was on her or he was merely observing how his sister got on, she could not say.

It was during the first remove that talk shifted to their stay at Pemberley, with Mr Darcy enquiring politely about Mrs Gardiner's brother and when they might expect his arrival.

"I believe on Monday next, sir," Elizabeth's aunt replied. "He has not far to travel, and as his practice does not permit him to be absent long, he will only trespass on your hospitality for a few days."

Mr Darcy nodded in reply. "He is most welcome here. And you are all at liberty to remain at Pemberley for as long as you wish."

From across the table, Elizabeth caught Colonel Fitzwilliam attempting to stifle an amused smile, but before she could interpret his response, Mr Darcy turned his attention to Mr Bingley.

"And what of you, Bingley? Of course, your presence is no imposition, but Leeds is a good fifty miles away—a full day's travel, even with favourable conditions."

Setting down his glass of wine, Mr Bingley chuckled. "Do not trouble yourself on my account, old man. My horses are sure-footed, and my aunt does not expect me until Christmas Eve. Besides," he added with a boyish grin, "I have been most eager to accompany Elizabeth and her relations on their tour of the area."

At his casual use of her Christian name, Elizabeth felt the unmistakable prickling of a flush creeping up her neck, and she could not help furtively looking around the table to see what anyone else had made of it. Her aunt and uncle exchanged a glance—though whether it was merely curious or disapproving, she could not discern—and Colonel Fitzwilliam appeared slightly taken aback.

It was Mr Darcy's black expression, however, that caused her gaze to drop instantly to her plate.

When at length the last bites of stewed fruits and spiced cakes had been consumed, Mr Darcy offered his sister a subtle nod, and she stood with some diffidence, leading the ladies into a small salon. Miss Darcy rang the bell, and before long refreshments were brought through. Mrs Gardiner began by asking the young girl about some of the people and places she remembered from the neighbourhood, and conversation flowed easily until the gentlemen joined them about a quarter of an hour later.

"So, how have you all fared since we were last in Hertfordshire?" Colonel Fitzwilliam enquired once they were all seated and coffee and tea had been poured.

Mr Bingley was quick to respond, eagerly recounting the latest developments at Netherfield and inundating Mr Darcy with a torrent of questions. Once this topic had been canvassed to Mr Bingley's satisfaction, Colonel Fitzwilliam turned his attention to Elizabeth and Jane.

"And what news from Longbourn? I trust you and your sisters have been in good health and spirits?"

Elizabeth laughed lightly. "Oh, we have been excessively diverted, to be sure," she replied, exchanging a knowing glance with her sister. "I do not believe we mentioned it, but while you were all at Netherfield, my father received a letter from a cousin, who was unknown to us—a clergyman, lately of Hunsford, in Kent, where he has the living of the local parish. By his proposal, the gentleman came to stay with us for nearly a fortnight in mid-November."

"Hunsford?" the colonel exclaimed. "Why, that is our

aunt's parish! How extraordinary that your relation should be her rector! What is the gentleman's name?"

"Mr William Collins," Jane supplied, and Colonel Fitzwilliam instantly turned to his cousin. "Darcy, have you made this Collins's acquaintance?"

Setting his cup down on the nearby table, Mr Darcy frowned in consideration. "I think I have, as it happens. When I last visited my aunt, she was entertaining some of the local gentry when I arrived. I believe her clergyman was among the company."

At this unexpected revelation, Elizabeth blinked in amazement. Although her cousin had spoken of his esteemed patroness many times during his visit, the fact that Lady Catherine de Bourgh was aunt to both Mr Darcy and Colonel Fitzwilliam was astonishing indeed.

"You were not pleased by your cousin's visit?" the colonel enquired, interrupting her thoughts.

"Oh, I would not say that exactly," Elizabeth answered with a small smile. "We were certainly entertained. My father, I know, enjoyed the gentleman's company a great deal, as he delights in the ridiculous."

Colonel Fitzwilliam barked a laugh. "That bad, was it?"

Elizabeth returned his grin. "Let us just say that my cousin is not a sensible man, sir. His every word and action seem dictated by his desire to curry favour, with little regard for propriety or merit. He is, I regret, a man whose conversation and conduct scarcely command respect, however much he strives to secure it."

"And you say you had never met the gentleman before? How came he to visit you now?"

"According to the gentleman himself," Elizabeth

answered, "the purpose of his visit was to extend an olive branch, of sorts, which I believe was to come in the form of an offer of marriage."

At the colonel's inquisitive glance, Jane quietly explained, "My father's estate is entailed, sir, and Mr Collins is to be the beneficiary."

"Ah," the gentleman replied with a nod of acknowledgement. "So he seeks to soften the blow by making one of you the future mistress of Longbourn."

"That would, indeed, appear to be his aim," Elizabeth agreed. "It seems that it was your aunt who encouraged the idea."

"That, I can readily imagine," the colonel said with a glimmer of amusement. "And tell me, was he successful in his quest?"

Elizabeth lifted her teacup, using it to shield her face as her skin prickled with the heat of embarrassment. What could she have been thinking to have raised such a topic of conversation? Surely it was evident that *she* could not be Mr Collins's object as she was all but spoken for by Mr Bingley, who sat not three feet away. This left Jane, as the eldest daughter, the natural choice to become her cousin's wife—though Elizabeth could scarcely imagine a more unfortunate fate for her beloved sister.

Stealing a glance at Jane, she felt a pang of guilt to see her staring resolutely at her lap, her fingers twisting nervously at the muslin of her gown. Elizabeth also noted that Mr Bingley had gone uncharacteristically still, his complexion pale, his lips pressed together in a tight line.

Cursing her carelessness, Elizabeth inhaled sharply, steadying her breath before responding with forced levity.

"Not as yet, sir, though I believe he intends to return in the new year."

To her chagrin, her aunt joined the conversation. "I still think you are too severe upon your cousin, Lizzy. It is to his credit that he wishes to make amends to your family in such a way."

"Indeed," agreed her uncle. "I know he has risen in my sister's estimation since his visit." After a moment's thought, he added, "Perhaps Mary might be persuaded to look favourably upon the gentleman. She has ever been a practical, steady sort of girl, fond of moral reflections. They might do very well together."

To this, Elizabeth merely murmured her assent, and to her relief, the conversation soon turned to other topics.

Chapter Twelve

⁂

D arcy closed the door to his chambers with a heavy sigh, leaning back against the solid oak panelling. What had begun as a day of eager anticipation had soon dissolved into a study in disappointed hopes and dashed expectations. Shrugging out of his coat, he tossed it onto the back of a nearby chair, loosening his cravat with an impatient tug.

The morning express from Bingley had brought with it a mixture of expectation and unease. Elizabeth Bennet, under his roof, walking the halls of Pemberley, her presence suffusing the house with a warmth he had long thought absent. The idea filled him with delight and dread, and as the hours ticked by, he had felt his composure fraying under the strain of his own expectations. When the party had finally arrived, he had steeled himself, determined to show Elizabeth—and her relations—the master of Pemberley at his most composed.

His first impression of Mr and Mrs Gardiner had been

reassuring. Despite being in trade, Mr Gardiner was gentle-manlike in both appearance and manners, while his wife was an amiable, elegant woman who was clearly a great favourite of her nieces. Darcy had found himself quite at ease in their company—an ease that faltered the moment Elizabeth stepped from the carriage.

Even now, the memory of her quick smile and luminous expression sent a jolt through him. She had looked radiant, her cheeks flushed from the cold, and for one wild moment, it had seemed as though time had stopped. Yet just as swiftly, reality had reasserted itself in the form of Bingley, who had swiftly moved to Elizabeth's side, his hand coming to rest with casual intimacy on the small of her back. The sight had sent an irrational surge of jealousy coursing through him, and he had barely managed to offer a polite welcome before retreating behind the familiar mask of civility.

Dinner had offered him some respite. His cook, Mrs Simms, apparently delighted to have a chance to prepare more than the simple fare he and Walsh favoured, had outdone herself, serving two full courses. The food was excellent, and conversation flowed easily amongst the group. He had been particularly gratified to see Elizabeth and Jane Bennet drawing Georgiana out of her shell, their gentle attentions coaxing his shy sister into genuine smiles and laughter. It was a sight he had not witnessed in many months, and for a time, it had soothed the ache in his chest.

Yet, as the evening wore on, the sight of Bingley and Elizabeth exchanging smiles and private glances rekindled a storm of discontent within him. The familiarity with which Bingley addressed her—using her Christian name in company, no less!—was like a dagger to his heart. For the remainder of the meal, Darcy's thoughts had been consumed by his own desperate yearning to be in Bingley's place. He wanted to be the one who basked in Elizabeth's attention, who teased her and received her playful retorts, as he had done in Yorkshire.

How he envied Bingley—the effortless ease with which he navigated the world, his ability to claim Elizabeth's regard without hesitation or fear. Darcy clenched his jaw, the ache of longing sharp and inescapable. Her smiles, her laughter, her warmth—all now seemed reserved for another man. The truth was undeniable, even as it mocked him.

Crossing into the adjoining sitting room, Darcy strode to the sideboard and poured a measure of brandy into a waiting glass. It had been months since he had indulged in drink, but tonight he craved the numbing reprieve it might offer. Settling into one of the winged chairs by the hearth, he exhaled deeply, his thoughts turning to the conversation in the drawing room.

The revelation of Mr Collins's connection to Mr Bennet had certainly taken him by surprise. That the Bennets' cousin and Longbourn's heir should be his aunt's rector was an almost absurd coincidence. Although Darcy had refrained from speaking ill of the clergyman in the presence of Elizabeth's family, his brief acquaintance with the man had left a decidedly poor impression. From what he had witnessed, Collins was obsequious, bumbling, and entirely devoid of sense. The prospect of Elizabeth—or any of her sisters—enduring his attentions was deeply unsettling. Whatever his faults, Bingley was a far worthier match. At the very least, Elizabeth would not be yoked to that buffoon.

Darcy took a long swallow of the amber liquid, its heat spreading through his body, though it did little to quell the turmoil within. He leaned back in his chair, closing his eyes. Well, it could not matter to him. The only young lady whose future he was obliged to secure was Georgiana's—and that duty, he vowed, he would see fulfilled.

Rising abruptly, Darcy set aside his drink and went to ring for his valet. He prayed that sleep, elusive as it often was, might grant him a reprieve from the chaos of his thoughts. Yet, as he crossed the room to pull the bell, his mind betrayed him once more, returning to the image of Elizabeth. The thought of her so near—and yet so unattainable—made his pulse quicken, and a bitter ache settled in his chest.

With a sharp shake of his head, Darcy forced the image from his mind, willing himself to master his unruly emotions. He could not afford to falter, not now. Tomorrow would bring another day, another test of his endurance. But for tonight, he resolved to banish her from his thoughts and find what solace he could in the oblivion of sleep.

Darcy stood at the front of a church, the warm glow of candlelight casting golden hues upon the vaulted ceiling. All eyes were fixed on the radiant figure of Elizabeth Bennet as she glided down the aisle, resplendent in a shimmering gown of yellow silk. Her steps were unhurried and graceful, her eyes sparkling with quiet happi-

ness. In her hands she carried a small posy of wildflowers, and Darcy could see lavender and devil's-bit mixed in amongst the winter blooms.

As she came closer, Darcy stretched out his hands, his heart soaring with an unfamiliar, unchecked joy.

But Elizabeth did not meet his gaze. Instead, she looked past him, her expression soft but distant, her attention drawn elsewhere.

Confused, Darcy turned to see what had captured her notice, only to feel his blood turn to ice. There, standing just behind him, was the one man he despised above all others.

"Wickham," Darcy hissed, his voice low but venomous. "You have no business here. Leave at once."

But Wickham only smirked, his expression one of practised insolence. "Ah, Darcy," he drawled, his voice dripping with mockery. "I am afraid you are mistaken. It is you who are the trespasser here. This is my wedding, after all."

To Darcy's horror, Wickham stretched out his arm, and Darcy saw his sweet sister emerge from the shadows, gazing up at his nemesis with unbridled adoration.

Darcy's stomach clenched in fury. "Unhand her, you scoundrel!" he bellowed, surging forwards. "You shall never marry her. I forbid it!"

Wickham's smirk only deepened as he placed a proprietary arm around Georgiana's slender shoulders. "Too late, old friend," he said, his voice laced with triumph. "The deed is done. And once you have scurried off to foreign shores, Pemberley will be mine—just as your father always intended."

JENNIFER ALTMAN

Darcy lunged for Wickham, his hands reaching for the villain's collar. But as his fingers closed on empty air, the scene around him shifted and dissolved. Suddenly, it was Bingley standing before him, Elizabeth by his side.

"Elizabeth, thank goodness!" Darcy cried. Relief and hope warred within him as he reached for her hands, but it was his friend she walked to, her cheeks flushed with a delicate warmth as Bingley's laughter echoed around him.

"No," Darcy whispered. Panicked, he turned to the rector, only to find the hulking form of the Reverend William Collins standing before him.

"You must stop the ceremony," Darcy called out. "Elizabeth Bennet is mine! She is to be my wife, not his!"

But Collins paid him no heed, his droning recitation of the liturgy continuing as though Darcy had not spoken. Spinning back round, Darcy called out to his friend.

"Bingley, what is the meaning of this? You know Elizabeth belongs to me!"

Bingley offered him a ready smile, and Darcy could see that all his teeth were made of gold.

"Sorry, old chap, you had your chance. She is mine now."

Before Darcy could respond, Bingley leaned in, his hands roaming possessively over Elizabeth's body, his lips moving along the alabaster column of her neck, inching towards the bodice of her gown...

Elizabeth's head tipped back, her eyes fluttering closed as she released a soft sigh of pleasure.

And Darcy screamed.

202

The sound of his own cry jolted Darcy awake, his body drenched in sweat, his chest heaving as he clawed at the bedclothes. The oppressive weight of the vision clung to him, the images still vivid and raw.

Running a trembling hand over his face, he forced himself to take deep, measured breaths. "A dream. It was only a dream," he murmured hoarsely, but the words rang hollow in the silent room. His heart continued to pound as if it had no intention of quieting.

Rising from the bed, Darcy moved to the window, drawing back the heavy curtains to reveal the dawn breaking over the Derbyshire hills. The horizon was tinged with hues of warm orange—a gentle promise of fair weather to come. The serenity of the view contrasted cruelly with the tempest inside him, and yet he found it grounding. He let the cold glass cool his palm as he leaned against the frame, staring out at the beginning of a new day.

Moving to the bell pull, he rang for his valet, his mind already on the day ahead. Elizabeth was an early riser, of that he was certain. Perhaps if he hurried with his toilette, he might join her in the breakfast room before anyone else awoke. The prospect brought him a small glimmer of hope.

After the morning meal, he would show his guests through the house, and if the weather held, perhaps they might walk the grounds. He glanced again at the view beyond the window, his frown deepening. If only Elizabeth could have visited in the spring or summer when Pemberley was at its most resplendent. He could so clearly imagine her wandering through the gardens, her keen eyes alighting on the riot of blooms and foliage, her expression filled with delight. The thought was both sweet and painful, knowing it could never be.

Shaking his head, he banished the image. What mattered now was the present—the opportunity to show her Pemberley as it was, even in the starkness of winter. There was one place in particular that he was most eager for her to see. He had imagined her standing within its walls countless times, her presence bringing it to life in a way he had never thought possible. But he would wait. He would bide his time until he could show it to her alone, relishing the moment free from the company of others.

For now, there was much to do. Straightening his shoulders, Darcy exhaled slowly, steeling himself for the day ahead. Whatever it brought, he resolved to meet it with composure and purpose.

They did not have much time, but he vowed to make the most of it.

As Darcy had hoped, Elizabeth was indeed in the breakfast parlour when he arrived, but she was not alone. Both his cousin and Bingley were seated beside her at the long table, chatting amiably as they partook of the spread.

Entering the room, Darcy struggled to keep the disappointment from showing on his face. Since when had Bingley kept such early hours? At Netherfield, the man had scarcely left his chambers before ten o'clock! Schooling his features into a mask of civility, he exchanged morning pleasantries with the group before crossing to the sideboard, where he poured himself a cup of strong coffee before taking his seat at the table.

"You are up early," he began, directing his words to Elizabeth, though his gaze flicked briefly to Bingley before continuing, "I trust you slept well?"

"Oh, yes," Elizabeth replied with a ready smile. "I do not remember when I have had a more restful night. I have always been an early riser, and while I am not sure I can say the same for Mr Bingley, during our travels we formed the habit of walking before breakfast, so perhaps that has inspired a newfound discipline in him."

Beside her, Bingley chuckled good-naturedly and interjected, "You see, Miss Elizabeth's presence has already been a steadying influence on me. We had a delightful ramble through the gardens earlier, and I pointed out some of the more picturesque spots."

Darcy's grip on his coffee cup tightened. Avoiding his friend's gaze, he kept his attention fixed on Elizabeth. "Have you plans for the day?" he asked stiffly. "I had hoped to take you and your relations through the house— unless, of course, Bingley has already undertaken that particular duty."

Elizabeth's cheeks turned a delicate shade of pink, and she glanced briefly at her plate before answering. "I should like that very much. Although I know my aunt is eager to call upon some old acquaintances in the area, I am certain she would enjoy the privilege of being shown through the house. She has often spoken of it as one of the finest homes in the country."

Darcy's chest swelled slightly at her words, and he inclined his head in acknowledgement. "It would be my pleasure," he replied with measured calm. "I have some business to attend to, but perhaps we might convene in the morning room afterwards. Would eleven o'clock suit?"

Elizabeth nodded with a warm smile. "Perfectly."

❧

Darcy arrived precisely at the appointed time to find the entire Hertfordshire party, along with his sister and cousin, already gathered in the morning room. He had entertained a faint hope that Bingley might excuse himself, given his familiarity with the house, but it seemed no one had any other engagements to occupy their time.

Clearing his throat, he offered polite greetings before gesturing for the group to follow him into the expansive entrance hall. Although his guests were already acquainted with several of the principal rooms, he began on the ground floor, moving from one space to another. As they strolled through each room, Darcy shared anecdotes and historical details about notable pieces, while his cousin and Georgiana occasionally contributed their own remarks.

The Gardiners and Miss Jane Bennet expressed all the admiration and politeness one might expect, but Darcy found himself distracted, his focus lingering on Elizabeth. He noticed how she spent more time gazing out of windows, studying the views of the grounds, than dwelling on the grandeur within. Her quiet attentiveness, so different from the exclamations of others, struck him deeply.

At last, they arrived at the library, a space that occupied much of the east wing. Drawing back the heavy oak doors,

Darcy stepped aside to allow his guests to enter first. Their collective intake of breath was as familiar to him as the room itself. The library, with its soaring shelves, intricately carved bookcases, and a domed fresco ceiling, was undoubtedly one of the house's most impressive features.

Darcy's gaze fixed on Elizabeth as she wandered farther into the room, her fingers lightly brushing the leather-bound spines. Her fine eyes, alight with wonder, seemed to drink in the endless rows of books. She was so entranced that she did not immediately notice her sister approaching.

"Oh, Lizzy! It is glorious, is it not?" Miss Bennet whispered, her voice reverent as she turned in a slow circle to admire the ceiling's painted artistry.

Elizabeth nodded, a radiant smile curving her lips, before looking in Darcy's direction. "I remember Miss Bingley speaking of your library on the evening we dined at Netherfield," she murmured, "but I never imagined anything like this."

Darcy inclined his head, his voice carefully measured. "Although I cannot claim any of the credit, I am gratified by your approval. I hope you will all make use of it during your stay. You are welcome to borrow anything you wish."

This suggestion led the guests to eagerly explore the shelves, and the next half-hour passed in a convivial manner, with everyone delighting in the discovery of old favourites and debating the merits of one author over another. Darcy watched with quiet satisfaction as his library, typically a sanctuary of solitude, came alive with the hum of animated conversation and the rustle of pages.

At one point, his attention was drawn to Georgiana,

who had ventured to a shelf in the far corner. Reaching up, she carefully extracted three handsome volumes and pressed them into Elizabeth's hands. Although Darcy could not hear their conversation from where he stood, the sight warmed him. Elizabeth's expression lit as she examined the books, calling her sister over to share in her discovery. Georgiana, for her part, seemed emboldened by Elizabeth's genuine delight, and her usual shyness gave way to an uncharacteristic ease.

When at last the exploration had run its course, Darcy suggested they step outside to enjoy the grounds. Both Mrs Gardiner and Elizabeth had expressed a desire to see the park, and the fair weather made the prospect all the more inviting. His suggestion was met with unanimous enthusiasm, and the group began moving towards the entrance hall.

They had just reached the threshold when Georgiana suddenly spoke up, her voice light but earnest. "Brother, you have neglected to show them the conservatory! Should we not take them there first?"

Attempting to maintain a neutral expression, Darcy turned to his sister with a forced smile.

"Yes of course. Forgive my oversight. Let us collect our coats and we shall visit it on our way out."

Georgiana beamed at his acquiescence, and Darcy nodded to the assembled party. With that, they set about preparing for the excursion, unaware of the subtle shift in their host's countenance as his thoughts turned inwards once more.

Mr Gardiner expressed an interest in seeing the entirety of the park, though he admitted it might be too ambitious for a walk, to which Darcy nodded his acknowledgement.

"The park is ten miles around, so such an undertaking would indeed be a formidable task. However, I would be delighted to show you the areas closest to the house. The north side of the property boasts some very picturesque views, though the gardens, I must admit, are its finest feature—particularly in the summer months." He paused, casting a pointed glance in Bingley's direction. "Unfortunately, there will not be much to see there at this time of year."

The group set off along the path, and Miss Jane Bennet soon fell into step beside him.

"Do you grow a great variety of flowers, Mr Darcy?" she enquired pleasantly.

Although he was at first surprised to be addressed by the lady, who had heretofore been mostly quiet in his company, Darcy replied with an easy nod.

"We do. Roses, of course—we have an entire garden dedicated to them. Beyond that, we cultivate hyacinths, daffodils, and lilies, as well as perennials like peonies, delphiniums, and foxgloves. My mother was very fond of flowers, and I have preserved the gardens much as they were during her time as mistress."

Miss Bennet murmured her approval, her voice warm and genuine. They walked on in comfortable silence for a time before Darcy, sensing that further conversation might be expected, turned back to his companion.

"Are you fond of flowers, Miss Bennet?" he asked, his

question eliciting a genuine smile. Looking into her clear blue eyes, bright with interest, Darcy suddenly found himself struck by the symmetry of her features; she was, he realized, a truly beautiful young woman. Were she of the peerage—or even from a distinguished family residing in town—she would undoubtedly have been well married after her first Season.

Catching himself staring, he quickly averted his gaze, a flicker of embarrassment colouring his thoughts. He forced himself to listen attentively as she spoke, though he realized belatedly that he had missed the beginning of her reply.

"...a variety at Longbourn," she was saying, "but we also have a stillroom, and I enjoy preparing herbal essences for myself and my sisters."

Darcy nodded politely, though he felt his earlier lapse keenly. Fortunately, they had just reached the river, and Mr Gardiner, who appeared to have a great fondness for fishing, eagerly asked after the best spots for the sport.

This was a topic Darcy was happy to discuss at length, and he even extended an invitation for the gentleman to return in the summer months and fish to his heart's content, should his travels bring him back to the neighbourhood.

The party continued along the edge of the water for some time before crossing a simple bridge and proceeding into a wooded grove. Their progress was unhurried, as Mrs Gardiner was not an adept walker, and her husband was engrossed in enquiring about every feature of the estate, from the lay of the land to the varieties of fish in the stream.

But as ever, it was Elizabeth who drew Darcy's attention. No leaf, plant, or bush seemed to escape her notice, her eyes alight with wonder at the natural beauty surrounding them. Darcy found himself suppressing a smile, captivated by the way she appeared to savour each sight as though experiencing it for the first time.

When they reached the crest of a small rise where gaps in the trees revealed sweeping views of the valley, the opposite hills, and the meandering stream below, the party paused to admire the prospect.

"Oh, it is lovely," Elizabeth breathed, stepping closer to Darcy's side. "How very fortunate you are to be surrounded by so much beauty. I can better understand now why you would never wish to leave here. I dare say if I were lucky enough to call a place like Pemberley home, I should feel the same."

Her words sent a jolt through Darcy's body, and he could only stare back at her. But after a moment, Elizabeth's cheeks flushed, as though she had just realized the unintended intimacy of her remark, and she quickly looked away.

The others soon joined them, offering their admiration for the view, but Darcy barely registered their words as his thoughts wandered.

When was the last time he had considered himself fortunate? How long had it been since he had looked at Pemberley with the same awe and reverence it had inspired in his youth, instead of seeing it as a weighty responsibility, a millstone around his neck? Certainly not for years. Oh, of course, he knew that many in his social circle envied his position—but it was merely his wealth and connections they coveted. None of that mattered to Elizabeth; she was entirely unaffected by material possessions. It was the natural world that enchanted her. Happiness for her was found in the gentle rustle of leaves on a summer's day, the cheerful babble of a stream carving its path through the countryside, or the bracing pleasure of a walk under an open sky. These were the things that had drawn him to her in the first place, all those years ago.

For the briefest moment, he allowed himself to picture the life he might have known: a marriage based on mutual affection, Elizabeth Bennet always by his side, filling every corner of Pemberley with her laughter and light.

But then Bingley called out, playfully chastising him for woolgathering, and the spell was broken.

Darcy moved to join the others, whereupon Elizabeth expressed a desire to ascend to higher ground, having learned from Georgiana that the village of Lambton could be seen from one of the nearby hills. Mrs Gardiner, however, who was already fatigued by the morning's exercise, stated she could go no farther, and Mr Gardiner and Colonel Fitzwilliam quickly volunteered to escort her back to the house.

The remaining party resumed their climb, eventually reaching a rocky plateau that offered a panoramic view of the valley below, with Lambton nestled at its heart and the village of Kympton visible in the near distance.

As he had anticipated, Elizabeth's enthusiasm for the scenery was unbridled. She described the view in glowing terms before linking arms with her sister and wandering towards the crest of the hill. There, the two engaged in quiet conversation until Bingley joined them, his presence drawing a light laugh from Elizabeth that carried on the breeze.

Darcy lingered where he was, striving to bring his unruly emotions under control, and a moment later, Georgiana appeared at his side, her cheeks pink from their exertion and the brisk breeze.

"Are you cold, sweetling?" he asked, surprised to hear himself use the endearment he had not spoken since she was a young girl.

Georgiana tilted her face up to him, her expression radiant. For the first time, Darcy truly saw her not as the child she had been but as the poised young woman she was in the process of becoming.

"Not at all," she replied with a happy smile. "I had forgotten how beautiful everything looks from up here. It almost makes one forget that there is anything disagreeable in the world."

Darcy nodded. "Indeed, it does." For a moment, they stood in silence, the crisp air carrying the faint scent of damp earth. Then, offering her his arm, he said, "Shall we rejoin the others?" His sister smiled and took it, and together they turned, leaving the view behind.

Elizabeth entered Pemberley's entrance hall in high spirits. Although she had thoroughly enjoyed her tour of the house —especially the library, where she could easily imagine spending many happy hours—it was their walk through the park that had truly invigorated her.

When they had stepped into the conservatory, her breath had caught at the sight of the exotic plants flourishing in the warm, sunlit space. The orangery, briefly pointed out by Miss Darcy, had seemed equally alluring, and she would have loved to explore it further. But once they had begun to walk through the grounds, she could see why Mr Darcy had hurried them along.

The park was vast, with natural beauty to be seen at every turn. Woodlands and groves gave way to lakes and rivers, gardens and follies, all seamlessly blending into the surrounding countryside. Although Elizabeth had visited grand estates before, nothing compared to Pemberley. She had never felt more at peace than when wandering its expansive lands, with Mr Darcy at her side and the quiet hum of nature around them.

Once their pelisses and greatcoats had been collected, Mr Darcy excused himself to attend to matters of business, and Elizabeth and Jane sought out their aunt and uncle.

Mr and Mrs Gardiner were easily found in the cosy sitting room near their chambers. Settled into armchairs before a crackling fire, they eagerly welcomed their nieces, and soon, the conversation turned to their impressions of the estate and its master.

With a mixture of admiration and delight, they each pronounced Pemberley unrivalled in beauty and elegance, and Mr Darcy infinitely exceeding expectations.

"He is perfectly well-behaved, polite, and unassuming," said Mr Gardiner. "I have been continually impressed by his attention to us. Why, to personally take us through the house and grounds when there was no need—it speaks to his character."

"There is something a little stately about him, to be sure," Mrs Gardiner added, "but it is in his bearing, and not unbecoming. And Pemberley itself is beyond my imaginings. I have often heard that its woods are among the finest in the country, but I never expected such a harmonious blend of grandeur and natural beauty." Her gaze shifted to Jane, and with a wry smile, she said, "I dare say it would be something to be mistress of all this."

Both Jane and Elizabeth flushed at the comment. Elizabeth looked away, while Jane lowered her eyes, murmuring with some discomposure, "The lady who one day calls Pemberley home will be fortunate indeed, but I hope you do not have ambitions for a match between Mr Darcy and me."

Mr and Mrs Gardiner exchanged curious glances before Mrs Gardiner said gently, "Do you not enjoy Mr Darcy's company, dearest? I noticed the two of you walking together in the gardens—you seemed to be conversing quite comfortably."

"Oh, I find Mr Darcy perfectly agreeable," Jane replied earnestly. "But I have never sensed any particular regard on his part. If anything, I would say he seems most at ease when speaking to Lizzy, do you not think?"

Mrs Gardiner's eyes widened slightly before she turned to Elizabeth with a lifted brow. "Well, yes," she said slowly, "but Lizzy is attached to Mr Bingley. Surely Mr Darcy would never be so ill-mannered as to seek the attention of a young lady already committed to his friend?"

"Indeed, he would not," Elizabeth hurriedly replied, eager to steer the conversation elsewhere. "And I happen to know, Aunt, that Mr Darcy is not currently seeking a wife.

So let us all enjoy our time here without trying to make more of his civility than it merits."

Her words were met with smiles, but Elizabeth could not help feeling the conversation had trodden uncomfortably close to matters she would rather not examine.

Chapter Thirteen

✿❀✿

The following day unfolded pleasantly for Pemberley's guests. Mrs Gardiner, eager to revisit Lambton, where she still had lingering ties, led the way with enthusiasm. Her friends and relations were more than content to explore the quaint town through her fond recollections; Elizabeth, in particular, was glad for the distraction, welcoming the opportunity to set aside her thoughts of Mr Darcy for a time.

They returned to Pemberley in high spirits, pleasantly fatigued from a day spent exploring all the nearby town had to offer, arriving just in time to dress for dinner. Upon reaching the drawing room a short while later, they were greeted warmly by Miss Darcy and Colonel Fitzwilliam. Mr Darcy, however, was notably absent.

When, in due course, they moved into the dining parlour, Mr Darcy finally joined them, his expression grim. After making his excuses and taking his place at the table, he then began, "Well, Miss Elizabeth, it appears that your wish for snow may soon be granted. I have just come from speaking with Atkins, my steward, as well as my game-keeper, and both are of the opinion that severe weather is on its way. The wind has shifted to the northeast, and the air has the rawness that often precedes a storm. The barom-eter in my study has been falling since this morning, and there are reports from Lambton of heavy clouds gathering to the north. Atkins informs me that the last time conditions were as they are now, the roads were impassable for days."

Across the table, Elizabeth widened her gaze. Although the idea of seeing Pemberley's grounds blanketed in snow was undeniably thrilling, she well knew the consequences such formidable weather would bring, and she could not help but notice the flicker of unease in her relations' expressions as they considered the news.

Mr Gardiner exchanged a glance with his wife before saying gravely, "If Mr Darcy's information is accurate, I fear we must resign ourselves to the likelihood that Harper will not be able to join us. I hope he is forewarned of the situation and does not attempt the journey in such perilous conditions."

Colonel Fitzwilliam frowned, leaning forwards slightly in his chair. "If the weather is indeed coming from the north, I dare say he will know of it before we do and find himself unable to travel."

Mr Darcy nodded. "He would be wise to stay put. Atkins has already instructed the tenants to see to their live-stock and lay in extra fuel. If the storm does come, I expect we shall see the signs within the next day or two."

Turning to Mrs Gardiner, he added, "If you wish to send word to your brother, madam, I can have a rider dispatched immediately. It cannot hurt to advise him that he would do well to remain at home, so he is not taken unawares."

Mrs Gardiner's lips pressed together in quiet concern, though her husband laid a reassuring hand over hers. "My dear," he said gently, "I know this is a disappointment, but Mr Darcy's suggestion is both practical and prudent. We would not want Harper to risk his safety, and even if he attempted the journey, he might not arrive before the roads are completely blocked."

Slowly, Mrs Gardiner nodded, releasing a sigh of resignation. "You are right, of course. I shall write to him at once. I only pray the message reaches him in time."

She rose from the table, excusing herself to pen the letter, as Mr Darcy beckoned a footman and quietly instructed him to inform the kitchens to delay the meal. Once the arrangements were made, he turned to his cousin, who let out a resigned sigh.

"Best not to take any chances," Colonel Fitzwilliam said. "I shall send word to have my carriage readied first thing in the morning."

Mr Darcy nodded, then turned to his friend with a look of quiet resignation. "Bingley, as you are bound for Leeds, you may wish to postpone your departure. If the storm travels faster than anticipated, the roads will become treacherous."

Far from appearing inconvenienced, Mr Bingley brightened. "Do you truly think so? Because I should not at all object to a delay. In fact, I must confess, I have been enjoying my time at Pemberley with Miss Elizabeth and her relations to such an extent, I was beginning to feel rather badly about having to leave."

Mr Darcy's mouth tightened, though he said nothing. Elizabeth, striving for composure, replied gently, "You are very kind, Mr Bingley. We should be pleased to have your company a while longer—but I do worry your aunt will be disappointed. I know how eagerly she must be anticipating your visit."

Mr Bingley let out a low chuckle. "Yes, of course. But I am certain she will understand, given the circumstances. I shall send an express to inform her of the change in my plans. With luck, it will reach her before the weather does."

Elizabeth nodded, just as Jane spoke up from her place across the table. "I suppose we shall have to cancel our trip to Youlgreave as well," she said softly, regret clear in her tone.

At Mr Darcy's curious look, Mr Gardiner added, "An acquaintance of mine runs a stud farm near there and graciously invited us to tour the place. We were to go the day after tomorrow."

Mr Darcy's gaze sharpened with recognition. "A stud farm near Youlgreave? Would that happen to be Mr Wainwright's establishment?"

"The very one," Mr Bingley interjected before Mr Gardiner could reply. "Miss Bennet was telling me about it over dinner the other evening. Gardiner acquired her mare there during one of his prior visits to Derbyshire."

"Indeed," Mr Gardiner confirmed with a pleased smile. "A fine animal she is too. I have known Wainwright for many years, and when he learned we would be in the area, he insisted we come to see the farm. I was unaware you were familiar with his business, Mr Darcy."

Colonel Fitzwilliam chuckled. "As one of the largest landowners in the county, Darcy rarely misses anything of significance happening in these parts."

Mr Darcy inclined his head slightly, his tone measured. "Wainwright has earned a fine reputation for himself. While not yet as established as some of the breeders in Yorkshire or Newmarket, his stock is excellent. Many locals prefer to avoid travelling so far afield for quality horses, and Wainwright's imports have already yielded impressive bloodlines. Several of the horses in my own stables come from his farm, as do some in Lord Matlock's."

Elizabeth noted her uncle's visible approval, though his expression grew thoughtful as he turned to his eldest niece. "It is a pity, but I fear we must postpone the visit if the weather proves as harsh as Mr Darcy anticipates. There is no help for it."

Just then, Mrs Gardiner returned to the dining room, and the conversation paused as Darcy called for his butler. He swiftly issued instructions to ensure an express rider was called to deliver her letter, then signalled for the dinner service to resume.

As the first course was laid before them, Mr Gardiner recounted their earlier discussion to his wife, who turned to Jane with a warm, sympathetic smile.

"I am sorry for you, dearest, as I know how much you were looking forward to the excursion, just as I was eagerly anticipating spending Christmas with my brother. But we are all at the mercy of the elements in situations such as these."

Jane nodded her agreement, though Elizabeth's spirits resisted such quiet acceptance. "But why must we abandon our plans altogether? Could we not go tomorrow morning, provided the day remains fair? The drive can be no more than an hour, so there should be ample time to return before the weather worsens."

Mr Gardiner looked sceptical, but it was Mr Bingley who spoke with enthusiasm.

"I think that a splendid idea! If you are able to alter your arrangements, I would gladly accompany you. To confess the truth, I was quite put out at the thought of missing such an expedition."

Mr Darcy continued to look grim as Elizabeth's uncle grew more thoughtful. "I suppose that could suit us well enough, provided the weather holds. I can send a note to Mr Wainwright before we set out. I am certain he would not object to our coming a day earlier than planned." Turning to his wife, he added, "That is, if you do not mind our going?"

Mrs Gardiner, who had not intended to join the excursion in any case, readily gave her blessing. Not particularly fond of horses, she was quite content to spend the day in Lambton with her friends.

"Then it is settled!" Mr Gardiner declared jovially. He turned to their host with a broad smile. "Mr Darcy, sir, we would be delighted if you could join us—should your plans allow it. And Colonel Fitzwilliam, of course, you would be most welcome as well."

The colonel gave an easy laugh, shaking his head. "Ah,

would that I could, but I am expected at Matlock. However, as I am travelling in the same direction, I can accompany you as far as Rowsley, if that suits?" Turning to his cousin, he then asked, "Darcy, what say you?"

Mr Darcy, his expression more reserved, shook his head. "I must decline, I am afraid. The impending storm requires that I see to my tenants and ensure proper preparations are in place." His gaze shifted to his sister as he added, "Georgiana, would you care to go? I know you are fond of horses, and Mr Wainwright's farm is in a particularly picturesque part of the county. That is, of course, if Mr Gardiner has no objection."

Mr Gardiner happily assented, and Elizabeth watched as Miss Darcy's eyes grew round, her face flushed with lively expectation.

"Oh, Brother, may I? I should enjoy that above all else!"

Mr Darcy responded with an indulgent smile, while Jane, seated across from Miss Darcy, immediately engaged the younger girl in animated conversation. Mr Bingley soon joined in, and the lively discourse carried on for the remainder of the meal, lending a pleasant note to an otherwise uncertain evening.

Once dinner had concluded, the entire party removed to the drawing room, and after tea was served, Miss Darcy was once again persuaded to move to the pianoforte. As the delicate strains of a Clementi composition filled the air, the assembled guests broke into smaller groups, some to listen to the music and others to engage in quiet conversation. Seated on a settee beside her sister and across from her aunt and Mr Bingley, Elizabeth set down her teacup, giving voice to an idea that had come to her during their earlier discussions.

"Jane, would you be terribly upset if I did not accompany you tomorrow?" she began. Seeing her sister's stricken expression, she hastened to add, "It is only that you know I do not share your fascination with horses, and now that you will have Miss Darcy for companionship, I thought I might join our aunt on her calls."

Mrs Gardiner regarded each of her nieces in turn before saying to Elizabeth, "You know I should be very glad for your company, Lizzy, if Jane and Mr Bingley do not object to your absence."

Jane's gaze darted briefly to Mr Bingley, a faint flush suffusing her countenance before she quickly lowered her lashes, her voice soft as she replied, "Of course. It is kind of you to think of our aunt, Lizzy. I shall not mind."

Elizabeth smiled warmly at her sister before turning her attention to Mr Bingley, who was presently fiddling with his cuffs, his eyes trained steadfastly upon the carpet.

"And you, sir? Surely you will not even notice my absence when surrounded by so many equine enthusiasts," she teased lightly.

Mr Bingley straightened, a flicker of uncertainty colouring his expression. "Well, I... That is, while I had greatly anticipated the visit, I should be most willing to forgo the excursion and accompany you and your aunt instead, if that is your wish. Truly, it would be my pleasure."

Although his words were polite and deferential, the quiet disappointment in his tone was impossible to miss. "That is a most generous offer, sir," Elizabeth replied, "but

I shall not hear of it. I know very well where your true interest lies, and it is certainly not sitting in a parlour in Lambton, listening to my aunt and her friends share reminiscences about their youth. Besides," she added with a pointed glance, "I am certain Mr Darcy will be counting on you to escort his sister, and Miss Darcy would be gravely disappointed if her brother were to rescind his consent."

Mr Bingley hesitated before offering Elizabeth a sheepish smile. "Well, if you are quite certain…"

"I am," Elizabeth assured him firmly. "And I shall brook no argument. Indeed, I shall eagerly await your return, ready to hear all about your grand adventure."

The after-dinner entertainment ended sooner than usual that evening, as everyone anticipated an early start on the morrow. Mr Bingley withdrew to pen a message to his aunt, informing her of his delayed arrival. Mr Gardiner composed a note to Mr Wainwright regarding their revised plans, while Colonel Fitzwilliam excused himself to pack for his imminent departure. Meanwhile, Mr Darcy went in search of his steward to begin preparations for the approaching storm.

The remainder of the party retired to their chambers with a mixture of anticipation and quiet resolve for the day ahead.

Having reached their apartment, Elizabeth and Jane curled up in their shared sitting room, the warm glow of the fire casting a soft light over their cosy retreat. A comfortable silence stretched between them as they both stared into the shifting flames, each lost in her own thoughts. It was Jane who broke the stillness, a faint furrow appearing at her temple as she turned to Elizabeth.

"Perhaps I ought not to go tomorrow," she said quietly, and Elizabeth's head instantly snapped round to face her sister, her eyes wide.

"Not go? But you have been looking forward to this excursion above everything! You could hardly speak of anything else on our journey here."

Jane flushed, lowering her gaze to her lap. "Yes, that is true. But that was before I knew Mr Bingley would be accompanying us—and *you* would not. How will it look if Mr Bingley and I are seen in company together without you? After all, he is your beau, not mine."

Elizabeth blinked at her sister in surprise before laughing lightly. "Jane, you are beginning to sound like Mama! A gentleman and a lady may enjoy each other's company without it sparking scandal or rumours of matrimony. Besides, you will hardly be alone. Do not forget that Miss Darcy will also be present, as will our uncle, so it will all be perfectly respectable. Besides, as you may recall, *I* was the one who encouraged Mr Bingley to go. There certainly can be no call for anyone else to object when I do not."

Across from her, Jane nodded slowly. "I suppose." Her cheeks coloured prettily, and she bit her lip as if reluctant to agree. "No, you are right," she admitted after a slight pause. "I do dearly wish to see the farm. I suppose I am only being silly."

Elizabeth leaned back against the settee with a tender smile. "Not silly, Jane. Just thoughtful, as always. But you must allow yourself to take some pleasure in this visit. I shall enjoy myself just as much in Lambton with Aunt Gardiner."

Jane gave her a tentative nod in return, the worry beginning to ease from her face. "Thank you, Lizzy. I do not know what I would do without your encouragement."

Elizabeth chuckled, releasing her sister's hand. "And I do not know what I would do without your good sense to temper my wild notions. Now, let us not waste another moment fretting. If the storm holds off, tomorrow promises to be a lovely day, and I fully expect you to tell me every detail of it when you return."

Jane nodded, her smile growing warmer as the fire crackled between them. For a little while longer, the sisters sat together, their conversation turning to lighter topics, until at last the flames burned low and the promise of rest called them both to their beds.

The party of four—with the addition of Colonel Fitzwilliam, who intended to ride with them for a portion of the way—departed for Mr Wainwright's farm immediately following breakfast. Mr Darcy excused himself soon afterwards, while Elizabeth accompanied her aunt upstairs to prepare for their morning calls. But it was not long before she found herself standing outside the Gardiners' apartment, knocking lightly upon the door.

"Come in," came the cheerful reply, and Elizabeth entered to find her aunt at the dressing table, fastening her gloves.

"Would you mind dreadfully if I did not accompany you this morning?" she began, before continuing with a slight frown, "I am afraid the change in the weather has brought on the beginnings of a headache."

Mrs Gardiner turned immediately, her expression shifting to one of concern. "A headache? Oh, my dear, I am sorry to hear that. Shall I call for some powders? Perhaps it would be best if I stayed with you."

Elizabeth shook her head, attempting a reassuring smile. "No, you must not alter your plans on my account. It is nothing serious, I assure you. A little rest and quiet is all I require."

Mrs Gardiner hesitated, her brows knitting with uncertainty. "Are you sure? I would hate to leave you alone if you are unwell."

Elizabeth's smile faltered slightly. In truth, the timing of her headache was far from ideal; it would render her the only remaining guest at Pemberley, in Mr Darcy's sole company—a thought hardly conducive to easing her discomfort. But as quickly as the notion formed, she dismissed it. No, she was being silly. She did not think it likely that she would leave her chambers, and Mr Darcy would undoubtedly be occupied with readying the estate for the better part of the day. He would have no cause to notice her presence in the house.

"Quite sure," Elizabeth replied softly. "It is just a mild discomfort. Truly, I would feel far worse knowing you missed the chance to visit your friends because of me. Please, go and enjoy yourself."

Her aunt studied her face, searching for any signs of greater distress, before relenting with a sigh. "Very well, but you must promise to send for me if the headache worsens or if you need anything at all."

"You have my word," Elizabeth said, her tone firm yet warm.

Satisfied, Mrs Gardiner gave her niece's hand a brief, comforting squeeze before turning back to gather her things. Elizabeth lingered only a moment longer, offering her aunt a parting smile before retreating to her chambers.

Once inside, she closed the door softly behind her, letting out a slow breath. The quiet enveloped her, and she moved to the armchair by the window, sinking into its comforting embrace. She gazed out over the frost-covered gardens, allowing the stillness to settle over her. Solitude, she reminded herself, was precisely what she needed—both for the throbbing in her temples and for the flurry of thoughts that had begun to weigh heavily on her heart.

❧

Darcy pushed open the conservatory doors, brushing the last traces of dirt from his coat and removing his hat and gloves. Warm air, rich with the scent of damp earth and blooming jasmine, enveloped him, a stark contrast to the biting wind outside.

He paused, taking a moment to appreciate the tranquillity of the space—the lush greenery, the colourful blossoms impervious to winter's rapid approach. Turning towards the entrance to the house, Darcy moved with deliberate strides, his mind already on the tasks awaiting him inside his study.

But then he saw her.

Elizabeth Bennet sat on a bench on the far side of the

229

room, a book open in her lap. The sunlight streaming through the glass bathed her in a golden glow, illuminating the gentle curve of her profile as she turned a page. Her presence here, so unexpected, caused him to startle, and his breath caught.

At the sound of his approach, Elizabeth looked up, her eyes widening in surprise. Darcy stopped abruptly, his pulse quickening as their eyes met.

"Mr Darcy!" Her voice, though steady, carried a note of apprehension. She quickly closed her book, rising to her feet.

"Miss Bennet." He inclined his head, striving to master the sudden unease that had stirred within him. "I— I did not expect to find you here. I thought you had gone into Lambton with your aunt."

Elizabeth coloured faintly before offering an apologetic smile. "I had intended to, but I found myself unwell this morning—a slight headache. I thought it best to remain behind and rest." She hesitated then, shifting her gaze before saying, "I am much improved now, however, and felt the need for a change of scenery. I did not mean to intrude."

"You could not," he said quickly, then added more evenly, "You are welcome to enjoy any part of the house for as long as you like."

"Thank you," she said quietly.

For a moment, neither spoke, the silence stretching between them. Darcy was acutely aware of every sound— the soft ticking of his pocket watch, the faint drip of water in the distance, and the steady rhythm of his heart.

He shifted his weight, struggling to gather his thoughts.

"I am glad to hear that you are feeling better. I wonder, if you are not otherwise engaged, whether I might take you to another part of the house, one that we did not have time to explore the other day…"

Elizabeth's eyes sparkled with curiosity, and Darcy continued at a rapid pace, "If you would permit me, Miss Bennet, I should very much like to show you the orangery. It is but a short walk through that passage over there, and I believe you may find it…agreeable."

Elizabeth tilted her head, her eyes bright. "Indeed, I should be most delighted to see it. I have often admired such places but have not had the pleasure of visiting one in some time." Setting her book down on the stone bench she had recently vacated, she regarded him again with an impish smile. "Pray, Mr Darcy, lead the way."

Darcy did as Elizabeth directed, extending his arm and gesturing for her to follow. As they proceeded down the long, softly lit corridor, his heart beat an erratic rhythm inside his chest. Each step along the polished wooden floors brought him closer to the moment he had imagined countless times—Elizabeth in the midst of the verdant greenery, her countenance alight with wonder.

As he opened the door and stepped aside to allow her entrance, Darcy's pulse quickened. The orangery unfolded before them, its lofty glass ceiling arching high overhead, bathing the room in golden light. Rows of fruit trees— orange, lemon, and fig—stood in stately symmetry, their glossy leaves catching the muted daylight and casting dappled shadows across the tiled floor. Pots of fragrant herbs lined the perimeter, their scents mingling with the sweet tang of citrus that filled the air.

Elizabeth drew in a sharp breath, turning to look up at him with wide eyes. "Mr Darcy, this is...exquisite. Indeed, I have never seen anything of its like before. It is simply remarkable!"

Darcy felt a smile pulling at the corners of his lips, though he struggled to find words that could match her expression. "I am gratified you think so. It is a place where I have always found solace—a haven if you will. And I thought perhaps you might enjoy it, given your affinity for nature."

She stepped farther inside, her fingers trailing lightly through the aromatic fronds of lavender and rosemary. "It is not merely the plants, though they are indeed lovely. It is the tranquillity of the place, the harmony of it. One could hardly feel anything but peace here."

Darcy followed her gaze as it wandered to the benches nestled amidst the greenery. Some were half hidden by tall ferns and trailing ivy, offering private retreats for quiet contemplation.

"It was designed with that very intention," he replied. "To allow one to sit and think, or simply to be. I have often found myself lingering here longer than I intended."

Elizabeth turned to him then, her eyes reflecting the dim light that filtered through the glass. "I can well imagine why. It is a space that invites thoughtfulness. And it is clear that great care has gone into its preservation."

He inclined his head, basking in the warmth of her praise as though it were the sunlight itself. "It has been a labour of love, I confess. And one that seems well rewarded in this moment."

Her colour deepened, but Darcy, emboldened by her

evident delight, offered her his arm. "May I show you the rest? There are some particularly fine specimens I should not wish you to miss."

Elizabeth nodded, slowly reaching out to place her hand lightly upon his sleeve. "Yes, Mr Darcy, I should be very glad to see more."

Chapter Fourteen

✿❖✿

W hen they had completed their stroll, Darcy led
Elizabeth to one of the polished wooden benches.
It was his favourite corner of the room, secluded behind a
cluster of orange trees, their leaves forming a canopy that
diffused the sunlight into shifting patterns upon the floor.

They sat, and for several moments, the gentle burbling
of water from the nearby fountain was the only sound in the
still space.

Darcy stole a glance at her, noting the slight furrow in
her brow and the way her fingers rested, motionless, upon
the folds of her gown.

He shifted his attention to a lemon tree, ripe with fruit,
mentally rehearsing a dozen different lines of conversation,
dismissing each as inadequate before the words could form.
The silence deepened until he could endure it no longer,
and he turned to look at her, clearing his throat.

"I have been meaning to thank you, Miss Bennet—you
and your sister—for your kindness to Georgiana. She

seems to have blossomed these last few days, under your care. Indeed, I confess that I have not seen her so at ease in a very long time."

At his words, Elizabeth lifted her gaze, offering him a genuine smile. "You need not express any thanks for that. Miss Darcy is a delightful young lady. Jane and I feel very fortunate to have made her acquaintance."

"Still, you have gone out of your way to make her feel comfortable. I wanted you to know that it has not gone unnoticed, nor unappreciated."

Elizabeth inclined her head, saying simply, "It is not difficult to be attentive to someone you genuinely like. From what I have observed, your sister is only exceedingly shy, and that is something that will likely improve the more she is out in society."

Darcy nodded slowly. "My sister has always had a gentle, unassuming nature. Like me, she has never performed well to strangers, but her reticence has increased significantly since the summer. I have recently found a new companion for her—an older gentlewoman with a mild manner—whom I anticipate engaging after the new year. I only hope that Mrs Annesley can help to coax Georgiana out of her shell, else she will never be ready for her presentation in the spring."

Elizabeth frowned slightly. "Forgive my impertinence, but must she be brought out so soon? At sixteen, she is still quite young. Might she not benefit from more time to prepare for all a first Season will throw her way?"

"I do not see the need to wait," Darcy replied curtly. "*Your* youngest sisters are out. And in Georgiana's case, it would not be prudent to delay. As things stand, she is too easy a mark for every scapegrace and wastrel in London society. She must be settled before— Well, let us just say that the sooner she is settled, the better."

Elizabeth looked up at him, a question in her gaze.

"Before you go away, you mean?" she asked guilelessly, and Darcy startled.

Elizabeth shrugged lightly. "Your housekeeper mentioned that you had plans to leave Pemberley."

"Ah, I see."

When he failed to explain further, Elizabeth continued, "You indicated that Miss Darcy had become more reserved since last summer. Did something occur to bring about this change in her behaviour?"

Darcy looked away. He had not meant to disclose anything about his sister's near ruin, but the gentleness of Elizabeth's tone, and the warm expression in her eyes, suddenly made him want to unburden himself, at least of the one thing he was at liberty to share.

With a deep sigh, he began, "About a year ago, Georgiana was removed from school, and an establishment was formed for her in London. Last summer, she travelled to Ramsgate with her companion, at her own request, where she encountered a man by the name of George Wickham." Darcy paused, the sharp heat of anger flaring within him before he pressed on. "Wickham was my father's godson and the son of a respectable man who managed the Pemberley estates for many years. Unfortunately, the son has proved to be nothing like his late father, and I have long since ceased to think well of him.

"In any case, my sister knew nothing of Mr Wickham's perfidy, and due to this ignorance, along with her affectionate heart, she was persuaded to believe herself in love, and to consent to an elopement. She was then but fifteen years old."

Elizabeth gasped, and Darcy's jaw tightened. "Wickham cared nothing for my sister. His aim was her fortune of thirty thousand pounds and control of Pemberley once I was out of the way. Thankfully, the elopement was thwarted when I arrived unexpectedly. Georgiana confessed everything, and Wickham left the place immediately. Her companion was removed from her post, and Wickham has since been dealt with.

"So now, perhaps you will understand both Georgiana's timorous comportment, as well as my motives for wanting to see her married to a respectable, upstanding gentleman as soon as may be."

Elizabeth's eyes widened as he concluded his tale, and for a moment she merely stared back at him in silence.

"Mr Darcy," she said at last, her voice low but trembling with feeling, "I can scarcely comprehend the anguish this must have caused you—and your poor sister!" She paused, her lips pressed together in a taut line. "For Miss Darcy to have endured such deceit from one she trusted—how her tender heart must have suffered under the weight of such betrayal."

Her gaze lingered on his, steady and searching before she continued, "And you, sir—how it must have grieved you, to see her so cruelly used and to feel all the burden of protecting her from further harm."

Elizabeth's eyes shone with unspoken emotion, and before he could register her intent, her hand rose, her fingers grazing his jaw before they brushed against his cheek. The warmth of her touch sent a shiver down Darcy's spine, and he sucked in a ragged breath, scarcely daring to move. When he had finished his confession—the weight of his family's near disgrace laid bare before her—he had expected her pity, perhaps even polite discomfort, but not this—never this.

He closed his eyes, leaning into the tender caress. Despite his best intentions, his resolve crumbled, and he slowly turned into her touch, pressing his lips to the centre of her palm.

Inhaling the intoxicating sweetness of her skin, he lifted his gaze, staring into the unfathomable depths of her eyes.

"Elizabeth," he choked out, and something in her expression ignited a fire within his very soul. In that moment, all rational thought flew from his mind, and despite every vow he had made, every restraint he had promised to uphold, he leaned forwards, his lips finding hers.

The first brush was hesitant, no more than a question, but the answering pressure of her mouth undid him. A wave of longing surged through his body, and his hand rose to cradle the back of her neck.

She tasted of sincerity and hope, and Darcy felt as if the very earth had shifted beneath his feet. Every sensation was heightened—the warmth of her breath, the sweetness of her scent, the softness of her skin as his thumb traced the curve of her jaw.

And yet, even as passion flared, there was reverence in his touch, as though he feared she might vanish if he held on too tightly. She was his undoing—she had been from the very first—and at this moment, he could not bring himself to care.

With great reluctance, Darcy drew back, his breathing ragged, and Elizabeth's eyelids fluttered open.

He studied her face with quiet intensity, and what he saw there—wonder, longing, and something that looked a good deal like disbelief—made his heart tighten painfully within his chest.

"Forgive me," he whispered, his voice thick with emotion. "That should not have happened."

Dropping his hands from where they had come to rest upon her shoulders, Darcy stood, pacing several steps away, his boots echoing against the tile floor. Shame burned through him, but even as it did, he could not entirely banish the memory of her lips against his, nor the way she had leaned into his touch...

He forced himself to face her again, though his composure was brittle at best. "Miss Bennet, I must beg your forgiveness. I have overstepped every boundary of propriety, and for that, I can offer no excuse. I know you have no reason to believe me, but I have never been the sort of gentleman to take such liberties with a lady—certainly not with you. I find such behaviour utterly abhorrent."

Her eyes lifted to his, and at length, she answered quietly, "I do believe you. Though, in truth, you have no cause for recrimination. If I am being entirely honest, your gesture was not...unwanted. I was merely surprised. I did not think...that is, I was under the impression that you did not have those sorts of...feelings for..."

Elizabeth broke off, shifting her gaze uncomfortably to

the floor, but Darcy reached out, gently lifting her chin with the tips of his fingers.

"For you?" he asked quietly, and Elizabeth lowered her lashes. "If that is indeed your meaning, then you would be mistaken. And if by *'those sorts of feelings'* you refer to desire, I have felt nothing but desire from the moment I first laid eyes on you, on that Yorkshire moor. God help me, Elizabeth, I want you with every fibre of my being."

At this declaration, Elizabeth visibly startled, blinking up at him with unconcealed astonishment.

"But then…I do not understand. In Hertfordshire, you made it abundantly clear that we could have no future together. You told me in no uncertain terms that you would never marry! Do you deny it?"

"No. I have no wish to deny it. But what I said was that I *would not* marry. I never told you that I did not *wish* to marry."

To Darcy's surprise, Elizabeth's blush deepened. "Yes, I remember. I believe if we are to be exact, you said that you were not *free* to marry. Is that not so?"

A small frown tugged at his brow. "I may have said something to that effect. I do not recall my precise manner of expression. Why? What difference does it make?"

Elizabeth looked away. "The way you said it… You seemed to imply that your feelings were engaged…elsewhere. And then later, when I…" She tilted her head, her expression pensive, before continuing, almost to herself, "I suppose it is possible to feel desire for more than one person. I simply did not…" Turning briefly away, she worried at her lip before once again boldly meeting his gaze. "What of Mr Walsh?"

Darcy stared back at her. "Walsh? What has he to do with this?"

"A great deal, I should say," Elizabeth replied, lifting her chin. "Are you not…attached to him, sir?"

"Attached?" Darcy blinked back at her before understanding struck, sharp and sudden. "Surely you do not mean…?"

Elizabeth flushed an even deeper shade of scarlet, and Darcy cursed beneath his breath. *Good God!* Had Elizabeth been under the misapprehension that *Walsh* was the reason he was disinclined to marry?

He turned slightly away, raking his fingers through his hair before coming to sit beside her on the bench.

"Elizabeth," he began gently, "Walsh has been an exceedingly good friend to me, and I owe him a debt of gratitude that I can likely never repay. But that is all. There are no…deeper feelings between us. I am sorry if anything I said led you to believe that I was presently attached to anyone at all. I certainly would never have kissed you as I did if that had been the case."

Elizabeth turned away, but Darcy could see the elegant column of her neck was stained a brilliant shade of pink.

"Well, now I feel exceedingly foolish," she murmured, still unable to meet his gaze. "I hardly know what to say. Can you ever forgive me for jumping to such an erroneous conclusion?"

Darcy chuckled. "There is nothing to forgive. In truth, I am certain you are not the first person to have made that assumption, though you *are* the first to have voiced it to me directly. That did surprise me."

"Why?" she asked, finally looking up at him with a wilful expression. "Because I am a lady, and therefore should know nothing about such things, or because I am not as worldly as the ladies of the *ton*?"

Shocked, Darcy sputtered, "Because it is not something that is generally spoken of! Certainly not in polite society."

At his words, Elizabeth's courage seemed to falter, and there was remorse in her expression even though her chin still tipped up a little when she spoke.

"I hope you know that I never would have broached the subject with anyone else. I am not one to spread gossip, which is more than I can say for others of your acquaintance."

At this, Darcy merely stared back at her with a quirked brow before she eventually sighed.

"If you must know, I did not come to that conclusion entirely on my own. It was Miss Bingley who first put the notion into my head, and *she* apparently received the intelligence from Colonel Fitzwilliam."

Darcy stiffened, his breath catching in his throat.

"What? Fitzwilliam would not…" His voice faded as he turned away, his jaw tightening. No, Richard would never fabricate such nonsense, but he might share Darcy's aversion to marriage if he thought it would help divert Miss Bingley's attentions. From there, it would have been all too easy for her to twist his words into a tale that suited her schemes—and plant it in Elizabeth's mind.

Damn Miss Bingley and her incessant meddling!

A low groan escaped him. "Hell hath no fury like a woman scorned," he muttered under his breath before meeting Elizabeth's curious gaze. "I should have realized she was up to something when she took such an interest in speaking to you after that dinner at Netherfield."

But Elizabeth quickly shook her head. "No, the fault is mine. I should have judged better than to have believed anything Miss Bingley said, especially when she did not scruple to sink your character after assuring me that she did not suffer gossip, as you were her brother's *particular friend*."

Darcy made to answer, but at that moment, the faint creak of a door opening on the opposite side of the room arrested their attention. He and Elizabeth froze, the sound of footsteps echoing faintly against the floor. Their eyes locked, tension threading between them as moments stretched into what felt like an eternity. The door opened again, and they heard one of the gardeners call out to someone before it banged softly shut.

Darcy exhaled slowly, relief washing over him as Elizabeth stood. "I should go. My aunt will be returning shortly, and she will worry if I am not in my chambers."

She turned, moving towards the corridor, but just as her fingers brushed the edge of the doorway, he found his voice.

"Elizabeth."

She halted mid-step, slowly turning back to face him.

"You should know that when I said I never should have kissed you, I meant it. But not because I regretted my actions. My feelings for you are not the work of a moment. You have stirred a longing in me unlike any I have ever known, and I shall savour the memory of that kiss for the remainder of my days. But there is no hope for any future between us, so it cannot happen again. Nor will it."

Elizabeth said nothing. Then, with a faint nod, she turned and slipped out of the room, leaving Darcy alone with the fading echo of her footsteps and the ache of words he wished he could take back.

❧

Elizabeth sat before the fire in her chambers, her hands resting in her lap, though her fingers absently twisted at the folds of her gown. The flickering flames cast shadows against the walls, but she scarcely noticed them. Her thoughts were far away—trapped in the orangery, in the lingering warmth of Mr Darcy's unexpected embrace.

What had she been thinking to have reached for him in such an intimate manner—she who had never touched *any* gentleman in such a way, not even Mr Bingley to whom she was practically betrothed!

The truth was, she had not been thinking at all. Or at least, she had not taken the time to meditate on her actions. All rational thought seemed to have flown from her head the moment she had placed her hand on Mr Darcy's coat sleeve, standing so close to him that she could smell the heady aroma of freshly pressed linen and shaving soap upon his skin.

And then he had looked at her with such a mixture of desolation and desire that it had seemed like the most natural thing in the world to press her fingers to his cheek, to offer him comfort in some small way. When he had kissed her palm, a searing fire had seemed to burn through her entire body. And then he had wrapped his arms around her, and his lips had touched hers with such tenderness and passion all rolled together, and she had been lost.

Standing from her chair, she paced to the nearby window, staring out into the gathering darkness.

Mr Darcy had begged for her forgiveness, but he could not bear all the blame for what had happened between them. She could not claim ignorance of her actions nor deny the yearning that had driven them. And yet, neither could she see a path forwards that did not end in sorrow. She had allowed herself to feel too much, too quickly, and now she could never go back.

Elizabeth closed her eyes, but the memory remained— the warmth of his hand, the strength of his embrace, the reverence in his voice when he spoke her name. She pressed her palm to the cool glass, and in the quiet of her bedroom, her heart whispered the one truth she had been unwilling to admit.

She was in love with Mr Darcy. And unless she was very much mistaken, Mr Darcy was in love with her.

For Elizabeth, the rest of the day passed in a haze of distraction. Dinner was a lively affair, with the travellers regaling those who had remained behind with tales of their adventures, but Elizabeth was hardly able to attend to the conversation. She could scarcely look Mr Bingley in the eye, and when her gaze connected with Mr Darcy's across the table, she could feel her entire body heat at the memory of his lips upon hers.

Her hands trembled slightly as she lifted her wine glass, forcing herself to focus on Jane's laughter as she responded to something Mr Bingley had said. But no matter how she tried, her thoughts betrayed her, wandering again and again to the orangery and the way her heart had quickened under Mr Darcy's touch.

What madness had possessed her to allow such liberties? What of Mr Bingley, whose attentions had been nothing short of honourable and whose devotion to her had never wavered? She thought of his easy smiles, his generous spirit, and the steadiness of his regard. How could she face him now, knowing that her thoughts—her very heart—had been so utterly disloyal?

Elizabeth's gaze fell to her plate, her appetite long since abandoned. Mr Bingley deserved more than her divided affections; he deserved a woman whose heart was wholly his, but could she truly forget what had passed between her and Mr Darcy? The way he had looked at her, as though she were the very air he breathed; the reverence in his voice, the unguarded passion of his touch—haunted her still.

And yet, his words continued to echo in her mind: they had no future together. He had said it so plainly, leaving no room for doubt.

Elizabeth inhaled an unsteady breath, pressing her hands together in her lap as if the motion might steady her wavering resolve. She had to make a choice.

Mr Bingley deserved better. He deserved honesty.

Which meant that an unhappy alternative lay before her

—either to bring an end to their courtship or to accept that what had occurred between herself and Mr Darcy was nothing but a fleeting moment, and could not—would not —be more.

If only she was certain that she had the strength to let Mr Darcy go.

Chapter Fifteen

T he snow began falling at midnight.

It was light at first—a gentle cascade of white, dancing in the moonlight. But soon, the flakes thickened, growing larger, tumbling faster, until the world outside dissolved in a flurry of movement.

Darcy knew all this because he spent the next two hours sitting in the high-backed chair by his bedroom window, the soft crackle of the fire doing little to relax the restless anticipation stirring in his chest.

He could not stop thinking about Elizabeth Bennet.

She had been quiet at dinner, and in the drawing room afterwards. Too quiet. And while her relations had readily attributed her behaviour to the headache she had claimed that morning, Darcy knew better. Judging by the deep flush that had overspread her cheeks every time their eyes met, he was certain she was reliving their time together in the orangery, just as he was.

What had possessed him to act upon his impulses in

such a way? He, who had always prided himself on his integrity and restraint, to have taken such liberties and then told her he had no intention of ever making her his wife—it sickened him to his very core. He was no better than the gentlemen he had always despised; men like George Wickham, who kept mistresses and used women for their own gratification with nary an honourable thought in their heads.

His breath fogged the glass as he exhaled, the warmth of the room meeting the cold beyond. Somewhere, under his roof, Elizabeth Bennet slept…

Or perhaps she did not. The thought unsettled him further, and he quickly stood, stalking to a nearby table and pouring a glass of brandy—an indulgence he only permitted himself on rare occasions, and then generally only in the privacy of his own rooms.

Returning to the window, he gazed out at the snow falling silently beyond the glass. Did Elizabeth lie awake, even now, staring into the darkness as he did? Did regret weigh as heavily upon her shoulders as it did upon his own?

He closed his eyes, but the memory of her touch returned unbidden—the softness of her hand against his cheek, the way her lips had yielded under his. Cursing himself anew, he took a long swallow of his drink, hoping it might banish the image that was now seared upon his mind.

He never should have kissed her—never should have let her set so much as a foot inside the grounds of Pemberley. Not when he could offer her nothing.

By the time Darcy finally sought his bed, the snowfall

had thickened, blanketing the estate in a pristine, unbroken layer of white. And though he settled against his pillows, sleep eluded him. Instead, his mind wandered, painting visions of Elizabeth strolling along snow-covered paths, her cheeks flushed from the cold, her joyful laughter carrying on the wind.

❧

Darcy awoke at daybreak to a countryside transformed under a shimmering cloak of snow. The pristine expanse seemed to stretch endlessly, reflecting the morning light and giving the grounds an ethereal glow.

Without waiting for his valet, he swiftly washed and dressed, eager to seek out his steward and ensure that his tenants had weathered the storm unscathed. His mind, however, was not entirely occupied with estate matters. Peering through the frosted glass, Darcy's thoughts once again turned to Elizabeth. Was she awake? What would she make of such a snowfall?

His lips curved upwards as he imagined her expression —eyes bright with wonder, her breath catching in anticipation as she gazed out at the altered prospect. It was still early, but he could picture her already up, perhaps seated in the breakfast room, marvelling at the view through the mullioned glass. The thought stirred a thrill of expectation within him, though he quickly chastised himself for indulging in such fantasies.

Leaving his apartment, Darcy descended the staircase at a brisk pace, his footsteps muted by the plush carpeting but quickened by a sense of purpose. He was just passing the library when a flicker of movement within caught his eye. Pausing, he peered through the partially open door and saw a lone figure standing by the tall front windows, her delicate profile framed against the silver light. To his surprise, it was not Elizabeth but her sister Jane.

Stepping into the room, Darcy approached quietly so as not to startle her. "Miss Bennet?" he said gently when he was a few feet away.

She turned at the sound of his voice, her pale features softening into a faint smile. "Oh, Mr Darcy. Good morning."

"Is anything the matter?" he asked, his gaze sharpening at the slight tremor in her voice.

The lady hesitated, her hands twisting together nervously.

"I…yes, that is no," she began haltingly before shaking her head. "What I mean to say is that it is Lizzy I am concerned about. She went for a walk over an hour ago, and she has not yet returned."

Darcy felt his pulse quicken, his earlier enthusiasm giving way to alarm. "Alone, in weather such as this? What could she have been thinking!"

To Darcy's chagrin, Miss Bennet blanched at the gruffness in his tone. He moved closer to the window, scanning the horizon. Snow had once again begun to fall in delicate, swirling ribbons. But even as he watched, it began to gather speed, obscuring the distant hills in a haze of white.

"It was not so terribly bad when she left. She promised she would not go far and that she would come back directly should the weather worsen. But now I am beginning to worry. Perhaps she merely walked a greater distance than she intended, but what if she has lost her way, or worse?"

Before she had even finished speaking, Darcy had stalked to the bell pull, giving it one brief tug and then summoning the footman who knocked on the door a moment later to enter.

"Have my horse saddled and brought to the east gate at once. And tell Pierce to lay out my warmest clothes. I shall be up directly to change."

The footman bowed his understanding before scurrying away to do his master's bidding, and Darcy returned to where Jane Bennet still stood, watching the quickly falling snow.

"Miss Bennet, pray, do not make yourself uneasy. I will find her. But it would be helpful to know where she went. Did your sister happen to tell you in which direction she intended to walk?"

"N-no," she stammered, her voice tight with concern. "She only said that she would not be gone long, so I assumed she would remain in the gardens, close to the house. But now…"

She turned her attention back to the frosted windows, and Darcy could see that the reality of her sister's predicament had truly set in. The temperature was dangerously low, and visibility was becoming increasingly poor. Pemberley was a vast estate, and Elizabeth could have gone in any direction.

Miss Bennet pulled her gaze away from the expanse of windows, shifting her attention to the clock on the mantel. Reading her thoughts, Darcy replied decisively, "If your aunt and uncle should awaken before I return, tell them what has happened, but pray, do not raise the matter with anyone else. There is no need to alarm the others unnecessarily. For all we know, your sister is even now on her way back and merely delayed by having to move at a slower pace. If all goes well, I shall be home with Miss Elizabeth before the conclusion of breakfast."

"And if not?"

Darcy frowned. "If I cannot locate her quickly, I shall return so that we can mount a proper search."

Jane Bennet nodded, and Darcy turned, moving towards the entrance hall with hurried steps. He had just reached the stairs when he heard the patter of slippered feet on the marble floors, and Miss Bennet's voice called after him in breathless tones.

"Mr Darcy, wait, I have just remembered something! I think I may know where Elizabeth has gone."

Darcy pushed his mount through the swirling snow. He could only hope that Jane Bennet had the right of it and that Elizabeth had indeed gone to the rise they had visited on their walk, where the village of Lambton could be viewed in the valley below. If not, he was wasting valuable time, riding off in completely the wrong direction.

He urged his horse forwards, the animal's hoofs crunching through the thick snow. The air was heavy with the weight of falling flakes, obscuring his vision and deepening the unease that had taken root in his chest. The chill bit at his cheeks, but he scarcely noticed it; his thoughts were consumed by Elizabeth.

She had been gone too long.

Shaking his head, Darcy cursed his own stupidity. What on earth had he been thinking, setting out to find her all on his own? He never rode alone, even in the best of circumstances. He should have apprised Mr Gardiner of the situation at once. Surely Elizabeth's uncle would have wished to join the search. Or, at the very least, he should have collected Atkins, his steward, to accompany him. What had possessed him to throw all caution to the wind when Elizabeth's very life might be at stake?

But even as the question formed, he already knew the answer. It was not his steward or Mr Gardiner he had been avoiding, but Bingley. Bingley, who was all but betrothed to Elizabeth, should have, by rights, been the one to search for her. Yet Darcy had taken it upon himself to play the role of her deliverer—compelled not only by concern but by the unbearable thought of Elizabeth turning to *Bingley* in gratitude for her salvation. If anyone was to be the recipient of Elizabeth's appreciation and regard, he had wanted it to be him.

And now his selfishness had endangered the life of the woman he loved.

He was so lost in his musings that he almost missed the turning that led to his destination. Tugging sharply on the reins he wheeled the horse about before spurring it into a gallop.

The skeletal branches of the trees loomed overhead, their limbs weighed down with snow, casting eerie shadows in the dim light. Darcy continued to scour the wintry scene, calling her name, but the wind seemed to snatch the words away, carrying them off before they could travel very far.

Then, through the silvery haze, he saw it—a flash of crimson—and his heart leapt.

"Elizabeth!" he shouted, urging his horse towards the splash of colour. As he drew closer, the shape became clear. It was her coat.

Elizabeth stood amid the trees, her arms wrapped tightly around her body, her head bowed against the wind. At the sound of hoofbeats, she looked up, and Darcy could see that her face was pale, her cheeks flushed from the cold, but relief overspread her features.

"Mr Darcy!" her voice called back to him.

He dismounted in an instant, striding to her side. "Thank God you are safe!" He grasped her gloved hands, feeling the icy chill that seeped through the fabric. "You are freezing."

"I-I lost my way," she said, her voice trembling along with her body. "The snow—I could not see where I was going."

"Come." Without hesitation, Darcy lifted her onto his horse, removing his greatcoat and wrapping it around her shivering body. "We must get you inside."

Taking the reins, he turned his mount and began leading it through the deepening snow.

After a few moments, Elizabeth glanced down at him as they pressed forwards, her breath unsteady.

"H-how did you k-know to come looking for me?" she called through chattering teeth.

"Your sister," Darcy called back. "She grew worried when you did not return from your walk. Then she remembered you had made a remark when we viewed Lambton from the nearby summit about how lovely the village must look in the snow, so I came this way first. I am glad her instinct was correct."

Elizabeth nodded, wrapping his coat more tightly around her body.

"I am exceedingly grateful to her, and to you. And thank goodness you found me when you did, as it appears I was walking in the wrong direction entirely."

"No," Darcy replied loudly over the roar of the wind, "you were not so far off. You were moving towards the formal gardens. But once you reached the next rise, you would have been able to see the house, so no doubt you would have corrected your course."

"I do not understand. Then why are we now going in the opposite direction?"

"Because I am not taking you back to the manor. At least not directly. We are much closer to the dower house. Indeed, you would be able to see it from here if the visibility were better. We shall be there within a matter of minutes."

It was not long afterwards that the stately stone edifice became visible through the gloom of the falling snow, its dark windows promising shelter and warmth. Although it had not served as a permanent residence since his grandmother's time, Darcy had always ensured it was kept furnished and ready, should the need for its use ever arise.

When they reached the door, Darcy gently lifted Elizabeth down from his mount. Her legs wobbled slightly, and he steadied her with a firm but careful grip.

"You are safe now," he murmured, his voice low and reassuring. "I shall have you inside in a moment."

Elizabeth managed a faint smile, her pale lips just

beginning to regain some of their natural colour. "Thank you," she whispered.

Leading the horse to the stables at the back, Darcy made quick work of securing the animal before returning to Elizabeth's side. From the inner pocket of his coat, he withdrew a heavy brass key, thanking providence that he had thought to bring it with him—though he would have broken a window to gain entrance had it been necessary.

The lock yielded with a solid click, and he pushed the door open, holding it so that Elizabeth could step into the dimly lit hall.

The air within was cool but dry, and Darcy wasted no time. Striding to the hearth in the front parlour, he set kindling and logs into place, striking a flame with practised efficiency and slowly coaxing it into a steady blaze.

Elizabeth moved closer, extending her hands towards the fire's warmth. The flickering light danced across her features, easing the tension that had been evident in her expression.

"You should sit," Darcy said with quiet insistence, motioning towards a nearby chair draped with a woollen blanket. "I shall fetch more wood in a moment and then see about tea." Elizabeth nodded, slowly lowering herself into the chair and pulling the blanket around her shoulders. Her eyes lifted to meet his, and there Darcy saw a mixture of gratitude and discomfiture in her gaze.

"Mr Darcy, I do not know how to thank you. I feel very foolish for having risked not only my own safety but yours as well."

Across from her, Darcy offered up a small smile. "We all occasionally do things we later come to regret. And there is no need to thank me. I am only glad to have found you before... Well, I am only glad to have found you, and to know that you are unharmed."

After that, they drifted into silence, Elizabeth curled up in the overstuffed armchair, and Darcy, standing before the hearth, staring into the shifting firelight.

The steady heat from the flames seeped into the room, but a sudden chill traced its way along his spine. He blinked, willing the sensation away, but his vision wavered, and the edges of the room suddenly seemed to pulse and quiver.

He gripped the mantelpiece, his knuckles whitening as a prickle of unease settled like a weight upon his chest. The faintest hum filled his ears, growing louder with each passing moment. A surge of dizziness washed over him, and he steadied himself, breathing deeply. *Not now,* he thought. *Not here.*

Darcy squeezed his eyes shut, but the sensations only intensified. Flashes of light burst behind his eyelids, and the tingling in his fingertips crept upwards, spreading through his arms.

He smelled the acrid aroma of smoke, sharp and disorienting, and he felt his knees begin to buckle. He opened his eyes, and the room tilted. And then the darkness swallowed him whole.

Chapter Sixteen

❧❀❧

"Mr Darcy? Can you hear me?"
    Darcy came back to himself slowly. He was lying on his back on the Brussels carpet, but there was something soft beneath his head. He swallowed, the dryness in his mouth sharp and unpleasant. Gradually, he realized his neckcloth had been removed, leaving his white lawn shirt gaping open at the throat. Turning his head, he saw Elizabeth sitting beside him on the floor, firmly clasping his hand.

Mortification surged through him as he tried to push himself up, his free hand instinctively tugging at the collar of his shirt.

"No, pray, lie still," Elizabeth murmured. Leaning forwards, she pressed a folded handkerchief to the corner of his mouth just as he became aware of the familiar metallic taste of blood. *Devil take it!* He had bitten his tongue. At least it did not appear that he had cast up his accounts, or worse. Slowly, he rolled onto his side, drawing his knees up slightly as he focused on taking slow, steadying breaths.

The silence between them stretched for several moments before Elizabeth broke it in a low voice. "Do you think you can sit?"

Darcy nodded, shifting his weight and wincing slightly as he propped himself up.

"I think you had a...spell of some sort," Elizabeth said hesitantly, and Darcy noticed that though her speech was cautious, her eyes were kind.

Again, he nodded. "How...how long...?"

"I do not believe it lasted more than a minute," she replied gently. "I am sorry I could not reach you in time to cushion your fall. I fear you might have struck your head."

Darcy's attention turned inwards as he attempted to take stock of his condition with slow, tentative movements. "No, it would seem I landed on my shoulder," he murmured, his voice rough. His attention shifted to his crumpled neckcloth lying on the carpet nearby, and his cheeks burned as he realized that must have been Elizabeth's doing.

Following his gaze, she flushed. "Forgive me. You appeared to be having some difficulty breathing, so I thought it best to remove it."

She reached out, retrieving the cloth and handing it back to him before averting her eyes.

Darcy accepted it gratefully, hastily wrapping the material around his neck and tying it in a simple knot. "You have no reason to ask for my forgiveness," he said quietly. "If anything, I must beg for yours. I cannot tell you how deeply sorry I am that you had to witness such a spectacle. You must have been..." He paused, the word *horrified* immediately leaping to mind, before continuing, "...very frightened."

Her eyes met his, the warmth of her expression easing a small portion of his shame. "You certainly owe me no apology, sir. While the episode was indeed unsettling to watch, I am sure it was far more frightening for you than it was for me."

"I beg to differ," Darcy replied, attempting a weak smile. "After all, I was unconscious for most of it."

A startled laugh slipped past Elizabeth's lips before she quickly composed herself, lowering her gaze to hide her smile. When her eyes returned to his, her voice was quieter, more cautious. "Am I correct in assuming something of this nature has occurred before?"

Darcy's gaze dropped, and he was silent for a moment before answering thickly, "Yes."

They sat in a charged silence before Elizabeth ventured tentatively, "Do you feel well enough to stand? I believe you would be more comfortable if we moved you to the sofa."

Darcy inclined his head, and she rose, extending a hand. He hesitated briefly before taking it, attempting to disregard the frisson of pleasure that jolted through him at the feeling of her bare skin against his. The sofa in question was only a few steps away, and it was not long before Darcy was settled onto it, his feet resting on a stool Elizabeth had pulled over.

"Is there anything I can bring you?" she asked. "A blanket? Or something to drink?"

"No, thank you," he said, his voice faintly slurred from the swelling of his tongue. "I only need to rest."

Elizabeth nodded, shifting awkwardly before he gestured to the nearby armchair. "Pray, sit. I am mortified beyond measure at what you have already observed without having to suffer the indignity of reclining here while you stand."

Elizabeth offered him a small, tentative smile before complying with his request and perching delicately on the chair by his side. For a moment, she bowed her head, her hands busily smoothing the fabric of her gown.

"Mr Darcy, I—"

"I hope you will—"

Elizabeth laughed lightly as they both spoke at once.

"Please," he said quietly, "I would like to explain, if I may?"

She nodded, her expression encouraging, and he looked away briefly, gathering his thoughts before speaking in a low voice.

"The first…episode occurred not long after my mother's death. I was thirteen, and it was early summer. My father and I had gone out riding on the estate. We had been out for some time when I began to feel as if something were not as it should be—I was suddenly light-headed, and there was a buzzing in my ears and a tingling sensation in my fingers. The next thing I knew I was lying on the ground with my father kneeling beside me, holding me by the shoulders. At first, I assumed I had been thrown, though I could not remember it happening. There was a blank space in my memory—nothing after the moment I began to feel unwell. However, when my father described what he had witnessed, it was clear that the horse was not to blame. I had experienced a convulsion of sorts, losing consciousness and slipping from my mount.

"We had been riding at a good clip, so in truth, I was fortunate not to have been trampled. In any case, we sat together for some time until I felt steady enough to ride home. My father stayed close, keeping our pace to a walk, and once we returned to the house, the matter was left behind. I think we both hoped—rather than truly believed—that it was an isolated incident. Perhaps I had been overcome by the heat or had eaten too little at breakfast.

"For some time afterwards, I avoided riding altogether. As a child, I had no fear of horses. I had been in the saddle nearly as long as I could walk. But suddenly, all I could think about was the attack—and that mayhap a hard ride would bring on another. My father saw my hesitation, though he never addressed it directly. Instead, he insisted that we ride together daily. I believe he was just as apprehensive as I—perhaps even more so—but he knew that if I did not conquer my fear immediately, it would only grow stronger.

"In any event, the days and months went by, and I did not experience another incident. In time, I began to believe that perhaps it was as my father said—no more than a unique occurrence—and I allowed myself to relax. Indeed, by the time it happened again, I had almost forgotten the first incident entirely."

Darcy paused, drawing a steadying breath, and Elizabeth interjected softly, "So, it did happen again?"

"Yes. About eight months later. It was nighttime, and I was in my bedchamber at Pemberley. There was a fire burning low in the grate, and I had pulled a chair up to the hearth to take advantage of the warmth and light. I was supposed to be in bed, but I was deep in *Gulliver's Travels* and could not resist finishing just one more chapter. Once again, I felt the strange creeping sensation—an uneasy fluttering in my chest and a faint tingling at the ends of my fingers. My vision clouded at the edges, and a hollow ringing began in my ears, growing louder with every breath. But this time, I had a sense of what might follow. I quickly stood and went to lie down on the bed.

"When I regained consciousness, the world felt disjointed, as though time had slipped past me without my consent. My limbs were heavy, weighed down as if I had run for miles, and my mouth felt dry, my tongue thick. I remember staring up at the ceiling, willing my breathing to slow and struggling to piece together how much time had passed.

"It was not fear I felt then, but shame—shame at my body's betrayal, and at my own helplessness."

Elizabeth reached out, gently squeezing his hand. "What did your father say," she asked, "when you told him it had happened again?"

Darcy turned his gaze aside, the memory settling heavily upon him. "I did not tell him. Not that night, nor after the next episode, which occurred some months later. As I said, I was deeply ashamed. By then, I was fourteen, and I was beginning to understand that there was something seriously wrong. Besides that, I could not bear the thought of placing yet another burden upon my father's shoulders. My mother had been gone scarcely more than a year, and he was already coping with his own grief while raising a son on the cusp of manhood and an infant daughter, alongside running an estate. I could not stand the thought of being yet another encumbrance for him."

Elizabeth's lips parted slightly, her tender gaze searching his face. "But…you did tell him eventually, did you not?"

"Yes," Darcy admitted. "But only because the next attack he witnessed for himself. After that, I confessed everything, and that was when he told me the truth."

Darcy looked away, his throat tightening as he continued, "The episodes I had been experiencing were not a complete surprise to him. It turns out there had been a great-aunt on his mother's side who suffered from a similar affliction. Her symptoms began much the same as mine, in her youth. Over time, however, her spells grew both more frequent and more severe. The family physician, lacking better understanding, diagnosed it as a form of lunacy." Darcy's voice thickened, and he hesitated before adding, "At the age of sixteen, her parents had her committed to an asylum. She lived out the remainder of her life there."

Silence settled heavily in the small sitting room until Elizabeth spoke, her voice tinged with disbelief. "How horrible. But that was generations ago! Surely your father could never have been so cruel?"

"No," Darcy replied, his tone steady but sombre. "But we both understood that we could not allow news of my condition to become generally known. Even within the family, it was discussed only sparingly. Fortunately, in my case, the spells did not appear to worsen. At the time, I was already studying with a tutor, having left school after my mother died the previous year. So, for a while, life continued much as it had before. I kept up with my studies and assisted my father with the business of the estate. The one thing of note is that it was during this period that I formed a friendship with George Wickham."

Elizabeth gasped, her expression incredulous. "Not the same Mr Wickham who tried to elope with your sister?"

Darcy inclined his head grimly. "Indeed, the very same. He was the son of my father's steward, and like me, he had lost his mother in childbed. That shared experience formed a bond of sorts between us. Moreover, there were few boys of my age in the area as my cousins and other peers were all away at school. It was my father's idea for George to join me in my studies. He was very fond of old Mr Wickham, and I think he felt responsible for keeping me at home. So, despite our differences in station, he did everything he could to encourage the friendship."

Elizabeth tilted her head, a faint crease forming along her brow. "Did Mr Wickham know of your condition? Did he ever witness one of these...episodes?"

"Thankfully, no. The spells were infrequent, and by then I had learned to recognize the warning signs. If I felt any of the usual symptoms, I would excuse myself and find a place to lie down until the worst had passed. There were a few narrow escapes, of course, but I always managed to avoid detection."

Darcy's voice grew quieter as he continued, "So, that was how I spent the next few years—until it was time for me to go to university. Although my father preferred that I continue my education at home, by that point, I was desperate to get away. Pemberley, as much as I loved it, was beginning to feel like a gaol, and I was eager to spread my wings—to meet new people and to see more of the world. It took months of persuasion, but eventually, my father agreed—on one condition."

Elizabeth leaned forwards slightly, her gaze fixed on him, as Darcy continued, his lips tightening, "That George Wickham accompany me. You see, his plan was to divulge my condition to old Mr Wickham and to strike a bargain. He would pay for George's education in return for his assistance in protecting my secret. At the time, I had little choice but to agree, though I did so reluctantly. Wickham had already begun to exhibit traits I found troubling, and I did not trust his discretion. Still, I was too eager for a change of scenery to refuse. And so, in the autumn of 1801, Wickham and I began our studies at Cambridge.

"It was at university that everything began to change— both for the better and for the worse. In the case of Wickham, the vicious tendencies and lack of principle I had glimpsed during our time at Pemberley began to flourish unchecked. His behaviour grew increasingly reckless, and I found myself more and more uneasy in his company, especially given his knowledge of my condition. I was torn about what to do—to confide in my father or to keep Wickham's proclivities to myself. Yet I feared that revealing the truth might lead to greater troubles, as it would involve Wickham's deceit as much as my own failings.

"An unexpected answer, however, came in the form of Mr Henry Walsh.

"Walsh and I became acquainted not long after arriving at university. He was a respectable young man from modest beginnings—the son of a schoolmaster with six children and scant means. However, Walsh had an uncle who had gone into the law, a bachelor who was able to fund his nephew's education. Henry was as clever as they come and had excelled in his studies from an early age. Still, as you might imagine, his background made him an outsider amongst those who prided themselves on their breeding.

"But I liked him instantly. Unlike Wickham, Walsh and I shared a great deal in common, and I found his company far more agreeable as I began to distance myself from my boyhood friend. By that time, Wickham had already abandoned any pretence of fulfilling the promise he had made to my father. He rarely attended lectures, instead choosing to squander his days in dissipation—late nights of gambling and drinking followed by long mornings spent in bed. While I was both appalled and saddened by his degeneracy, I confess I felt a measure of relief as well. His self-indulgence effectively freed me from the burden of his custody, and I could finally move through life without the weight of his judgment or interference.

"So, it is not surprising that when I had my first attack while at university, it was Walsh who was with me, not Wickham."

Elizabeth tilted her head, her brow furrowed. "What happened? Mr Walsh must have been alarmed if he was unprepared for such a thing."

Darcy exhaled, his gaze distant. "He was startled, certainly, as anyone would be, but he responded with remarkable composure. It was during the Michaelmas term, a particularly demanding period with examinations approaching. We had gone for a walk, to clear our heads, and I began to feel the now-familiar signs that an attack was imminent. Walsh must have noticed something was wrong because I remember him looking at me with some concern, asking whether all was well."

He hesitated, his tone subdued. "I barely managed to shake my head before everything went dark. When I woke, Walsh was there, kneeling beside me. He helped me up and escorted me back to my rooms. He asked no questions, demanded no explanation—only enquired whether I felt steady enough to make the short walk."

Elizabeth's expression gentled. "He sounds like a remarkable friend."

Darcy nodded. "He was—and is. The next morning, I told him everything, and his response was simple—he only asked how he might be of help.

"After that, Walsh quickly replaced Wickham in almost every respect—accompanying me to lectures, encouraging me in my studies, and ensuring that I did not push myself too far when I felt the early warning signs of another episode. Meanwhile, Wickham became increasingly... disreputable. I shall not go into the particulars in the presence of a lady, but suffice it to say that the company he kept was abhorrent, and he spent little time in the classroom. I saw less and less of him, which was a relief, though it also left me uneasy. By that time, I had begun to doubt his trustworthiness, though I had reason to believe he could be persuaded to hold his tongue so long as my father controlled the purse strings."

Darcy exhaled slowly, his jaw tightening. "And so, we reached an unspoken agreement. Wickham would say nothing of my ailment, and in return, I would not inform my father of his exploits. While I do not regret my choices

—especially as they allowed me to distance myself from him—there were consequences."

Darcy paused here for breath as Elizabeth waited patiently for him to continue.

"Due to my concealment of the truth," Darcy began again, "my father's attachment to Wickham never wavered. To the very last, he thought of him as the same charming boy who had been a friend to me when I needed one most, and because of that, he provided generously for Wickham in his will—a legacy of one thousand pounds. More than that, he made it known that he wished Wickham to inherit a valuable family living, should he choose to make the church his career." Darcy's voice grew tight, his frustration barely contained, as he bit out, "But now I digress."

Elizabeth did not press him further, her expression one of quiet understanding as he gathered himself before continuing.

"It was my intention to return to Pemberley upon grad-uation, while Walsh planned to study the law, hoping to eventually join his uncle's practice. What George Wickham planned to do I neither knew nor cared. Certainly, he had no intention of making the church his profession, despite my father's wishes. But before any of these paths could be settled, my father fell ill, and within a matter of months, he was gone."

"How dreadful for you," Elizabeth whispered.

Darcy nodded grimly. "It was one of the darkest periods of my life if truth be told. While my condition had remained somewhat manageable during my time at univer-sity, the strain of my father's illness—and the grief that followed his death—took its toll, and my own health began to decline at a rapid pace. The attacks increased in frequency, sometimes occurring as often as twice in a single week, and the warning signs I had come to rely upon were brief—if I noticed them at all.

"Before he died—and with my knowledge and permission—my father shared the details of my affliction with my uncle, the Earl of Matlock, and later with my cousin Colonel Fitzwilliam, with whom I had always been close. He also arranged for me to consult with a physician in Edinburgh, a man reputed to have success in treating cases like mine. It was my father's final wish, and my uncle vowed to see it through. Five years ago this summer, Lord Matlock fulfilled that promise."

Across from him, Elizabeth's eyes grew round as realization struck. "Five summers ago... That was where you were going? When we met in Yorkshire?"

He hesitated before nodding. "Yes."

For a moment, her expression grew distant, and Darcy wondered whether she was thinking back to that long ago day, but after a moment she merely nodded, prompting gently, "And the physician? Was he able to help you?"

Darcy's lips pressed together, the memory drawing a scowl. "The *physician*—if I can even use such an appellation to describe the gentleman—was little more than a charlatan. His methods were crude, and his conclusions were of little use. He declared there was nothing to be done beyond avoiding strain and keeping to a quiet life. Worse still, he *helpfully* informed me that there were still those in the medical profession who viewed my condition as a form of madness—grounds for being cast into Bedlam."

Elizabeth's breath hitched, her shock evident, but Darcy

pressed on, his tone grim. "You will understand, then, why I resolved that I could not remain on English soil. To become fodder for gossip—to risk tarnishing the Darcy name, or worse, finding myself consigned to a madhouse—was something I could never endure. Were it not for Georgiana, I would have left these shores long ago."

"So, that is why you wish to see her married so soon," Elizabeth murmured, and Darcy nodded in reply.

"My father entrusted Georgiana's guardianship to Colonel Fitzwilliam, along with myself, for reasons you can no doubt appreciate. As I did not wish to leave the full burden of her care to my cousin, I agreed to remain in England long enough to see my sister happily settled. But that decision was not without risks. If anyone were to discover the truth…"

Elizabeth stared back at him, nodding her understanding. "And that is why you rarely leave Pemberley," she said quietly, her expression serious. "To minimize the chances of anyone finding out."

Darcy inclined his head. "Can you imagine what hope Georgiana would have of securing a respectable husband if rumours of lunacy within the family ever arose? The only gentlemen who would even look at her would be the ones with pockets to let, or worse. And once they gained control of her assets…who knows what would become of her—or of Pemberley? They could drain the coffers within a year."

"But, I do not understand," Elizabeth replied. "You would leave her Pemberley?"

Darcy responded with a solemn nod. "It is already done. Once I am gone, everything will pass to her, save a modest sum I shall use to establish myself far away from here."

"I see. And Mr Walsh?"

Darcy inclined his head, considering her words. "He will not be accompanying me, if that is your question. He has already rendered me a great service—one I can scarcely hope to repay." He paused for a moment before continuing in a low voice, "Upon my return from Scotland, once I realized that a cure was not possible for me, I sought out Walsh and made him an offer. I would hire him to take charge of my financial affairs, and in return, he would reside here at Pemberley to be of service in a more...personal capacity. His compensation has been generous, ensuring that by the time I am prepared to depart England, he will have the means to pursue whatever course he chooses—be it the law, continued financial consultancy, or even the purchase of a small estate, should that be his inclination."

Elizabeth nodded, her expression pensive. When she did not speak, Darcy looked away, before continuing in a brusque manner.

"Well, now you know everything, and I can only beg your forgiveness. It was never my intention to humble myself in such a way, nor for you to witness..." His voice faltered, his jaw tightening as the memory of the humiliating scene returned unbidden. "...what you observed here today. But perhaps it is for the best. I have no reason to doubt your discretion, and now you will understand what I told you in the orangery—that there can be nothing further between us." He hesitated, then added, his tone edged with bitterness, "No doubt you will leave here counting yourself most fortunate to have escaped unscathed."

Elizabeth arched a brow, incredulity sharpening her voice. "Unscathed? Forgive me, Mr Darcy, but no—I am afraid I do not understand you in the least."

Darcy exhaled sharply, his fingers curling into fists at his side. *Does she not see? Can she not comprehend what I am trying to spare her?* His chest tightened, torn between reason and the unbearable pull of longing.

"Elizabeth, please! You are far too clever not to recognize the imprudence of such a match. Surely, you must see that I can never marry."

She stared at him for a long moment before rising abruptly, the sweep of her skirts brushing against the floor. Crossing to the window, she stood with her back to the room, the tension in her frame betraying her struggle for composure. When at last she turned, her expression was one of quiet defiance.

"You are right about one thing," she said, her voice brimming with intensity. "I shall never speak of what happened here today, nor of what you have confided in me, if that is your wish. But you are utterly mistaken if you believe any of it justifies your refusal to marry."

"Refusal?" His laugh was bitter. "Is that what you believe this to be, after everything I have told you? I am *damaged*, Elizabeth! Can you not see that? Marriage is out of the question. I could never—*would* never—saddle any woman with such a burden, least of all a woman I—" He broke off, his throat tightening as he turned away. "Least of all you. And even if I were selfish enough to make you my wife, there would be no children. On that, I am resolved. I could never risk passing on an affliction such as this to any offspring of mine."

To his astonishment, when he finally dared to meet her gaze, there was no pity in her dark eyes—only a fiery resolve. A blazing challenge that stole his breath.

"And if I should choose to marry you in any case?" she enquired. "Should that not be my decision to make?"

"No. You are young, and you are not thinking clearly. Can you not see what your future would be? In the best of circumstances, you would be nursemaid to a recluse who rarely leaves his rooms. And in the worst, you would be bound to a madman committed to Bedlam. Is that truly the life you would choose for yourself?"

Elizabeth parted her lips, a retort already forming, but before she could speak, Darcy turned away, his tone clipped and final.

"This conversation is over. I have nothing more to say on the matter. Marry Bingley, Elizabeth. He will give you the life you deserve."

Chapter Seventeen

E lizabeth was spared the need to respond to Mr Darcy's pronouncement when he abruptly stood, declaring his intent to seek sustenance in the kitchens. And while her first impulse had been to offer to accompany him, she quickly dismissed the idea. No doubt he was already deeply embarrassed that she had observed his earlier episode, and her presence would likely only heighten his discomfort. So, she simply nodded and let him go.

In truth, Elizabeth did not mind being left to herself for a time. She needed the quiet to reflect upon all she had witnessed—and all that Mr Darcy had shared. Although she had managed to maintain some semblance of composure for his sake, the episode had shaken her more than she cared to admit. To see a man so powerful, so controlled, brought so low had touched something in her she could not easily banish. For one terrible moment, she had feared he might die before her very eyes. And when he had finally stirred, her relief had been so profound that she had nearly wept. But it was his confession afterwards that had truly unsettled her. His words—spoken with such raw honesty—continued to echo in her mind.

Now, seated alone in the dower house's cosy front parlour, with the fire crackling softly in the hearth, Elizabeth exhaled a trembling breath. The memories clung to her—the unnatural stillness of his body, the sharp pang of helplessness that had seized her as she knelt by his side, powerless to do anything but wait and pray. Yet even amidst her terror, a fierce determination had risen within her. She had known instinctively that any display of distress on her part would only deepen his humiliation, and she could not bear to wound him further.

Despite her best efforts to appear collected, the weight of the moment lingered. How deeply must such a proud, private man feel the strain of his malady? Certainly she could not imagine anyone, save perhaps her beloved Jane, observing her in such a vulnerable state.

The thought stirred an ache within her, mingling pity with a burgeoning respect for the courage it must have taken for him to share his story.

He had carried this burden for so many years, living in fear of his own body, haunted by shame and a sense of inadequacy. And now, to hear him declare that he would never marry, never father children, for fear of passing this affliction on—it tore at her heart.

Elizabeth rose and began to pace the room, her thoughts in turmoil. How could he believe himself unworthy of love? Did he not see the strength it had taken to endure such trials, to build the life he had, despite them? And yet, she understood his fear—the cruel judgments of society, the whispers that would surely follow if his condition were known. She longed to shield him from all of it, to stand beside him and bear the weight of it with him.

But what could she do? He had made his decision. He had drawn a line between them, not out of indifference but out of a misguided sense of duty. To defy that decision would mean challenging his very sense of honour.

Elizabeth sank back into the chair, her hands clenched against her skirts. She would not give up on him. She could not. Whatever it took, she would find a way to make him see what she already knew.

He was not damaged. He was not broken.

He was the strongest, most honourable man she had ever known. And somehow, she would show him that he was deserving of respect, of happiness, and above all, of the love she was ready to offer him.

※

It was with no little relief that Elizabeth had managed to compose herself by the time Mr Darcy returned some twenty minutes later, carrying a tray laden with a teapot, cups and saucers, a bowl of apples, and a wedge of cheese. His entrance filled the room, though he hesitated just inside the doorway, as if uncertain how to proceed. She stood awkwardly, smoothing her skirts, while he set the tray down on the nearby table.

"I, ah...I hope this will suffice," he said, his voice unusually stiff. "There was little to be found in the larder. Indeed, there would not even be this much, had my steward not hosted a hunting party here in the autumn."

Elizabeth nodded, quickly stepping forwards in an attempt to ease the tension that had thickened between them. "It is more than sufficient, Mr Darcy. Thank you for taking the trouble." She began arranging the cups and saucers, her hands oddly aware of his presence as he moved to stand by the window.

Behind her, Mr Darcy cleared his throat. "It seems the snow is beginning to subside. Once we have rested a while, I believe we should be able to return to the house." He paused momentarily before adding, "Your family will no doubt be anxious for your return."

"Yes, I am certain my aunt has been beside herself," Elizabeth answered. "I can only hope she has not taken ill with worry."

From the corner of her eye, she saw him glance over at her, his gaze lingering for a moment before shifting back to the frost-covered pane. "If the snow stops soon, we may yet spare them undue distress," he said quietly. His voice gentled at the end, and an uneasy silence settled over the room.

Elizabeth busied herself with pouring the tea, acutely aware of every sound—the clink of the china, the crackle of the fire, the soft hiss of wind against the windowpane. But then she saw Mr Darcy stiffen, the change in his posture drawing her attention. She turned slightly, catching sight of his sharp gaze fixed on something beyond the glass.

"What is it?" she asked, grateful for the distraction.

Mr Darcy did not answer immediately, his shoulders stiffening as he peered out at the snow-covered grounds. "It appears someone else has been caught in the storm. They must have seen the smoke from our chimney."

Elizabeth set the teapot down and moved to join him. She could just make out the form of a lone rider, his cloak billowing slightly in the wind as his horse trotted up the drive.

To her surprise, Mr Darcy turned to her abruptly. "Elizabeth, pray, go upstairs and wait for me there. I do not recognize the gentleman as anyone from the estate—it would be safer if you were not here when I admit him to the house."

Elizabeth hesitated, shifting her weight, but the urgency in his tone prompted her to nod. She began to step away, but as the horseman drew closer and slowed his mount, a gasp escaped her throat.

"Mr Darcy!" she exclaimed, her hand clutching the edge of the windowsill. "The gentleman is no stranger—it is my uncle!"

Darcy startled at Elizabeth's proclamation, shifting his gaze from her joyful expression to the figure outside the window, who was now dismounting and tying his horse to a nearby post.

Damnation! He should have anticipated that Mr Gardiner would not be content to sit quietly at Pemberley when his niece was in danger. How the man had managed to track them down was anyone's guess, but more importantly, how was Darcy to explain bringing Elizabeth to the dower house and remaining alone with her, unchaperoned, for all this time?

His thoughts churned, but Elizabeth, her eagerness

overriding his growing panic, reached out to tug lightly on his sleeve. "Come. He must be half frozen!"

Darcy nodded absently, stealing one last glance out of the window at the approaching man before drawing to a halt. "Elizabeth, wait!" His voice was sharp, causing her to pause mid-stride. "Do not open the door. I can see the gentleman clearly now, and it is most certainly not your uncle."

Elizabeth turned back to him, a small frown puckering her forehead before a laugh escaped her lips. "Oh! No, it is not my uncle Gardiner. The gentleman is Mr Harper, my aunt Gardiner's brother."

Relief mingled with renewed anxiety as Darcy apprehended the meaning of her words, but before he could respond, Elizabeth, already halfway across the room, reached for the latch. A gust of cold wind swept into the room, stirring the flames in the hearth. A tall, broad-shouldered man stood on the threshold, stamping snow from his boots and shaking the damp from his coat. Darcy noted the resemblance to Mrs Gardiner immediately—the kind expression in his eyes, the ease of his manner—as he looked up and caught sight of Elizabeth.

"Lizzy!" the man exclaimed, his face breaking into a broad smile before he stepped forwards and pulled Elizabeth into a warm embrace. "What on earth are you doing here?"

Elizabeth laughed, beckoning him inside before shutting the door firmly behind him. "I might ask you the same thing," she replied as they all stepped farther into the room. "Did you not receive Aunt Gardiner's express, entreating you not to come? We had reason to believe a storm might be on the way, and she was worried for your safety."

The man pulled back, a flicker of uncertainty crossing his features. "Express? No, I must have left before it arrived. As soon as I saw the weather beginning to worsen, I departed straightaway. I was able to keep ahead of the storm for the better part of the journey, but it caught up to us in Bakewell yesterday afternoon. The post coach could go no farther, but I was lucky enough to find a horse for hire, and here I am."

He grinned broadly as Elizabeth blinked back at him.

"You rode all that way in the midst of a storm? You might have become lost, or frozen to death!"

Mr Harper shrugged good-naturedly. "I am no stranger to the area, nor to riding in inclement weather. And I certainly was not about to miss Christmas with my sister and her family after all our careful planning. But pray, tell me how I have come to find *you* here and not at the great house. I had not anticipated stopping, but then I saw the smoke from the chimney and thought whoever was within might allow me to warm up before riding the remainder of the way. I had no notion of finding you here. Nor you, sir," he finished with a bow in Darcy's direction.

Darcy opened his mouth to explain, but it was Elizabeth who spoke first.

"Oh, goodness, I have not even introduced you! Forgive me—Mr Darcy, may I present my uncle, Dr Harper?"

Darcy inclined his head in greeting. "It is an honour to make your acquaintance, sir."

Dr Harper shook Darcy's hand firmly, his eyes discerning but not unkind. "Mr Darcy. The honour is mine.

I cannot thank you enough for affording me the privilege of being a guest in your home." He then turned back to Elizabeth, concern evident in his expression. "Now, tell me, what is all this? I find you here, in the midst of such harsh weather. What has happened?"

Elizabeth's cheeks coloured faintly as she cast a glance at Darcy. "It is rather a long story, Uncle. Let us just say that you are not the only one who is intrepid—or foolish—enough to venture out in the middle of a snowstorm. I am ashamed to say that I set out this morning for a walk and got hopelessly turned around. If Mr Darcy had not come after me, I dare not think what might have happened."

Harper's expression instantly sobered as he took Elizabeth's measure. "Lizzy, good Heavens! How long were you out in this weather? Never mind, let me see your hands. And your feet! Do you know how quickly one can develop frostbite in temperatures such as these?"

Elizabeth laughed lightly, though she did extend her hands for his inspection. "I am quite well. I assure you we have been sitting by the fire for some time, and Mr Darcy has just brought tea. Speaking of which, it is you whom we must worry about now! Come, let me take your coat, and we shall move closer to the hearth, so you may recover from the chill." At Elizabeth's words, Darcy reached for his greatcoat, offering to stable Dr Harper's horse. When he returned to the warmth of the parlour, he found Elizabeth and her uncle sitting by the fire, each with cups of tea held tightly between their hands.

"Mr Darcy," Dr Harper began as soon as he was seated nearby, "I owe you a great debt for coming to my niece's aid this morning. Pray, forgive me for not expressing my gratitude at once. Elizabeth has been telling me about her adventures, and I cannot thank you enough for your prompt intervention."

Darcy offered the gentleman a slight tilt of his chin, saying seriously, "There is no debt, sir. Miss Bennet is a guest in my home—I could not have done otherwise."

Dr Harper nodded his understanding, then paused, his gaze narrowing slightly in confusion. "But is there no one else with you, sir? Surely you did not go in search of my niece all on your own?"

Darcy could feel the heat building in his cheeks at the man's near accusation, but when he spoke, it was with his usual quiet authority.

"I did, yes. It was still early when I set out, and I did not want to lose a moment by awakening any of the other gentlemen to accompany me. Besides, I know the property better than anyone, and I felt that I could cover more ground on my own. Luckily, I was able to locate Miss Bennet quickly, else I certainly should have returned to the house to gather up a larger party."

Across from him, Dr Harper nodded slowly. "I see. Well, again, you have my thanks for your timely intervention, though I would still like to look Elizabeth over more thoroughly once we return to the main house."

Elizabeth sighed, fixing her uncle with an indulgent smile. "Very well, if you must. But while you are at it, I would appreciate it if you would see to Mr Darcy as well. He fell earlier and hit his shoulder."

At Elizabeth's words, Darcy sucked in a breath, but if she noticed, she did not let on. For Dr Harper's part, he merely glanced over at Darcy, nodding easily before saying, "I am not surprised. The walkway outside is a sheet of ice. I was lucky to have made it to the front door in one piece. It would be my privilege to take a look, sir, if you will allow it?"

They stayed until the snow stopped falling—just long enough for Elizabeth's uncle to shake off the winter's chill and for Mr Darcy to return the tea things to the kitchen. Although the fire had been extinguished, a trace of heat still lingered in the air, momentarily dulling the memory of their earlier peril.

Elizabeth stood beside her uncle, wrapped once again in her thick pelisse, which was now mercifully warm and dry, waiting for Mr Darcy to return with the horses so they could make their way back to the great house before the snow began falling again. Though the room was no longer cold, her fingers trembled as she tugged her gloves more snugly into place. "Uncle," she began slowly, "I hope… That is, you will not say anything, will you? About finding me and Mr Darcy alone here together?"

Her uncle gave her a measured look, his head tilting slightly in question, and Elizabeth hurried to add, "Nothing untoward occurred, I can assure you—Mr Darcy has always been a perfect gentleman. But I would not wish for him to feel any sort of pressure to… That is, people might assume…" She looked away, her cheeks warming as she struggled to find the right words.

Her uncle's expression gentled as he gave her shoulder a reassuring squeeze. "Very well. I see no reason to incite rumours where no just cause exists. You have nothing to fear from me."

Elizabeth exhaled quietly, though her heart still fluttered at the thought of what might have been whispered had they been discovered by someone else. After a moment, her uncle added with a knowing glint in his eye, "As far as I can recall, I believe we all converged on the dower house at precisely the same time, did we not?"

The smile he turned on her was light and playful, and she could not help but smile back.

"Yes, sir," she answered, "Indeed, I believe we did."

Chapter Eighteen

Elizabeth awoke on the morning of Christmas Eve to the muted glow of sunlight filtering through the curtains of her bedchamber at Pemberley. The fire in the hearth had burned low but still cast a gentle warmth that wrapped around her like the counterpanes piled high upon her bed. She stretched beneath the covers, savouring the comfort and security.

As the memories of the previous day crept back into her mind, Elizabeth rolled over, gazing at the embers glowing in the grate. What a day it had been. She, Mr Darcy, and her uncle Harper had returned to the house to find it in a state of uproar. Mr Bingley and her uncle Gardiner had already donned their greatcoats and were preparing to set out on horseback, joined by half a dozen of Mr Darcy's footmen, to search for them. The look of relief on their faces when they saw her step inside, safe and unharmed, had been nearly enough to bring tears to her eyes.

And then there had been the astonishment—followed

quickly by joy—when Mrs Gardiner noticed her brother. Dr Harper had been swept into the cheerful embrace of the family gathering, and Elizabeth had been swiftly bundled off to her chambers with orders to rest and recover.

She could still feel the luxurious heat of the bath water that had been promptly brought up, easing the chill from her bones and washing away the remnants of her ordeal. Afterwards, she had spent the day nestled in her bed under a mountain of blankets, comforted by the fire and the steady stream of visitors who rarely left her side. Jane, her aunt, and even Miss Darcy had taken turns sitting beside her bed, pressing cups of tea into her hands and bringing her hot broth and porridge until she protested that she could eat no more.

But it was in the quiet moments, when her visitors had retreated and left her alone with her thoughts, that Elizabeth truly began to comprehend everything she had learned at the dower house. Mr Darcy's confession, his fears, and his relentless determination to shield his sister—it all fell into place like pieces of a scattered puzzle. Behaviours she had once found peculiar, even frustrating, now made perfect sense in light of what he had shared.

She thought back to the Meryton assembly, where his unwillingness to stand up with Jane—and his general reluctance to dance—had provoked widespread offence. How he had spent the evening at the periphery of the room, lingering in shadowed corners or gazing out of darkened windows, as though the light and noise were somehow unbearable.

By his own admission, he avoided social gatherings whenever possible, and when obliged to attend, he never danced. His preference for walking rather than riding, unless necessity dictated otherwise, had once seemed an oddity in a gentleman of his station. But now, she understood.

Then there were the subtler details—those she had observed without considering their significance. She had never seen him partake of more than a sip of wine, much less the stronger spirits most gentlemen favoured. His aversion to sitting too near a roaring fire. His rigid self-control, his unshakable reserve, the way he deflected attention in a crowded room—all bespoke a man deeply attuned to his own limitations and determined to avoid anything that might test them.

How often had she heard others remark on his aloofness, his absence from society, his apparent disdain for all but his closest confidants? Yet now, with the truth laid bare, she saw it for what it was: Pemberley was more than his ancestral home—it was his refuge. Within its walls, he found the solitude he craved, the company of trusted companions like Mr Walsh and Colonel Fitzwilliam, and the freedom to live without the relentless scrutiny of society's expectations.

And then there were his episodes—those moments when his body betrayed him—which struck most often in times of great strain or heightened emotion. The death of his mother. The pressure of university exams. The torment of watching his father's final illness, followed by the crushing weight of managing a vast estate alone. Even the storm that had driven him into the woods in search of her—exacerbated by the firelight in the dower house—had likely precipitated yesterday's attack.

His reserve, his pride, even his perceived indifference—all seemed to be born not from arrogance but from a deep-rooted vulnerability and an implacable need to shield himself from the judgment of the world.

As these revelations settled upon her, Elizabeth felt her heart clench with an ache she could not quite name.

In the short time she had known Mr Darcy, she had come to admire his strength—his unflinching sense of duty, his loyalty to his family, his unwavering principles. But now she saw that his fortitude ran deeper still. Every measured action, every carefully weighed decision, was a testament to his courage. He had spent half a lifetime waging a quiet, unseen battle against his own body, carrying a burden few could begin to comprehend. And yet, through it all, he had persevered—not for himself, but for those he loved.

A wave of humility washed over her. How hasty she had been to judge him, to assume arrogance where there was only pain, to mistake restraint for indifference. She thought of the way he had carried himself as he spoke at the dower house, his voice steady even as he recounted the most vulnerable moments of his life. He had not sought compassion. He had not asked for understanding. Yet, as she sat in the stillness of her room, Elizabeth resolved to give him both.

It was Christmas Eve, and if this was to be Mr Darcy's last festive season at Pemberley, she intended to do everything in her power to make it one he would not soon forget.

Darcy stepped into the entrance hall, shrugging off the winter chill as a rush of warmth washed over him. Outside, the wind still howled across the grounds, carrying with it the sting of ice and snow, but within the house, all was calm. He had just handed his greatcoat off to a waiting footman when his attention was caught by the unexpected sight before him. Garlands of fresh greenery adorned the balustrades, their dark leaves gleaming in the golden light of the chandelier. The air was tinged with the crisp scent of pine and holly, mingling with the faint trace of beeswax polish. He stood motionless for a moment, taking in the scene before him with measured thought. He had not given Hastings or Reynolds any directives regarding the decorating of the space, and it was unlike either of them to take such an initiative without his explicit instruction. The hall, though striking in its festivity, seemed suddenly unfamiliar —Pemberley shaped by a hand other than his own.

A burst of laughter rang out from deeper within the house, prompting Darcy to follow the sound to the library doors. There, he paused at the threshold, momentarily taken aback by the sight before him. The expansive room, with its towering shelves of leather-bound volumes, was bathed in the amber light of late afternoon, the warmth of a fire crackling cheerfully in the hearth. Furniture had been pushed aside, and Elizabeth Bennet and her sister Jane knelt upon the Persian rug, their hands weaving ivy and holly into wreaths, their laps littered with sprigs of fir and laurel. Beside them sat Georgiana, her delicate fingers fumbling slightly as she attempted to secure a wayward branch of yew into a garland. Scattered around them were a multitude of ribbons in deep crimson and forest green, a pair of pruning shears, and an array of freshly cut greenery. A small basket of scarlet berries rested beside Elizabeth, and as he watched, she deftly secured a spray of them to her work, her eyes bright with merriment. Shifting his gaze back to his sister, he noted the rosiness of her cheeks and the gentle smile that played upon her lips, though her eyes remained fixed upon her task.

For a long moment, he just stood, transfixed by the tableau before him, but then Elizabeth turned, catching him out. Her smile seemed to falter slightly when their eyes met, but when she spoke, it was with her usual good humour.

"Ah, Mr Darcy! I hope you do not mind that we have transformed your library into our workshop for the afternoon."

Stepping farther into the room, he once again surveyed the scene before saying slowly, "Not at all, but…I do not understand. Where did all this come from?"

Georgiana instantly stood, hurrying to meet him, her voice spilling forth in a breathless rush, "From the grounds, of course! Well, except for the ribbons. Those came from the attics. It was all Elizabeth's idea! To decorate the house, I mean. Mr Bingley and Dr Harper helped us to cut everything down, and Mr Hastings sent two footmen to assist with carrying it all home."

Darcy blinked back at her. To say that he had never seen his usually reticent sister this exuberant would be an understatement, and for a moment, he was at a loss for words.

Apparently, he was silent too long, for as he watched, Georgiana's face fell, and her cheeks grew pale. "You are not angry, are you?" she asked in a voice scarcely above a whisper.

"No, not at all," he replied at once. "Forgive me for my reserve. I was merely surprised…and concerned that all you young ladies might have been out so long in the cold, but especially you, Miss Elizabeth, after your adventure yesterday morning," he added, turning in her direction.

Elizabeth flushed slightly at his words, but when she looked up at him, her eyes were bright.

"Oh, I am well recovered, I assure you. And it was done for the good of Pemberley, after all. Even the grandest of houses deserves a touch of festive cheer, do you not agree?"

Despite his best intentions, Darcy smiled back at her.

"Well then, I suppose I shall leave you to it." Taking a few tentative steps towards the door, he then turned to enquire after the remainder of the party.

"My aunt was helping us for a time," Elizabeth replied, "but she has gone up to rest. I believe you will find the gentlemen in the billiards room. That is, unless you would care to assist us in our work?" Turning to his sister, she continued in a playful tone, "Georgiana, do you not think your brother would make an excellent hand at securing these ribbons?"

"Indeed," his sister answered, her cheeks dimpling with evident delight, "and he is tall enough to help us hang the garlands in the places we cannot reach."

Darcy's lips quirked, though he made a show of considering her words. "Very well," he said, already beginning to remove his coat. "I cannot promise my creations will meet such exacting standards, but as my sister so kindly pointed out, I do have the advantage of height on my side. Now, tell me, where are we to place these wreaths?"

೫

Once the remainder of the greenery had been hung, everyone retired to their respective chambers for some much-needed rest and to ready themselves for dinner and the evening's festivities.

While the Christmas feast would take place the following day, Cook had still managed to prepare a meal that included hearty dishes of roasted venison and beef and a variety of savoury pies, which were served alongside a spiced wassail punch and mulled wine to warm everyone's spirits.

Afterwards, they retired to the drawing room, which had taken on a festive air. A fire blazed in the marble hearth, while candles were lit throughout the space, casting a cheerful glow. But it was their earlier handiwork that truly completed the alteration: evergreen garlands adorned nearly every surface, while wreaths studded with bright red berries hung over the mantelpiece, and the air was scented with pine, mingled with the heady aromas of baking spices wafting up from the kitchens below.

Georgiana and Elizabeth took turns at the instrument, and they all sang carols. After some time, Mrs Reynolds came in with several footmen carrying silver trays laden with coffee, tea, mulled wine, and chocolate as well as small cakes and biscuits, roasted chestnuts, and candied and fresh fruits, and they all ate and made merry.

Next there were parlour games, including *Hunt the*

Slipper, charades, and a lively round of *Snapdragon*, which Elizabeth easily won.

Afterwards, they all settled around the dwindling fire, and Dr Harper—who had a sonorous baritone—read aloud from William Cowper and Shakespeare's sonnets.

Now, as the evening drew to a close, Darcy stood near the hearth, his glass of port untouched, surveying the room. The evening had been a joyful one—laughter and lively conversation weaving through the space as the group gathered to celebrate. Even Georgiana, typically reserved in company, had seemed unusually at ease, her soft laughter ringing out more than once.

Yet for all the warmth of the gathering, Darcy's thoughts continually led him back to Elizabeth. Since their return to the house late yesterday morning, they had not shared a moment alone, and the absence of any private conversation weighed on him more than he cared to admit. Although she had displayed her usual cheerful demeanour, effortlessly charming those around her, he could not shake the feeling that she was avoiding him. Her glances had been fleeting, her attention carefully fixed elsewhere whenever he drew near.

So, when she deliberately approached, his heart quickened, though he schooled his features into calm composure. She stopped a few paces away, her posture poised yet her expression unreadable.

"Mr Darcy, I wonder whether I might solicit your opinion on a book I recently finished?" she asked lightly, but her dark eyes carried a weight of earnestness that belied her casual tone.

"Of course," he replied, his voice low but steady. "If I may be of service, I am happy to oblige."

Elizabeth nodded, before sharing the title. "It is a novel Georgiana was kind enough to lend me when we first arrived. I found it most engaging. Have you read it?"

"I regret to say I have not," Darcy admitted, his curiosity piqued by the subtle shift in her tone. To his surprise, her smile deepened.

"Well then, I think you must," she said, her gaze holding his for a fleeting moment. "I believe you would find it extremely enlightening."

Darcy inclined his head, murmuring his thanks, but before he could say more, Elizabeth offered him a brief curtsey and turned away, moving across the room to rejoin her aunt. He watched her retreat, her words lingering in his mind with curious persistence. What had she meant? And why had the encounter felt so charged with unspoken significance?

When, not long afterwards, the clock struck midnight, happy tidings were exchanged, yawns were stifled, and cups were set aside as everyone made their way towards the staircase to retire for the evening.

Darcy, who had stayed behind to speak to his butler, noticed upon reaching the landing that Elizabeth hung back from the others, and she called to him as he reached the upper floor.

"Mr Darcy," she said once he was within earshot, "might I ask you to wait just a moment? I should like to fetch that book for you."

Still slightly puzzled by her sudden interest in sharing the novel, Darcy agreed. He waited at the top of the stairs as she retreated down the guest corridor, reappearing moments later with three handsome leather volumes in hand.

He accepted them with a slight bow, once again wishing her a good evening before turning in the direction of his chambers. But he had not gone more than a handful of steps before he heard Elizabeth call out quietly behind him.

"I particularly think you will enjoy chapter twenty, in the first volume," she said, her eyes holding his for the briefest of moments.

Darcy blinked but quickly recovered his composure. "Thank you, Miss Elizabeth. I shall look forward to reading it."

She nodded, her expression indecipherable, and then added softly, "Good night, Mr Darcy. And a very happy Christmas."

Before he could respond, she turned and disappeared down the passageway, leaving him standing there with the books in his hands.

Once Elizabeth had vanished from sight, Darcy made his way to his chambers with all due haste, chasing away his valet and perching on the edge of one of the armchairs in his sitting room as he turned the pages of the first volume with clumsy fingers.

Chapter twenty… When he finally landed on the appropriate page, he began eagerly skimming the text. He could not fathom why Elizabeth had taken such pains to mention that particular part to him, but he knew her well enough to believe that if she had done so, it was not by chance.

It was not until he was four pages into the chapter that he noticed something written faintly in pencil in the right-hand margin. Holding the book closer to the fire, he could just decipher the faint inscription: *Two o'clock.* Darcy's gaze quickly shifted to the sentence beside it: *I shall be glad to have the library to myself as soon as may be.*

His heart began to pound, the steady rhythm quickening as the implications of the note took shape. The library, at two. This morning, he had to presume... His eyes darted to the clock on the mantelpiece. Twenty past twelve.

Was Elizabeth attempting to arrange an assignation, of all things?

He closed the book, but his fingers lingered on the cover, tracing its embossing as his thoughts raced. Surely he had misunderstood. Elizabeth Bennet would never be so reckless as to summon him to meet her in the middle of the night. Would she? And yet, she had made a very specific point of pressing this volume into his hands and had even emphasized the chapter specifically. Could it have been a mere coincidence? No, he could not believe that it was.

Rising abruptly, Darcy crossed the room, his steps restless. He paused before the window, his gaze fixed on the moonlit grounds, though his thoughts were far from the quiet scene beyond the glass. What could Elizabeth wish to say to him at so late an hour and in such secrecy? Was it something she dared not speak of in daylight, or in the presence of others?

Unbidden, an image from their time together at the dower house appeared in his mind: her touch, warm and steady, grounding him in his most vulnerable moments. Her words—gentle but fierce in their defence of his character—echoed in his ears.

Darcy briefly closed his eyes, the memory searing. Her

kindness, her courage, her ability to look beyond his flaws and see the man beneath—it was a gift he had neither expected nor deserved. And now this.

His hands flexed at his sides before he turned back towards the fireplace, his jaw tightening. If he went, what would it mean? Could he risk another moment alone with her, knowing the strength of his feelings? And yet, if he did not go—if he let this chance slip away—would he regret it for the remainder of his days?

The mantel clock chimed, marking the half-hour. Darcy's gaze returned to the book, still resting on the table where he had left it. The decision loomed before him, weighted with uncertainty, yet in the deepest recesses of his heart, he knew it was no decision at all.

Drawing a steadying breath, he straightened, his resolve hardening. Whatever awaited him in the library at two o'clock, he would face it. He was helpless to do otherwise.

Darcy moved silently through the dimly lit corridors, the faint glow of the wall sconces casting long shadows that flickered as he passed. The house was strangely quiet, the footmen who stood watch by day now absent, as though the great house itself had hushed in anticipation of what was to come.

His footsteps slowed as he approached the library doors. Pausing, he drew in a steadying breath, his fingers tightening briefly before he lifted the latch and stepped inside.

The library was shrouded in a golden glow, the fire in

the hearth reduced to a bed of smouldering embers, its weak light casting faint shadows against the high ceiling. And there, standing near the centre of the room, was Elizabeth.

She was simply dressed, her gown a modest departure from the finery she had worn earlier in the evening. Her hair, while neatly arranged, lacked the elaborate adornments of a formal gathering, and the effect was one of quiet elegance. But it was her expression—nervous, yet resolute—that captured Darcy's attention and set his pulse quickening.

Closing the door, he offered her a shallow bow before moving farther into the large space. "Miss Bennet," he greeted, his voice low, though the stillness of the room carried it easily to her.

"Mr Darcy." She inclined her head, her hands clasped before her. "You came."

"I did," he replied.

Her lips curved faintly, but her eyes remained fixed on his. "I was not certain whether you would decipher my message, or agree to meet me, even if you did."

"I was not sure myself. You are putting your reputation at great risk, contriving such an assignation—in the dead of night, unchaperoned."

Elizabeth regarded him with a measured look, her chin tipped up ever so slightly. "I am aware of the risks. However, I needed a moment alone with you, and I could not be certain I would have another opportunity."

Before Darcy could respond, she brushed past him, crossing to the door and, with deliberate intent, turning the key in the lock. The click of the mechanism falling into place echoed in the silence, and Darcy's heart began to hammer inside his chest.

His breath hitched as his gaze followed her movements. "If you are thinking to force a proposal," he began, his voice thick with emotion, "I warn you, it will not work."

Elizabeth turned back to him, her expression calm, though her cheeks were flushed. "Rest easy, Mr Darcy," she answered simply. "I have no desire to win you by force."

"Then what—" Darcy's words died in his throat as Elizabeth turned away. As he watched, she reached behind her neck, her slender fingers deftly beginning to work the buttons at the back of her gown.

His throat tightened, panic—and something far more potent—surging through him. "What—what are you doing?" he croaked, his voice hoarse and barely audible.

Elizabeth did not respond, her fingers continuing their task with a practised ease that made his heart pound erratically. He stood rooted to the spot, torn between alarm and a helpless fascination. His breath quickened, each inhalation shallow and uneven, as he struggled to regain his self-control. He knew he should stop her, or at the very least look away, but he could scarcely move.

"Elizabeth, pray, do not…" he whispered at last, his voice breaking, just as the bodice of her gown slipped from one shoulder. The curve of her collarbone and the smooth expanse of her skin glowed in the firelight, drawing his gaze as though compelled by an unseen force.

She turned to face him then, and her eyes, steady and unflinching, met his. For a moment, he could do nothing but look back at her, the space between them taut with something unspoken, something that crackled like a gathering storm. But then his eyes drifted, drawn irresistibly to the pale skin laid bare before him.

And there, just below her shoulder, was a mark—irregular in shape, like a splash of ink, its edges softened as if faded by time. It stood in stark contrast to the otherwise perfect smoothness of her skin.

Elizabeth's voice broke the silence, low but steady. "It has been with me since birth. I have always hated it, though my mother used to tell me I should be grateful it was in a location that was so easily concealed." She paused for a moment before looking back at him with a steady resolve. "So, you see, Mr Darcy, none of us is perfect."

Darcy's throat tightened, and he swallowed hard. "You are so beautiful," he whispered, the words escaping before he could think better of them. His gaze lingered, reverent and awestruck, before he continued, "And I love you for revealing this. For trusting me and for trying to convince me that, in some small way, this makes us equals in our imperfections. But it is not the same."

"Is it not?"

"No," he replied firmly, even as his voice trembled. Tearing his gaze away, he paced back a step, as if distance might lend clarity to his thoughts. "Your mark is superficial —a curiosity, nothing more. Whereas I—" He broke off, his hands clenched at his sides. "I am not whole, Elizabeth! I am deeply, irrevocably flawed—on the inside. Can you not see that?"

Her expression gentled, her lips parting as though to respond, but Darcy cut her off, his voice rising. "And before you say it does not matter, it does. It matters to me."

Elizabeth's expression turned distant, her gaze falling as

she looked away. With careful movements, she reached for the bodice of her gown, tugging it back into place before briskly fastening the buttons.

"Very well," she said, her voice resolved. "You have made your wishes abundantly clear, and I now see that there is nothing I can do to alter your opinion. But I would like to ask something of you, just the same." She turned back to face him, her eyes steady, and Darcy inclined his head in reply.

"If it is in my power to give, then you know that you will have it."

"You may not feel that way when you have heard what it is," Elizabeth answered. "I would like you to speak to my uncle Harper...in a professional capacity."

Darcy began to shake his head, and Elizabeth immediately raised a hand to forestall his refusal.

"I know what you would say, but you saw that physician *years* ago. And if you are worried for your reputation, I assure you, my uncle would never reveal your secret."

Darcy released a ragged breath. While he could not fault Elizabeth for grasping at straws, he knew agreeing to her request would only raise her hopes—a cruelty he wished to spare her. Yet, despite himself, he hesitated, her determination making it nearly impossible to refuse.

"It is not that I do not trust your uncle's discretion," Darcy answered slowly, "but you must understand, the physician I saw was an expert in maladies of the mind. I mean no disrespect, but Dr Harper is a country doctor. It is unlikely that he has ever encountered a case such as mine, and even if he has, Dr Abernathy was very clear on my prognosis—there is no cure."

"I know. And I am sure you think me very foolish, but I just... I would still wish for you to speak to him, if you are willing. It certainly cannot make things any worse, and he is right here at Pemberley, after all."

Once again, Darcy sighed. He knew better than to believe that Elizabeth's uncle would have anything to offer by way of assistance, but she was right about one thing: speaking to him could certainly do no harm.

"Very well. If it pleases you, I shall do as you ask. But Elizabeth, I beg you not to expect too much. My prognosis will not change, nor will my intentions."

Chapter Nineteen

◆◆◆

After parting with Elizabeth the previous night, Darcy had returned to his chambers and dashed off a brief note to Dr Harper, handing it to his valet at first light and asking that it be delivered without delay.

As was his custom, he had awoken early, washed, and dressed. But instead of breakfasting, he made his way to his study. It was there that the physician found him, arriving promptly at the appointed time and knocking lightly on the open door.

Darcy immediately stood, beckoning the gentleman in and motioning for him to take one of the two chairs opposite his desk.

"Thank you for coming," he began, moving to close the heavy mahogany door before returning to his own seat.

Across from him, Dr Harper dipped his chin. "Of course. I am at your disposal, sir. Indeed, it sounded like a matter of some urgency."

Darcy offered the gentleman a single nod, but beyond

that, he found himself momentarily at a loss, his practised eloquence deserting him in the face of the task before him. He opened his mouth to speak but faltered, and Harper's perceptive gaze softened.

"Your note mentioned you had a question of a medical nature," the physician gently probed, his tone one of encouragement. "Is your shoulder still bothering you, from your fall the other day?"

"Ah, no." Darcy looked away, shuffling some papers on his desk before saying, "Though I do have a medical issue on which I would welcome your advice. But first, I wish to thank you," he began, "for your discretion regarding the events at the dower house, the day you arrived. I know that what you witnessed could easily have been misconstrued, and I am grateful for your circum-spection."

Dr Harper waved the words away with a small smile. "You owe me no thanks for that. Elizabeth's character speaks for itself. If she says nothing untoward occurred, I believe her." He paused for a moment before continuing, "Does the matter you wished to speak to me about have to do with my niece?"

Darcy hesitated. "Not directly, no, although she is aware of all I am about to relate. It was at Miss Elizabeth's prompting that I asked to see you," he admitted. "She believed—believes—that you may be able to offer guid-ance on a...personal matter."

And so, Darcy began. He kept his account brief, recounting the essentials of what he had already told Eliza-beth. He spoke of his first attack, of the fear and confusion it had wrought, and of his father's efforts to find help. The ineffective treatments he had already tried, and the years of secrecy and shame that had followed.

Dr Harper listened intently, stopping Darcy occasionally to ask for clarification or to follow up on something he had said.

When Darcy finished his recitation, silence stretched between them for a moment before the physician leaned back in his chair, his expression thoughtful. "So, it is the falling sickness," he eventually offered, "or epilepsy, as it is more properly called."

Darcy's gaze remained fixed upon the pile of correspondence in front of him. "Yes."

The doctor regarded him carefully before speaking again. "Well, you are in good company. Great men throughout history have been thought to have suffered from the affliction—Socrates, Julius Caesar, Alexander the Great, as well as many others. In fact, the ancient Greeks used to refer to epilepsy as 'the sacred disease'. But then, I suspect you know all this already."

Darcy nodded, pulling his lips up into a humourless smile. "I have read everything I can find on the subject. But nothing I have learned has offered much in the way of hope when it comes to controlling the disease, or more importantly, uncovering a cure."

"And the physician you mentioned? The one in Edinburgh?" Dr Harper enquired.

"Tonics and tinctures—none of which proved effective. Although he was touted as an expert in the field, his knowledge was rudimentary, at best. All he could tell me was that it was a malady of the mind and was likely hereditary."

Dr Harper was silent for a long moment, a crease

forming along his forehead as he considered. Finally, he began speaking in a low tone. "This is not my area of expertise," he admitted, "but I have colleagues—trusted men—whose work does venture into such matters. If you wish it, I would be more than willing to write to them on your behalf."

"You would do that?" Darcy asked. "Of course," the physician replied without hesitation. "No man should carry such a burden alone."

Darcy swallowed hard, the words settling heavily in his chest. He was not yet certain what such an offer might yield, but for the first time in a very long while, the path ahead did not feel entirely impassable.

Lost in his thoughts, he startled when Dr Harper spoke again.

"You mentioned earlier," he began, his tone measured, "that you had taken Elizabeth into your confidence. However, am I correct in assuming that your condition is not widely known?"

Darcy responded with a curt nod. "Only a few trusted members of my household and a handful of close relations are aware of it. I have taken great care to ensure it remains that way."

"And yet, you chose to tell Elizabeth."

Heat prickled at the base of Darcy's neck, but when he spoke his reply was even. "Yes, though I did not set out to do so. Elizabeth witnessed an episode at the dower house. I could not let her leave without an explanation."

At the use of his niece's given name, Dr Harper lifted a brow but chose not to remark on it. Instead, he shifted the conversation. "Ah, the fall you mentioned?"

Darcy inclined his head in acknowledgement.

"Well," the doctor said with a faint smile, "you could not have chosen a better confidant. Elizabeth is, as I am sure you have noticed, an extraordinarily sensible young lady. My sister has often spoken of her remarkable composure. And, if I may add, she is also quite lovely."

"That she is," Darcy murmured, his gaze dropping to the floor. When he glanced up again, Dr Harper was studying him with an expression that bordered on amusement.

"You are in love with her."

Darcy noted that it was not a question, and he briefly looked away, his shoulders sagging under the weight of unspoken thoughts. When he turned back to face the lady's uncle, all he could seem to manage was a tentative nod, before saying in a hoarse whisper, "More than I can bear to admit."

"I see." After a moment he added, "And unless I very much miss my guess, it would seem she is in love with you."

Once again, Darcy was taken aback by Harper's quiet certainty.

"I cannot think why she would be, given all I have confessed. But the matter is immaterial. If you are asking whether I intend to marry her, the answer is no."

Harper's expression grew solemn; however he did not immediately argue. Instead, he regarded Darcy thoughtfully, as though deliberating the best way to proceed.

"I see," he repeated, his voice carefully neutral. "Forgive me for my presumption, but I feel compelled to ask. Is there any reason you *should* marry her?"

Darcy tensed at the implication, and heat crept into his cheeks as a fleeting memory of their kiss rose unbidden in his mind.

"Certainly not! If you are insinuating that I would debase Elizabeth in such a way, I would never show her such disrespect."

"So, you are prepared to let her go?" Dr Harper asked, his voice sharp. "This woman you love beyond all reason?"

Darcy straightened, startled by the intensity in the other man's tone. Yet, when he replied, his voice remained steady. "I am. Unless you have some magical potion to make me whole again, then yes. I shall let her go."

Dr Harper's eyes flashed, and he leaned forwards in his chair. "Then you are a fool."

Darcy flinched at the harshness of the words, but before he could object, the man pressed on.

"I am sorry, Mr Darcy, but if you are looking for sympathy, you will receive none from me. Do you have any idea how fortunate you are to have found the kind of mutual affection you share with my niece and to be able to act upon it? To have the right to join your life with hers, openly, as man and wife? To build a family and a future together?" He paused, his voice breaking. "Dear God, I would give *anything*…"

The doctor abruptly stood, pacing several feet away, his voice faltering as he struggled for composure. Meanwhile, Darcy sat in stunned silence as the pieces slowly began falling into place. Dr Harper's vehemence, his sudden loss of equanimity—it was too personal, too raw.

Realization struck, and with it came understanding. This—this was why Elizabeth had so easily misinterpreted his relationship with Walsh. She knew someone who bore the scars of a secret life, and she had witnessed its toll. The physician's sudden loss of composure revealed far more than the man likely intended.

He regarded the physician, his features soft. "I am sorry," he said quietly. "Truly sorry."

Dr Harper did not meet his gaze immediately, but when he finally turned, his expression was carefully guarded. "Such is the way of things," he said, his tone resigned. "I apologize for my outburst. I should be accustomed to it by now."

Darcy slowly inclined his head. "And your family? Are they aware of how things stand?"

The physician hesitated before nodding. "The relations I trust, yes. I confided in my sister long ago, and I gave her leave to tell Gardiner before they married. To his credit, my brother-in-law has never treated me with anything but kindness and respect, for which I shall always be grateful."

"And Elizabeth?" Darcy asked, though he felt he already knew the answer.

Dr Harper exhaled, his shoulders easing slightly. "Yes. Elizabeth and Jane know. But I would not have the rest of the Bennets informed."

Darcy managed a faint smile, nodding his comprehension. He could all too easily imagine Mrs Bennet's hysterics and the youngest sisters' careless gossip.

They fell into a contemplative silence, the crackle of the fire the only sound between them. Darcy reflected on the other man's burden—a lifetime spent concealing the truth, navigating the world under the weight of society's judgment, shaping every choice around what would be deemed acceptable. Was it so different, he wondered, from his own fears? The relentless effort to conceal his affliction, to move through each day with the quiet dread of being discovered?

And yet Harper had endured. He had carved out a future for himself despite it all.

Darcy's gaze returned to the man standing before him, and something shifted. A kinship. Perhaps better than anyone, Elizabeth's uncle knew what it meant to live with a secret.

And in that moment, Darcy was certain that he could trust Harper with his own.

Elizabeth awoke on Christmas morning far later than usual, the pale winter light doing little to dispel the shadows left by a restless night. Sitting up slowly, she pressed her fingers to her temples as memories of her meeting with Mr Darcy came rushing back. The heaviness in her chest threatened to pull her into a spiral of melancholy, but a knock at the sitting room door drew her from her thoughts.

Quickly wrapping herself in her dressing gown, Elizabeth went to answer. But when she entered the adjoining chamber, she found Jane, dressed and ready for the day, opening the door to the corridor. To their mutual surprise, Georgiana stepped inside, her cheeks flushed and her eyes bright with anticipation.

Elizabeth's nightclothes drew a brief falter in the girl's expression, and she instantly began stammering an apology, but Elizabeth waved it aside.

"You do not need to beg *my* forgiveness. I am the one at fault for oversleeping. Give me just a moment, and I shall be ready to join you both downstairs."

Once Elizabeth was dressed and refreshed, the three ladies descended to the breakfast room, where the rest of the household had already gathered. The scent of fresh rolls and spiced tea mingled with the faint aroma of greenery adorning the house, filling the room with a cheer that matched the lively conversation. For a time, Elizabeth allowed herself to be swept up in the merriment.

Although it was Christmas morning, the heavy snow made attending church services impossible. Instead, the party assembled in the saloon, where Mr Darcy stood before them, the family Bible in hand. His rich, steady voice filled the air as he read passages appropriate to the season. Elizabeth watched him intently, noting the calm authority with which he commanded the room's attention.

Afterwards, the pianoforte was opened, and the ladies took turns exhibiting. Georgiana's playing, as always, was exquisite, her slender fingers weaving beautiful melodies. Elizabeth, though she contributed a lively tune, found her heart was not truly in it. She worked to keep her smiles warm and her spirits high, yet a faint pall seemed to linger over her. She could not help but notice that Mr Darcy, too, appeared more subdued than usual, his moments of quiet reflection almost palpable.

The Christmas feast that followed was a lavish affair. The table was laden with roasted pheasant, venison, spiced puddings, and cakes, all prepared with exceptional care. Candles flickered in polished silver holders, casting a golden glow over the faces of those gathered. Laughter rang out, and glasses were raised in toasts to health and happiness; but for Elizabeth, the joy of the moment felt just out of reach.

As the afternoon waned and the party separated into smaller groups, Elizabeth sought a reprieve. Noting that Jane had secured Mr Bingley's attention—the pair were settled contentedly before the fire, where Jane was sharing her newly acquired copy of Berenger's *The History and Art of Horsemanship*—while Mr Gardiner and Mr Darcy were sitting in a corner discussing political matters as Miss Darcy and Mrs Gardiner kept themselves amused at the pianoforte, she sought out her uncle Harper.

Having made arrangements to meet in one of the small sitting rooms on an upper floor, Elizabeth soon slipped away, where she found the gentleman already waiting. The intimate space was warmed by a crackling fire, its gentle light softening the lines of her uncle's face as he regarded her carefully.

"You look tired, Lizzy," he said at last, a slight frown playing across his countenance. "I suspect you did not sleep well last night."

Elizabeth managed a faint smile. "No, Uncle, I fear I did not." She paused, her hands folding tightly in her lap. "But I have been hoping we might have a moment alone. Have you... That is, did you speak with Mr Darcy?"

He nodded, leaning back slightly in his chair. "I did. We spoke at length." He hesitated, his gaze resting on her, as though considering how best to proceed as Elizabeth's fingers fidgeted with the fabric of her gown.

"While I do not know Mr Darcy well," her uncle continued, "I can sense that he is a very proud and private man. I think it took a great deal of courage for him to come to me as he did, in no small part due to your encouragement, it would seem."

Elizabeth lowered her lashes, saying, "I only wished for him to have someone he could confide in. Someone who might offer him some assistance, where I could not."

"I appreciate your faith in me, but I must admit that Mr Darcy's malady is beyond my province. However, as I assured him, I have colleagues whose work does delve into such matters. I have offered to write to them on his behalf."

"Thank you," she replied, once again meeting his gaze. "That is more than I could have hoped for."

They were both quiet for a moment before Dr Harper began hesitantly, "Elizabeth, while I applaud you for wanting to be of service, you must understand that a man like Mr Darcy will not easily accept assistance. A gentleman such as he has likely been taught to value strength, independence, and self-reliance above all. To admit vulnerability, even to himself, must be profoundly difficult for him, I think."

Elizabeth's fingers tightened in her lap, her mind turning over his words. "I know," she answered quietly. "He guards his pride fiercely. But I cannot stand by and do nothing."

Dr Harper's expression warmed. "You care for Mr Darcy—a great deal."

Elizabeth's eyes dropped to her hands, her voice barely above a whisper. "I do."

Her uncle regarded her thoughtfully before saying, "Forgive me, Lizzy, if I speak out of turn, but I must confess that your aunt led me to believe that it was Mr Bingley who held your affections. Was she mistaken?"

A flush crept up Elizabeth's neck as she said haltingly, in a low voice, "No. It was never my intention to cause Mr Bingley any pain. My feelings for Mr Darcy have been coming on so gradually, I was in the middle before I knew I had begun. Now I fear I have made a muddle out of the entire situation."

Her uncle smiled gently back at her. "Not one that cannot be remedied, I suspect."

When Elizabeth did not answer, he continued, "Elizabeth, none of us possesses the power of choice when it comes to whom we love. I should know that better than most. But, if you have made your decision, you owe both gentlemen your honesty."

Elizabeth nodded miserably as Dr Harper continued, "And there is something else. With regard to Mr Darcy's condition, your path, should you choose to move forwards, will not be an easy one. There is no cure for what ails him, and should you continue to grow…closer, you must be prepared for the reality of what a life with him could require."

Elizabeth managed a faint smile. "I believe it is too late for caution, Uncle. My heart, I am afraid, already belongs to him."

"Yes, I suspected as much. However, as someone who has your best interests in mind, I would be remiss if I did not speak my piece. Marriage is not always easy, Elizabeth, even in the best of circumstances, but when one person has a debility such as Mr Darcy's…" His voice faded, and he looked away briefly before continuing, "Let us just say that

I have seen even the strongest relationships crumble under the weight of such trying circumstances."

Elizabeth nodded solemnly, feeling his words settle over her. Yet beneath the apprehension, her heart remained steadfast.

"Thank you, Uncle," she replied softly, "for your counsel and your kindness. But my mind is made up. I cannot turn away from Mr Darcy. Not now."

Her uncle sighed but offered her a small, approving smile. "Then I only hope he will let you in. That, my dearest Lizzy, may be the greatest test of all."

Chapter Twenty

E lizabeth and Jane returned to their apartment late that evening, the gentle light from the fireplace casting a soothing glow about the space. To their surprise, they found a silver tray resting upon the low table in their sitting room, bearing a pot of chocolate and a neatly arranged plate of biscuits. A brief note, penned in a careful hand, lay beside it.

Jane picked it up. "It is from Georgiana, thanking us for contributing to a most delightful Christmas."

Elizabeth smiled, touched by the young lady's thoughtfulness. "How very kind of her," she murmured, settling into a chair as Jane poured the rich, fragrant chocolate into their cups. The comforting aroma filled the room, mingling with the faint scent of pine and winter air that crept through the windowpanes.

For a time, they sipped in silence, savouring the warmth of the drink and the sweetness of the biscuits. However, her sister's thoughtful expression did not escape Elizabeth's attention.

At length, Jane set down her cup, saying with quiet concern, "Lizzy, are you well? I could not help but notice you have seemed…not quite yourself these past few days. Are you certain you are fully recovered from your ordeal in the snow?"

Elizabeth paused, the cup halfway to her lips, before attempting a reassuring smile. "I am perfectly well, I promise you. You need not trouble yourself on my account." Seeking to divert the conversation, she tilted her head thoughtfully before continuing, "Though, if we are speaking of such things, I might say the same of you. You seemed a bit melancholy this evening. It is not like you, especially as I know Christmas has always been one of your favourite days of the year."

Across from her, Jane sighed softly. "Forgive me, I did not mean to worry you. It is nothing of consequence. Only…I have been thinking a good deal about the future of late. Everything will change soon, I expect."

Elizabeth's lips parted slightly in confusion. "Change?"

Jane nodded, offering a wistful smile. "If you are to marry Mr Bingley, you will leave Longbourn, and I dare say I must soon follow suit. So, this may be our last Christmas together for some time."

Elizabeth felt her breath catch, a flicker of unease tightening in her chest at Jane's mention of Mr Bingley. Although she had come to accept that a marriage between them was out of the question, she could not, in good conscience, confide in Jane before addressing the matter with the gentleman himself.

Keeping her voice light, she replied evenly, "As Mr Bingley has yet to propose, our understanding is far from settled. But even if we were to marry, I should only be at Netherfield, which is scarcely three miles away. So I see little reason to worry over such a thing now."

But to Elizabeth's surprise, instead of appearing relieved, Jane offered up a wan smile.

"Perhaps it will be I who lives too far away to return for Christmas. If, say, I was to marry Mr Collins and make my home in Kent," she finished in a low tone, her gaze fixed upon her lap.

At Jane's words, Elizabeth startled, staring back at her sister with unconcealed alarm. "What? Marry Mr Collins? Jane, you cannot be serious!"

"And why not? I shall have to marry someone, after all, and with Mr Collins, at least Longbourn would remain in the family. He would be a prudent choice."

Elizabeth's distress deepened with every word. The very notion turned her stomach. "Jane, I absolutely forbid it!" she burst out, her agitation impossible to contain. "Mr Collins is an insufferable imbecile who would make you wretched for the rest of your days. You could not bear such a life."

Jane exhaled sharply. "And whom shall I marry, then, Lizzy? The butcher in Meryton? Or perhaps Uncle Philips's clerk? I think we both know there is no one in Hertford-shire who would suit me. And time does not stand still—for any of us."

Elizabeth's heart twisted, but Jane pressed on, her voice turning sombre. "I had thought, perhaps, Mr Darcy might be a worthy prospect, but that has come to nothing. In truth,

I dread returning home only to confess to Mama that I did not manage to secure his interest during our stay."

At her sister's words, Elizabeth's breath caught, and it took all her strength to ask gently, "Jane...do you care for Mr Darcy?"

Jane let out a small, humourless laugh before shaking her head. "No, Lizzy, I do not. And he has certainly never shown the slightest inclination towards me. But Mama..." She paused, exhaling slowly. "Mama has built castles in the air, and I know not how to restore her to reality."

Elizabeth's expression softened, and she reached out, taking her sister's hand in a reassuring grasp. "Jane, you must not think yourself bound to fulfil Mama's every whim. And most certainly not with Mr Collins."

"I know," Jane replied. "I spoke in jest, at least in part. But there is truth in my worries. Before long, I shall have to marry someone."

"Yes. But you deserve a husband who will cherish you, not merely offer you security. As for Mr Darcy, he would not have suited you, in any case."

Jane tilted her head, studying Elizabeth with a contemplative expression. "No, he would not. I do *like* the gentleman, of course," she hurried to add, "and I know you are fond of him. It is only that he is so very serious, and his countenance is severe most of the time. I do not think I could ever be entirely easy in his company."

Elizabeth offered her sister a wry smile before saying kindly, "You need not justify your feelings to me, Jane. I do like Mr Darcy—very much. But I can see that his temperament would not be agreeable to everybody."

To this, her sister nodded her agreement, saying

hurriedly, "It is just that I had always imagined my husband to be a gentleman of a more social disposition—one who delights in conversation, shares my interests, and whom I might speak to freely and easily."

Elizabeth blinked, her sister's words falling into place like the soft click of a latch, finding its hold.

"Someone like Mr Bingley..." she murmured.

"Well, yes!" Jane said with feeling before her cheeks turned rosy and she stammered, "That is not to say—of course, I do not mean Mr Bingley *specifically*."

"No, of course not," Elizabeth answered absently. She allowed her thoughts to drift for a moment longer before shaking them away with a measured breath. Then, turning to Jane, she offered a reassuring smile before pressing her hand with gentle affection. "In any case, you need not worry. The right gentleman will come along soon enough, I am certain of it. With your beauty and sweet disposition, how could it be otherwise?"

But to Elizabeth's surprise, Jane frowned back at her. Pulling her hand away, she rose from her seat, pacing across the carpet.

"Is that what you think I want? For some gentleman to offer for me simply because my appearance and manners are pleasing to him, without ever taking the trouble to learn anything about me?"

Elizabeth's mouth opened, but no words came, and Jane carried on, her cheeks flushed with emotion. "And as for being sweet and demure—did you ever consider that I am reserved in company because I have always been terrified of putting a foot wrong? That every word I utter feels like a trial?"

"Oh, Jane," Elizabeth whispered, her voice thick with emotion. "Forgive me for speaking so thoughtlessly. I had no idea—"

But Jane cut in, her voice rising. "But that is just it, Lizzy! You cannot begin to understand what it has been like for me—to feel as though the future of our entire family rests upon my shoulders. Since I was old enough to comprehend our situation, I have known that it would fall to me to raise our fortunes. For as long as I can remember, Mama has made it all too clear that my beauty is to be our salvation. That I must marry well or risk seeing our family reduced to ruin the moment Papa is gone."

Her breath quickened, and she turned away, her arms crossing tightly against her chest. "Do you have any idea what it has felt like to live under such a burden? To know that my mother sees me as nothing more than a means to an end? That I am to be bartered away to the highest bidder, like some prized thoroughbred, regardless of my own wishes?

"And you—" Jane's voice wavered before she steadied it once more, "—you have always declared that you would marry for nothing less than the deepest love. But I have never had that luxury. I shall marry where I must, despite my inclinations."

Elizabeth stared back at her sister, stunned into silence. A cold realization settled over her, guilt twisting sharply in her chest. Without a word, she rose swiftly and crossed the room.

"Oh, my dearest Jane," she murmured, pulling her sister into a fierce embrace. "Why did you never say any of this to me before? No, do not answer that. You should not have had to say it—I should have had the presence of mind to understand. But I was blind, like all the others. All I saw was your serenity, your grace, and your sweet disposition. I did not see because I did not take the trouble to see."

Jane trembled in her arms, silent tears slipping down her cheeks. "I did not wish to burden you," she whispered brokenly. "You have always had such a lively, carefree disposition, and I would never wish for that to change."

Elizabeth shook her head firmly, drawing back just enough to meet Jane's tear-filled eyes. "You should never have borne that weight alone. I see you now, Jane, *truly see you*. And I shall never forgive myself for failing to notice your pain."

Jane gave a small, choked sob and leaned into her sister's embrace. Elizabeth's arms tightened in a protective hold, as though she could shield Jane from every unkind expectation placed upon her slender shoulders.

The fire crackled quietly, casting a warm glow over them as they stood entwined, two sisters bound not just by blood but by a newfound understanding. In that quiet moment, Elizabeth silently promised that she would do everything in her power to help Jane find happiness—on her own terms.

The morning of Boxing Day dawned crisp and clear over Pemberley, the frost clinging delicately to the window-panes. Darcy had risen early, taking his breakfast alone in his chambers. It was a calculated retreat, one he knew was cowardly, but avoiding Elizabeth Bennet seemed the wisest course—for both their sakes.

Ever since their return from the dower house, his attraction to her had become a quiet torment—one he dared not indulge. He reminded himself that any attachment between them was impossible, and lingering in her company would only stoke feelings that could never be realized. Worse still, he feared that offering her even the faintest glimmer of hope would be a cruelty he could not permit himself.

With these thoughts pressing upon him, Darcy strode resolutely through the great hall. Having spent the morning overseeing the accounts with his steward, he was intent on sequestering himself in his study for the remainder of the day. However, as he turned the corner, a sudden movement caught his eye.

Bingley emerged from the library with an air of barely contained exuberance, his step unusually light and brisk. As Darcy advanced, he noticed the faint blush on his friend's cheeks and the uncharacteristic brightness in his eyes. Not noticing Darcy's presence, Bingley adjusted his cravat before turning and hurrying off in the opposite direction.

With measured steps, Darcy advanced along the corridor, stopping at the threshold to the library and peering inside.

There, seated alone by the window, was Elizabeth Bennet. The faint morning light danced across her features, and there was a composed stillness about her. He knew he should continue on his way, but something made him step inside the room.

Darcy cleared his throat quietly. "Miss Elizabeth," he

greeted, inclining his head with careful politeness. "I trust you are well this morning?"

She turned at the sound of his voice, and the faint flicker of a smile brightened her expression.

"Mr Darcy," she greeted with a formal nod. "Yes, I am quite well, I thank you."

He lingered near the doorway, hesitant, yet something continued to compel him to speak.

"I just saw Bingley in the corridor," he began, his tone casual though his heart had quickened. "He appeared— exceedingly happy."

"Yes," Elizabeth answered with an enigmatic smile, "I expect he did. That is often the result of anticipating a life-time spent with the woman you love."

Darcy's stomach clenched as a cold sense of dread surged through his body. So, it was over, then. The moment he had both anticipated and dreaded had come to pass. Bingley had finally offered for Elizabeth—and been accepted.

"Ah. I see. Well, in that case, pray allow me to be the first to wish you joy," he forced out through stiff lips.

To his further mortification, Elizabeth's smile broadened.

"Thank you. I could not be more delighted. Indeed, I can think of very little that would bring me more joy than the happiness of a much-beloved sister. As for myself, I have always wished for a brother, and I dare say Mr Bingley will make an excellent one."

Darcy blinked, stammering at length, "I-I beg your pardon. I had assumed—"

"That Mr Bingley had come here to make an offer of

marriage to me?" she finished smoothly, and Darcy gave a curt nod.

"I expect he did. However, I did not give him the opportunity. It has recently become clear to me that Mr Bingley is far better suited to my sister Jane. In fact, I now believe him to be quite in love with her, and I am confident that she returns his affections. I simply let Mr Bingley know that I would much prefer to welcome him to the family as a *brother* rather than a husband."

As Elizabeth's words took hold, Darcy's mind churned with a storm of conflicting emotions, but anger won the day, and his jaw tightened as he stared back at her.

"You should not have done that. Despite any feelings he may harbour for your sister, Bingley would have been a steadfast husband to you had you given him the chance."

Elizabeth gazed back at him with an arched brow. "Mr Darcy, were I merely in search of a loyal companion, I should just as soon have selected a puppy."

Darcy's jaw tightened. "While I generally admire your wit, this is hardly the time for humour. Have you given any thought to the consequences of your actions? How will you explain the transfer of Bingley's affections to your sister when you return to Longbourn? You will be a laughingstock!"

Elizabeth's smile faded at the harshness of his tone, but she replied with equanimity, "I am not in the habit of managing the opinions of others, Mr Darcy. Those who know me well will understand, and those who do not may think as they please. In any case, I would rather endure the censure of my neighbours than a lifetime of being married to the wrong man."

Darcy stared at her, torn between admiration for her boldness and frustration at her recklessness. His chest tightened with the knowledge that he could not shield her from the consequences of her own choices—and that he had no right to try.

Releasing a strangled sigh, he brusquely raked his fingers through his hair. "If you truly feel you could not have been happy with Bingley, I suppose I must respect your decision. But pray, tell me you have not done this for my sake, Elizabeth, because on that score, nothing has changed, nor will it."

"So, that is it, then?" Elizabeth replied, her voice laced with anger. "You refuse to marry me, even though you love me?"

Her accusation hit Darcy with startling force, and he took an involuntary step backwards. "That is not—" he began, but the words caught in his throat.

Elizabeth stood, her eyes flashing with the fire he had always associated with her. "Can you deny it, Mr Darcy? Can you stand there and tell me truthfully that you do not love me?"

Despite his best intentions, Darcy's defences crumbled beneath the weight of her challenge. Closing his eyes briefly, he whispered, "No, I cannot. I do love you. More than you know. And I shall carry that love with me until my dying day. But it is not enough to build a life on—at least not the sort of life you deserve."

Elizabeth's lips parted, as though to speak, but Darcy raised a hand, his throat taut with restrained emotion.

"Please, do not make this any more difficult than it is already. I have done all that you have asked of me. Now it is my turn to request something of you." Stepping closer, he continued, "You must move on from this, Elizabeth. Find someone worthy of your regard, someone who will cherish you and care for you. You are wasting your time with me."

The words tasted bitter on his tongue, but he knew them to be necessary. She was too far above him, and there were shadows within that he could never allow to touch her. The risk was too great, the cost too dear.

Elizabeth's eyes shimmered, but she did not look away. For a fleeting moment, Darcy thought she might argue— might refuse to let him retreat into this cold resolve. But then, slowly, she inclined her head, the smallest of acknowledgements.

The air between them grew heavy, and Darcy felt the weight of all he was sacrificing press down upon him. Without another word, he turned and left the room.

On the fourth day after Christmas, word reached Pemberley that the roads were clear, and plans for the departure of the Hertfordshire party were soon underway.

It was decided that Elizabeth and Jane would journey to London with their aunt and uncle, stopping only briefly at Longbourn to collect the Gardiner children. In confidence, the sisters had spoken privately with their aunt regarding Mr Bingley, and all agreed it would be best for them to remain away from Hertfordshire for a time.

This arrangement would grant Mr Bingley and Jane the opportunity to court in relative privacy and, perhaps, reach an understanding before her return home. Mr Bingley, for his part, would continue on to Leeds to visit his aunt as planned, though he eagerly anticipated a swift return to town.

Meanwhile, Dr Harper would depart for Yorkshire to resume his own affairs.

The days that followed her conversation in the library with Mr Darcy had been difficult ones for Elizabeth. She avoided the gentleman as much as possible, spending her time in the company of Georgiana and her own relations. Despite her outward composure, Elizabeth could not quiet the lingering ache within her heart. Each moment in Mr Darcy's presence felt heavier than the last, and so she kept her distance, knowing it was for the best.

When the day of their departure at last arrived, emotions ran high. Tears were shed and embraces shared between Elizabeth, Jane, and Georgiana with promises to write and plans to reunite in London in a few weeks' time.

Elizabeth's farewell to Mr Darcy was far more subdued. He was the picture of civility, offering genuine farewells to her aunt and uncle and wishing them a safe journey. When it came time to bid Elizabeth goodbye, he merely dipped his chin before handing her into the carriage. Elizabeth felt a familiar start as her gloved hand met his, but their parting words were devoid of emotion.

As their carriage made its way down the winding drive, Elizabeth stared out of the window, watching the rolling fields unfurl before her. She was under no illusion that Mr Darcy would one day change his mind and offer for her; she knew that he would not. He was a gentleman of strong convictions, and he would stand by the decision he had made. Still, she would always be grateful for the time she had spent at Pemberley. It had afforded her the chance to see Mr Darcy as he truly was, as few would ever be granted the privilege of doing, and it had opened her eyes to her own feelings. She believed Mr Darcy when he said that he would never marry, and she knew now that neither would she. But even if they spent the remainder of their lives apart, she would take comfort in the fact that a piece of her would always be his, just as a part of him would forever belong to her. And of course, she could not forget the one other thing that had come out of their journey to Derbyshire: Jane had found her heart's desire and the companion of her future life. For one had only to look into the eyes of the happy couple when they beheld one another to know that they would be together for the remainder of their days.

As for Elizabeth, she would never have the future she had once imagined, but securing the happiness of a most beloved sister was enough.

It would have to be.

Chapter Twenty-One

Early March 1812, London

"Mama, there is a carriage pulling up at the gate!" Samuel Gardiner called out, his nose pressed against the window in the front parlour as his younger sister struggled to claim her own spot on the narrow bench.

"It is Mr Bingley!" cried Margaret. "And there is another gentleman with him. Oh, he is very handsome. And very tall!"

Across the room, Jane set aside her embroidery, lifting her head to exchange a glance with Elizabeth. The quiet understanding that passed between them was tinged with curiosity.

"Children, hush! And come away from that window," Mrs Gardiner softly admonished, hurrying over to lay a gentle but firm hand on each child's shoulder. "Now upstairs and back to your studies. You will see Mr Bingley tonight at dinner."

Groaning in unison, the children reluctantly allowed themselves to be guided from the room, their joyful chatter fading as they ascended the stairs.

Jane turned to her sister, her voice barely above a whisper. "Mr Bingley did not say anything about bringing another gentleman to call. Do you suppose Mr Darcy has returned to town?"

Despite every effort to retain her composure, Elizabeth felt her heart leap a little in her chest, her pulse quickening in a most unwelcome manner. Schooling her features into calm neutrality, she lifted her chin. "I suppose it is possible," she replied, her tone carefully even.

It had been above eight weeks since their departure from Pemberley, and in that time, their entire world seemed to have shifted on its axis.

True to his word, Mr Bingley had reached London a fortnight after Elizabeth, Jane, and the Gardiners, becoming a frequent and welcome visitor at Gracechurch Street. In his company, Jane radiated happiness, her countenance brighter than Elizabeth had ever seen it, and she took genuine comfort in observing her sister's steady joy. Mr Bingley, with his easy manners and attentive care, continued to endear himself to the Gardiners, often joining them at the dinner table and lingering long into the evenings.

As for Elizabeth, she was quietly relieved to find no awkwardness between herself and Mr Bingley. Whatever fleeting discomfort might have existed had quickly dissipated, leaving in its place an easy companionship. He truly was the brother she had always dreamt of, and she could not be happier with the way everything had transpired.

Yet, the letters from Hertfordshire brought news of even greater changes.

Mr Walsh had, quite unexpectedly, proposed to Charlotte Lucas—and been swiftly accepted. Stranger still, upon returning to Longbourn and finding Jane and Elizabeth absent, Mr Collins—at their mother's urging—had redirected his attentions to their sister Mary. Yet, when an offer of marriage was made, Mary, in an uncharacteristic display of resolve, had refused the gentleman outright—to Mrs Bennet's indignation and Mr Bennet's wry amusement. Humiliated, Mr Collins had retreated to Hunsford with uncharacteristic haste.

However, of Mr Darcy, they had heard little. To everyone's surprise, Georgiana had chosen to remain at Pemberley rather than return to town. Though warm and cheerful, her letters were curiously vague, revealing nothing of her brother's movements or intentions. Mr Bingley himself had received only one brief letter from his friend, sparse on details and offering little beyond the usual civilities.

And so it was with a prickling unease that Elizabeth now looked up to see Caldwell, the Gardiners' butler, stepping into the front parlour to announce their guests.

"Mr Bingley," Caldwell intoned with his usual dignified calm, before turning slightly to gesture towards the gentleman stepping out of the shadows to stand at his friend's side. "And Mr Darcy."

Elizabeth's breath caught. She rose slowly, feeling Jane still beside her, poised and serene. Mr Bingley strode forwards with his familiar, affable ease, his face alight with pleasure at the company. But it was the man beside him— taller, graver—who drew Elizabeth's gaze.

Mr Darcy was precisely as she remembered and yet, somehow, entirely changed. His countenance was composed, though a certain tension lingered in the set of his shoulders. His eyes—dark and searching—met hers, and Elizabeth felt a curious stillness settle in the space between them.

Turning, she offered Mr Bingley a genuine smile before inclining her head politely in the direction of his friend. "Mr Bingley," she greeted. "And Mr Darcy. This is unexpected."

Mr Bingley beamed back at them, while Mr Darcy's bow was rigidly formal, as was his voice, even as he addressed both sisters by name. However, any further conversation was forestalled by Mrs Gardiner's cheerful entrance, her gaze immediately drawn to their visitors. "Mr Bingley! Mr Darcy! What a pleasant surprise."

Mr Darcy acknowledged her with a respectful nod. "I beg your pardon, madam, for arriving unannounced. Having returned to town only yesterday, I called upon Bingley, who mentioned his intention to visit. As I had wished to pay my respects, I took the liberty of accompanying him."

Mrs Gardiner smiled graciously. "You are most welcome, Mr Darcy."

A brief exchange of civilities followed, filled with cordial enquiries about Mr Darcy's journey south. Elizabeth, though outwardly composed, could not overlook the subtle tension in the air.

"Shall I ring for tea?" Mrs Gardiner offered at length. "I imagine you gentlemen must be in need of some refreshment after your drive."

Mr Bingley brightened, but Mr Darcy, with a slight shake of his head, countered lightly, "The weather is rather mild today, and, as such, I was wondering whether Miss Bennet and Miss Elizabeth might be inclined to walk out with us. I noticed a park nearby."

Perceiving that her nieces were in favour of the scheme, Mrs Gardiner gave a nod of approval, and soon after, the four of them stepped out into the early afternoon air.

They made their way towards the small park across the street, the sound of carriage wheels fading in the distance as they set out on the winding path. The natural ease between Jane and Mr Bingley carried them ahead, leaving Elizabeth and Mr Darcy to follow at a more measured pace.

For several moments, the silence stretched between them, broken only by the crunch of gravel beneath their feet. Clasping her hands, Elizabeth was contemplating how best to begin, when Mr Darcy quietly enquired, "I trust you have been well, Miss Elizabeth?"

She cast a glance up at him from beneath the brim of her bonnet. "Yes, thank you. I am quite well. And you, Mr Darcy? I trust your journey to town was uneventful?"

"Indeed, it was," he replied, his gaze firmly fixed on the path ahead.

A moment passed before Elizabeth spoke again. "I imagine you have come for Mr Walsh's nuptials?" she offered, and Mr Darcy nodded in reply.

"I have, yes. However, I confess my reasons for stopping in London were twofold. I have come for the wedding, of course, but I also wished to see you."

Elizabeth's breath hitched, and she briefly looked away. "Oh?" she queried, unsure how else to respond.

He seemed to hesitate, as though weighing his next words. Then, his gaze shifted, and Elizabeth followed it to a secluded bench nestled beneath the bare branches of a great oak.

"Would you care to sit for a moment?" he asked, his tone gentler than before.

Elizabeth, surprised by the sudden request, nodded her agreement.

They crossed the lawn in silence, the air carrying with it the distant laughter of children and the whisper of shifting branches. The bench, while weathered, offered a secluded sanctuary from the hum of the city beyond the wrought iron gates. As they settled, Elizabeth took in the scene before them—the skeletal trees casting long shadows across the grass, and the pale sky stretching endlessly above. For a moment, neither spoke.

At last, Mr Darcy broke the stillness. "Bingley seems happy with your sister."

Elizabeth started slightly at the abrupt shift in conversation, knitting her brows together for the briefest moment. "Yes," she replied, her tone sharper than she intended. "As I suspected, they are perfectly matched. I have never seen Jane so content, and I dare say Mr Bingley is equally so."

Mr Darcy inclined his head, his expression thoughtful. "That is well. In fact, it is one of the reasons I wished to speak with you."

Elizabeth turned to him, curiosity flickering in her eyes.

He drew a slow breath, as though steadying himself. "I wished to apologize for the harshness of my words during our conversation in the library at Pemberley. It was never my intention to cause you distress—I only sought to act in what I believed to be your best interests." He hesitated, his gaze shifting briefly away before continuing with measured deliberation. "However, I see now that the choices you made were justified, given the circumstances."

Elizabeth studied him in silence for a moment, noting the sincerity in his manner. "Thank you, Mr Darcy. I appreciate your candour. And I assure you, I understand your concerns were kindly meant."

He gave a slight nod but did not look away. "But more than that, I wished to thank you—for everything. For your assistance that day at the dower house and your discretion afterwards, but most importantly, for encouraging me to seek your uncle's counsel. Harper and I have maintained a steady correspondence since his departure from Pemberley, and I now understand why you hold him in such esteem, and why you urged me to put my trust in him. Meeting your uncle has been one of the greatest gifts of my life. He has helped me to better understand my feelings…about many things."

Elizabeth's surprise melted into something warmer. "I am glad to hear it," she said gently.

The air between them shifted subtly, no longer weighed down with hesitation but rather something unspoken, poised delicately in the space they shared.

Mr Darcy cast his gaze downwards for a brief moment, his gloved hands resting on his knees. "Your uncle has done far more than lend a sympathetic ear. He has written on my behalf to several esteemed acquaintances and has been able to locate a physician in Dublin who is conducting research into conditions of the brain. Disorders similar to…mine. We have been corresponding, and he has agreed to see me at my earliest convenience."

Elizabeth's breath caught, and the smile that lifted her lips was warm and sincere. "That is wonderful news," she replied with great feeling. "I am truly pleased to hear that my uncle was able to assist you, and that you have found someone who may be able to offer the answers you seek."

Darcy regarded her with a slow nod. "I do not want to expect too much, but I am hopeful. The gentleman, a Dr Patrick Doyle, worked under a prominent physician at the Salpêtrière Hospital in Paris, before the war. He has a particular interest in epilepsy, and similar disorders of the nerves, and his approach is far more enlightened than that of most others in his profession."

Elizabeth considered this before replying, "Dublin is a long way to travel, but it will be worth the journey if this physician can offer you some ease of mind. But…will you be able to manage on your own? I cannot think that Mr Walsh will wish to leave Charlotte so soon after they are wed."

"No, nor would I ask it of him. But I shall not be travelling alone. Georgiana is to accompany me, along with Mrs Annesley, her new companion."

Elizabeth's lips parted in surprise, and Mr Darcy nodded back at her, continuing, "I have told Georgiana everything. Indeed, it was unfair of me to keep the truth from her for so long. And she has handled the intelligence with the munificence and grace of one well beyond her years. She is more resilient than I supposed and stronger than I gave her credit for."

"I am so glad. Then, you will not bring her out this year? I know you had hoped for her to make a match during the forthcoming Season."

Mr Darcy shook his head, a flicker of embarrassment crossing his features. "I was mistaken about that as well. It was never Georgiana's desire to enter society so soon, nor to have a grand come out at all. I should have heeded her wishes instead of trying to dictate her future. Pressing her towards marriage before she was ready is an error I deeply regret."

Before Elizabeth could offer a reply, the sound of hurried footsteps captured her attention. Turning towards the sound, she was alarmed to see Jane rushing along the nearby path, tears flowing freely down her cheeks, with Mr Bingley in anxious pursuit.

Apprehension rising in her chest, Elizabeth darted in her direction. "Jane! What is it?" she cried, reaching for her sister's hands.

But as Jane drew closer, Elizabeth could see that her face was radiant, even through her tears. "Oh, Lizzy," she gasped, breathless and laughing all at once, "'tis too much —far too much! I do not deserve to be this happy!"

By this time, Mr Bingley had come to stand at her side, beaming with unrestrained delight. "Miss Bennet has just made me the most fortunate of men, by consenting to be my wife!"

Elizabeth let out a startled cry before stepping forwards to envelop her sister in a warm embrace, her own eyes stinging with emotion. Nearby, Mr Darcy inclined his head, offering his quiet congratulations.

Jane thanked him with her usual good grace; however, Elizabeth noticed that Mr Bingley shifted awkwardly on his feet, his smile faltering as he avoided his friend's gaze.

The tension was soon broken, though, as Jane stated her desire to return to Gracechurch Street to share her glad tidings with her aunt and uncle. Mr Bingley immediately acquiesced, and the pair set off in the direction of the house.

Elizabeth and Mr Darcy followed behind at a more leisurely pace. They walked in silence for a few moments, each lost in thought until Mr Darcy spoke, his voice low and contemplative.

"Is it my imagination, or did Bingley seem uneasy just now? I hope he does not think I am displeased at the news of his engagement."

Elizabeth glanced up at him, studying his countenance for a moment before shrugging lightly.

"From what Jane has related, it seems that you were quite severe with him for showing any partiality towards my sister, so I suppose it is not an unreasonable assumption." There was a brief pause before she tilted her head slightly. "*Are you* displeased?"

"No! Quite the contrary. I can see now that they are well matched, and I hope they will be very happy. I shall tell Bingley as much at the first opportunity." After a brief pause he continued, "If I was cross with him in the past, it was only for your sake. I could not bear the thought of you suffering embarrassment or heartache due to the withdrawal of his affections. But I realize now that I had no right to meddle in the lives of others."

Elizabeth looked up at him sharply, wondering whether the astonishment she felt was plain in her expression. Words hovered on her lips, but for once, she found herself hesitant to speak. At length, she began slowly, "Mr Bingley is engaged to dine at Gracechurch Street this evening. Will you and Miss Darcy not join us?"

Mr Darcy's posture straightened, and for a brief moment, Elizabeth thought she glimpsed a flicker of pleasure in his eyes before he answered steadily, "That is kind of you, but I would not wish to intrude."

"I assure you, it would be no imposition. Truly, after the generous hospitality you extended to us at Pemberley, I know my aunt and uncle would be delighted to return the kindness. And as for Miss Darcy, I would be most pleased to see her again. Jane and I have both felt the loss of her company."

Sensing his hesitation, she continued, "It is only to be a small family dinner. Aside from you and your sister, Mr Bingley will be our only guest."

"Ah, I see," Mr Darcy answered carefully. "Will *Miss* Bingley not be joining the party?"

Elizabeth offered up a small smile, her voice light with mischief. "Oh, did Mr Bingley not tell you? Miss Bingley remains in Scarborough with the Hursts. Apparently, she has taken a keen interest in the local scenery and is in no great hurry to return to town."

At this revelation, Elizabeth watched as Mr Darcy visibly relaxed, the tension in his shoulders easing. The corners of his mouth lifted into a genuine, unguarded smile —a rare sight indeed.

"Then I thank you. My sister and I would be very pleased to join you for dinner."

෫෴

After the gentlemen's departure, Elizabeth retreated to her chambers feeling curiously unsettled. The crisp afternoon air had done little to cool the quiet tumult within her, and though her steps were steady, her thoughts were far from composed.

Earlier, upon returning to the house, she had informed her aunt of the invitation she had extended to the Darcys to join them for dinner. As expected, Mrs Gardiner received the news with delight and had promptly excused herself to the kitchens to notify the cook of the additional guests.

Now, seated by the window, Elizabeth allowed the distant hum of the city to recede, her thoughts drifting inwards. Despite her efforts, questions continued to stir. What did she hope to gain from Mr Darcy's company this evening? And what could account for the change in his manner since they had parted at Pemberley two months before? Her mind, so often quick and agile, felt weighed down with uncertainties she could not name.

When the hour drew near to prepare for dinner, Elizabeth rose and dressed with deliberate care. She selected the gown she had worn on Christmas Eve, smoothing the delicate fabric as if it might somehow settle the nervous energy thrumming beneath her skin. Regarding her reflection in the glass, she noted that she appeared as composed as ever, yet there was an apprehension in her chest that she could not shake.

Making her way downstairs, she was pleased to see that their guests had already arrived. Jane, standing beside Mr Bingley, seemed to emanate a quiet joy, and their affectionate glances left little doubt as to the depth of their understanding.

Georgiana stood behind on the arm of her brother. For a fleeting moment, Elizabeth's eyes found his, but then his sister stepped forwards, drawing Elizabeth's attention. The lively discourse that followed revealed noticeable changes in Georgiana—her shyness had eased since their time at Pemberley. She returned Jane and Elizabeth's warm greetings with unfeigned delight, her manner poised yet sincere. There was a quiet strength about her now, a newfound composure that spoke of growing confidence.

Dinner that evening was a truly festive affair, brimming with light-hearted conversation and laughter, much of it revolving around Jane and Mr Bingley's recent engagement. Elizabeth smiled and contributed where she could, yet her usual vivacity felt muted, replaced by a quiet introspection. Her thoughts drifted, and more than once, her eyes sought Mr Darcy's across the table. Each time, she was startled to find his gaze already resting on her, his expression unreadable.

When the meal concluded, the entire party rose to repair to the parlour, having already decided to forgo the usual separation of the sexes. As they moved to depart, Elizabeth lightly touched Mrs Gardiner's arm.

"Aunt, I have just recalled—I left my shawl in the garden earlier this morning when I was out with the children. Perhaps Mr Darcy might accompany me to fetch it. I would hate for it to sit overnight in the damp air."

Mr Darcy, who lingered nearby, responded with some surprise but quickly murmured his consent before seeking Mrs Gardiner's approbation.

"Very well," her aunt replied after a brief pause, her brows lifting ever so slightly. Then, with a pointed glance at Elizabeth, she added, "But do not tarry." Nodding her understanding, Elizabeth went to collect her pelisse, as Mrs Gardiner instructed the maid to retrieve the gentleman's greatcoat.

With Mr Darcy beside her, they made their way towards the door, the quiet stir of conversation from the parlour fading behind them.

The cool air greeted them as they stepped into the garden, the glow of lanterns casting flickering light over the grass. Elizabeth drew in a calming breath, acutely aware of Mr Darcy's steady presence as they made their way along the gravel walk. The distant murmur of conversation and laughter from the house slipped into the background as they followed the familiar path to a small clearing, where a cluster of wooden benches sat, nestled among the garden's hedges. It was a favourite spot of hers, one she had often retreated to during her visits in Gracechurch Street. Here, lantern light barely touched the shadows, casting the secluded corner of the garden in a quiet intimacy. With measured steps, Elizabeth moved to one of the benches, seating herself and smoothing her skirts with deliberate care before folding her hands lightly in her lap.

Mr Darcy hesitated at the edge of the clearing, his posture rigid, his hands buried deep in his coat pockets. His eyes, dark and unreadable, met hers briefly before shifting away.

"Should we not be searching for your wrap, Miss Elizabeth?" he intoned gravely.

Across from him, Elizabeth met his steady gaze. "There is no wrap, Mr Darcy. Or at least, not one that I have left in this garden. I simply wanted a moment to speak with you. Alone."

A flicker of confusion crossed his countenance, swiftly replaced by a carefully guarded composure. "I see," he murmured, though his stance remained wary.

Elizabeth tilted her head, studying him intently. "Tell me, Mr Darcy, do you respect me?"

His head tilted slightly, seemingly caught off guard by the question. "Of course. I hold you in the highest esteem."

"Do you believe me intelligent?" she pressed, her voice even but firm.

He shifted slightly, his unease apparent. "Undoubtedly."

"And capable of making my own decisions?"

He hesitated, understanding illuminating his expression. "Yes," he answered slowly.

"Good. Since we spoke earlier this afternoon, I have given the matter a great deal of thought and have come to a decision." She inhaled deeply, steadying herself before continuing, "I wish to accompany you and Miss Darcy to Dublin. I would like to be there when you meet Dr Doyle."

Mr Darcy stared back at her, his guarded demeanour fracturing as a series of emotions crossed his face— surprise, a fleeting spark of hope, and then, inevitably, regret. He turned slightly, as if to distance himself, though his voice was gentle when he spoke.

"Elizabeth, please believe me when I say that there is nothing I would like more," he admitted quietly. "But you must know that such a thing is impossible. Your father would never permit it."

Elizabeth lifted her chin, her tone firm despite the heat rising in her cheeks. "He would. That is to say, he would not have a choice…if we were married."

Mr Darcy froze, his breath catching as the weight of her words settled between them. For a long moment, he said nothing, only searching her face—as though unsure he had heard her correctly.

He looked away, then turned back, searching her eyes.

"Elizabeth…" he began, but she stopped him with a shake of her head.

"No, pray, let me speak."

Her voice was even, though her heart hammered within her chest. She rose from the bench, her eyes never leaving his.

"In Derbyshire, you accused me of not listening, but I assure you, nothing could be further from the truth. I feel as if I have done nothing *but* listen. I listened to Miss Bingley tell me you had formed an attachment to Mr Walsh, and I listened to my mother tell me you were destined for Jane. And most importantly, I listened to you tell me you would never marry. Now it is *your* turn to listen."

She took a step closer, regarding him with quiet defiance.

"I love you, Fitzwilliam Darcy, exactly as you are. Broken or whole, damaged or intact, rich or poor. I love *you*, the man you are inside, and there is nothing about you that I would change, even if I could. What is more, there is no other gentleman in all the world whom I could ever be prevailed upon to marry. I want you for my husband, and nothing you say or do will change my mind."

For a long moment, the silence stretched between them, then, to Elizabeth's surprise, Mr Darcy's mouth curved into a slim smile.

"Are you making me an offer of marriage, Miss Bennet?" he asked, his voice laced with wry amusement.

Elizabeth flushed slightly but lifted her chin. "Yes, Mr Darcy, I believe I am. As you do not seem inclined to make an offer to me, it seems I must take matters into my own hands." Then, in one swift movement, she dropped to her knees, causing Mr Darcy to visibly startle before barking out a laugh.

"Elizabeth, what are you doing? The ground is damp, and you will stain your gown."

She shot him a pointed look, her lips pressing into a knowing smirk. "Quiet. You are ruining my proposal."

Mr Darcy fell silent, though his astonished grin remained. Elizabeth reached for his hand, her fingers curling lightly around his.

"Fitzwilliam Darcy, I love you with all my heart, and that will never change. I promise to stand beside you in all things, to cherish you, just as you are, and to face whatever comes our way. Will you do me the immeasurable honour of becoming my husband?"

Mr Darcy stared back at her intently, before lifting their joined hands and pressing a tender kiss upon her knuckles.

His gaze softened, yet there was an intensity behind his eyes that made Elizabeth's breath catch.

"Elizabeth," he murmured, his voice low and rough with emotion, "you astonish me beyond words. I cannot—"

"Ahem," Elizabeth interjected, clearing her throat with a pointed expression. "Mr Darcy, if you are inclined to make a speech, might I at least request an answer to my question before you do so? As you have remarked, the ground is rather wet."

Mr Darcy's surprise melted into a deep, earnest laugh. Without hesitation, he gently drew her to her feet, his hands steady and warm on hers. His palms rose to cradle her cheeks, his thumbs brushing lightly against her skin.

"My dearest, loveliest Elizabeth," he began, his voice a tender caress, "the honour, as you must know, will be all mine. But yes, I will marry you. I could hardly refuse after such a magnificent performance."

A playful smile tugged at his lips before one hand slid to the nape of her neck, the other tilting her chin upwards. His eyes, dark and intent, searched hers for the briefest moment before he leaned in, capturing her lips in a searing, breath-stealing kiss.

For Elizabeth, the world seemed to fall away, leaving only the quiet rustle of the garden and the rapid beating of her heart. It was several long moments before Mr Darcy finally drew back, his breath mingling with hers.

"Thank you," Elizabeth whispered, and Mr Darcy chuckled, letting his forehead rest lightly against her own. "Are you thanking me for kissing you or for agreeing to be your husband?"

Elizabeth grinned back at him. "Both, I should imagine."

His smile deepened, and he had just opened his mouth to speak when the calm, clear voice of Mrs Gardiner rang out across the garden, startling them both.

"Lizzy, pray come along now. Your uncle and I are waiting."

Elizabeth's cheeks heated, and she winced inwardly, wondering exactly how much her aunt had seen.

"Coming, Aunt," she called back, her voice pitched with feigned cheer. Turning to Mr Darcy she continued quietly, "I suppose we ought to return to the house before my uncle comes after us with a pistol."

Mr Darcy's lips twitched, but his features soon sobered. A prickle of unease stirred in Elizabeth's chest at the shift in his expression. "What is it?" she asked. "Is something troubling you?"

"No... It is only that I wish to be certain—that this is truly what you want. You know it is very unlikely that my prognosis will change."

Elizabeth's eyes narrowed. "Fitzwilliam Darcy, are you trying to renege on our agreement already? We have not yet been betrothed a full five minutes!"

Laughter rumbled in his chest, the sound low and warm. "No, nothing of the sort. You have my word—I shall happily marry you if that is your wish. I only want to be certain that you will have no regrets."

Elizabeth's expression softened as she reached up, fingertips grazing his jaw in a feather-light touch. "There could be no regrets. I have wanted this from the first day we met—when you led me to believe I was about to pick a poisonous flower."

Mr Darcy's lips quirked into a tender smile, but his eyes searched hers with quiet intensity. "Have you?" he asked.

Elizabeth nodded slowly. In the pale moonlight, she could see the subtle shift in his eyes, a flicker of vulnerability, chased swiftly by something deeper: unbridled joy.

"Lizzy!" Mrs Gardiner called again, her tone firmer this time, drawing them back to reality.

Elizabeth sighed, casting Mr Darcy a reluctant smile. "We should go."

The gentleman, however, did not release her hand. His grip tightened ever so slightly, as though he was grounding himself in the moment.

"Yes," he murmured. His eyes lingered on her face, as if memorizing every line. "But not before I steal one last kiss."

And with that, he leaned in once more, sealing their future with a kiss as soft as a promise.

Chapter Twenty-Two

Early April 1812, Hertfordshire

F our weeks after their understanding was sealed, Fitzwilliam Darcy and Elizabeth Bennet, along with Charles Bingley and Jane Bennet, were married from Longbourn in a joint ceremony.

The small church brimmed with warmth and light, its simple elegance adorned with garlands of spring greenery and delicate blooms. Sunlight streamed through the stained-glass windows, casting a soft wash of colour across the pews filled with family and friends. The air was rich with joyful anticipation, murmurs of admiration, and the rustling of fine muslin and lace, as all gathered to witness the union of two devoted sisters to two equally besotted gentlemen.

After the ceremony, the newly wedded couples and their guests returned to Netherfield Park for an elaborate breakfast, assiduously arranged and overseen with pride by an enraptured Mrs Bennet.

Although it had taken the matriarch some time to fully comprehend that it was Elizabeth who had ensnared the wealthy Mr Darcy, while her most deserving daughter, Jane, was to marry the affable Mr Bingley, at length, Mrs Bennet had come to realize that the precise pairings mattered little. Both gentlemen had been caught, and in the end, that was all that truly mattered.

As Elizabeth moved through the crowd, she could not help but marvel at the transformation Netherfield had undergone in only a few short weeks. The principal rooms overflowed with fragrant arrangements of spring flowers—tulips, hyacinths, and daffodils—their radiant hues lending a romantic air to the bright morning. Laughter echoed through the halls as guests mingled, offering well wishes and basking in the glow of the occasion, while servants made their way through the throng, balancing trays of sumptuous confections and glasses of sparkling wine.

Across the room, Elizabeth caught sight of her new husband, and a genuine smile lit her expression. Mr Darcy stood in relaxed conversation with his cousin Colonel Fitzwilliam and Mr Walsh. All three gentlemen appeared equally pleased with the celebrations, and Darcy's expression—so often composed and guarded—was now wholly unreserved. His laughter was easy and unaffected, the crinkle at the corners of his eyes softening his countenance in a way that made Elizabeth's heart swell with joy.

Nearby, she could see Georgiana standing with her new companion, Mrs Annesley, a genteel older lady whose gracious and steady presence Elizabeth had come to admire in their brief acquaintance. She was pleased to see her new sister perfectly at ease, conversing quietly with a small circle of guests, her cheeks flushed with happiness, the earlier strains of anxiety replaced by serene contentment.

Elizabeth's attention drifted around the room until it settled on Jane, who stood in a corner, engaged in conversation with Mr Bingley.

With steady purpose, Elizabeth moved in their direction. Mr Bingley, ever attentive, straightened at her approach.

"Elizabeth," he greeted warmly, though there was a trace of distraction in his smile. "I shall leave you two to talk."

Fixing his bride with a tender gaze, he gave Jane's hand a reassuring squeeze before disappearing back into the crowd.

Elizabeth turned to her sister, her brows lifted in gentle enquiry. "Is everything well?"

Jane offered a gentle smile before casting a cautious glance around, as if ensuring they would not be overheard. "Yes, of course. It is just…well, I was not to speak of it until matters were more certain, but…Charles has had a letter from Mr Wainwright."

Elizabeth tilted her head in mild surprise. "The owner of the stud farm, in Derbyshire?"

Jane nodded. "He and Charles have been corresponding regularly since our visit. It seems that Mr Wainwright is looking to sell. He is advancing in years, and his daughter has been urging him to join her in Somerset. Mr Wainwright had hoped to keep the land in the family, but he has no sons, and his daughters are well settled elsewhere… So, he has offered the farm to Charles."

For a moment, Elizabeth could only stare, her delight rendering her briefly speechless. "Oh, Jane! That is wonderful! I know it has long been his wish to explore something along those lines, and I dare say you will be happy in such a venture as well. And, selfishly, I cannot help but rejoice at the thought that you might be settled so near to Pemberley. Do you think Charles will accept?"

Jane's smile deepened, her earlier unease dissolving. "I believe he will. He seems very much inclined to pursue it. By the time you return from Dublin, I hope all will be settled to everyone's satisfaction."

Elizabeth, overcome with emotion, drew Jane into a tight embrace. "I am so very happy for you. Truly, this is the best possible news."

As they stepped apart, a familiar voice interrupted their quiet moment. "I hope I am not intruding," came Charlotte Walsh's warm greeting.

Elizabeth turned with a smile for one of her dearest friends.

Charlotte, now the picture of contentment as Mrs Walsh, extended her hands to each of the sisters. "My sincerest congratulations to you both. What a lovely ceremony."

Jane thanked her friend before excusing herself to return to Mr Bingley.

Left alone, Charlotte shifted her attention fully to Elizabeth, saying with heartfelt admiration, "Eliza, you look beautiful."

Elizabeth smiled back. Months ago, she might have

deflected such a compliment, insisting that Jane was the true beauty in the family. But now, with a heart overflowing with joy, she could only grin more broadly and say, "Thank you, Charlotte. As did you, at your own nuptials last month. I am only sorry that remaining in Hertfordshire for the ceremony meant that you and Mr Walsh were forced to postpone your journey north."

A light laugh escaped Charlotte's lips. "Nonsense," she said, shaking her head. "Henry would not have heard a word about missing your wedding. Nor would I. You know that you and Mr Darcy will always be family to us."

Elizabeth felt a swell of emotion and fought to keep her composure. "As you will be also," she replied softly, her voice steady despite the tears threatening to fall.

Shaking away her melancholy, Elizabeth regarded Charlotte with a lifted brow. "So, are you ready to be Mistress of Pemberley?" she teased lightly.

Charlotte laughed. "You know I shall never be that. Nor would I wish to be. But I shall do my best to be a helpmate to Henry and to serve your tenants until you and Mr Darcy return—which I hope will be very soon!"

"I hope so too, as I shall miss you and Jane desperately. But who knows? Perhaps I shall become enraptured with the beauty of the Irish countryside, and we shall never leave."

"Bite your tongue!" Charlotte chided playfully.

Elizabeth grinned. "Well, whether our stay is long or short, I know we shall rest easier knowing that Pemberley is in such capable hands. Fitzwilliam already trusts your husband implicitly, and by the time we return, I have no doubt you will know the estate far better than I do!"

Charlotte's cheeks coloured as she demurred, "You know we shall not be residing at the manor house. Though, from what Henry has told me, the dower house is every bit as large as Lucas Lodge, so I think I shall have quite enough to keep me occupied."

Elizabeth laughed lightly, but her amusement softened when she caught the telltale sheen of tears in Charlotte's eyes.

Concerned, she reached for her friend's hands, leading her gently to a quieter corner of the room. "What is it, Charlotte? Are you uneasy about moving to Pemberley? I imagine it will be difficult, being in an unfamiliar place with new people, but—"

"No, no. It is not that." Charlotte sniffed, wiping away her tears with trembling fingers. "It is just... Oh, it is silly, really!" She shook her head, but Elizabeth gave her a patient, urging look.

"If you must know," Charlotte continued hesitantly, "I am crying because I am so happy! Lizzy, never in a million years did I believe I could be as happy as this."

Elizabeth opened her mouth to reply, but Charlotte pressed on. "Oh, I know how I used to talk. I always proclaimed I was not romantic, and that all I desired was a comfortable home. But that was only because I believed that was all I could expect. I have never been handsome, and at seven-and-twenty, my chances of making any match —let alone a love match—were painfully slim. But now, I have found a gentleman I respect and admire—as he does me—and all I can think about is how differently things might have turned out for me."

Elizabeth gave Charlotte's hands a reassuring squeeze.

"Nonsense. You were never destined for spinsterhood. You are far too clever and kind not to have secured a husband eventually."

Charlotte offered a watery smile, dabbing at her cheeks. "Perhaps. But now I know that there are far worse fates. In truth, I shudder to think whom I might have accepted under different circumstances."

Fitzwilliam Darcy stood slightly apart from the jubilant crowd, his dark gaze sweeping over the scene before him. Netherfield's principal rooms were festively adorned, and the great hall rang with cheerful chatter. Yet despite the revelry surrounding him, Darcy felt an unexpected stillness settle within. Never in all his imaginings had he thought he could be so content—so filled with eager anticipation for the life that lay ahead. And all of it, every precious second, was owed to Elizabeth Bennet.

His musings were interrupted by a firm clap on the back, and a moment later, Bingley's grinning countenance came into view beside him.

"So, Dublin, is it?" he enquired, his eyes alight with good humour. "How long will you be gone?"

Darcy turned towards his friend, a small smile tugging at the corners of his mouth. "We set sail in a fortnight, and I do not think we shall return until the autumn, at least. Georgiana wishes to see some of the Irish countryside, and Fitzwilliam has already arranged to visit when next he is on leave."

At the mention of his name, Colonel Fitzwilliam sauntered over, a glass of wine in hand and a wry grin brightening his expression. Raising his glass slightly, he said, "To your health and happiness, gentlemen. And may Dublin survive the Darcys."

Bingley chuckled, shaking his head. "You really should have said something before arranging such a grand wedding trip, Darcy. I had only thought to take Jane to Bath this summer!"

Darcy's cheeks heated slightly as he said, "It was rather a last-minute decision. But tell me, what are your plans after your return? Will you remain at Netherfield for the time being?"

Bingley's gaze flickered across the room to the spot where Mrs Bennet held court, loudly extolling the virtues of her new sons-in-law to anyone within earshot, and he winced slightly. "Ah...I am not certain. Jane and I have discussed the matter and believe we may find it more comfortable to settle a bit...farther afield."

Darcy and his cousin exchanged an amused glance before the colonel leaned in slightly, a glint of curiosity in his eyes. "And what of *Miss* Bingley? I could not help but notice that the lady is not in attendance. I hope her absence does not signify her displeasure with your choice of a wife?"

To Darcy's surprise, Bingley's expression instantly brightened. "Oh, not in the least! Caroline wished to be here, but she has been detained in Scarborough for the most delightful reason—she is engaged to be married! My sister is to wed Lord Ashcombe as soon as the banns can be read."

"Indeed?" Darcy enquired with a lifted brow. Although

he was not intimately acquainted with the gentleman, Lord Ashcombe—a widower of some five-and-thirty years who held the barony of Moorhaven—was known to be a steady, respectable man. "A most advantageous match," he added, shaking his friend's hand. "I am pleased for her."

Fitzwilliam grinned broadly. "As am I. Who would have thought Miss Bingley would so swiftly settle?"

They shared in Bingley's obvious delight for a few moments more before Jane's gentle voice called to him from across the room. Bingley smiled fondly at his bride.

"Ah, if you gentlemen will excuse me, my wife awaits."

He had taken but a few steps when he paused, turning back.

"Oh, Colonel! I nearly forgot. Caroline asked me to deliver a message to you. She wrote that I was to say 'thank you' when next we met. She did not offer any further explanation, but indicated that you would understand."

Fitzwilliam's easy smile faltered for just a moment before he recovered, raising his glass in silent acknowledgement.

Bingley, intent on rejoining his wife, offered a final grin and disappeared into the crowd.

Darcy cast a sidelong glance at his cousin. "Should I enquire?"

Fitzwilliam smirked, swirling the wine in his glass. "No, Cousin. I believe some mysteries are best left unsolved."

❧

Afternoon sunlight bathed Netherfield's drive in golden hues as Darcy assisted Elizabeth into the waiting carriage. The crisp spring breeze carried the scent of blooming flowers, mingling with the cheerful murmur of family and friends gathered to bid them farewell. Darcy cast one final glance over the assembled crowd—Jane and Bingley stood arm in arm, Mrs Bennet was dabbing her eyes with a lace handkerchief, and Mr Bennet offered a rare, approving nod —before climbing in after his wife.

Elizabeth settled onto the forward-facing seat, smoothing the folds of her travelling gown. After the briefest hesitation, Darcy ducked his head, choosing the seat beside her. As the vehicle swung into motion, the rhythmic clatter of hoofbeats against the gravel drive echoed behind them. Elizabeth leaned into his side, and he wrapped his arm around her shoulders, drawing her close. To his delight, she nestled into his embrace, the gentle rocking of the carriage blending with the steady cadence of her breaths.

For a time, they rode in silence, watching the countryside unfurl beyond the window in a rush of verdant green fields and budding hedgerows. Darcy tilted his head, gazing down at the woman by his side. He breathed in the subtle fragrance of lavender and rose that clung to her, and his heart swelled with quiet wonder. She was his. Elizabeth Bennet—now Elizabeth Darcy—was his wife.

The thought still astonished him. From the moment he had first laid eyes on her, on that Yorkshire moor, she had unsettled him, challenged him, and ultimately transformed him. Her wit had pierced through his pride, and her warmth had melted the walls he had built around his heart. And yet, it was more than that. She had introduced him to a different way of seeing the world—of seeing himself. Her encouragement to seek counsel from her uncle, Dr Harper, had irrevocably altered the course of his life. He felt lighter, freer, more himself than he had ever been.

Today was the first day of their future, and tonight, there would be no more secrets, no more barriers between them. He would know her fully, just as she would know him.

Elizabeth stirred beside him, tipping her chin to look up at him with a winsome smile. Her dark eyes, bright with curiosity, met his.

"What are you thinking about?" she asked, her voice scarcely rising above the gentle clatter of the horses' hoofs.

Darcy's lips curved into a faint smile. "You," he admitted simply. "How fortunate I am. And how profoundly grateful I shall always be to have you as my wife."

Elizabeth's expression softened, tenderness flickering in her fine eyes as she gazed back at him with obvious affection.

He studied her intently for a moment before his thoughts turned inwards. A contemplative stillness settled over him as he murmured, "I looked for you, you know."

Elizabeth's smile faltered, her forehead creasing in confusion at the unexpected shift in the conversation.

"Of course," she answered, sitting straighter against the plush squabs. "And I am very grateful for it. Had you not ventured out to find me I cannot imagine—"

"No," Darcy interrupted. "You mistake my meaning. I

do not refer to the day of the storm. I looked for you, after our first meeting, all those years ago."

For a moment, Elizabeth said nothing, her eyes widening in surprise. Darcy glanced away, his gaze drifting to the passing scenery before continuing in a low voice, "Once I returned to Pemberley, I could not stop thinking of you. I knew—or believed—that there could be no future for us, yet the idea of never seeing you again..." He swallowed hard. "It was unthinkable. I told myself I was being foolish, that I ought to put you from my mind, but still, I searched. Every time I had cause to travel to London, I took a different route through Hertfordshire, stopping in village after village, hoping against reason that I might find you." A wry smiled touched his lips. "Of course, with nothing more than your approximate age and Christian name— which ultimately proved to be incorrect—to go on, it is no wonder that I never had any success."

"Oh, Fitzwilliam," Elizabeth whispered, lifting one hand to caress his cheek, "can you ever forgive me? If I had only known..."

Her voice faltered, and Darcy reached for her hand, placing a reverent kiss to the back of her wrist.

"It is of no significance now, and I do not tell you this to burden you with regret. I only wished for you to know that meeting you that day...it altered me. You mattered to me from the very beginning. You always will."

Elizabeth nodded solemnly, momentarily silent before lifting her eyes to his.

"As we are sharing confidences, there is something I have been meaning to ask you."

Darcy inclined his head, regarding her with quiet

curiosity. "Of course. You must know that you may ask me anything."

"Well," she began hesitantly, "it is to do with that evening, in my uncle's garden—"

"When you proposed to me?" Darcy interjected. To his satisfaction, Elizabeth's cheeks flushed a becoming shade of pink.

"Fitzwilliam Darcy, might I remind you that you solemnly swore never to speak of the circumstances surrounding our engagement?"

He chuckled, tightening his arm around her shoulders. "I believe, madam, if you recall our conversation, I only promised never to reveal those details to another soul. I did not surrender the right to tease you on the topic from time to time."

Elizabeth sighed, though her eyes sparkled. "You are incorrigible."

"So you have told me."

She shook her head in mock exasperation. "In any case, I have been wondering… When I…asked you to marry me, what made you agree so readily? When we parted ways at Pemberley, you seemed determined to avoid marriage at all costs, so I cannot account for your change of heart. I confess, I thought I would need to exert far more effort to persuade you."

Darcy smiled back at her with quiet amusement. "To tell the truth, I had already realized that I could not bear to let you go. That evening, when I came to Gracechurch Street for dinner, I intended to ask whether I might make my addresses once Georgiana and I returned from Dublin. You simply spoke before I had the chance."

Elizabeth shifted in her seat, blinking up at him. "Are you saying that you had already changed your mind about marrying me before you even arrived in town?"

From his seat beside her, Darcy gave a sheepish nod. "I had."

Elizabeth drew back, her eyes widening in disbelief. "Do you mean to tell me that I made a complete cake of myself for no reason at all? Why on earth did you not stop me and speak your piece?"

A rich chuckle escaped Darcy's lips. "It is not often that a gentleman is made love to by the woman he admires, and rarer still to receive an offer of marriage. I was enjoying myself immensely. Besides, once you had begun, you were going along so charmingly that I did not have the heart to interrupt."

Elizabeth stared at him for a long moment before releasing an incredulous laugh. But before she could speak, Darcy leaned in and captured her lips in a tender, lingering kiss. The steady rhythm of the carriage faded into the background as the world narrowed to just the two of them.

When he finally drew back, Elizabeth was breathless, her dark eyes lit with passion.

"You are incorrigible," she whispered again, and Darcy smiled against her temple.

"And yet, you still married me."

Elizabeth sighed, sinking deeper into his embrace. "Yes, I did. And I shall never regret it."

Epilogue

❧

July 1814, Derbyshire

I t was a glorious summer day at Pemberley, the sky a
brilliant expanse of blue with only the faintest wisps of
clouds drifting overhead. The estate thrummed with activity, both inside and out. Servants bustled about the manor
house, carrying linens and polishing silver, their hurried
footsteps echoing through the halls. Amid the carefully
maintained grounds, gardeners trimmed hedges and tended
to the blooming flowers, while the distant murmur of
voices carried on the warm breeze. The house, dormant for
two years, was awakening at last.

Elizabeth Darcy moved briskly through the entrance
hall, pausing only to direct a footman to carry a chest up to
the master chambers. A sense of anticipation coursed
through her as she oversaw the remaining tasks of

reopening the house. Entering one of the front rooms to speak to Mrs Reynolds about the evening's arrangements, something beyond the window caught her eye—the glint of polished wood as a carriage wound its way down the long drive.

Her heart leapt. Without a second thought, she lifted the hem of her gown and hurried from the room, her footsteps echoing lightly on the marble floors. Bursting through the great oak doors, she descended the stone steps, laughter already rising in her throat.

The carriage rumbled closer, its wheels crunching over the gravel. As the coachman pulled the horses to a halt, Elizabeth's breath quickened. A moment later the door swung open, and one of the dearest faces in her world emerged, radiant and smiling.

"Jane!" Elizabeth called, her voice bright with joy.

"Oh, my dearest Lizzy!" Jane exclaimed, her eyes shining as she carefully stepped down. "I cannot believe it has been above two years since I have heard your voice, and yet looking at you now, it feels as if no time has passed at all!"

Elizabeth let out a breathless laugh, gathering her sister in a tight embrace. "I must beg to differ, Sister. In fact, a great many things have changed," she teased, her gaze drifting pointedly to Jane's gently rounded belly.

Her sister flushed, one hand resting protectively over the small swell. "Oh, you must not tease me so, Lizzy."

Elizabeth's smile only widened as she turned towards the carriage, peering inside expectantly. "But where is my namesake? Do not tell me you have come without her!"

Jane released a wry chuckle. "I knew you would chide

me for that. But little Eliza is teething and has not been sleeping well, so I thought it best to leave her at home with Nanny." She levelled her sister with a pointed look. "Now, Lizzy, do not pout! You will have ample opportunity to see her, now that we are to be practically neighbours."

"Oh, very well," Elizabeth replied, slipping her arm through Jane's. "Come inside. You must be fatigued, and this heat will do you no favours. I shall have tea brought immediately."

They ascended the steps together, Elizabeth guiding her sister through the bustling entrance hall. Navigating the pleasant chaos, Elizabeth led Jane along a side corridor into a smaller, sunlit parlour. The room offered a peaceful reprieve from the household commotion, its tall windows open to invite in the summer breeze.

Crossing to the bell pull, Elizabeth gave it a light tug. "We shall have tea here, I think, as the drawing room is still under dust sheets. Then you must tell me everything I have missed!"

Jane smiled fondly, lowering herself into a chair. "Only if you promise to tell me all about Dublin—every last detail. But first, how is your husband? I know you have been cautious about putting too much in your letters, and Charles and I have been desperate for news."

Settling across from her sister, Elizabeth met her gaze with quiet affection, her thoughts drifting back to those early days in Dublin and their arrival at Dr Doyle's offices.

The memory unfolded vividly. How heavily the stigma surrounding Fitzwilliam's condition had weighed on him when they arrived—the fear of public scorn ever present. But Dr Doyle, enlightened in his studies, had provided a different perspective. He spoke not of madness but of management—helping her husband to discern the warning signs of an impending attack, avoid overexertion and anxiety, and embrace habits that might lessen the frequency and severity of his convulsions.

Elizabeth remembered the cautious hope that had begun to kindle in him as he absorbed this knowledge. The understanding that epilepsy was a disease, not a reflection of his character or worth, began to lift the shadow that had long hovered over him. For the first time, he had seen a path forwards—not a cure, perhaps, but a way to live without fear and shame dominating his every decision.

What pleased Elizabeth most, however, was how this understanding had emboldened him to be more open with those dearest to him. Before long, he had given Dr Harper —by then a trusted friend—leave to disclose his diagnosis to Jane, her husband, and the Gardiners, and had directed Colonel Fitzwilliam to confide in those among his family whose discretion he could trust.

This quiet act of faith marked a profound shift in how her husband perceived his own value, and the knowledge that he no longer concealed an essential part of himself from those he loved filled Elizabeth with unutterable joy.

Her smile deepened as she returned her focus to Jane, saying, "He is well, truly. His time in Dublin has done him much good. I promise we shall tell you and Charles everything we have learned at dinner tonight…that is, if you have been able to persuade your husband to abandon his horses for an evening!"

Jane laughed lightly at Elizabeth's jest, before saying,

"He will be here, I assure you. He would have come with me this morning if we did not have a mare about to foal."

They were briefly interrupted then as tea was brought in, and Elizabeth graciously turned hostess, directing the footman with quiet ease. Once the tea was poured and the silver tray removed, she settled back into her seat, cradling the cup between her palms. But when she looked up, she was startled to see tears in her sister's eyes.

"Oh, Lizzy, forgive me. It is just so wonderful to see you! I can scarcely believe we are sitting here together, having tea! Charles and I were both quite astonished to receive your express, saying that you had already arrived in Liverpool!"

"I know," Elizabeth answered, with an arch smile. "Poor Mrs Reynolds has apologized at least half a dozen times for not having the house ready for us, though we have told her repeatedly that she is blameless—considering that we arrived six weeks before we originally intended!"

Jane's expression turned thoughtful "And Georgiana? How is she faring after leaving Captain Spencer behind? It must have been difficult, especially so soon after their engagement."

Elizabeth sighed. "It was not easy, no. But she has such a generous spirit, when she learned…that is, when Fitzwilliam explained the difficulties he was facing over-seeing everything here, now that the Walshes have gone to Hertfordshire, she readily agreed to indulge him and leave earlier than planned."

Jane nodded, and Elizabeth absently stirred her tea as her thoughts wandered. What was meant to be a brief sojourn in Ireland—no more than half a year to consult with Dr Doyle regarding Fitzwilliam's health—had stretched far beyond their original intentions. And it was no secret that it was for Georgiana's sake that her husband had continued to delay their departure.

In those early months in Dublin, Georgiana had met Captain Edward Spencer, the second son of an earl, at a musical salon. Elizabeth could still recall the way her newest sister's eyes had brightened upon their first introduction and the hesitant yet eager dialogue that passed between them after the performance. What began as a shy acquaintance had soon blossomed into deep and abiding affection. Darcy, ever protective, had made discreet enquiries, but to everyone's delight, the gentleman proved to be of good family, sound character, and steady temperament. Once assured of his sister's happiness, the decision to prolong their stay had been an easy one.

"And where is Georgiana now?" Jane asked, drawing Elizabeth from her musings. "I was so looking forward to seeing her."

"Oh! Did I not say? She returned to London with Colonel Fitzwilliam. She and Mrs Annesley are to visit the warehouses so that Georgiana might purchase the remainder of her wedding clothes—though I can scarcely imagine what more she could need after the multitude of gowns she acquired in Dublin!"

Jane laughed softly, helping herself to another iced cake, as Elizabeth's gaze drifted to the open windows. In Pemberley's vast gardens, roses in full bloom swayed gently in the breeze, and butterflies flitted amongst the foxgloves and sweet Williams.

Inhaling the fragrant scent of freshly cut grass, she

returned her attention to Jane, saying lightly, "Speaking of new sisters, do you see much of Miss Bingley—forgive me, Lady Ashcombe? You wrote that she and her husband scarcely leave Scarborough these days."

Jane sipped her tea, answering with a single nod. "Yes, though she seems quite content with country life. She continues to keep herself busy with the renovation of the house, and now of course there are the children. Charles and I spent Christmas with them last year, and you would be surprised to see the change in her! She was a most gracious hostess, and she simply dotes on her husband. Charles said she is happier—and kinder—than he has ever known her to be."

Elizabeth smiled, though her attention was momentarily diverted by the sight of a gardener walking past the windows carrying a large basket of freshly cut blooms. When she turned back to face her sister, she found Jane smiling at her with dry amusement.

"Lizzy, would you like to go for a walk?"

Elizabeth's cheeks heated under her sister's knowing gaze, and she released a quiet chuckle.

"Was I that obvious?" At Jane's nod, she continued, "In truth, I have been longing to take a turn about the gardens. I have scarcely left the house since we arrived yesterday afternoon. But I did not think…that is, I would not have you walking out in this heat, in your condition…"

To Elizabeth's surprise, Jane laughed. "And what do you imagine I do all day at home, Lizzy? Lie about while the world passes me by?" At Elizabeth's guilty flush she continued, "In truth, a walk will do me good, and the weather is still quite tolerable. Come," she added, setting down her teacup, "let us go out."

The sisters rose and made their way into the gardens, where the summer sunshine enveloped them in its golden embrace. The breeze carried the heady fragrance of roses, mingling with the sweet scent of honeysuckle. Bees droned lazily amongst the blossoms, and the rustle of leaves added a soothing melody into the tranquillity of the afternoon.

They strolled along the gravel paths, passing neatly trimmed hedges and flowerbeds bursting with colour. In time, they came upon a secluded bench nestled beneath the boughs of an ancient oak, offering a serene view of the lake shimmering in the distance. Settling there, they breathed in the fresh air, basking in the peacefulness of the moment.

At length, Elizabeth turned to ask after the Gardiners, and Jane gazed back at her with a genuine smile.

"They are all well, and Mary seems to be flourishing. She is working with a music master, and my aunt has even persuaded her to purchase some new gowns that are far more flattering to her figure. Indeed, now that she has the opportunity to mix more in society, and is not constantly being compared to the rest of us and found wanting, I have every hope that she will soon be happily settled."

Elizabeth nodded her agreement. "I am so glad you were able to persuade her to go. I know it was not easy to convince her to leave Longbourn, especially as she has never been fond of London."

"Yes, that is true. However, that first year after you left was difficult for Mary, what with Mama constantly berating her for refusing Mr Collins. Though for my part, I am very glad she did! I cannot think even Mary would have been happy with such a gentleman."

"Having heard the particulars of his proposal from Mary, I must agree," Elizabeth replied. "It is a wonder he was able to secure a wife at all, though I suppose the promise of one day being mistress of Longbourn could not have hurt his cause."

"No, I suppose not. Still, it seems that he did have to rely upon his benefactress to secure the match."

Elizabeth frowned. "Lady Catherine? What had she to do with it?"

"Oh, did you not know? Apparently, she was most seriously displeased when our cousin returned to Kent and had to admit that he had been rejected not once but twice in a matter of days! I was sure you would have heard of it."

"No. Fitzwilliam has ceased all communication with his aunt. He cut her off entirely after that scene she made before our wedding, demanding he break off his engagement to me and marry Anne." Elizabeth paused before saying, "But what did you mean when you said that Mr Collins had been twice rejected? Did he offer for Kitty or Lydia after Mary refused him? I cannot think Mama would have neglected to mention it if he had."

To Elizabeth's surprise, Jane's lips curved into a most uncharacteristically sly smile. "No, it is even worse than that. He offered for Charlotte! The day after Mary turned him down. Can you believe the temerity?"

"What?" Elizabeth gasped. "Charlotte never mentioned anything about it! Mama must have been beside herself."

"She did not know! Nobody did. Charlotte did not tell a soul. She felt it would embarrass Mary and upset everyone involved, so she kept the matter to herself. I only found out about it recently, when we had them to dinner before they left for Hertfordshire, and she let something slip. In any case, once Mr Collins returned to Kent and told his patroness all, Lady Catherine was forced to secure a match with someone from the local parish, lest he bungle things for the third time."

Elizabeth laughed lightly before saying, "How is Charlotte, by the way? She has only written once since settling in Hertfordshire, but she seemed genuinely pleased with her new home. I still cannot believe that she and Mr Walsh have let Netherfield!"

"Nor can I! Though I suppose it makes a certain kind of sense. Once Mr Walsh had determined to lease an estate, he was eager to find something convenient to town and within easy distance of Charlotte's family—and his in Bedfordshire. So, Netherfield suited perfectly. And Charlotte has taken to the house splendidly—you know how practical she is. She has already overseen several improvements to the principal rooms and gardens."

Elizabeth nodded, yet her mind had already begun to drift elsewhere. After a thoughtful pause, she spoke. "I have been considering something—what would you think if I invited Kitty to stay at Pemberley for a time? She has sounded quite melancholy in her recent letters, and I cannot help but feel she would benefit from some distance from Lydia. Perhaps the Gardiners might bring her when they travel here with Mary later in the summer."

To Elizabeth's delight, Jane readily approved of the idea, even suggesting that Kitty might stay with them should she ever prove too much for the Darcys to manage.

The sisters fell into a comfortable silence, each savouring the tranquillity of a summer afternoon. Elizabeth allowed her gaze to wander, drinking in the vivid colours on display around her and watching a pair of butterflies dance idly amidst the lavender.

Suddenly, something beyond the stone wall caught her eye—the familiar glint of pale golden-green berries. She sat upright, eyes alight. "Jane, look!" she cried, rising swiftly to her feet and crossing the lawn at a hurried pace. "Gooseberries!"

Without hesitation, Elizabeth rose onto her toes, reaching for a branch heavy with newly ripe fruit spilling over the low wall. Turning back triumphantly, she held up the cluster with a broad smile.

Jane, however, remained rooted to the spot, wide-eyed —not at the berries, but at something else entirely.

"Elizabeth Bennet Darcy!" She gasped, climbing to her feet and striding towards her sister, her sharp eyes scanning Elizabeth's form. "Are you... Are you *expecting*?" she finished in an eager whisper.

Heat rushed to Elizabeth's cheeks, a startled laugh escaping her lips. "I am," she admitted, her eyes shining. "I did not think it noticeable yet, but I suppose the time has come to commission some new gowns," she added with a low chuckle.

Jane reached out, squeezing her hand. "Oh, Lizzy, how wonderful!"

"Yes, but you must promise to keep this between us, at least for now. No one knows yet—save Georgiana. We had to tell her, to explain our desire to leave Ireland sooner than planned."

Jane nodded knowingly. "So that explains why you travelled home with such haste."

Elizabeth laughed lightly. "Indeed. I assured Fitzwilliam there was no need to hurry, as we still have many months before the baby arrives, but he would not hear of it. He was quite determined that our child—and heir—be born at Pemberley."

Jane smiled, but Elizabeth's thoughts turned inwards. It had not taken her husband long to abandon his firm stance against having children. Yet despite their shared longing and countless hopeful attempts, no child had come. Fitzwilliam, naturally, had blamed himself—convinced that his condition was at fault. They had nearly resigned themselves to a quiet life together when, to Elizabeth's astonishment, after nearly two years of marriage, she had finally conceived.

Her hand instinctively rested on her slightly rounded stomach, a quiet joy settling over her. She looked back at Jane and smiled, certain that this secret, for now, was perfectly safe in her sister's keeping.

It was then that Elizabeth heard it—a deep baritone that was unmistakably her husband's, drifting towards them on the breeze.

Turning, she spotted Fitzwilliam standing by the glittering lake, engaged in conversation with one of the gardeners. Beyond him, Pemberley's high, wooded hills stretched into the distance. The sunlight cast a golden glow upon him, illuminating the strength in his posture and the easy confidence in his gestures. Her heart gave a leap at the sight.

Noticing the warmth in Elizabeth's gaze, Jane took the

sprig of berries, turning away with a knowing smile. "I think I shall return to the house. The walk has left me rather tired."

Elizabeth squeezed her sister's hand. "Of course. Go and rest, dearest."

As Jane departed, Elizabeth gathered her skirts and set off in the direction of her husband, her steps quickening with anticipation. She wove her way through the gardens, past bowers of roses and hedges alive with colour, the breeze stirring the petals in her wake.

Darcy looked up as she approached, and a slow smile broke across his face, filling her with a sudden, inexplicable joy. Without hesitation, she closed the distance between them, falling into the familiar haven of his embrace.

Held securely in his arms, Elizabeth felt a profound sense of contentment—a quiet certainty that this was where she was meant to be. Their journey had not been without its struggles, but every step had led them here, to this moment, this life they were building together.

Resting her head against his chest, Elizabeth breathed deeply, the scent of summer flowers mingling with the warmth of the man she loved.

Whatever joys and trials lay ahead, she knew they would face them together. And for Elizabeth Darcy, that was more than enough.

It was everything.

The End

A Note of Thanks

Thank you so much for reading! I'm truly grateful that you chose to spend time with this story. Whether you read it in a single sitting or savored it over several days, I hope it brought you enjoyment.

If you found something to love in these pages, I'd be so thankful if you would consider leaving a brief review on the site where you made your purchase. Reviews make it easier for new readers to discover books they might enjoy and allow writers like me to keep creating stories to share.

Whether it's a few words or a longer reflection, your thoughts truly make a difference.

With heartfelt appreciation,

Jennifer

Also by the Author

To Conquer Pride

The course of true love never did run smooth...

When Fitzwilliam Darcy departs Hunsford after his disastrous proposal to Elizabeth Bennet, he does not expect their paths to cross again. Indeed, knowing the lady's true feelings for him, he makes every effort to see that they do not. But when a chance encounter leaves him stranded in an abandoned cottage with the one woman he can never have, Darcy quickly realizes there is more at risk than just Elizabeth's reputation.

Elizabeth Bennet knows Mr. Darcy is the last man in the world whom she could ever be prevailed on to marry. Until the morning he hands her a letter, his countenance as dark and forbidding as the windswept sky. Now, trapped in a snowstorm with the one person she was certain she despised, Elizabeth is startled to discover that her feelings are not at all what she expected.

But is one night alone together enough to alter the course of their future?

Can any man as proud as Mr. Darcy be expected to offer for the same woman a second time?

In this tale of serendipity and second chances, literature's unlikeliest couple must conquer pride, prejudice, and faulty first impressions in the elusive quest for their own happily ever after.

Faults of Understanding

"I have faults enough, but they are not, I hope, of understanding."
--Mr. Darcy, Pride and Prejudice

When Fitzwilliam Darcy makes an impetuous offer of marriage to Miss Elizabeth Bennet, he is convinced they have as good a chance as any for a harmonious life together. That is, until an overheard conversation changes everything, and Darcy realizes he is now joined in perpetuity to a woman who loathes the very sight of him.

Elizabeth Bennet's expectations for matrimonial accord were never very high, having accepted Mr. Darcy's proposal in a fit of pique, not love. Still, she is determined to make the best of her situation, despite having tied herself to such an arrogant, disagreeable man.

But life at Pemberley is not at all what she imagined, and Elizabeth soon finds herself with more questions than answers about the enigmatic gentleman she agreed to wed.

Trapped in a marriage founded on misunderstandings, Fitzwilliam and Elizabeth Darcy struggle with deepening attraction while confronting self-doubt and old betrayals. But is love enough to heal the wounds of the past? What will it take for two people bound by duty to find their way home to one another?

Acknowledgments

I am deeply grateful to Jo Abbott, whose sharp editorial insight and steady patience helped shape this story into its best form. I was incredibly fortunate to have her guidance throughout the process.

Many thanks as well to Susan Adriani, whose stunning cover design far exceeded my expectations. Her attention to detail and creative vision made the final cover more beautiful than I could have imagined.

And to every reader who has joined me on this journey, once again, thank you for allowing me to tell you a story. Your support and encouragement makes all the difference.

About the Author

Jennifer Altman is a novelist, an anglophile, and a lover of all things Regency. After a long career in the television industry, Jennifer shifted to book publishing in 2016 and hasn't looked back. She currently makes her home just north of New York City, where she lives with her three-year-old Cavapoo, Penny. When she's not writing, Jennifer can be found reading, watching British period dramas, and not cleaning her house. *More Than You Know* is her third novel.

Printed in Dunstable, United Kingdom

68534162R10231